"Fresh, original, and fall-out-of-your-chair funny, Lisa Shearin's *Armed & Magical* combines deft characterization, snarky dialogue, and nonstop action—plus a yummy hint of romance—to create one of the best reads of the year. This book is a bona fide winner, the series a keeper, and Shearin a definite star on the rise."
—Linnea Sinclair, RITA Award–winning author of *Games of Command* and *The Down Home Zombie Blues*

"*Armed & Magical* is the kind of book you hope to find when you go to the bookstore. It takes you away to a world of danger, magic, and adventure, and it does so with dazzling wit and clever humor. It's gritty, funny, and sexy, a wonderful addition to the urban fantasy genre. I absolutely loved it. From now on Lisa Shearin is on my auto-buy list!"
—Ilona Andrews, author of *Magic Bites*

"*Armed & Magical*, like its predecessor, is an enchanting read from the very first page. I absolutely loved it. Shearin weaves a web of magic with a dash of romance that thoroughly snares the reader. She's definitely an author to watch!" —Anya Bast, national bestselling author of *Witch Fire*

Magic Lost, Trouble Found

"Take a witty, kick-ass heroine and put her in a vividly realized fantasy world where the stakes are high, and you've got a fun, page-turning read in *Magic Lost, Trouble Found*. I can't wait to read more of Raine Benares's adventures."
—Shanna Swendson, author of *Damsel Under Stress*

continued . . .

"A wonderful fantasy tale full of different races and myths and legends who are drawn so perfectly, readers will believe they actually exist. Raine is a strong female, a leader who wants to do the right thing even when she isn't sure what that is . . . Lisa Shearin has the magic touch."

—*Midwest Book Review*

"Shearin serves up an imaginative fantasy . . . The strong, well-executed story line and characters, along with a nice twist to the 'object of unspeakable power' theme, make for an enjoyable, fast-paced read." —*Monsters and Critics*

"Lisa Shearin turns expectation on its ear and gives us a different kind of urban fantasy with *Magic Lost, Trouble Found*. For once, the urban is as fantastic as the fantasy, as Shearin presents an otherworld city peopled with beautiful goblins, piratical elves, and hardly a human to be found. Littered with entertaining characters and a protagonist whose self-serving lifestyle is compromised only by her loyalty to her friends, *Magic Lost* is an absolutely enjoyable read. I look forward to the next one!" —C. E. Murphy, author of *Coyote Dreams*

"Lisa Shearin has the potential to become the Janet Evanovich of fantasy. She writes with a fun, unpretentious style, and she has mastered writing with humor."

—*SFFWorld.com*

"[An] edgy and fascinating first-person adventure. In her auspicious debut, Shearin populates her series with a variety of supernatural characters with a multitude of motives. Following along as this tough and feisty woman kicks butt and takes names is a most enjoyable way to spend your time." —*Romantic Times Book Reviews*

"Nicely done. I actively enjoyed the characters and their banter." —*Critical Mass*

Ace Books by Lisa Shearin

MAGIC LOST, TROUBLE FOUND
ARMED & MAGICAL

Armed & Magical

Lisa Shearin

ACE BOOKS, NEW YORK

THE BERKLEY PUBLISHING GROUP
Published by the Penguin Group
Penguin Group (USA) Inc.
375 Hudson Street, New York, New York 10014, USA
Penguin Group (Canada), 90 Eglinton Avenue East, Suite 700, Toronto, Ontario M4P 2Y3, Canada
(a division of Pearson Penguin Canada Inc.)
Penguin Books Ltd., 80 Strand, London WC2R 0RL, England
Penguin Group Ireland, 25 St. Stephen's Green, Dublin 2, Ireland (a division of Penguin Books Ltd.)
Penguin Group (Australia), 250 Camberwell Road, Camberwell, Victoria 3124, Australia
(a division of Pearson Australia Group Pty. Ltd.)
Penguin Books India Pvt. Ltd., 11 Community Centre, Panchsheel Park, New Delhi—110 017, India
Penguin Group (NZ), 67 Apollo Drive, Rosedale, North Shore 0632, New Zealand
(a division of Pearson New Zealand Ltd.)
Penguin Books (South Africa) (Pty.) Ltd., 24 Sturdee Avenue, Rosebank, Johannesburg 2196, South Africa

Penguin Books Ltd., Registered Offices: 80 Strand, London WC2R 0RL, England

ARMED & MAGICAL

An Ace Book / published by arrangement with the author

PRINTING HISTORY
Ace mass-market edition / May 2008

Copyright © 2008 by Lisa Shearin.
Cover art by Aleta Rafton.
Cover design by Judith Lagerman.
Interior text design by Kristin del Rosario.

ISBN: 978-0-441-01587-0

ACE
Ace Books are published by The Berkley Publishing Group,
a division of Penguin Group (USA) Inc.,
375 Hudson Street, New York, New York 10014.
ACE and the "A" design are trademarks belonging to Penguin Group (USA) Inc.

PRINTED IN THE UNITED STATES OF AMERICA

10   9   8   7   6   5   4   3   2   1

For Derek,
husband, business manager, arm candy.

In loving memory of my mother,
Jeanette Starnes.
You gave me my love for books
and the written word.
I wish we'd had more time. I miss you.

For my dad,
Joseph Starnes,
who proudly tells everyone
that his little girl writes books.
Love you, Dad.

Acknowledgments

To my amazing agent, Kristin Nelson. You always go above and beyond the call of duty, and I can write secure in the knowledge that you've got my back. Thank you for everything.

To my wonderful editor, Anne Sowards. Thank you for believing and for giving my books a loving home.

To Linnea Sinclair, romantic sci-fi author extraordinaire, book-promo genius, mentor, and gal pal. Thank you for always being there for me.

To Aleta Rafton, astounding cover artist. Thank you for bringing Raine to vibrant life.

To editorial assistant Cameron Dufty and Ace publicist Valerie Cortes. Thank you for all of your hard work.

Chapter 1

"Once again I'm glad I'm not welcome in polite society," I muttered.

Phaelan grunted in agreement. My cousin wasn't welcome in polite society, either, but for a different reason. He was a pirate. Excuse me, seafaring businessman. I was a seeker. Among some magic users, seeking didn't rate much higher than pirating. I didn't care what some magic users thought.

There had to be a better way to spend our first day on the Isle of Mid than listening to overeducated mage professors making long-winded speeches, but our guards hadn't asked us what we wanted.

Our guards were a pair of Guardians from the Conclave of Sorcerers. We were in their citadel's tower, overlooking the town's main square, where the boring speeches were being made. We weren't prisoners, but we weren't exactly guests.

My accommodations in the citadel were bright, airy, and more than comfortable, with a sweeping view of Mid's harbor. Being a member of the Benares family, I kind of expected something along the lines of dark and damp, with a view of iron bars. Sometimes it's nice to be disappointed.

Phaelan had opted to stay on his ship anchored in Mid's harbor. Good choice. At least he had one.

Phaelan was here because he'd come with me. I was here because I had to be.

My name is Raine Benares. I'm an elf and a seeker—a finder of things lost and people missing. I can now add "finder of stones of cataclysmic power" to my resume. I found one last week, and I can't get rid of it, or the cataclysmic power it gave me as some sort of sick and twisted finder's fee.

The stone with the warped sense of humor is called the Saghred. It's a black rock about the size of a man's fist that fell from the sky a millennium ago, more or less. I ancient times, armies that carried the Saghred before them were indestructible—and their adversaries were annihilated. You'd think something as small as the Saghred couldn't cause all that much trouble, but you'd be wrong—apparently size really doesn't matter.

Every magic user who'd been bonded to the Saghred had gone crazy. Not crazy like an eccentric aunt, but take-over-the-world-and-kill-millions kind of crazy. The Saghred and I were bonded, but I couldn't sense it now. It was locked in a containment room in the lowest level of the citadel, under heavy guard, and spellbound under layers of the strongest bindings the Guardians could weave. But it'd already done its damage to me. I no longer needed the Saghred's help to do the things I could do now. My magical skill level used to be marginal. I didn't know what my limits were now—or even if I had any limits. I didn't know if the Guardians were keeping me in the citadel for my own protection or for everyone else's. I didn't think the Guardians were all that sure, either.

I didn't want a link with a legendary stone of power. That's why I was here. One of those fancy-robed speech-making mages trying to impress new students and their parents with a lot of long words might be my only hope of getting rid of it. That thought alone was almost as scary as the stone I was attached to.

The Isle of Mid was home to the most prestigious college for sorcery, as well as the Conclave, the governing body for all magic users in the seven kingdoms. Classes for the fall semester were starting in a few days, hence the pompous speeches. Parents with magically talented kids had to shell out a lot of gold to send their darlings to the Conclave's college. I guess the faculty wanted to assure the parents they'd be getting their money's worth.

A tower room in a citadel was the last place I wanted to be. However, my guards looked downright content. Vegard and Riston were both big and human, and Vegard was endearingly homicidal. The Guardians' sworn duty was to protect the members of the Conclave and defend the Isle of Mid against any outside threat, but they spent most of their time protecting the Conclave's students and citizens from each other. The Guardians were sorcerers and warriors, and keeping the peace in a city of sorcerers gave them plenty of practice at being both.

Vegard and Riston's job today was to guard and protect me. And considering that I was in a tower room in the Guardians' citadel, it looked like a pretty plum assignment. I mean, how much trouble could a girl get into under heavy guard in a tower room? Notice I didn't ask that question out loud. No need to rub Fate's nose in something when I'd been tempting her enough lately.

Phaelan had generously offered his guard services as well, just in case something happened to me that my Guardian bodyguards couldn't handle. Phaelan's guard-on-duty stance resembled his pirate-on-shore-leave stance of leaning back in a chair with his feet up, but instead of a tavern table, his boots were doing a fine job of holding down the windowsill. I don't know how I'd ever felt safe without him.

My cousin looked like the rest of my family—dark hair, dark eyes, dark good looks, equally dark disposition. I stood out like a flaming match at night with my long red gold hair, gray eyes, and pale skin. Considering my present circumstances, I was surprised there weren't a few white hairs among the red.

Phaelan leaned forward, looking down into the square. "What's he saying?"

"That's Loran Abas, professor emeritus of chanting," Vegard told him.

My cousin blinked. "There's a class for that?"

"Afraid so. Trust me—you don't want to hear what he's saying. Though if you'd like, I can fix it so you can."

Vegard didn't say if that fixing would involve magic, but I suspected it did. Phaelan wasn't a big fan of magic.

"No, thanks."

We were about four stories up, and the window was just an opening in the fortress wall, so I could hear snatches of what some of the professors were saying, but that was about it, and that was fine with me.

The blond Guardian shrugged. "Your choice, but you're missing out on some of the finest-quality droning bullshit you'll ever hear."

Phaelan's expression never changed. "My world will go on without it."

"Sat through more than your share of those?" I asked Vegard.

"Stood through is more like it—at attention. Over the years, I've learned to block out the voice of virtually anyone. It's a gift I'm glad to say I have."

"It also makes it easier to hear the audience's comments," Riston added. "That's the entertaining part right there."

I looked back down at the sea of humanity, and elves, goblins, and dwarves. A tall and leanly muscled elf in the steel gray uniform of the Guardians stood on the raised stage just behind Archmagus Justinius Valerian's chair at his right hand. Mychael Eiliesor. I couldn't make out his expression, but I was sure it was a perfect, polite, professional mask.

Mychael Eiliesor was the paladin and commander of the Guardians. He was also an enigma, wrapped in a riddle, coated in yum. The yum was apparent to any female with working eyes. What wasn't apparent was what was going on behind Mychael's tropical sea blue eyes.

I liked Mychael. I think Mychael liked me, but he wasn't about to let liking me get in the way of his duty. As paladin, protecting the Saghred was his responsibility. And since the Saghred and I were psychic roommates, that protection extended to me. He took that job very seriously. Regardless of how Mychael felt about me, he wasn't taking any chances. That caution took the form of Vegard and Riston, tower rooms, and plush and all-too-secure accommodations. The words "gilded cage" came to mind. I didn't like cages; it didn't matter what they were made of.

Archmagus Justinius Valerian rose and approached the podium as the final speaker. The archmagus had absolute authority over the Isle of Mid and everyone on it. He was also the mage Mychael had deemed most likely to help me sever my link with the Saghred.

The audience greeted their archmagus with cheers and whistles. I didn't know if the cheers were for Justinius, or because he was the final speaker, or both. Either way, the wall of sound was almost deafening.

A slow grin spread over Vegard's face. "This is usually good. In our younger days, if we weren't on duty, we'd meet at the tavern across the street to listen to the old man."

I must have looked unenlightened at his source of amusement.

"We did shots at every sarcastic remark," Riston clarified.

Vegard grinned. "We got so drunk."

The archmagus stepped up to the podium. The other speakers had used notes; Justinius Valerian used his brain. As to sarcasm, his speech had plenty to go around. The old man spared no one. The loudest cheers from the student section came after snarky comments aimed directly at them. The worse the abuse, the louder the cheers. I smiled. They were probably doing shots down there, too. The students loved him.

I wasn't the only one taking advantage of an upper-floor window as a vantage point. Nearly every window of houses, shops, and businesses around the main square were filled with spectators. The window directly across from ours had been empty.

It wasn't anymore.

Oh hell.

The archmagus's voice faded into the background as Banan Ryce gave me a casual salute.

Banan Ryce was commander of the Nightshades. Nightshades were elves—they were also assassins, kidnappers, blackmailers, or whatever they had been given enough gold to do. I knew Banan; he'd met me. Let's just leave it at that.

Thanks to my Saghred-enhanced skills, I knew that Banan's salute was more than a greeting for me; it was a signal, and his people in the crowd below responded. Some moved into position; others were already where they needed to be to do whatever it was they were going to do. I knew exactly which ones were there at Banan's bidding as surely as if they had a bright red spot painted on top of their heads.

I stood. "We've got trouble."

I felt Vegard and Riston's power flare behind me. It would be way too little, far too late.

Vegard tried to shield me, with both body and wards. "Where?"

I didn't let him do either. "Everywhere. At least thirty Nightshades. They're all over the square and they're moving. That's Banan Ryce in that window there. You know him?"

Vegard looked, saw Banan, and spat an obscenity that described him perfectly. Sounded like Vegard knew Banan, too.

I could see into the collective minds of the Nightshades. Their intentions were as clear as if they had yelled them up to me. They were going to collapse the stage. They weren't aiming for the stage itself or the dignitaries seated on it; they were going for the supports under the stage. The stage was a good dozen feet above the street. The Guardians posted around the base of the stage would be crushed under the combined weight of falling wood and people. The fall from the stage might kill some; but the Nightshades were there to ensure their two main targets didn't survive.

Justinius Valerian and Mychael Eiliesor.

"Target?" Riston was suddenly at my other side.

"Mychael and the archmagus. The Nightshades are collapsing the stage," I said.

And a lot of people were going to die when they did.

Vegard saw Banan's people moving. "Riston, alert—"

Riston was already charging down the stairs. "I'm on it!" he yelled back.

I dimly heard him shouting orders. Everything below had melted into slow motion. Banan's men stopped, and I felt their power quickly building. Armed Guardians were pouring out of the citadel, but they wouldn't get there in time. The spells of Banan's people weren't silent, but there were too many of them. If only a handful of them survived, it would be enough to do what they'd planned.

Kill the archmagus and the paladin, and take a lot of innocent people with them when they did it.

I didn't think; I just reacted. I could move small objects with my mind; the same went for stopping. That was what I could do before the Saghred. From my vantage point, the Nightshades were just small objects in need of moving and stopping. I didn't have to break *them*, just their concentration. I struck, and the ones who hadn't bothered to magically shield themselves went flying. None of them landed on their feet, and some of them were thrown against buildings. None of those got back up. That maneuver alone cut Banan's numbers by half.

Banan laughed and applauded in the window across from me. Panicked screams came from below. The stage was collapsing on itself. My hand instinctively shot out to stop it. Four stories up made no difference. I'd always used gestures when moving anything bigger than myself; it helped me to focus my magic. The stage wasn't a small object. The screams faded in my ears, and all I could hear was the hissing in and out of my own breathing. I didn't know how long I'd be able to keep the stage from falling, but I suspected it wouldn't be long. What I was doing was mind over matter. Problem was, my mind couldn't get past how heavy that matter was. And I was doing it alone. No Saghred, just me. The new, improved, really scary me.

Mychael was helping Justinius Valerian off the stage. I had no idea how Mychael managed to steady them both on the pitching and collapsing platform, but he was paladin for a reason. Out of the corner of my eye, I saw a crossbow bolt fly toward them. Valerian saw it, too. He viciously spat something at it and the bolt reversed direction and hit the sniper in the chest, sending him off the rooftop and down to the street.

The stage was coming down whether I wanted it to or not. Gravity would only be defied for so long. My hand shook violently as I let what was left of the stage come to rest on the cobbles, praying that everyone around the perimeter was out of the way. My breathing was ragged and I heard gasps and whimpers I dimly recognized as mine.

"Good job, ma'am," I heard Vegard say. His voice was tight with awe and maybe fear.

Phaelan looked a little wild-eyed. "Shit."

Yeah. I felt the same way.

I leaned over and rested my hands on wobbly knees, trying to get my wind back. I could barely lift my head, let alone another stage. I looked out the window.

Banan Ryce was on the street and in a big hurry to get somewhere, and it looked like that somewhere was away from me. He vanished into the student section.

I pushed Vegard and Phaelan out of the way and stumbled down the stairs. Black speckles danced on the edges of my vision and I felt woozy. I pushed that out of the way, too.

"Stop!" Vegard yelled.

I didn't stop, but I didn't get away from him, either. I'd just lifted a stage; he hadn't.

He stopped me with a hand on my arm. I noticed that it was a very respectful hand, no hard grip.

"I'm going after him." My strength was coming back, and my rage had never left me. "I'm a seeker. I can track the bastard."

Vegard hesitated, clearly torn between duty and getting his hands on Banan Ryce.

"Go." His voice was more growl than words. "We've got your back."

I didn't stop to ask who besides Vegard had my back. I assumed it was Riston and Phaelan. Truth was, I didn't care. I'd have gone after Banan Ryce alone. It wouldn't have been smart, but I was too angry to worry about smarts and my own safety right now.

The square was chaos. Wading through a crowd of panicked people was bad enough, but multiply that times ten when those people were magic users. They were scared, they were angry, and they were looking to protect themselves. The magical distortion from their shields should have negated any tracking I could do. It didn't. Banan Ryce's magical scent rode the air. Time to remind the bastard just how good a seeker I was, new powers or not.

I tracked Banan to a side street that was little more than an alley. He wasn't trying to hide; he was trying to run. I didn't blame him. You didn't try to kill that many people and hang around for kudos.

"Wait," Vegard told me. He scanned the crowd over my head. "Jori!" he bellowed.

Moments later, a young Guardian pushed his way through the crowd to us. His eyes were borderline panicked. "Sir Vegard, what happened? Who—"

"Later," Vegard yelled over the screaming and shouting people surging around us.

The kid had a crossbow. He didn't look old enough to use it. I was, and better yet, I had a target. I didn't need magic to take out Banan Ryce.

"I need your bow," I told him.

The young Guardian looked to Vegard.

"Give it to her," Vegard ordered. "And your bolts, too."

He obeyed. Vegard was getting downright handy to have around.

"Riston and Captain Benares are somewhere behind us," Vegard told him. "Find them and tell them we've gone in there." He jerked his head toward the alley. "We want backup."

The young man's eyes went wide. "Benares?"

"Yes, *that* Captain Benares," Vegard barked. "Get over it."

"Yes, sir. Over it, sir. I'll find Sir Riston."

Vegard and I crossed the street and stopped with our backs against the wall leading into the alley. I knew Banan had stopped somewhere in that alley. I could feel him. Turning that corner just might get our heads blown off.

"How many ways out of that alley?" I asked Vegard.

"One exit, one courtyard."

I somehow knew Banan wasn't going for the exit. "He's in the courtyard waiting for something, and I don't think it's us."

Vegard drew his ax off his back. His hands and the ax blade flickered with blue fire. Now that's what I called backup.

I checked around the corner. The alley was empty. We went in. The entrance to the courtyard was about halfway down the alley.

The heat from two furnaces against the far wall hit us head-on. Leaning against walls and lying on tables were mirrors in various stages of completion. There were piles of sand for making them, and crates for shipping them.

A mirror factory. Just my kind of place.

Some of the mirrors were man height. They could have been mirrors to admire yourself in, or they could be an exit for Banan—or an entrance for his backup. I hated mirrors.

Mirror magic took a lot of discipline and a lot of concentration, and could make a lot of trouble if the mage were so inclined. Mirror mages could use mirrors to translocate people, manifest creatures, or move objects from one place to another. Then there was the spying and peeking that could be done from any bespelled and unwarded mirror. I was sure there were perfectly moral mirror mages—I just hadn't met any.

Banan was there and he wasn't alone. He could never resist leaving a crime scene without a souvenir. In this case, his souvenir was also a hostage.

She was young, blond, and terrified. From her age and the simple robes she wore, she was probably a student.

As leader of the Nightshades, Banan had spent a lot of time outdoors and looked it. His dark hair and tanned face were a startling contrast to his pale green eyes. He was rugged, he was handsome, and he knew it. He also fancied himself a ladies' man. Unfortunately the ladies he fancied didn't always fancy him back, and that was just the way Banan liked it. Murder was his job; rape was what he did for fun.

Banan didn't look concerned in the least to see himself on the business end of my crossbow. "Ah, Raine, you found us. I should have known you would sniff me out. You were magnificent back there. You performed just as I'd expected—and as my clients were promised. Everybody's happy."

The bastard had set me up. Someone wanted to see what I could do, and Banan had set up the audition.

"Well, almost everybody." Banan's grin was crooked. He thought it was charming. "My two targets survived, didn't they?"

"They did."

The elf shrugged. "Well, if at first you don't succeed . . ."

I pushed down the urge to pull the trigger. The girl was too close to Banan for comfort, either mine or hers. The urge didn't go without a fight. That was fine; I didn't plan to keep it locked down for long. As soon as I could get her out of my line of fire, I'd give Banan a performance *I* could be proud of. I'd even put a little magical something extra on the tip of the bolt that'd slice through his shields like hot butter.

I gazed down the bolt's shaft. I had a gratifyingly clear

shot at the space between Banan's green eyes. He pulled the girl tighter against him. Vegard growled low in the back of his throat, and his magic clawed the air with the sound. Banan ignored him, all of his attention on me. He didn't consider Vegard much of a threat. His mistake.

"Wouldn't it be easier to use the Saghred?" Banan taunted me.

"I only use the rock against big trouble. You don't make my list." I kept my concentration where it belonged—on the sweet spot between Banan's eyes. "Let her go."

The elf smiled. "Not going to happen."

I held the crossbow steady; my finger tightened on the trigger. "Never hurts to ask first."

A familiar fire bloomed in the center of my chest. Fire to consume Banan Ryce, and anyone who might step out of a mirror to help him. The fire and the Saghred's power that fed it blazed under my breastbone, white-hot and raging. Just call it, came the whispered impulse in my mind. The power was mine for the taking. I shoved down the fire and the impulse. I swallowed them hard and held them down. The fire flickered and writhed, trying to get around my will. I pressed harder and it stopped. The tip of the crossbow bolt wavered.

Banan saw it and laughed.

"You want the power—and I know you want me." His voice was low, compelling. "Put down the crossbow and take me, Raine. Like you have a choice."

The fire had diminished to a warm, soft glow, a harmless glow, a glow that only wanted to help me protect the girl. Just to help. Help me. My hands were sweating.

The Saghred was talking to me inside my head. That was impossible. The Saghred was spellbound, under guard, and under lock and key.

Only as long as you want it to be.

It wasn't a whisper; it wasn't even a voice. It was the truth. If I willed it, the Saghred would shake off its bindings and destroy Banan Ryce.

Banan faded into the background; so did Vegard and the

girl. It was just me and the Saghred. The fire burned and the temptation grew. I clenched my jaw against them both. I would not be used.

My finger tightened on the trigger.

A flash of reflected mirror light blinded me.

I dropped to the ground and rolled. If I couldn't see, I was a target. Banan had been doing more than admiring his reflection. Strong hands grabbed me. I tried to bring the crossbow up.

"It's me!"

Vegard.

"I've got you." Vegard took the bow and hauled me to my feet, pulling us both behind a stack of packing crates. I couldn't see the crates, but I could smell the wood.

The girl screamed.

"Stay!" Vegard ordered me.

I nodded past the tears streaming down my face. I wasn't crying, but apparently my eyes were. Vegard let me go, and I heard him step out from behind the crate. He swore.

I blinked my eyes back to working order and looked where Banan had been.

He was gone and the girl along with him. The surface of one of the big mirrors rippled from recent use. Banan had just dragged his prize out of another mirror somewhere on the island, the mirror this one had been linked to—and there was no way in hell of finding out where it was. Mirror magic left no trace or trail. As a seeker, *that* was why I really hated mirrors.

Guardians ran into the courtyard; Riston and Phaelan were with them. An officer I didn't recognize approached us. He saluted Vegard; then he looked at me. I was tear streaked, dust covered, and I imagine I wasn't much to look at.

"Ma'am, I need you to come with us."

Chapter 2

I knew I wasn't being arrested—at least I didn't think I was. It's just that certain members of my family have had extensive experience with what being arrested looked and felt like. What had just happened to me met both criteria. You know what they say—if it looks like an arrest and feels like an arrest, chances are it is an arrest.

I was sitting on a bench outside Justinius Valerian's office. Now that I was out of the screaming crowds and actually sitting down, it felt less like an arrest and more like sitting outside the headmaster's office, waiting to get yelled at. Vegard was sitting next to me. I wasn't sure if he was there as a guard or as an accused accomplice. I didn't want to ask. These were Conclave walls; they probably had ears.

I sighed, leaned back, and closed my eyes. That felt good. Too good. "I am in so much trouble," I muttered, my voice sounding as tired as I felt.

"No, you're not," Vegard said.

I opened one eye and looked at him. "What makes you think that?"

"I've been in trouble." He glanced around. There was no one in the archmagus's outer office but us. "This ain't it. Besides, you just saved the archmagus, the paladin, and every dignitary on that stage—and all the Guardians on duty around it. There's some grateful men in our barracks right now who think mighty highly of you."

The Guardian punched me affectionately on the shoulder. I winced. Amazing how using magic can even make your hair hurt.

The big lug was grinning like a maniac. "I think you're about to become the old man's pride and joy."

I smiled a little. It sounded like I was Vegard's pride and joy, too.

I leaned back against the wall and closed my eyes again. "Then why are we sitting out here?"

Vegard didn't have an answer for that one.

I did. I'd just magically cut loose in a packed city square, and I was related to the most notorious criminal family in the seven kingdoms. It probably didn't matter that I was just trying to help. Someone had paid Banan Ryce a lot of money to kill Mychael and the archmagus. Someone who didn't get what he paid for. And that kidnapped girl was in the worst kind of danger. My mind kept going over what had happened in that courtyard. And I kept telling myself that I never had a clear shot at Banan. Telling myself that didn't make it any easier to take. When I heard the office door open, I didn't want to open my eyes and look, but I thought it might be a good idea if I did.

Mychael Eiliesor was standing in the open doorway. He looked pissed. I wasn't particularly cheerful, either.

Mychael's hair was rich auburn, his features strong and classically handsome, and his eyes were tropical-seas stunning—and lock-up-your-daughters-and-wives trouble. The outer package was gorgeous; the man inside was dangerous. You didn't get to be commander of the Conclave Guardians by being any other way.

He looked at my dust-covered self, and then at Vegard.

"Vegard, you're dismissed. You're off duty until the evening watch. Get some rest; you've earned it."

I didn't ask what I'd earned. I'd be finding out soon enough.

Vegard saluted his commander and left. I stood up. I was stiff and achy, but I got there.

"Are you hurt?" Mychael asked.

I shook my head, and managed a weak grin. "But that stage sure was heavy."

Mychael's eyes were unreadable. "Yes, it was."

"I take it the archmagus wants to see me now." I didn't ask it as a question.

"He wants to see you."

Justinius Valerian was the supreme head of the Conclave of Sorcerers, commander in chief of the Brotherhood of Conclave Guardians, and the craftiest spellslinger in the seven kingdoms. I'd heard he was a foul-tempered, nasty old man.

I'd only seen the archmagus of the Conclave at a distance. The old man sitting in front of me holding a glass of whiskey wasn't quite what I'd imagined. What once might have been lean had turned grizzled. What might have been a luxurious head of hair was now a fringe of downy, white tufts on a liver-spotted head. Only a pair of gleaming blue eyes gave a clue to the man himself.

"So you're the one who's giving me ulcers," he said.

"It's the least I can do since I've driven you to drink."

Valerian snorted, a sort of laugh. "This job did that years ago. Or at least it gave me a good excuse. After this morning, you probably want to join me."

"I'll pass." I didn't think dulling my wits around this man would be a good idea.

He took a sip of whiskey, savored it, and swallowed. "I've been archmagus for a long time—some people say too long. Dealing with sons of bitches like the Nightshades is part of my job; I knew that coming in. Most times it's just an annoyance." His bright blue eyes were hard as agates. "This morning went beyond that, and right now I'm way the hell beyond annoyed. No one endangers my people—especially not my students." He leveled those eyes on me. "Do you know what you did out there?"

"Death, destruction, and chaos—all courtesy of yours truly." Nothing like a nice, public display of Saghred-enhanced power to get me all the attention I never wanted.

"You let the cat out of the bag is what you did," he said point-blank. "You also didn't cause the destruction and chaos; the Nightshades did that. And because of you, the only people who died today were Nightshades. We have wounded to take care of, but not one of my people was killed, and for that you have my thanks."

"You and Mychael were his intended targets," I told him.

"I know."

"He intends to try again."

"Of course he will. He didn't do his job. Whoever hired the bastard isn't happy with him right now."

"Any idea who that might be?"

The old man chuckled dryly and took another sip. "That list started when I took office and gets longer every day. The same is true for Mychael here."

I looked from one of them to the other. "So who's at the top of the list this week?"

The archmagus leaned forward. "There's a couple of front-runners," he said quietly. "Mychael and I will deal with it. You're a nosy little thing, aren't you?"

I shrugged. "I've been called worse. If that bolt had hit you, you'd be dead, and I'd be screwed. I understand you've been voted the mage most likely to get me out of this mess. I don't want anything to happen to you."

He grinned broadly. "That makes two of us. But this isn't your fight. If you see another bolt coming at me, just duck. I'll take care of it—and Banan Ryce."

"I couldn't keep him from kidnapping one of your students." I couldn't keep the anger out of my voice, either.

"So I heard. I also heard you did what you could."

"Tell that to the girl Banan Ryce took. He wanted a human shield against me, so he took one. And he probably picked this particular one because she was beautiful and blond." I paused. There wasn't any easy way to say this. "Banan Ryce likes blondes—a lot."

"I know." Mychael's voice was carefully emotionless. "We're doing everything we can to find her as quickly as possible."

"Who's we?" I asked bluntly.

"The Guardians and the city watch."

"He took her through a mirror. Good luck."

"There are several likely locations for an exit mirror of that size. They're all being checked."

"And if you don't find it—or her?"

"We'll expand our search as far as necessary."

"Does your city watch have any seekers?"

"They do."

"Are they any good?"

If my question offended him, he didn't show it. "Yes, they are."

I looked at Mychael; he looked at me. I hadn't asked whether they were good enough. Mychael knew what I was thinking, and what I wanted to do. I felt directly responsible for that girl's kidnapping and whatever was happening to her now, and I wanted to be the one to find her. Mychael knew how good a seeker I was. He also knew that my connection to the Saghred made me one of the most dangerous people on the island. As paladin, Mychael wasn't about to let me loose on his island. He didn't have to say anything; I could see it in his eyes.

The only sound was the ice clinking in Justinius Valerian's glass. "Yes, we do think you're dangerous."

I could add mind reading to Justinius Valerian's list of talents.

"What I did with that stage today was all me, no help from the rock," I told them point-blank. "Just my own skills enhanced by contact with the Saghred. I was completely in control the entire time. Collapsing that stage was more than an assassination attempt for the two of you; it was an audition for me. Someone wanted to see what I could do, and apparently they got what they wanted. Banan said I performed perfectly and that he had a happy client."

"You're sure you didn't use the Saghred?" Justinius asked.

I snorted. "Positive. I didn't get dizzy, fall down, and throw up. When I chased Banan Ryce into that courtyard, the Saghred offered to help. Insistently. I told it I didn't want its help." I looked at Mychael. "The Saghred's wide-awake. I thought it was bound."

"It is." His lips were set in a grim line. "It *was* as of this morning."

"Before Miss Benares took on the Nightshades?" Justinius asked him.

I didn't like that question, or what it implied about my future.

"I checked the containment room myself just after sunrise," Mychael said. "And got a report from the guards on duty. At that time, the Saghred was spellbound and quiet."

Justinius leaned back in his chair. The only sound in the room was the wood creaking.

"Then bindings aren't enough," he told Mychael. "We need more."

"I'll take care of it, sir."

The old man's bright eyes narrowed as he looked at me. "The Saghred's got you where it wants you. The Nightshades want you where they can get you. And Eamaliel Anguis is your papa."

I took a shallow breath. "That hits the high spots."

The Saghred was also known by its pet name, Thief of Souls, which pretty much described its favorite activity of slurping souls and sometimes the bodies they came in. One of those souls trapped inside was my father—a Conclave Guardian named Eamaliel Anguis. He had been the Saghred's protector, until the Saghred decided to turn its protector into its next meal.

"He's in there?" Justinius asked.

I nodded.

"Has he been talking to you?"

"Sometimes. Mostly it's Sarad Nukpana."

Sarad Nukpana was a goblin and the high priest of the Khrynsani, an ancient goblin secret society and military order. He was also chief counselor to the goblin king, Sathrik Mal'Salin. But most of all, Sarad Nukpana was a first-rate psychopath. Nukpana and his boss wanted to get their hands on the Saghred and bring back the good old days of annihilating armies. Thanks to me, Nukpana was imprisoned inside the Saghred, but a shaman that powerful wasn't about to let a little thing like being a disembodied soul get in the way of vengeance. He didn't want me dead, just tormented for eternity.

Justinius took a healthy swig of whiskey. From the way my morning was going, joining him was sounding better by the second.

He set the glass down. "Sarad Nukpana's not someone I'd want in my head."

"No one asked what I wanted."

"And you want me to change that."

"It'd be nice if you could help."

Justinius straightened in his chair. "My not-so-illustrious predecessors didn't have any luck turning that rock to dust, but then I like to think I'm a better mage than they were."

"Do you have any immediate ideas?"

"Not a one. But Mychael just dumped this on me late last night. Brilliance takes time."

"Time's something I'm running out of."

"Mychael said the rock's not affecting you, and from what I'm seeing I'm inclined to agree."

"I beg to differ."

"Feeling evil?" Justinius asked.

"No."

"Having an urge to overthrow governments, kill thousands?"

"No and no."

"Take over the world?"

"Too much work."

He laughed, a bright bark. Then the laughter was gone. "You sure you want to be rid of it?"

I knew the "it" he was referring to. Power. "What I was born with was working just fine as of last week," I told him. "I'm a *very good* seeker," I said with a meaningful glance at Mychael. "I'm an average sorceress. That was good enough for me, and I'd like to have that back."

"Some of my mages would be foaming at the mouth to have what you have now."

Justinius Valerian's eyes had never left mine, but they changed focus, and I felt the barest hint of the power that'd earned him his title. He was seeing me inside and out. It was the type of seeing that'd earn any other magic user the business end of my fist. Considering who Justinius was, I thought I'd let him finish. He was just assuring himself that I wasn't actually on the verge of a world-domination rampage.

"You'll be fine," he concluded. "But considering who your papa was, that's not all that surprising."

"Who my papa *is*," I corrected him.

"You're absolutely sure about that?"

My father was alive. Nine hundred years' worth of alive. The last year or so had been inside the Saghred, the other eight hundred and something years the result of an extended lifespan from too much contact with the Saghred. A fate I really wanted to avoid.

"Unfortunately certain," I said.

"Poor bastard."

I nodded in agreement. "His daughter's not in too great of a state, either. But at least I'm not sharing his accommodations—or his roommate."

"Sarad Nukpana isn't someone I'd want to spend eternity with."

I didn't have a response for that.

I'd been in the Saghred once before. It had only been for a few moments, but it'd been enough time for me to see that it wasn't a vacation destination, more like someplace you went after a lifetime of pulling wings off of flies, then working your way up to things that screamed. A Sarad Nukpana kind of place. I had met Sarad Nukpana up close and personal last week, and was in no hurry to repeat the experience. It was looking more like I was my father's only chance at freedom—or resting in peace.

"Girl?"

"Sir?"

"Let's keep that bit of information to ourselves for now."

"Nukpana or my father?"

"Both, but especially who's little girl you are. That doesn't need to leave this room."

"I wasn't about to yell it from the battlements. I'm not sure how I feel about it myself."

"Contrary to how old I look, I'm not old enough to have known your papa in his early Guardian days. But history's told me plenty about the bastards he was up against. I'm ashamed to say the archmagus back then was one of them; and a couple of his top mages were a few more. History has an annoying tendency to repeat itself. I'm going to see what I can do to keep that from happening. The Conclave did your papa wrong. I'll do whatever I can to make up for it."

"Thank you." And I meant it.

"Though the first help I might be giving you is of a legal nature." He glanced at Mychael. "I heard from your friends the Khrynsani last night."

I swore silently. Mychael tried not to look concerned, but I wasn't buying it.

"Actually, I didn't see their representatives directly," Justinius continued. "They filed their formal complaint with the magistrate. He brought the papers to me. Your ship hadn't docked yet."

"What papers?" Mychael's voice betrayed no emotion.

"The papers charging Miss Benares here with grand larceny, attempted murder, kidnapping, and false imprisonment."

I blinked. "Of who?"

"Grand Shaman Sarad Nukpana. The Khrynsani have requested that we turn you over to them for prosecution."

"What?"

"We won't do that," Mychael assured me.

"I should hope not!"

"Actually, we can't do that," Justinius said. "Not legally, anyway."

"For the Khrynsani to have any legal claim, they would have to go through the elven embassy," Mychael told me. "That would take time; no doubt they want to resolve this quickly."

Justinius cleared his throat. "Actually, I just heard from Giles Keril this morning."

The name sounded vaguely familiar. "Who?"

"The elven ambassador to Mid," Justinius said.

Oh, that Giles Keril.

"Keril got an identical set of papers this morning," Justinius continued. "The sight of goblin lawyers on his embassy doorstep probably made the little weasel crap his pants. The goblins are claiming that Miss Benares here has stolen the Saghred, which is a treasured possession of the goblin people, attempted to murder a counselor of the royal House of Mal'Salin, and has kidnapped and falsely imprisoned said royal counselor." He winked slyly at me. "Not a bad week's work, girl."

I'm sure if I listened closely enough, I'd be able to hear Sarad Nukpana laughing.

"By the way, you're listed as an accessory," Justinius told Mychael. "They claim your actions in Mermeia were outside of your legal jurisdiction as paladin."

At least I'd have company when I was hung out to dry. Last week Mychael had come to my home city of Mermeia to enlist my services as a seeker, but mostly as Eamaliel Anguis's daughter, to help him and his Guardians find the Saghred before Sarad Nukpana could get his hands on it. Both Mychael and Sarad Nukpana suspected the Saghred was in Mermeia. They were both right. I found the Saghred, and the Saghred promptly attached itself to me like a psychic leech. I'd definitely gotten the raw end of that deal.

Like father, like daughter.

"I'm not hanging either one of you out to dry," Justinius told me point-blank.

Further confirmation that the old man could read my mind.

"In terms of legal strength, you may not have any choice, sir," Mychael told him.

"The hell I don't."

"The Seat of Twelve will have to be convened, and you only have two votes to their twelve. Given that enough of them vote in our favor, the situation won't escalate any further."

The Seat of Twelve was the name given to the twelve mages who made up the governing Conclave council. In terms of firepower, they ranked right up there with Justinius Valerian.

"And if you're not too popular right now?" I didn't want to ask, but I had to.

"The goblin government could begin extradition proceedings," Mychael said. "If they prove just cause with the elven embassy, they could begin the same against you."

I wondered just how fast Phaelan could set sail.

"They would have to prove that you had malice of intent on all counts," Justinius told us both. "And I don't think anyone who knows—or knew—Sarad Nukpana would call any treatment he received at your hands unprovoked."

I couldn't be bonded to just any old stone of cataclysmic power.

Mine had lawyers.

Chapter 3

"I want to help find that girl," I said as soon as Mychael closed the archmagus's office door behind us.

Mychael sighed. He looked about as tired as I felt. I wasn't the only one whose day had gone down the crapper.

"I know you want to help," he told me. "And under normal circumstances, I would welcome that help, but—"

"I'm dangerous," I finished for him. "And unpredictable, and infected with the Saghred."

Mychael's lips curled into a weary smile. "I knew you were dangerous and unpredictable the moment I met you."

That had been last week. Our first meeting had been mistaken identity, followed by misunderstanding, ending in me kicking Mychael in the balls. Not one of my glowing moments.

"What happened today just further proves my point," Mychael was saying. "The Nightshades are here; so are the Khrynsani. The safest place for you is in this citadel. The Khrynsani want to get their hands on you. And the same people who hired Banan Ryce to collapse that stage could have also paid him to kidnap you." His blue eyes were hard. "Neither is going to happen."

I took a breath and told myself to calm down. Mychael didn't respond to emotional tirades. He was the paladin; he demanded cooperation, and respected logic. I knew a way I could give him both and still get what I wanted.

"I don't want Banan yanking me through a mirror, either," I told him. "I also don't need to leave the citadel to help find that girl. Lock me in the highest tower you've got, have Vegard sit on me, just get me something that belongs to her, something she's worn recently, or used, like a hairbrush. Hairbrushes are great. I don't need to do the footwork. Your men and the city watch know this island better than I do. Just let me point them in the right direction."

I stopped, mainly because I'd run out of air. Mychael didn't say anything, but I could tell he was wavering.

"You can link to a victim through objects?" he asked.

"Yes, I can link through objects. It'll be like I'm inside the girl's head."

For a seeker, one of the best ways to find a missing person was to hold an object that belonged to them. The closer the person was to that object, the better. Before I'd picked up more magical mojo courtesy of the Saghred, my seeking talents were good, better than most, but still pretty basic. I could use an object to track the person who owned that object, but most of what I got were just impressions, not a direct link. I could then use those impressions—and some good old-fashioned footwork—to find the missing person. Thanks to the Saghred, what's normal for me now is unheard of for most seekers. I can link directly to the person. Last week, I got a murder victim's final moments in full color, sound, smell, and touch. I felt like I was being murdered right along with him. Not pleasant, but neither was being murdered. That was the first and only time I'd done it. I assumed it would work even better with a living subject. I wasn't about to tell Mychael that I'd only done it once. Show no doubt, know no refusal.

"Can any seeker on your city watch do that?" I asked quietly.

From his silence I knew none of them could. I waited.

"I'll get you her hairbrush."

•   •   •

An hour or so later someone knocked on the door to my room. I ex-
pected a hairbrush. It was Riston.

"The paladin would like to see you in his office."

When I got there, Mychael wasn't alone. I took one look
at his guest and I think my mouth fell open.

The man's robes were a riot of silk and color. Red, orange, amber, gold—every color that flame could be at one
point or another in its capricious existence—this man managed to wear them all at once and wear them well. It was
nothing short of a stunning fashion achievement.

"Maestro, this is Raine Benares," Mychael said. "Raine,
this is Maestro Ronan Cayle."

If you were a magic user, you'd heard of Ronan Cayle.
The spellsinging master. The legend who only taught future
legends. The maestro who turned out the finest spellsingers
the Isle of Mid and the Conclave had to offer. Mychael's
teacher.

Mychael was a spellsinger and a healer. Each was a
highly desirable magical talent, and Mychael was gifted
with both. With the power of his voice alone, a spellsinger
could influence thought with a quietly hummed phrase, or
control actions with simple speech or carefully crafted tune.
One person or thousands—the number didn't matter. One
spellsinger could turn the tide of battle. Gifted spellsingers
were highly prized and sought after—not to mention rare
and dangerous. Mychael could do virtually anything he
wanted to with that baritone of his, and not only would his
intended victim not mind in the least, he'd enjoy it. I know
I had.

His spellsinging teacher's appearance didn't match his
reputation. Ronan Cayle's features were strong and solid,
but it was the kind of face that would go unnoticed in a
crowd. He was human, but from the amber glint in his hazel
eyes, there was elf in there somewhere.

The maestro extended his hand for mine. I gave it to him
and was treated to a most proficient hand kiss.

So this was Piaras's future teacher.

Piaras Rivalin was an elf, my Mermeian landlady's grandson, and the little brother I'd always wanted. He'd also attracted unwanted attention last week as a result of the Saghred. Piaras had fought off that attention with a level of spellsinging talent unheard of for a seventeen-year-old. His singing voice was magnificent, but it was also an incredibly powerful weapon that he needed to learn to control. My godfather, Garadin Wyne, had been Piaras's first voice teacher. He knew Ronan Cayle from his Conclave days and had sent the maestro a letter of recommendation. Mychael added his recommendation to Garadin's, effectively securing an audition for Piaras.

Tarsilia Rivalin and Garadin had come with us to Mid, but at my insistence had returned to Mermeia. Piaras and I were surrounded by hundreds of Guardians; we were as safe as we were going to get, so there was no reason for them to stay. Plus Piaras would be going to school; I would be looking for a way out of my Saghred predicament. Neither were short-term activities. I snorted to myself. The way my luck was running, Piaras would graduate before I was out of this mess.

Piaras was practicing downstairs in the citadel's music room for his audition tomorrow with the maestro. The poor kid was already scared to death. Hopefully he hadn't heard the maestro was in the citadel.

"We need your help," Mychael was saying. He didn't sound too happy about it.

I didn't move. "With what?"

"The Saghred. Since spellbinding isn't containing it, I asked Ronan if he knew a spellsong that would work. He does. You can sense that the Saghred is awake." His expression darkened. "Unfortunately, we cannot. It would be helpful to know whether the spellsong is working." He paused uncomfortably. "We need you to go down into the containment rooms with us."

That was the part he really didn't like.

I hadn't been down to the Guardians' containment

rooms, and I didn't want to go now. But I also didn't want the Saghred awake and in my head.

"I'll go," I told him. "What kind of spellsong are you going to use?" I asked the maestro.

"A sleepsong," Cayle told me. "Since binding the Saghred itself was ineffective, Mychael and I thought that the souls inside would be a better target."

I bristled. I didn't like hearing my father described as a target.

"The song I'll be using is for the binding of wayward souls," he continued.

"Binding?" My voice was tight with restraint. My father was not a wayward soul. Being trapped in the Saghred was torture enough; I did not want him bound and unable to move.

Ronan Cayle sensed my growing anger. So did Mychael.

"Raine, it's like sleep," Mychael explained.

"I would think you would want Sarad Nukpana bound," Cayle said, clearly puzzled at my reaction.

"I'm not talking about Sarad Nukpana," I said, my voice low and quiet.

"Ronan knows about your father," Mychael told me.

"Ah, then I understand your concern," Cayle said. "I can guarantee that your father will not be harmed."

"Have you ever been hit with this sleepsong?"

"No, but—"

"Then you can't guarantee me a damned thing."

Mychael stepped between us. "Raine."

"This is my father we're talking about!"

"And Sarad Nukpana," he reminded me sternly. "And who knows how many others just like him. Raine, your father gave over eight hundred years of his life to keep the Saghred out of the hands of people like Sarad Nukpana." Mychael's intense blue gaze never wavered. "It can't remain active. Your father is a Guardian; he knows his duty. He would want us to do this." Mychael's voice lost some of its edge. "He's trapped inside the Saghred. You've been in there; you know what it's like. Sleep would be a mercy."

I remembered what I had seen. Those who had been in the Saghred the longest had been reduced to filmy, faceless wraiths. Other prisoners seemed to be more solid, but their bodies looked ravaged and wasted as if from disease. I had seen my father. Elegantly pointed ears, a beautiful, pure-blooded high elf. His hair was silver, and his eyes were the gray of gathering storm clouds. Eyes identical to my own. He had only been inside the Saghred for a year, and he had already begun to fade.

I had been able to see through him.

I gritted my teeth and stifled a sniff. I would not tear up in front of Mychael, and I sure as hell wouldn't in front of a stranger.

Mychael looked at me. I stared at him. I didn't say anything because I knew he was right. My father had been taken by the Saghred while trying to hide it from the Khrynsani and Sarad Nukpana. He would want us to do this.

"Is it really like sleep?" I asked Mychael quietly.

He gave me a sad smile. "Yes, it's like sleep."

I looked from Mychael to Ronan Cayle. "Tell me what you need me to do."

The Guardians' containment rooms were beneath the basements of the citadel. They were rooms that could be locked down tight enough to hold something as powerful as the Saghred. The corridors were cold stone; the doors to various rooms were thick wood and banded with some serious iron. There was nothing supernatural beasties liked less than iron. I wondered if those supernatural occupants had included the two-legged variety from time to time. Considering that Mid was an island full of sorcerers, I would be willing to bet these rooms had also been used as prison cells.

The farther into the depths of the citadel we went, the thicker the air got. Chilled and constricting. Breathing became an effort. It wasn't the closeness and thickness of the walls that gave me that impression; it was something else.

"What kind of containments do you have on this place?" I asked Mychael, using more breath than I could actually spare.

"Level ten here, level twelve on the next two floors down."

Containment spells only went up to twelve. Mychael had arranged housing for the Guardians' newest guest on the bottom floor of the citadel. Bottom floor, subterranean, level-twelve containments, plenty of experienced Guardian chaperones—and someone was trying to break curfew. I bet I knew who the bad boy was. I didn't need any proof to know that Sarad Nukpana would have turned ringleader the moment he was inside the Saghred.

"Level twelve should be reassuring," I said.

Mychael's expression was grim. "It usually is."

I prided myself on being in good shape. Most times being a seeker just demanded that you be in better shape than what was chasing you. I had always aspired to go beyond that. Yet here I was, going *down* flights of stairs, and I was out of breath. That was just plain wrong.

I took a ragged gasp of air. "Is this normal?"

To my satisfaction, Mychael did look a tad flushed himself, and so did Ronan Cayle. Being paladin meant he had to be in better shape than everyone, and Ronan Cayle's lung capacity was as well-known as his voice.

"To a degree." Mychael took a deep breath. "We layer our shields. When they've just been replenished, it can thicken the air somewhat."

"Somewhat like this?"

"Nothing like this."

Not only was the air thick, it was cloying in my mouth, my throat, my lungs, threatening to choke me, and it didn't smell too great, either. Though the smell was the least of my problems. Sliding up from below along the chilled stone walls came a sibilant whisper. I knew that voice. I didn't know if I heard it with my ears or in my head, but I knew who it was and where it was coming from. The language was Goblin, as was the speaker.

"Good morning, my little seeker," Sarad Nukpana murmured.

Those five silky little words were all it took to start my skin crawling on the soles of my feet and keep going until it reached my scalp. The voice sounded husky from sleep, carried the warmth of the bed, and was way too intimate under any circumstances, especially since Sarad Nukpana was the last person I wanted to open my eyes and find sharing my pillow.

I took a slow and careful breath, not daring to move. "Do you hear that?" I asked Mychael.

From my expression he knew I had heard something bad. "Hear what?"

"He cannot hear my words or thoughts, little seeker. Only you."

Mychael scowled. "Nukpana?"

I nodded in the smallest motion possible.

"Give your paladin my regards."

The goblin's voice felt like a cat rubbing up against my face—not a sensation I used to mind. Until now.

I swallowed. "He says hello."

We picked up the pace. Nukpana's warm laughter bubbled up around us.

"Our power grows." I could almost feel the goblin's languid stretch. *"Tell your paladin and his maestro that they cannot stop us."*

"Mychael, unless Sarad Nukpana's taken to referring to himself in the royal 'we,' he's found some like-minded friends in there."

"I'm not surprised."

"I am. He never struck me as the friend-making type."

"Allies, little seeker. Allies. All of a like mind; all with the same goal."

If Sarad Nukpana could talk to me in my head, the least I could do was return the favor. I knew how.

"So, what kind of club are you and your new friends starting?" I asked.

"We merely wish to ensure our survival—and our prosperity. You will help us accomplish both."

"Fat chance."

"You cannot refuse us any more than you can refuse to breathe. You are a bond servant to the Saghred, like your father before you." There was a knowing smile in his voice. *"Even now you do its will."*

That was unwelcome news. I tried to find breathable air and go down the stairs, while my mind raced to find what I could have done to make the Saghred happy. I'd lifted the stage this morning with the power the Saghred had already given me. I didn't tap the stone. And when it tempted me in that courtyard, I didn't give in. I couldn't see how either was doing the Saghred's will.

"Soon its desires will become your own, and you will have an eternity to fulfill them. You are strong enough to serve, but too weak to resist."

The sense of Sarad Nukpana abruptly vanished. "So much for him ignoring me," I said out loud.

Concern flashed in Mychael's blue eyes. "What did he say?"

"Oh, nothing much, just promised me eternal servitude." I made a little dismissive waving motion with my hand. I saw that it was shaking. "He's just trying to scare me."

"Scared is the smartest thing you could be right now."

"That must make me the smartest person on the island."

"Are you all right?"

"If I said yes, I'd be lying. Having an evil madman popping into my head isn't something I want as a permanent arrangement."

"And it won't be." Mychael promised, his intense expression telling me he'd never broken a promise and wasn't about to start with me.

"It's my new life's goal, too. By the way, he's found some new friends to play with, and they have plans."

That earned me a couple of words I didn't expect to hear from a paladin.

Sarad Nukpana's low laughter bubbled up again in my head. I told myself it was only the memory, not the real thing. It didn't lessen the creepies. And I didn't share with Mychael that Nukpana considered me his new helpmate. One catastrophic problem at a time.

We arrived at the citadel's lowest level. The Saghred's containment room's door was just a door. It didn't look like a portal to the bowels of hell or the entrance to the unspeakable. It was just a thick wooden door, banded with iron, and flanked by a pair of burly Guardians who didn't look happy to be there. I didn't blame them.

Sarad Nukpana wasn't going to go to sleep without a fight. I thought the comparison to an obnoxious child was oddly appropriate. I'd threaten to spank him, but unlike a child, Sarad Nukpana would probably enjoy it. In fact, I was sure of it.

"Once we're inside, let us know if the subject begins to misbehave," Cayle reminded me.

It looked like I wasn't the only one using a naughty schoolboy analogy.

"Trust me—when the Saghred misbehaves, you'll know about it whether I tell you or not. But I'll be glad to mention the obvious when it happens."

"You mean *if* it happens."

"Well, we can all hope for that."

Mychael had been speaking in low tones with the Guardians on duty at the door. He crossed the corridor to where we waited. "Are we ready?"

"To get it over with," I said.

Mychael nodded, and the Guardians posted on either side of the door unlocked, unlatched, and opened it.

The stairs and the room below were brightly lit, but only for the benefit of the Guardians on duty. Being its own self-contained little world, the Saghred made its own interior light. The outside world was not visible from inside. Unfortunately, I had this knowledge firsthand.

The room contained only the essentials—four Guardians and the object they guarded. One look at the Saghred sitting on its pedestal told me that the stone had its figurative eyes closed, but it was far from asleep. Unlike with a child pretending to be asleep, Mychael, Ronan, and I weren't just going to turn off the bedroom lights and close the door on our way out.

Sarad Nukpana was nowhere to be heard. Maybe he'd rolled over and gone back to sleep. Maybe he and his new friends were up late last night plotting world domination.

I didn't like any of it, no maybe about it.

The Saghred sat on a small table in the center of the room, still in the translucent, white stone casket Mychael had used to transport it to Mid. It was still translucent, but it sure wasn't white.

I couldn't ever think of a time when a red glow was a good thing.

The Saghred's glow reminded me of an angry, red eye. I half expected to hear a warning growl to go along with it. The rock was clearly not amused, which told me the shields might be holding. Barely.

I had heard about the kind of power Conclave-trained Guardians could put into their containment spells. It was an accepted fact that if a Guardian clamped something or someone down, it stayed put. I didn't think the Saghred had heard the same stories—and if Sarad Nukpana had, he was delighting in ignoring them.

The Saghred's glow faded to a softly pulsing pink, and I felt the faintest tug, like a child's hand wrapping around my little finger, a soft insistence, a come-watch-what-I-can-do kind of invitation. Sweet and innocent and perfectly harmless.

"You can bat your eyelashes at me all day," I told the Saghred. "I'm not buying."

I could only describe what happened next as a tantrum.

The containment box lid sprang open and a beam of blood-red light shot out and engulfed one of the Guardians. He screamed, and I lunged for the box. I knew it was a bad idea. I also knew it was exactly what Sarad Nukpana wanted. But I knew the Guardian was dead or worse if I did nothing.

As soon as my hand touched the open lid, I realized just how bad an idea it was. The last voice I heard from outside the Saghred was Mychael's shout.

Chapter 4

My world turned gray and silent.

More of a twilight fog actually, the kind you see on a waterfront pier—just before you step off the edge. Last time I had been inside the Saghred, it had been a gray void filled with filmy figures. This almost looked the same, but with the notable and welcome absence of the figures. I wasn't going to complain; some of the figures had wanted me dead. Besides, there was no one to complain to. Then I saw movement through the shimmering silver light, movement that resolved itself into a tall figure. I looked around. There was no cover, no place to hide; I was half tempted to close my eyes. If I couldn't see it, maybe it couldn't see me.

"It doesn't work that way," the figure murmured.

I knew that voice. The speaker emerged from the shifting mist. Sarad Nukpana. I wasn't surprised, but I sure was disappointed. Of all the Saghred's residents, he was the one I least wanted to run into.

With a negligent wave of Sarad Nukpana's elegant fingers, the fog retreated.

No mere featureless wasteland would do for Sarad Nukpana.

We stood in a space filled with sensual comforts. A low bed covered with pillows. A plush chaise upholstered with fabric that looked too soft to be real, a low table with two chairs, the table set with glasses and a heavy, cut-crystal decanter of dark, ruby liquid. My feet sank into a fur rug so soft and decadent, I had to resist the urge to drop and roll. Not the sort of surroundings you'd expect of someone plotting world domination.

Sarad Nukpana himself didn't look any worse for wear, and he also looked amazingly solid. Going from corporeal to disembodied soul hadn't diminished his dark beauty one bit. His long black hair was shot through with silver and fell loosely around his strongly sculpted face; the tips of his upswept ears were barely visible through the midnight mass of his hair. Nukpana's pearl gray skin set off what was any goblin's most distinguishing feature—a pair of fangs that weren't for decorative use only. The danger didn't detract from the race's appeal; some would say it fueled it. I guess all that sinuous grace and exotic beauty can make you overlook a lot, and Sarad Nukpana was certainly devastating. He was also insane—that I couldn't overlook.

"You redecorated," I remarked, my mouth dry. "Not my taste."

His eyes were bottomless black pools. "It suits my taste—and my needs—perfectly."

I didn't move. "So the newest inmate gets to choose the color scheme?"

He laughed, a dark, rich sound. "In a way of speaking. I am the newest here—and the strongest."

I couldn't help but notice that the plushness extended only so far. I wondered if the same was true of his influence. Where the room's walls should be, the void with its shimmering waves of mist resumed.

"Did someone else not agree with your taste?"

The goblin's flawless face remained expressionless. "The most intimate surroundings are small. I have all that I need here."

"Or are you using all the strength you can spare?"

The goblin's dark eyes narrowed. "Still playing dangerous games, little seeker?"

"They seem to be the only kind available." I helped myself to the plush chaise. "You wanted me here, and you went to a lot of trouble to make it happen." I leaned back and crossed my legs. It really was very comfortable. "What do you want?"

"To make you an offer."

"No."

He smiled. " 'No,' I can't make you an offer, or 'no,' you refuse?"

"Oh, you can make me an offer; I just won't have any part of it."

"Just like that." His smile broadened, his fangs peeking into view. "No hearing me out and then casting my offer back in my face?"

"That's right. Regardless of what you say, I already know I'm going to turn you down. And since you've turned my mind into your personal bedroom, I'm sure you know what I know. So it seems counterproductive to prolong this conversation any more than it has to be."

"I do know your thoughts. See what you see." He paused suggestively. "And feel what you feel. Shall I hazard a guess as to why you fear what I can offer you—what the Saghred can give us both?"

"Insanity and prolonged death? Just because you're merrily skipping down that path doesn't mean I want to join you."

"I merely want to give you what you truly desire."

"You and the rock are going to go away?"

"That is not what you really want."

This promised to be good. I crossed my arms. "And just what is my heart's desire?"

"Power."

"No, power is what *you* want. *I* want you to vanish."

Sarad Nukpana made himself at home on the bed, and took his time doing it. "There are many kinds of power— with many uses. So we can both desire power, but have different uses for it. That does not change the fact that we essentially want the same thing."

I'd heard enough and sat up. "I've seen what your idea of power does. There isn't anything I could want less."

"Even if you had the power to protect?" His smile was slow and confident. "The power to defend those in danger, the ones you love? The power you scorned this morning. If you had accepted what the Saghred offered, that girl wouldn't be in Banan Ryce's hands." The smile reached his black eyes. "That means whatever is happening to her this very moment is entirely your fault. You could have prevented it with one word."

I didn't move. "The Saghred doesn't offer that kind of power." I said it, but I wasn't sure of it.

"Oh, but it does." His voice rubbed over me like the soft fabric beneath my fingertips. "The power is the same; the only difference is how it is used. You could choose how you use your gift. That is what the archmagus fears; it is the fear your paladin won't admit. The strength the Saghred gives you also gives you the strength to choose."

"Whether to become a disembodied soul now or later? I don't consider that much of a choice."

"Your choices are the Saghred's choices. Do you think you and your paladin chose to bring the Saghred to Mid? Hardly, little seeker. The Saghred chose where it would go, and who would take it there. We are all instruments of its will; I have merely found a way to make that will work to my advantage."

"So you want to live like an evil genie in a bottle?"

"It will not be forever."

"I'm sure your buddies in here felt the same way—for the first hundred years or so." I looked out into surrounding grayness. There were slender forms all around us. They weren't the screaming wraiths I'd encountered last time I was inside the Saghred; these were standing perfectly still, patiently waiting for something. Creepy. I could feel the power coming off of them, though the force from Sarad Nukpana was stronger. He was definitely the big dog in the pack. For now. I wondered which one out there was second in the pack order. Disturbingly, my father was nowhere to be seen.

I'd had enough, and stood. Sarad Nukpana rose and came toward me with predatory grace, quicker than any mortal creature had a right to move. He caught my wrist in his hand. I had to remind myself that the goblin wasn't mortal anymore. However, his hand was strong and all too solid around my wrist. I felt his will meld with the Saghred, stretching outward, beyond the room, beyond the void.

I dimly heard an agonized scream. The Guardian.

Two could play at that game. With my free hand, I grabbed the front of his shirt and twisted my fingers until the silken fabric was firmly knotted in my fist. "Release him. Now."

There was a flicker of surprise in the goblin's dark eyes. He expected me to be afraid. I was. But I was a hell of a lot more angry. In my family, rage wins out over fear anytime.

"Such a small request," he murmured. "You are certain you do not wish anything more?"

"Let's see . . . You gone, the rock gone, your lawyers gone. That would pretty much cover it for me."

"Those are not within my power, or yours." He moved his body slowly against mine, and it was all too obvious he liked being this close. "But the Guardian is within your power to free," he whispered against my ear. "The Saghred is yours to command. Tell it to release him, and it shall be done. Immediately. You only need to will it." He drew back just enough to gaze down at me, his dark eyes shining. A slow smile formed, fangs visible. The goblin's smile told me that he would love to see me do it. Probably because the moment I asked the Saghred for one favor, it could demand one right back. I had a feeling that the rock's idea of a small favor would be something along the lines of my eternal soul on a platter, like a bunch of grapes to be plucked one at a time. I wasn't about to be served up to anything or anyone.

If I did nothing, the Guardian would die. And I had a

feeling he would be the first of many until the Saghred, or Sarad Nukpana, got what they wanted.

I had another feeling. Actually it was more like a realization. Sarad Nukpana couldn't have decorated all by himself. Nor could he be attacking that Guardian all by his lonesome. He and the Saghred were connected in some way and feeding off of each other.

If I hurt one of them, the other should at least blink. I was counting on Mychael acting when the rock blinked. Nukpana was standing close enough; his breath was warm against my cheek. I'd wonder later about how disembodied souls could breathe, let alone be warm. Wonder later; act now. His hand on my wrist had felt solid enough. Let's see how solid the rest of him was.

My knee was ready to find out when the floor buckled beneath our feet and the silvery void rippled with an unseen impact. Nukpana and I landed hard on the floor, and I rolled clear and came to my feet before the goblin could get his hands on me again.

The void beyond Nukpana's bedroom was lighter now, like the sun trying to force its way through heavy fog. The light faded and then flared again with increased intensity.

Nukpana looked up into the void and laughed. "Your paladin is trying to rescue you. An impressive effort. He must fear for your safety."

That made two of us.

I was standing on the edge of Nukpana's bedroom, and my hand brushed against the void.

It was solid, not mist.

It was also cold and brittle beneath my fingers, like a sheet of translucent ice. Fog could be penetrated, and ice could be broken. Breaking it could also let the wraiths in— or let me out. There was only one way to know for sure.

I grabbed one of the chairs and swung it with everything I had.

Nukpana's world shattered. The void engulfed Sarad Nukpana, the room, everything. I felt myself being pulled backward. The goblin's wordless scream came to me through the racing mist, dim from distance, but raw with undiminished fury.

In an instant, my feet went from plush fur to stone floor. Mychael was holding me pressed tightly against him, his hands on either side of my head.

"She's back," I heard him say to someone. He sounded out of breath. I didn't know who he was talking to; my eyes wouldn't exactly focus.

The room got lighter and the blurred images sharpened into Ronan Cayle and the Guardians. I shuddered, a full head-to-toe event. Then the shuddering turned into shaking and some shallow breathing. I couldn't stop the shaking, and I didn't even try. Breathing, I made an effort to do. Mychael's hands went from my head to around my waist. They were strong and warm, and they were all that was between me and a quick and unpleasant trip to the floor.

The Guardian who the Saghred had attacked was on the floor, half-conscious, and trying to sit up. He was determined and his brother Guardians had their hands full trying to stop him. His first words blistered the air blue. I'd found if a man could swear that expressively, the insides of his head couldn't have been too rattled. With only a little help from his brothers, he got to his feet.

I steadied myself with my hands against Mychael's chest. He was standing close enough to kiss. I could feel his heart pounding beneath my palm.

I took a panting breath, then tried a smile. "You tried to break into the Saghred."

"I did." His eyes reflected concern, relief, and rage all at the same time. "He didn't hurt you, did he?"

I shook my head. "You breaking in gave me the idea to break out. It worked."

Mychael's hands tightened briefly around my waist; then with a quick glance at his men, he loosened his hold and stepped back, much to my disappointment.

To my surprise, I stayed on my feet. "Did I vanish or something?"

"You were here the whole time," Ronan Cayle said. "All five seconds of it."

I blinked. "Seconds? That's it?"

"It felt like longer?" he asked.

"About a half hour's worth. I guess time's different on the inside." I'd heard that from some of my formerly incarcerated family members. I never thought I'd have my own experience to draw from. "What happened out here?"

Mychael's expression darkened, and I think it was aimed at me. "You went for the box's lid before I could stop you. Then you closed the lid and took a step back." He paused uncomfortably. "You stopped breathing; that was how I knew he'd taken you inside."

I stared at him. "I stopped breathing?"

"It's the first sign of an out-of-body experience," he told me. "And considering what you'd just touched, I knew where you'd gone."

I felt the residual tingle of his hands pressed to the sides of my head. "You used your hands to—"

A muscle twitched in Mychael's jaw. "Attempt to retrieve your soul."

"My soul was gone?" My voice sounded very small.

"It was."

I didn't say anything. I couldn't say anything. Though there was a good chance that I'd scream later.

"What happened in there?" Mychael asked quietly.

I swallowed. "Nukpana tried to tell me that being bonded to the Saghred was a gift, not a curse. It wasn't a very convincing argument. It's also a discussion I'd rather not have with him again—in my body or out." I looked from Mychael to Ronan. "Are you two ready to do what we came for and get the hell out of here?"

"More than ready," Mychael said. He looked at Ronan. "Sir?"

In response, the maestro tossed aside his outer, merely flamboyant robe, exposing the inner, if at all possible, more outrageous robe. I guess it was the sort of thing a legendary spellsinger wore to a legendary stone of power figurative ass kicking. I didn't know if Ronan Cayle was getting comfortable to sing, or getting unburdened by all that silk should running become necessary. Either one sounded like a good idea. But I didn't want to be the one to tell the maestro that if the Saghred decided to fight back, his little brocade-booted feet weren't going to do him any good.

"The melody is more effective in a lower range," Ronan told Mychael. "You start. I'll come in with the countermelody."

"Is everyone able to shield themselves?" Mychael addressed the question to his Guardians and me.

I nodded. The Guardians responded by speaking their personal shields into place. I followed suit. We weren't shielding ourselves against the Saghred; we were protecting ourselves against what Mychael and Ronan were about to do. I had no doubt that their sleepsong would be one of the most potent. We weren't wayward souls, but it was still a sleepsong sung by a pair of masters. If we didn't shield ourselves, we'd be on the floor snoring. With shields, we would still be able to hear the song, but the spell wouldn't affect us.

Mychael began to hum, the softest, most soothing sound I'd ever heard. Even standing across from him, I could feel the sound resonating from deep in his chest. I could only imagine what it would feel like to be held there, listening to that sound, feeling that music. The humming resolved into whispered words, the syllables melding one into the next, the pitch low and constant and warm.

He had a deep, molten, luscious baritone that made me think of melted chocolate. Decadent and delicious, not to mention hypnotic. If that voice had been persuading me to go to sleep—or do anything else—I don't think I'd have been able to resist. Hell, I don't think I would have even tried.

I'd only heard Mychael's singing in snippets. But I knew enough about spellsinging to know that his voice was doing some very intricate and impressive work. I couldn't tell yet if the Saghred was impressed enough to be sleepy, but it made a fan for life out of me. The tune was simple and heartbreakingly beautiful, but it was the words of the spell-song that would have tripped up a lesser spellsinger.

Ronan's tenor seamlessly merged with Mychael's baritone, flowing underneath in a strong countermelody. Not surprisingly, I didn't feel the same way about Ronan's voice, but I knew enough about spellsinging to tell that his pipes more than matched his reputation.

Their spellduet was essentially a lullaby for one, soft and soothing. Volume wasn't needed, just intensity.

I just wanted to stand there and bask in the rolling waves of scrumptious sound, but I had work to do. It was my job to see if Sarad Nukpana had stopped listening because he couldn't keep his eyes open. I felt the Saghred begin to waver. The soft light illuminating the stone never changed, but what I sensed from it definitely did. It was working.

Then it wasn't. Something or, more to the point, someone, was fighting back.

I'd give Mychael and Ronan three guesses and the first two didn't count.

I saw Sarad Nukpana with others I had only seen through silver mist—his new friends, his allies. Only now they were just as solid as Nukpana himself. There were goblins and elves and humans, with a couple of creatures whose race or species I didn't recognize. The evil inside the Saghred didn't restrict itself to Sarad Nukpana. They were down, but they weren't going out. I heard laughter, muffled but still mocking.

I didn't want my voice to possibly disrupt what Mychael and Ronan were doing, but I made sure my expression spoke volumes. They knew as well as I did what was happening—and what was not happening. They were getting the message without my help. Professionals that they were, their spellduet never faltered.

Suddenly, a disembodied voice floated in the air around us, a voice of staggering strength and power, a baritone like Mychael. It was deep, vibrant, and impossible to ignore.

It was Piaras.

Maintaining one particularly glorious low note while Cayle's tenor danced above it, Mychael indicated a small square opening, almost hidden in shadow near the ceiling. Of course, an air vent. I thought the containment rooms were sealed, but that was ridiculous. If they'd been sealed, we wouldn't have been able to breathe. I assumed that like in most large buildings, the vent led to a network of tiny tunnels running throughout the citadel. Piaras was practicing on the citadel's main floor in the music room. I recognized it as one of his sleepsongs. But unlike Mychael and Ronan, Piaras wasn't singing a lullaby for one. The kid was trying to knock out a platoon. It was a sleepsong for use on a battlefield—and if we could hear it down here, so could the rest of the citadel.

Oh shit.

Magnified by the ducts, his voice was as hypnotic as Mychael's—and as sleep inducing. I heard what sounded like a sigh of smug, sensual contentment from Sarad Nukpana. If the Saghred had been a cat, it would have been purring. I didn't want the rock belligerent, but I didn't want it happy, either. Piaras's singing made it just a little too happy.

Then the Saghred simply drifted off to sleep. I felt like a lead weight had been lifted from the center of my chest. All sense of the Saghred was gone. I hadn't felt this good in a long time.

Piaras's voice went silent with the end of the spellsong. I didn't know how he'd done it, but I couldn't deny what he had done.

An untrained teenage spellsinger had just put the Saghred to sleep.

Chapter 5

We ran up the stairs in what must have been record time. The wards on the containment levels had protected the Guardians there, but once the three of us reached the citadel's main floor, Piaras's handiwork was sprawled all around us.

Dammit.

Piaras knew to shield his voice when he practiced. More important, he knew how. I didn't know what had happened here, but it couldn't have been Piaras's fault. I'd never seen Mychael that angry, and Ronan Cayle looked like he'd skipped angry and gone straight to enraged.

Dammit to hell.

We saw three kinds of Guardians on the way to the music room: asleep, stunned, and mostly awake. The asleep ones had been caught completely unawares. The stunned ones had probably heard a couple of notes before they could get their shields up. The mostly awake ones were the experienced Guardians who knew what they heard and immediately protected themselves.

There were way too few of those.

This morning I'd thought I was in trouble. I knew Piaras was in trouble.

The corridor in front of the music room looked like the aftermath of a bad bar fight or a good night out—some of the Guardians were snoring; some were happily curled on their sides; and one had slid down the closed music room doors. He wasn't asleep, but he wasn't quite with us, either.

Mychael stepped over the Guardians on the floor, pushed the dazed one aside, and flung open the doors. Piaras was there and, surprisingly, so was Phaelan.

Piaras looked up from his music stand, his big brown eyes like a deer caught in torchlight. He knew from the looks on our faces that something was deathly wrong, and it was his fault. Then he saw the Guardians on the floor behind Mychael, and every bit of color drained from his face.

Phaelan was sprawled in a chair reading a book—completely conscious and utterly clueless.

I jerked the book out of his lap. He plucked the plugs out of his ears, and sat up indignantly.

"What?"

I pointed to the pile of Guardians outside the open door. One Guardian staggered by, leaning on the wall for support.

Phaelan whistled. "Damn, looks like my crew on shore leave. Did the kid do that?"

"Apparently."

Phaelan grinned at Piaras and gave him a thumbs up. "Good work, kid." He stopped and took in everyone's expressions, including Piaras's. The grin vanished, and the thumb wilted. "Not good work?"

Mychael pushed past Piaras and went to the air vent near the ceiling. Apparently that was how Piaras's voice had traveled throughout the citadel, so that's where Mychael aimed his. He took a deep breath and sang. The spellsong was loud; it was discordant; and it commanded every sleeping Guardian to wake up. Now. When he finished, he turned on Piaras, his eyes blazing.

"Did you disable the shields on this room?" he demanded.

"No!" Piaras was horrified. "The shields were down?"

"We could hear you in the containment rooms, through the air vent."

"I checked the shields before I started," Piaras protested. "They were up the entire time."

From the moment he came through the door, Ronan Cayle had been stalking around the edge of the room like a hound on a fresh scent. "Not for your last song, they weren't." He never took his eyes off the walls. "And the shields on this room weren't disabled. They were cut." Cayle stopped in front of a section of wall near the air vent. "A careful, surgical cut," he said, sliding his hand up the wall. His hand stopped. "A cut that started right here." He quickly pulled a chair over, stood on it, and moved his hand slowly over the metal grille of the vent, careful not to touch it. "And it extended right into the air vent."

Piaras looked like he had stopped breathing or had forgotten how. "A cut? But I would have known if someone slashed the shields."

"Not if someone very talented didn't want you to know," Cayle said, never taking his eyes off the vent. He carefully placed his fingertips on the grille. "And that someone took great care so you would not know—and chose the air vent so your song would reach the most people." Cayle sounded like he almost admired the bastard's work.

"Where could they have cut the shields from?" I asked.

"Since they were cut while Piaras was singing, it wasn't from inside this room," Mychael said. "They would have worked from the other side of the wall."

"What's back there?"

"Two rooms. The reception area for visitors and a common room where the men relax when they're not on duty."

"So it was guests or Guardians."

Mychael's eyes were blue frost. "None of my men would have done this," he said quietly.

"Then one of your guests was up to no good," I told him.

"Who'd want all the Guardians to take a nap?" Phaelan asked.

Mychael and I looked at each other. Nightshades or Khrynsani. Take your pick. The Nightshades wanted to kill Mychael. The Khrynsani wanted me alive. Both would love to get the Saghred. Sleeping Guardians would make getting any of the above a whole lot easier.

Mychael glared at the wall. "Whoever did it simply walked out through sleeping Guardians."

"Or has blended back into the woodwork," I said. A lot of things didn't make sense to me right now, but two questions demanded asking. "Well, whoever it was, how would they've known Piaras would be in here, and what spellsongs he'd be practicing?"

Piaras cleared his throat. "I reserved the room last night, and I had to give a reason." He paused apologetically. "I wrote 'sleepsongs.' "

"The logbook is on a desk down the hall," Mychael told me.

I was incredulous. "Anyone could have seen it?"

"It's a book to reserve time in a music room, Raine. A spellsinger practicing is hardly a state secret." Mychael looked at the air vent. "Is it still asleep?"

I didn't need to ask who "it" was. There was no pressure in the center of my chest from the Saghred. I still hesitated before answering. "Yes."

"You don't sound sure."

"I'm sure it's asleep. I just don't trust it."

Cayle spoke. "If it is asleep, the king's ransom question is how long will it stay that way."

"A century or two would be nice," I muttered.

Piaras looked from one of us to the other, now scared *and* confused.

"Should we tell Piaras what he just did?" I asked Mychael.

"He needs to know."

Out in the corridor, Guardians were getting to their feet in response to their paladin's voice; some of them had thrown an arm over a brother's shoulder for support. It was starting to look less like nap time and more like the morning after a night out.

"You mean that?" Piaras asked. He sounded a little sick.

"I'm afraid you did more than that," I told him.

"I did *more*?"

"Mychael and Maestro Cayle were spellsinging the Saghred to sleep, but you beat them to it."

"Maestro?" Piaras whispered in sheer terror.

Somehow I didn't think Piaras had heard anything past "Maestro."

Mychael spoke. "Ronan, this is your audition for tomorrow."

Cayle's amber eyes were locked on Piaras. "So you're Master Rivalin. Audition, hell. There'll be no audition."

Phaelan came to his feet. I was about to punch Ronan Cayle.

Piaras stood perfectly still, his breathing shallow. "I no longer have an audition." He didn't ask it as a question, and he clenched his jaw against any further show of emotion. He was devastated, but he was going to keep his dignity. "I understand, sir."

Phaelan stepped up beside me, and I laid a restraining hand on his arm. If he was going after Cayle, he'd have to get in line behind me.

"No, you don't understand," Cayle told him. "You don't knock out half the Guardians in the citadel and then audition." He walked slowly around Piaras, assessing what he saw and what he could not see.

The Piaras I saw was tall, had liquid brown eyes and tousled dark curls, and was on the verge of becoming a handsome young man. Piaras saw awkwardness and a voice that would always be less than perfect. I think Ronan Cayle was seeing a powerful, loose cannon who'd taken out most of Mid's main line of defense.

"Yes, you're very dangerous," the maestro said softly. His voice was velvet-covered steel. "With the right song, you'd be lethal. You're unpredictable, impulsive, and you have absolutely no idea of your potential."

Piaras swallowed. "Potential, sir?"

"Potential." Cayle stopped in front of Piaras and smiled slowly. "For the good of the seven kingdoms, I'd better take you as a student." His smile broadened and those amber eyes glittered. "As to auditioning, you just did."

Piaras gaped in disbelief. "You're accepting me?"

"I am." Cayle chuckled softly. "You've left me no choice."

"And without a formal audition," Mychael told Piaras, his lips curling into a small smile. "That's a first, isn't it, Ronan?"

"It is. Be at my tower at exactly eight bells tomorrow morning," Cayle told Piaras. "Mychael can tell you where it is." The smile vanished. "And come prepared to work."

Piaras smiled like the sun had just come out. "Thank you, sir."

Ronan Cayle laughed, a short bark. "We'll see how thankful you are after tomorrow. And by the way, my students are expected to sprint to the top of my tower in three minutes or less. Builds lung capacity." There was an evil glint in those amber eyes. "You're going to need it."

"A cut shield explains Piaras spellsinging my men to sleep," Mychael said. "But it doesn't tell me who did the cutting, or why. It also doesn't tell me how Piaras sang the Saghred to sleep. That was a battlefield sleepsong; it shouldn't have worked."

Piaras blinked. "I did what?"

"Your voice put the rock to sleep," I told him. "*That* was that other thing you did."

"How could . . . ? I never meant to . . . I was up here; the Saghred is down there." Realization dawned on him. "There are air ducts in the containment rooms."

Mychael nodded. "We could hear you loud and clear."

"Sir, I'm sorry," Piaras hurried to explain. "I never meant to—"

Mychael held up a hand. "I know you didn't, and I'm not blaming you. This room stays shielded to prevent exactly what just happened. The sabotage was not your fault. And regardless of how you did it, you did put the Saghred to sleep, and for that you have my thanks."

"It was almost like the Saghred wanted to go to sleep once it heard you," I told Piaras. "It liked what it heard." I paused uneasily. "A lot."

"It *liked* Piaras's song?" Phaelan asked.

"The Saghred and those *inside* the Saghred liked Piaras's song," I clarified. "And I'm not sure if either is a good thing."

Piaras didn't move. "What do you mean?"

"I got the feeling the Saghred's inmates enjoyed your song a little bit too much—and so did the rock."

"Is the rock asleep?" Phaelan asked.

"Yes."

"If it's asleep, it doesn't really matter what its taste in music is."

Logic was all well and good, but Phaelan wasn't the one with a growing, evil fan base.

Piaras was clearly creeped. "I don't want the Saghred's inmates to like me." He lowered his voice. "Especially you know who."

"I don't want him to like you, either." Neither one of us felt the need to say the name out loud. Sarad Nukpana was asleep. Probably. Saying his name right now didn't seem like a good idea, kind of like summoning an evil genie out of a bottle.

Last week, Sarad Nukpana had given me a choice: either I gave him a demonstration of the Saghred's power, or he would sacrifice Piaras to the Saghred. Piaras was alive. Nukpana was inside the Saghred. Now Nukpana let Piaras sing him to sleep. I needed to know why, and I needed to know now. If the Saghred had gone to sleep of its own volition, it'd probably wake up the same way.

I pulled Mychael aside. "So, is there a user's manual for the Saghred?" My words were for his ears alone. Thanks to our saboteur, I didn't know who could be listening.

He looked honestly baffled. "A what?"

"User's manual, directions, instructions, why the damned thing fought two master spellsingers, but rolled over and went to sleep when Piaras sang to it."

"The Scriptorium has several books on the Saghred."

"Good. I want to read them."

"They're in Old Goblin."

"Not a problem. I read Old Goblin."

Mychael seemed reluctant. I knew why.

I waited a few seconds until my voice wouldn't sound as exasperated as I felt. "Yes, the Saghred's been in my head," I said through only partially clenched teeth. "And I am well aware that you can't entirely trust me as long as there's a chance it will come back. But do you really think it's going to help our cause to keep me locked away *and* stupid? If any of those books can tell me how to unhook myself from that rock, I want to know about it. And I'm not the only one in danger here." I glanced at Piaras; he was talking earnestly with Ronan Cayle. I lowered my voice even further. "I want to know everything that Sarad Nukpana knows, and then some."

Mychael hesitated, but not for long. "I'll make the arrangements."

"Sir?" came a familiar voice from the doorway.

It was Riston. I couldn't help but notice that he had a bad case of bedhead, and he still looked a little dazed. Piaras winced apologetically. Phaelan's laugh came out as a snort.

"Sir, the chief watcher is here to see you." Riston looked puzzled. "And he said he brought you a hairbrush."

Chapter 6

The man in Mychael's office was wearing enough leather armor and blades to make him feel secure in the nastiest sections of town. I'd once found out the hard way that when a man was that big and that heavily armed and wearing an expression that grim, it was good to wait and be properly introduced.

Mychael greeted him with a warm handshake. I couldn't help but notice that Mychael's entire hand vanished in the man's enormous paw.

"Raine, this is our chief watcher, Sedge Rinker. Sedge, this is Raine Benares."

I crossed the office and cautiously extended my hand. Members of my family were generally greeted with hand-*cuffs* by law enforcement, not hand*shakes*. Rinker hesitated a moment, then took my hand in a firm yet surprisingly gentle handshake.

"I was in the square this morning and saw what you did." Rinker's voice was a basso rumble. "Impressive work—and I don't mind saying a little scary."

I grinned. I couldn't imagine anything scaring this man. "I scared me, too," I told him.

Sedge Rinker didn't look like a man who sat behind a desk all day. His dark beard was trimmed neatly enough, but he hadn't fussed with it. His hair was efficiently short, but style wasn't something he bothered with or cared about. However, his armor and weapons were of the highest quality and in immaculate condition. I'd seen his like among watch officers many times—they were utterly devoted to their work and the people they protected.

"Did you get anything useful from those two Nightshades?" he asked Mychael.

I gave Mychael a sharp look. "You took two alive?"

"We did."

"And?"

"And our investigation is ongoing."

It was his paladin voice, the voice that wasn't about to tell me anything. His expression wasn't volunteering information, either.

Rinker looked uneasily from Mychael to me. He'd assumed Mychael trusted me. So had I.

"Janek Tawl is a friend of mine," Rinker told me, deftly changing the subject. "He says you're the best seeker he knows. I was glad to find out you were visiting us."

Janek Tawl was a friend of mine, too. As chief watcher of the Sorcerers District back home in Mermeia, Janek's path had crossed mine on a regular basis. Janek occasionally sought my expertise as a seeker, and from time to time he was able to give me leads on cases I was working on.

"Janek's a top-notch watcher and a fine man," I agreed. "I'm honored that he thinks so highly of me." I tossed Mychael a meaningful glance.

"Mychael tells me you want to help us find one of our missing students."

Small talk was over. I liked a man who got right down to business. "I want to do everything I can to help," I told him.

Rinker pulled a cloth-wrapped object out of a leather bag. He carefully handed it to me without unwrapping it. Good man. He knew his business, and more important, he knew mine. More than once I'd been called to a crime scene only to find that the object I most needed to use had been handled by nearly every watcher on-site, contaminating it and rendering it useless for seeking. It was their emotional imprint I'd get, not the victim's. So the only person I'd find was the stupid watcher who'd last picked it up.

I took the wrapped hairbrush. "Did anyone touch this before it was wrapped?" I asked him.

"No one," he assured me.

I smiled at him. "Thank you, Chief Watcher. It's always a pleasure to work with true professionals."

He nodded. "I understand you were there when Miss Jacobs was taken through that mirror."

"Megan Jacobs is the student's name," Mychael clarified.

"Yes, I was," I told the watcher. "Unfortunately, I wasn't in a position to do anything to prevent it." I frowned. "I can't make up for what happened, but I want to help you find her—and the man who took her."

"You're familiar with Banan Ryce?" Rinker asked.

"We've met," I said flatly. "It wasn't professional, but it was hardly social."

The watcher didn't ask me to explain, which was good, because I had no intention of doing so.

I turned to Mychael. "May I use your couch? Hopefully I won't need it, but better comfy than concussed."

"Of course."

I went to the couch, sat down with my back against the cushions. Even before my Saghred-enhanced seeking skills, I made it a point to try to sit someplace soft when working. The impressions I got from an object could be vague or jarring, and since I was attempting a direct link with a hopefully still-living person, the disorientation from that link could very well put me on the floor.

I held the wrapped hairbrush in one hand and peeled back the fabric with the other. It was a small silver brush of fine quality. Even better, there were a few long, blond hairs caught in the bristles. Last week, I got to experience a murder victim's last seconds right along with him—all courtesy of the power boost the Saghred had given me. The victim had been killed the day before, so I'd gotten nothing from his personal object but last impressions and a mild case of the whirlies.

Megan Jacobs was still alive, as far as we knew. I'd never been inside a living person's head before. I was pretty sure I could do it; I just didn't know what to expect. Being the control freak that I am, I always want to know what to expect. Too bad I rarely get what I want.

I picked up the brush and clasped it in both hands.

The connection was immediate, crystal clear, and unnerving as hell.

I was disoriented, but what I felt was sick. I took shallow breaths and blew them out in short puffs, willing the contents of my stomach to stay right where they were. My stomach listened, and I saw the world through Megan Jacobs's eyes.

The girl was alive, conscious, and scared to death. The scared part seemed like an appropriate enough response to being dragged through a mirror by Banan Ryce. As best I could tell, Banan hadn't been keeping her company. That was good. What wasn't so good was that she wasn't in any place I could easily identify.

It was cold, damp, and almost completely dark. A single small candle in an iron holder was on the floor with her. The floor and walls felt like stone to me, probably subterranean, judging from the temperature, though whether it was natural or a man-made structure such as a cellar I had no way of knowing—and neither did Megan. She wasn't tied up and could have gone exploring. I know I would have. She just huddled in a corner, shaking. The shaking I could deal with, but if she didn't stop breathing like she was trying to outrun a demon from the lower hells, she was going to pass out and take me right along with her. She certainly had the right idea about Banan Ryce, but he wasn't in the room with her now.

But that didn't mean she was alone.

There was another girl with her. The meager light showed a slender figure, curled on her side. She was turned away from me, so I couldn't see her face, but I could see her hair. She was a blonde. The slight rise and fall of her back told me she was breathing, so she was either asleep or unconscious.

Megan's panicked breathing was making me lightheaded. Though it might have been less from Megan, and more from what I was about to try. In the good old days of last week, when I was just a simple seeker for hire, I could use an object from a missing person to get an idea of the direction they'd been taken. A vague idea. That's what I could do in my pre-Saghred professional life. Megan had been taken through a mirror. Mirrors didn't leave a trail to follow; but since I had successfully linked with Megan, I should be able to pinpoint for Sedge Rinker exactly where those girls were—and better yet, where he could get his hands on Banan Ryce, if the smug bastard was nearby.

Maybe.

Knowing the mechanics of how something was done and actually doing it yourself were two entirely different things. Sometimes those things turned out to be merely unpleasant—sometimes they were lethal.

Ah, the joys of my chosen career.

I loosened my grip ever so slightly on the hairbrush, likewise loosening my direct link with Megan Jacobs. I maintained contact with the girl, although I was no longer inside her head. The impression of the girl remained, strong and clear. It was like keeping someone in your line of sight, but no longer touching them. I kept my eyes closed and my breathing even. I was now back in the citadel, no longer where Megan was being held.

Step one successfully completed.

I felt myself start to smile and stopped it. Don't get cocky, Raine.

I almost didn't dare to breathe. As a seeker, I knew what to do now; I just didn't know how far I could go. Logic and the strength of my contact with Megan Jacobs told me I should be able to go from the citadel directly to where Megan was being held.

Sometimes logic didn't work. And sometimes it bit you in the ass.

I gripped the brush again, but resisted a direct link, instead focusing on direction. I'd just been with Megan; now I needed to know where she was.

The impression of the girl was like a scent. I followed it.

I felt myself leave the citadel and go out into the square where the stage had collapsed this morning. Men were working by torchlight to clear the last of the debris. I followed Megan's scent into the twisting, cobbled mazes of Mid's streets, through the college campus, and into the center city.

And lost her.

Not lost as in I lost the trail, but lost as if Megan Jacobs had suddenly ceased to exist. If the girl's trail had been a lit candle, someone had just blown it out.

I gripped the brush harder. Still no Megan.

I backtracked and tried again. No dice.

Dammit.

Rami Pirin was the son of a bitch who'd taught me everything I knew about seeking. I called him a son of a bitch because his lessons had been unrelenting and most times downright mean. He was also the best seeker I'd ever known or heard of. He could have done what I was trying to do. With my new Saghred-powered magical mojo, I should have been able to do it easily. Rami had taught me that only three things could have caused what had just happened: Megan had been killed; I'd screwed up and lost the trail; or a powerful someone didn't want me finding Megan and had done some fancy magical footwork to ensure I didn't.

One, I would have known if Megan had been killed. Two, I knew I hadn't lost the trail. That left option number three. Rami had always taken that particular option personally. Like teacher, like student. If that meant I had to find Megan and Banan Ryce the old-fashioned way, so be it.

"I'm just an old-fashioned girl," I muttered through clenched teeth.

"What?"

It was Mychael's voice.

I took my hands off the brush and completely broke contact. I slowly opened my eyes. Everything was a little swirly there for a moment, but I was still on the couch and still upright. I was safe, but those girls weren't. And worse yet, someone packing mage-level power didn't want them found.

"Where is she?" Mychael asked.

"Cut right to the chase, don't you? I'm fine, by the way."

"Good. Where is she?"

"Relatively small room, completely dark, stone walls and floor. She's not tied up, but she's too scared to do anything about it. She's alive and unhurt—for now." I paused and glowered. "And as best I can tell, she's being held in the central city."

Mychael glowered back. "Best you can tell?"

I resisted the urge to snap. "Yes, as best I can tell." I told them both about the trail vanishing, and Rami's three reasons why it could have happened.

"Do you know if Banan Ryce has that kind of power?" Mychael asked me.

"He's been known to pack a punch, but he can't do anything like that."

Mychael was silent for a moment. "That's a lot of trouble to go to for a getaway hostage."

"Yeah, it is. But Megan Jacobs isn't alone. There's another girl being held with her." I looked at Sedge Rinker. "Did you know that you have two kidnapped girls?"

Mychael looked sharply at the chief watcher.

The watcher clenched his jaw. "Megan Jacobs was the second victim," he told Mychael. "The first was taken last night."

"Why wasn't I notified?" Mychael wanted to know.

"Her parents are here and want to keep it quiet." It sounded like Rinker liked saying that as little as Mychael liked hearing it. "If it was a random kidnapping, they don't want the abductors to know who she is. They also don't think we're working quickly enough, and have hired their own investigators."

Mychael scowled. "Who's the girl?"

"Ailia Aurillac."

Mychael's scowl deepened. "Her father is Gerald Aurillac," he told me.

"The shipping magnate?" I certainly recognized that name. Phaelan had helped himself to several of Gerald Aurillac's ships over the years. Rich takings, quality merchandise. No doubt Aurillac would be put out at the Conclave college losing his little girl. I thought I'd keep my family's connection to the Aurillacs to myself. If Sedge Rinker didn't know, I wasn't going to be the one to tell him. He had a good opinion of me; I thought I'd let him keep it a while longer.

"She's petite and blond, right?" I asked.

"Yes," Rinker said.

"That's probably her then." Even worse for local law enforcement—a missing heiress.

"When two of my men went to the Aurillacs' yacht to inform her parents, Magus Silvanus was already there and had broken the news."

Mychael didn't swear, but his eyes sure did.

"Who's that?" I asked.

"Carnades Silvanus," Mychael told me. "The senior mage on the Seat of Twelve."

"How does he know the girl?"

"He's her faculty advisor," Rinker told me. "As soon as her dorm housemother discovered she was missing, she notified the magus and then the watch. The magus went directly to the girl's parents."

And stepped hard on some city watch toes when he did. Bet that hadn't earned him any popularity points with Rinker's people.

"What's in it for him?" I asked. "Besides a brown nose?"

"A black eye for local law enforcement," Mychael said. "Guardians included."

I carefully wrapped the hairbrush. "Banan Ryce took

Megan Jacobs. Since Ailia Aurillac is with her, I think it's safe to say that Banan or his Nightshades are responsible for her as well. Where was Ailia taken from?"

"Her dorm room."

So much for campus security.

"By any chance does she have a large mirror?" I asked. I couldn't imagine a wealthy heiress who wouldn't.

"She does," Rinker said.

The girl I saw with Megan wasn't dead, but she wasn't moving, either. "Were there signs of violence found in the room?"

"None. But we did find a rag soaked with wiccbane."

"Good," I said.

That earned me an odd look from both men.

"I'd rather get wiccbane than clubbed over the head," I told them. "Linking with her might make me woozy, but that'll be it."

"But you've already seen Miss Aurillac," Mychael said.

"I saw her, but I didn't see how she got there. Megan Jacobs is conscious and scared to death. The only thing I'm getting from her is light-headed. Ailia Aurillac is asleep or unconscious. That means a link with her just might let me see the last people she saw before the wiccbane got to her."

Rinker's dark eyes shone. "You can do that?"

I met his gaze. "I can do that." Then I leaned forward with a conspirator's smile. "And I'm betting you have something of hers in that bag."

"I do. I was one of the first watchers on the scene. I found a gold locket on the floor of her room. The chain was broken."

"Any blood on it?"

"A little."

Bad for Ailia, good for me. That should make my link all the more powerful. I held out my hand. Rinker dropped the pouch into it.

I opened the bag and dumped its contents onto the couch beside me. I picked it up by the chain, careful to avoid for now the specks of blood on one section. I'd found through unpleasant experience that a chain conducted images a lot less than a pendant. I didn't know why; it just did. I looked at Ailia's pendant—gold, high quality, beautiful workmanship. The pendant was large enough to contain engraving inside or even a tiny painting. My money was on the latter. The Aurillacs could certainly afford a miniature portrait, or perhaps it was a gift from the girl's fiancé.

"Is she engaged?" I asked Sedge.

"Not that I am aware of."

Probably a gift from her parents then.

I hesitated a moment longer, then dropped the locket and chain into my hand and closed my fist around both.

I had been grabbed from behind before. I knew what to do. I had a couple of responses that had served me very well. Ailia had never been attacked. Panic was the only response she knew. I didn't enjoy feeling it along with her. Panic, terror, frantic struggling against at least three attackers in the near darkness. She didn't stand a chance and they knew it. They were laughing. She managed one muffled scream before they'd made sure she couldn't. Two wore masks; one didn't. I knew the one not wearing a mask. Ailia didn't, but she saw him. That wasn't good. Generally kidnappers who let you see them might be planning on collecting a ransom, but they weren't planning on letting you go once they did.

The unmasked kidnapper was Banan Ryce. That made it even worse.

The last thing both Ailia and I saw was Ryce's green eyes.

The next thing that blurred into focus was Mychael's concerned blue eyes, which was a vast improvement.

"Are you all right?" he asked.

I nodded, then shook my head to clear it. "Do you know if Banan still has those two mirror mages working for him?" I asked Mychael.

"He does."

"Looks like they're earning their keep."

Banan's two mirror mages were identical twins, bound to each other by more than appearance. To take something or someone through a mirror took a pair of mages working in perfect unison—one at a receiving mirror, one at the origin mirror. Anything less and a mirror was just a mirror. Banan's twins were good, the best I'd ever seen. One of the twins had probably been hiding in that courtyard this morning, keeping the getaway mirror warm and running for his boss. A lot of stolen goods—or two kidnapped girls—could be passed through two magically connected mirrors.

"Are Megan Jacobs's parents wealthy?" I asked.

"They're well off," Rinker told me. "But not anywhere near the Aurillacs."

"Banan Ryce could still be after a ransom," I said. "But I doubt it. Even the Aurillacs would be small change for him. And Banan Ryce doesn't take a job unless he's paid a lot of gold up front with more on the way." I paused uneasily. "He's got some—shall we say—expensive tastes."

Neither man asked me to elaborate and I was grateful. I still felt queasy enough from the link.

"I don't care how good they are—Nightshades can't completely go to ground," Rinker said. "They have to eat, and eating means supplies. I know of a few houses where they've holed up in the past. I'll have my men stake those out. Miss Benares, is there anything else you can tell me?"

"Hurry."

"That's a given."

I indicated the brush and locket. "May I keep these for now? I'd like to use them again. Maybe next time I can catch Banan's mage employer off guard and get some specifics for you."

"Of course." Rinker retrieved his cloak and headed for the door. "I'll be in touch. Let me know if you find out anything else."

I nodded and rubbed my temples. I had a hell of a headache coming on. No surprise there. I squeezed my eyes shut and pinched the bridge of my nose.

"Headache?" Mychael asked.

I didn't open my eyes. "Not yet, but I've got a doozy on the way."

Mychael had walked Sedge to the door, but didn't close it after him. "Vegard?" he called.

I opened my eyes.

"Sir?"

"Could you have the kitchen send up something for Raine?"

"Yes, sir." Vegard glanced in and gave me an encouraging smile. I returned the favor as best I could. "You okay, ma'am?"

"I'll get there. I'm not hungry," I told both of them.

"You need to eat," Mychael said.

"Is that your healer's voice I hear?"

"It's one of them." He turned to Vegard. "It doesn't have to be anything fancy, just food and make it fast."

"Yes, sir."

Mychael closed the door.

I leaned back on the couch, and let the quiet grow for a few moments. "Why didn't you tell me you'd taken a pair of Nightshades?"

"We have yet to gain any useful information from them."

"Useful information? Or any information you're willing to share with me?"

Mychael didn't answer. Sometimes silence said more than a whole mouthful of words.

I took a breath and let it out slowly. "That's what I thought."

Mychael's eyes softened a little. "Raine, I'm telling you the truth. We haven't learned anything from them. But if we do—"

"You still couldn't tell me."

He hesitated. "I'm under direct orders not to." From his tone, he liked saying it as much as I liked hearing it.

I just looked at him. "Justinius. The old man doesn't trust me as far as his bony arms could throw me."

"He didn't get to where he is, and stay there for as long as he has, by taking unnecessary risks," Mychael told me.

"So telling me what's going on would be both unnecessary and a risk."

"In Justinius's opinion, yes."

"What about yours?"

"If I learn anything that tells me you're in more danger than you already are, then I will share that information with you. I feel responsible for getting you into all of this, and I will protect you."

"I know, because it's your job."

His eyes were on mine, steadfast and resolute. "It's more than my job," he said softly. "I think you know that."

I did.

Mychael sat down next to me, and raised his palms toward me.

"I can help with that headache. May I?"

I hesitated only a second before nodding. I didn't know what he was going to do, but I had a feeling I'd like it and my budding headache wouldn't.

He placed his thumbs against my temples, his strong hands wrapping around my head, his fingertips a warm pressure against the base of my skull. His thumbs started doing wonderful, circular things to my temples and his fingertips were doing likewise to the back of my neck. Oh my. I dimly heard myself make a little sound of contentment. No headache could survive that tactile onslaught.

"How's that?" Mychael's voice was a bare whisper, a deep, rich, wonderful whisper. It was his spellsinger's voice. I closed my eyes and let it work its magic.

"Good," I murmured. "Perfect even." I might end up in a puddle on the floor, but I was fine with that. Puddles couldn't have headaches, or not be trusted, or worry about kidnapped girls, or connections to soul-sucking stones.

I took a breath and let it out on a sigh. "So what do you think Banan wants with—"

"Shhhhh. Relax."

I smiled a little. "That's easy for you to say."

"Apparently it's not easy for you to do." I heard the humor in his voice.

I opened my eyes. Mychael's eyes were close to me—and so was the rest of him. I remembered what had happened last week at the goblin king's masquerade ball when we were this close and my face was cradled in Mychael's hands. My heart did a double thump at what we had done next.

"This isn't relaxing," I breathed.

Mychael's blue eyes had darkened. "No, it's not." His voice was deeper, huskier.

I swallowed. "Relaxation's way overrated."

Mychael was close enough to kiss for the second time today. This morning we had Ronan Cayle and four Guardians watching us. No kiss then. No one was watching us now.

Mychael bent his head until his lips barely brushed mine. I felt the warmth of his breath and the rapid pulse of his wrists against my face. We stayed that way, breathing, barely touching. Then Mychael slowly moved his lips to my forehead, resting them there in a lingering kiss, a kiss that banished my headache, erased my tension, exiled my fatigue, and made my toes tingle. Spellsinger *and* healer. Nice combination.

"You're a really good kisser," I whispered, kind of dazed.

I felt Mychael's lips curl into a smile. He gently tilted my face up to his.

"You should go to bed." His voice was low and vibrant.

"Bed?" I was dazed, but I was liking it. Actually what I felt was a little tipsy. If this was what a master spellsinger could do to a girl, he could keep right on doing it.

"Bed," he repeated, like he thought he wasn't getting through to me. "You need to rest."

I felt a giggle bubbling up. "Whose bed?"

Mychael blushed and lowered his hands from my face to my shoulders. Much to my disappointment, the tipsiness immediately started to go away.

"That would be your bed," he told me.

I grinned crookedly at him. It might have been leftover tipsies, but I do believe I detected regret in that yummy voice.

Mychael took his hands off of my shoulders. "I'll have Vegard bring your dinner to you there."

Chapter 7

Thanks to Mychael's attentions, and my own exhaustion, I slept all night, and way later than I'd planned the next day. It was early afternoon before I left the citadel for the Conclave Scriptorium armed with a full Guardian escort and a letter from Mychael to get me past the front doors.

I could have easily found my way there by myself, but I played by Mychael's rules and took Vegard, Riston, and a ridiculous number of additional Guardians with me. Vegard and Riston were uniformed, armed, and virtually plastered to my sides. If I had to draw a blade in a hurry, I'd have to knock one of them out of the way first.

The rest of my Guardian escort was there to keep anyone who might be after me from getting through their outer perimeter and into my immediate vicinity. They were keeping watchful eyes on the faculty, parents, students, and various visitors crowding Mid's winding streets this time of year. Not surprisingly, everyone gave us a wide berth.

The Conclave Scriptorium never failed to make me stop and gawk like a tourist. Light reading was not something you came to do in the Scriptorium. Inside those granite walls was the largest and most complete collection of books, scrolls, tablets, and anything else you could write, scratch, or engrave words on in the seven kingdoms. Impressive would be an understatement. Overwhelming sounded about right. Not to mention the place stank to high heaven, magic-wise. I'd spent time in some mages' private libraries, and while their bedtime reading material could pack quite a magical punch, it had nothing on the Scriptorium. Too long in this place could send a sensitive into magic overload that'd make your worst hangover pale in comparison.

I must have winced or something because Vegard nodded in understanding.

"Yeah, it gives me a headache, too," he said. "Nontalents do most of the book retrieval in the stacks. The reading rooms are separate. Only certain mages are allowed to spend time in the stacks themselves. Though I don't see why they'd want to."

We passed through massive, iron-banded doors into a cavernous, cool interior lit by lightglobes recessed into the walls. The counter at the far end was a wall-to-wall monolith of black marble manned by librarians who looked less like academics and more like a black-robed line of defense for the precious books that lay beyond. There was a single opening in the center to allow mere mortals to pass into what the librarians no doubt considered their inner sanctum. I didn't think trying to stroll through without permission would be a good idea.

Something moved above us, and I looked up.

There was a kid stuck to the ceiling.

I blinked. "What the . . . ?"

Riston and Vegard looked up. Riston winced; Vegard chuckled.

"It's a student," Vegard told me.

I gave him a look. "I can see that. How the hell did he float up there like a human balloon?"

"He didn't float," Riston told me. "It's detention." He didn't sound like he approved of it. "He was put there by a librarian, probably Lucan Kalta."

"Lucan who?"

"Kalta. The chief librarian."

"What'd the kid do?" Whatever it was, he didn't look all

that sorry that he'd done it. He grinned and waved at me. I did a little finger wave back.

"Could be anything," Vegard said. "But usually ceiling tacking is reserved for trying to take a book without checking it out. Kalta takes that personally."

"So take the book to the desk and check it out—what's the problem?"

"Certain books can't be checked out," Riston explained. "And other books students aren't qualified to get their hands on, for their own safety."

Vegard grinned. "Everyone coming and going can see you up there—it's one hell of a deterrent." He looked up and chuckled again. "Let's hope the kid paid attention during levitation classes. When the librarians release you, sometimes they catch you before you hit the floor; sometimes they don't."

I was careful not to walk directly under the dangling student. "You have Mychael's letter saying we can be here, right?"

Vegard followed in my footsteps. "I wouldn't have set foot in here without it."

Since I wasn't a Conclave mage or faculty, I needed a sponsor to vouch for me. Vegard had a letter from Mychael that should get me access to the books I needed.

A black-robed, bespectacled man virtually scrambled around the edge of the massive counter to greet Vegard.

"Sir Vegard. It's good to see you again. How are you?"

"Doing fine, Nelek. Doing fine."

"How may I assist the paladin today?" Nelek asked.

I muffled a smile. It's all about who you know.

Vegard passed him an envelope. I noticed it carried the seal of the Guardian paladin. Apparently Mychael wasn't taking any chances on the Scriptorium's staff giving us the cold shoulder. The librarian glanced at the seal and surreptitiously secreted it in an inner pocket of his black robes.

"Follow me, please."

We were in.

The looks that met us as we passed through the opening in

the counter were curious at best and downright hostile at worst. I felt like I was violating sacred territory. Once inside, there was a lot of marble and granite, with doors that looked suspiciously like vaults. Drawers slid out of stone walls on silent rollers. Then there were the stacks—long, tall, dark shelves arranged in narrow rows containing bound volumes. I wouldn't want to be anywhere around if one of them suddenly decided to fall. The place reminded me of a mausoleum. It definitely set my teeth on edge. Though what probably made my teeth hurt was the undercurrent of a nearly overwhelming scent of parchment, old leather, and magic. It wasn't the sense of stagnant magic, of just words or runes written on parchment; it was waiting magic, sometimes not patiently, for the leather covers containing them to be opened and read and given life beyond what already pulsed impatiently against their parchment restraints. I sensed spells shifting restlessly against the animal hides they had been written on. The outside of the Scriptorium had given me a headache; the inside made my skin want to crawl.

Nelek the librarian strode purposefully ahead of us. He must have been a nontalent. If I had to work here, I know I'd want to be.

"Uncomfortable?" Vegard asked me.

"To say the least."

"We'll be working in a shielded room," he assured me. "You won't be able to sense the manuscripts out here in the vault."

I glanced around. "It's actually called that?"

"Not officially, but that's what it looks and feels like, so that's what we call it."

I had a thought, and it wasn't comforting. "What's going to shield us against what we'll be reading?" If level-twelve wards hadn't held against the Saghred, I didn't know what'd work against the probably insane scribbling of the goblin shamans who had spent their short and mad lives living and working with the Saghred.

"There's plenty of security precautions in the reading rooms," he assured me.

Right. Now where had I heard that before?

The reading room the librarian unlocked for us was just a room with a table and four chairs. That was normal. What was not normal was a clear cubicle next to the table. It looked like glass, though I suspect it wasn't. It was tall and wide enough that a man could have stood upright in it. Inside was a sturdy lectern to hold a manuscript or document being examined. I sensed a charge in the air surrounding the cubicle. Containment wards. Not level twelve, but still impressive. They were inactive now, but then the cubicle was empty. No menacing manuscripts inside whose mere touch would turn the staunchest mage into a cackling lunatic bent on an island-wide killing spree.

Nelek opened and read Mychael's request. Mychael had reviewed the list of books with me before I left the citadel. There were two history volumes of the goblins' Fifth Age, which was about a thousand years ago—when the Saghred had surfaced and had done its worst damage. The other was the journal of Rudra Muralin, the Fifth Age's version of a young Sarad Nukpana. Unlike Nukpana, Rudra Muralin had actually gotten his hands on the Saghred and had used it extensively.

"It will take a few moments to gather what you require, Sir Vegard," the librarian said. "And since the paladin's request involves highly restricted volumes, the chief librarian must be informed."

"Of course."

With a little servile bow, the man left, closing the door behind him.

"Shit," Vegard said mildly.

"What?"

"Lucan Kalta's gonna foam at the mouth when he sees that list."

"Are you saying we won't get the books?" That didn't make me happy.

"It might get dicey."

What seemed an eternity later, Nelek came back with two assistants carrying what I assumed to be the books

Mychael had requested for me. A fourth man followed. He was tall, black robed, spectrally thin, and didn't look happy to see any of us. I experienced the sensation of a kid caught with his hand in the cookie jar.

Vegard inclined his head respectfully. "Chief Librarian Kalta."

"Sir Vegard."

Lucan Kalta turned those basilisk eyes on me. I stood my ground. Show no fear; know no fear. Kalta was likely used to cowering students and probably most of the faculty with that gaze. I'd imagine he'd had a lot of practice over the years. But I'd been sucked inside the Saghred yesterday; it was going to take a lot more to intimidate me than one man questioning my right to merely read about it.

"You are Paladin Eiliesor's consultant?"

If that was what Mychael was calling me, I'd play along. "I am."

"May I inquire as to your qualifications to view these books?"

I didn't hesitate. "Did Paladin Eiliesor include them in his request?"

"He did not."

"Then he probably didn't think it necessary to make them public knowledge."

From the way Lucan Kalta's face reddened, you'd think I'd slapped him. One of the librarians with him gasped and stopped breathing. A muffled snort came from Vegard. This was Kalta's turf, but I wasn't about to buckle to any territorial posturing. The Benares' definition of diplomacy was putting cannon shot across someone's bow rather than through their waterline. Any finer points of civilized behavior were lost on my family—and right now I didn't feel like trying to be an exception.

Kalta recovered, something he probably didn't get too much practice doing. I could feel the frost coming off him. "It may not be necessary for the public, but it is for me, Mistress . . ."

Apparently Mychael hadn't given him my name. I had no problem providing it.

"Benares."

The librarian next to Lucan Kalta managed to find a little air, but he sucked it in with a strangled squeak. Sometimes I got intense satisfaction out of telling people my name and then watching the reaction. This was one of those times. I know it was petty, but a girl has to take her fun where she can get it.

Kalta's red face faded all the way to an outraged white, and his lips pulled so tight they vanished entirely. I think any sense of humor he may have possessed vanished with them. I was curious to see if the books I needed did likewise.

There were many things Lucan Kalta could have said or done. Apparently the list was too long for him to make an immediate selection, so he turned to Vegard.

"Sir Vegard, if you would please tell Paladin Eiliesor that I require any future requests for restricted manuscript study to be *preapproved* by me, along with the names and scholarly qualifications of those who will be viewing the books. I will officially relay my wishes in writing by the end of the day." With that, he turned and left the room, sweeping the three librarians along in his wake like a little flock of startled crows. The door closed behind them all with a resounding boom.

Vegard lost it.

I'd never seen the Guardian doubled over with laughter before, and I had to admit it did suck the tension right out of the room. Even the normally stoic Riston couldn't stifle a couple of chuckles. Lucan Kalta must not be in danger of winning any popularity contests.

I glanced at the door, expecting it to fly open. I really didn't want to get kicked out of the Scriptorium without reading one word of what I'd come to see.

Riston was smiling. "Don't worry, ma'am. The room's soundproof."

So I joined them. Laughing felt good.

•   •   •

Unlike the Saghred itself, the books about the stone behaved them-
selves. No attempt to influence, no writhing runes trying to
crawl off the page and jump on my face.

The Fifth Age goblin history books were massive and
predictably dry reading. There were a lot of names and
dates, but no personal commentary or interesting asides. I
skimmed them both, stopping only for detailed reading
when I saw the character for "Saghred." History was written
by the victors, and during the time the goblin royal family
had the Saghred in their arsenal, they had more than their
fair share of victories. There was plenty of smiting, laying
waste, conquering, and enslaving going on, but no explanation of how the Saghred had actually done any of the above.
What I did get was an all-too-comprehensive picture of
just how much damage the Saghred had done during its
heyday—and how much damage I might be able to do now.

Rudra Muralin's name was mentioned often, which
made sense, seeing that he was the one telling the Saghred
who to smite and what to lay waste to. On one page, he was
called something else.

Saghred bond servant.

My hand had been resting on the page just below those
words. I moved it, resisting the urge to wipe my hand on
something, anything. Sarad Nukpana had told me yesterday
that I was the bond servant to the Saghred, like my father
before me.

I set the history book aside and quickly reached for Rudra
Muralin's journal. It was a much smaller book, its pages yel-
lowed with age and held together by a band of leather
wrapped around the middle. From what I knew about him,
Muralin had been like a bully on a playground—except his
playgrounds had been cities or battlefields, and thousands of
people had died for the sake of his childish curiosity. It
sounded like Sarad Nukpana hadn't fallen far from the crazy
shaman tree that had sprouted Rudra Muralin.

The paper of Muralin's journal was brittle and dry with

age, but the information was anything but dry reading. There was page after page of what he had asked the Saghred to help him do. None of Muralin's antics were anything I'd ever repeat—and I would never do what he did to get that power. Before he did anything significant with the Saghred, Rudra Muralin would sacrifice captives to the stone, feeding its power with all the consideration one would give to throwing logs on a fire.

Sacrifices fed the stone, but it wasn't what Muralin had used to awaken the Saghred, direct its power, and then put it to sleep afterward.

Rudra Muralin had been a spellsinger. A young, talented, really powerful spellsinger.

Like Piaras.

There was a knock at the door. I almost jumped out of my skin.

Vegard looked at me and I nodded once. I closed Muralin's journal and put my hand over it. Vegard partially opened the door and looked out.

He stepped back and Nelek slipped through and closed the door quickly behind him.

From the look on his face, he wasn't the bearer of good news. "Ma'am, Chief Librarian Kalta has requested that I collect the books. He said to tell you that three hours is ample time for your study."

Vegard said the exact word I was thinking.

"I'm sorry, sir."

"Not your fault, Nelek."

The librarian pulled a slender leather-bound book out of his robes and handed it to me.

"I thought this might be of interest to you," he said. "It was written in the last century by a goblin historian named Okon Nusair. It's an obscure work about the legends surrounding the Saghred. Since Nusair didn't document the sources of much of his information, it's considered fiction by serious scholars. It's rarely checked out. Paladin Eiliesor may not have been aware of its existence." Nelek looked nervously at the closed door. "The chief librarian is in a meeting and I could tell him I was unavoidably delayed in fulfilling his request."

I gave him as much of a smile as I could. "Thank you. I appreciate your help."

The librarian smiled shyly and shrugged. "At the very least, it's a good companion volume to Rudra Muralin's work."

The book felt smooth and almost pliant under my hands. Creepy.

I opened it and flipped through the still-crisp pages. I shouldn't have any problem reading it since it was written in modern-day Goblin.

In Rudra Muralin's handwriting.

Oh hell.

I opened Muralin's journal on the table. The handwriting was identical—and written nearly a thousand years earlier.

I carefully closed both books, and told myself I was not going to scream.

My father had been nearly nine hundred years old before the Saghred had taken him last year. History said Rudra Muralin died about a thousand years ago as the result of a dare.

On a challenge from the goblin king, Rudra Muralin used the Saghred to create the Great Rift in northern Rheskilia. The Great Rift was a mile-wide, nearly fifty-mile-long tear in the mountains of the Northern Reach. In one of the aftershocks that followed, Rudra Muralin fell off the highest edge into his newly created gorge, bringing an abrupt end to a notorious shamanic career. A couple of his more devoted disciples followed him like lemmings.

So said history. History's been wrong before.

And if history was wrong, the greatest and craziest shaman to ever wield the Saghred was alive and well and could be anywhere—including here.

"I'd like to check both of these out," I told Nelek, my voice surprisingly calm.

The librarian looked at me like I'd just asked him to run naked through the stacks. I didn't want to get him in trouble, but one way or another I was leaving here with both of Rudra Muralin's books. They were small enough to fit under my jerkin if necessary. I remembered the kid tacked to the ceiling. I smiled, and Nelek swallowed nervously. I'd like to see Lucan Kalta try tacking me anywhere.

"But the books are from the restricted section," he said as if that explained everything. It didn't.

"Restricted books can't be checked out?"

"Only those with the highest scholarly qualifications can—"

Time for a change of tactic. "How are Paladin Eiliesor's scholarly qualifications?"

"Impeccable, but—"

"The paladin needs to see these." I gave him my most earnest look. "Nelek, isn't it?"

"Yes, ma'am."

"Nelek, you heard what happened yesterday in the square?"

"I wasn't there, but I talked to some who were." He paled. "Terrible business."

"Yes, it was. And as you can understand, the paladin is working hard to find who was responsible. He would have come here himself, but he simply couldn't spare the time. Information in these books could really help him."

He looked incredulous. "Those books?"

"These books. But it needs to be kept secret. Get these books for the paladin and keep it quiet, and you'll have the gratitude of the paladin and the archmagus."

Nelek's eyes widened. "The archmagus?"

"The archmagus."

Nelek glanced nervously at Vegard.

"Their *undying* gratitude," Vegard told him.

That man was unbelievably handy to have around.

The librarian hesitated a moment longer, then drew himself up. "I'd be proud to help. I have a good friend at the checkout desk. Let me see what I can do."

Chapter 8

"Quick thinking, ma'am," Vegard told me, after Nelek had gone.

"I do what I have to. I'm sorry I had to lie to your friend."

The Guardian shrugged. "You did what you had to. Are those two little books that important?"

"They are. I need to read them, and seeing how Lucan Kalta feels about me, if I let them out of my sight, I'll probably never see them again. Just how much pull does Nelek really have around here?"

"Usually enough."

"You've checked out books on the sly before?"

"All the time in my student days. A lot of stuff I wanted to know was in books I couldn't get my hands on." There was a gleam in Vegard's sky blue eyes. "Make friends in high places, or distribute coin in the right places."

"So how does Lucan Kalta know if someone walks out with his books?"

"My student days were before Lucan Kalta."

"Damn."

"Yeah," Vegard agreed.

"Kalta just seems to know," Riston said. "We're still not sure how."

I picked up both books and considered the available space in my jerkin. There wasn't as much room as I would have liked. "I'd like to see him try tacking me to the ceiling," I muttered.

Vegard's chuckle was downright evil. "I *want* to see him try."

Nelek came back in record time, but he wasn't alone. The two assistants who had brought the books stood behind him.

"We're here for the books, ma'am," he said, brisk and professional. Then he gave me a quick wink. "Marten and Cecil, if you would take the history volumes, I'll take care of the other two."

After the assistants collected the two goblin histories, Nelek held out his hand. I hesitated and then gave him the journals, never taking my eyes from his. He got the message loud and clear. If he tried to go anywhere with those books other than the front desk, I was going to tackle him.

"The chief librarian requested that I escort you to the front desk," Nelek said, watching the two librarians walk around the corner and into the stacks. His mouth curled in a tiny, conspiratorial smile. "If you'll follow me, we'll take care of your request."

Vegard and I traded a look. You gotta love friends in high places.

A tall figure stepped out of the stacks, blocking our way.

His hair was the color of winter frost, eyes the pale blue of arctic ice, an alabaster complexion, a cold, sharp beauty. Pure-blooded high elf. His black and silver robes were understated and elegant, and clearly cost a small fortune.

Nelek instinctively clutched the books to his chest. "Magus Silvanus, always a pleasure to see you." The librarian didn't sound pleased in the least; he sounded terrified.

So this was Carnades Silvanus, senior mage on the Seat of Twelve, Ailia Aurillac's faculty advisor, and parental brownnoser.

I sensed Vegard and Riston come to reluctant attention behind me. They had to. The Guardians' main duty was the protection of the archmagus and the mages of the Seat of Twelve.

Silvanus was as tall as Mychael, which put the top of my head level with his jaw. He looked down on me—in more ways than one. I've always made it a point not to dislike someone on first sight, but I was willing to make an exception for this one. Gleaming against the black silk of his robes, a mirrored disk dangled at the end of a silver chain. A high elf *and* a mirror mage—no wonder I didn't like him.

"You must be Raine Benares, the seeker we've heard so much about." Silvanus smiled, revealing perfect teeth. The smile was as fake as the charm he tried to put into his voice. "I'm Carnades Silvanus."

He extended his hand for mine, palm up, his long fingers slightly curled. He was going for a hand kiss, not a handshake. I was brought up to believe that it's rude not to shake someone's hand. I was also brought up to trust my instincts. The touch of a hand was all it took for some mages to assess another's magical strengths or weaknesses. I didn't want Carnades Silvanus knowing either of mine.

I inclined my head; I tried for gracious. "Magus Silvanus."

He left his hand out a moment longer, then slowly lowered it, never taking those arctic eyes from mine. "I understand you're assisting the city watch in their investigation of Ailia Aurillac's disappearance."

"I understand it's a kidnapping."

"So it appears. Have you made any progress in your investigation?" he asked politely.

"The paladin and chief watcher are aware of my findings. Since the investigation is ongoing, I can't discuss them publicly."

His smile was back. "But you are a private consultant—and I'm hardly the public."

"The paladin or chief watcher will have to determine who knows my findings." I tried a fake smile of my own. "That decision's not mine to make. I'm only a consultant on this case and a guest on this island."

"My apologies, Mistress Benares. I meant no offense. I

merely asked out of concern for Miss Aurillac's safe return."

"We're all concerned about that. I understand you're her faculty advisor."

"I am. Miss Aurillac is a splendid young lady and one of our top scholars."

I glanced at his mirror pendant. "So her specialty is mirror magic?"

"Ailia is gifted in many areas and has yet to choose a specific area of study. But yes, one of them is mirror magic."

"And the others?"

"She has an interest in spellsinging and alchemy."

I snorted to myself. Like her daddy's coffers didn't have enough gold. I'll bet I knew what he wanted her to major in.

"I want to thank you for what you did in the square yesterday," Silvanus said. "I was on that stage. Your skills are very impressive—your strength even more so."

"You're welcome." Thanks was the last thing I expected from him. It's been my experience that if one hand is extending an olive branch, the other hand is about to stab you in the back. "I'm glad I was there to help."

Carnades saw the books in Nelek's hands. "Ah, Rudra Muralin's journal. I understand you've been studying all afternoon, Mistress Benares. Study is admirable."

One of my hands curled into a fist, ready to fight for that journal if I had to. "You're familiar with Muralin's works?"

"I have a keen interest in goblin history. It's a hobby of mine."

"An elf studying goblin history. That's unusual."

"Understanding your enemy is the first step to defeating him. Education is the key to that, not ignorance. We bury our past at our peril."

I could add bigot to the list of reasons why I didn't like Carnades Silvanus.

"My interest is academic," Silvanus said. "What is your interest?"

"The same as yours," I shot back smoothly. "Education."

A boom shattered the silence and I almost jumped out of my skin. A black-robed librarian quickly bent and scooped up the massive book that had landed flat on the marble floor.

I felt the barest touch on my wrist. Silvanus.

My memories of the past week flashed through my mind in an instant.

I reacted instinctively, which meant in the next instant Silvanus's hand was twisted at what I knew to be a painful angle. Any hand that touched me without permission got treated the same way; it didn't matter if he was man or mage. No means no.

Vegard and Riston weren't at attention anymore, and I think Nelek was about to faint. I held up my other hand indicating that they should not interfere. To my surprise, they stayed put.

"I'm not that kind of girl," I told Silvanus quietly. "If you have a question for me, ask it."

The mage's breath came in a pained hiss. "You're infected with that filthy goblin rock."

I leaned in close. "And you're rude. You don't touch anyone with a questing spell. If I wanted you to know my memories, I'd tell you."

Silvanus thought a word. It wasn't a very nice word. I'd also been called worse before.

Neither one of us moved or blinked. After another moment or two, I released Silvanus's hand and took a step back. I liked Vegard and Riston, and I didn't want them to magically bite off more than they could chew. Carnades Silvanus was the senior mage on the Seat of Twelve, and if the power I'd felt coming off him was any indication, my two Guardians would be in way over their heads. I didn't want a fight. I wanted to take my books and get out of there.

Silvanus's pale eyes glittered. "You are a danger to everyone on this island. You should be locked up—and I'm going to see to it that you are."

With that, he turned and left, the heels of his boots echoing sharply on the marble floor.

Vegard stepped up beside me. "Are you all right, ma'am?"

I never took my eyes off of Silvanus's retreating back. "Never been better."

The big Guardian shifted uneasily. "If anything happens to Justinius Valerian, he's in charge."

That was one more scary thought.

"We try to take *really* good care of the old man," he assured me.

Silvanus's silk robes swept around the corner. I kept my eyes on the spot. "Let me know if I can help."

Lucan Kalta's meeting must have ended early. He was waiting for us at the front desk. Nelek's good friend must have been the sick-looking librarian standing behind Kalta.

Crap.

On the upside, Carnades Silvanus couldn't lock me up until Lucan Kalta unpeeled me from the ceiling. I glanced up. The student wasn't on the ceiling anymore, which left plenty of room for me, my inner pessimist chimed in.

I turned to Nelek. "Give me the books. I'll take it from here."

His eyes went enormous under his spectacles. He presented the books to me like I was condemned and the books were my last meal.

I sighed. "Yeah, I know. It's not going to be pretty."

I turned and stepped up to the desk and Lucan Kalta. "I would like to check out these two books for the paladin."

Kalta smiled. I'd never thought of Death as the smiling sort, but give this guy a scythe, set him at the gates of the lower hells, and no one would know the difference.

"I understand checking out books for the paladin is done quite often," I said reasonably. "As I'm sure you know, the paladin is a busy man."

Kalta's smile broadened and he held up two sheets of paper. I recognized them.

The chief librarian leisurely glanced at one, then the

other. "Let's see, Mistress Benares. The first is a letter from the paladin granting you access to the Scriptorium. The second is the list of the books the paladin requested that you see." He carefully folded both pages and put them in the envelope we'd brought them in. His black eyes narrowed gleefully. "Neither page mentions allowing you to remove any book from this Scriptorium." He held out a skeletal hand. "The books, if you please."

I made no move to hand them over. Kalta's smile turned from satisfaction to anticipation. My smile told him to bring it on.

"An oversight on my part," Mychael said from behind Lucan Kalta. "As Mistress Benares said, I am a busy man."

Kalta's breath came out on a hiss. I think I might have growled. When I started a fight, I wanted to finish it. I know; it's not one of my better qualities. I hesitated, then took one step back from Kalta. I had to take the civilized high road sometime. Kalta's professional mask slid back into place.

"Are there checkout forms prepared for my signature?" Mychael asked mildly.

Nelek's librarian friend held out two pieces of paper. His hands were shaking.

Mychael took them, and looked around the desk. "Does anyone have a pen?"

Chaos ensued as all of the librarians on duty scrambled to get the paladin a pen. Their cooperation warmed my heart. Kalta shot a withering look at Nelek. The little librarian quickly looked down at his shoes and then resolutely met his boss's eyes. He didn't look away again. Someone had just grown himself a backbone. I resisted the urge to wink at him. I didn't want to get him in any more trouble than he already was.

Mychael signed the checkout forms, and gave them to an expressionless Lucan Kalta. I walked through the opening in the counter with my two books, Vegard and Riston right behind me. The books didn't vanish, and I didn't float up to the ceiling.

"Thank you for your assistance, Lucan," Mychael said. "I will have these returned as soon as I've finished with them."

He fell into step next to me.

"Your timing is impeccable," I whispered as we walked toward the doors and freedom.

Mychael's voice was next to my ear. "Timing had nothing to do with it. Though I was hardly surprised to find you nose to nose with Lucan Kalta."

"What's that supposed to mean?"

"Just what I said. You are who you are; he is who he is. I was not surprised. As to my timing, I received a report that Carnades Silvanus was seen hurrying into the Scriptorium; you weren't seen coming out. The Seat of Twelve knew about the Saghred even before we docked with it. And knowing how Carnades feels about anything goblin . . ."

I felt a little smile coming on. "So you came after me."

"I came after you."

My little smile widened to a grin. "I hope you left your white charger outside."

Mychael's blue eyes lit with boyish humor. "I did. I didn't think our chief librarian would approve of the mess he'd make."

"The chief librarian doesn't approve of me, either."

Mychael chuckled. "So I saw."

"Sorry about that."

"Don't be. Lucan Kalta's a fine librarian, but he can be a pompous ass. What books did I go to all that trouble to check out?"

"Highly restricted books. I'll tell you more when we're out of here."

Mychael sighed. "Lucan doesn't let go of those lightly."

"Especially to people like me. That's why I was glad a person like you came along to check them out for me. It kept Lucan Kalta from trying to tack me to the ceiling. It would have gotten ugly. No one tacks me anywhere."

"If you had crossed through that counter with restricted

books, Lucan would be well within his legal rights to tack you to the ceiling—or since you're not a student or faculty, he could have had you arrested."

I grinned. "Would you be the one doing the arresting?"

"Not under normal circumstances. But since I was there, my duty would call on me to be the arresting officer." There was a smile tugging at the corners of his mouth.

My grin broadened. "Would there be cuffs involved?"

"Only if you resisted arrest."

"Oh, I can guarantee you I'd resist arrest. You'd have your hands full."

"I already do," he muttered.

Chapter 9

It was dark when we left the Scriptorium. I guess time flies when you're not having fun. Yesterday I'd been inside the Saghred and pissed off Sarad Nukpana. Today I'd been inside the Conclave Scriptorium and pissed off its chief librarian and one of the Seat of Twelve. Not exactly the ending I had in mind for my second day on the island.

I heard a snort and smelled sulfur. There was a Guardian holding a pair of reins. The reins weren't attached to Mychael's white charger—or maybe they had been and the dragon had eaten him. The insides of the dragon's nostrils glowed orange with restrained flame. If he sneezed, the Guardian holding his reins was toast.

Mychael saw my look. "His name is Kalinpar."

"That's not a white charger."

Mychael smiled. "No, he's not, but he is the quickest way to get around the city."

"You came here on that?"

"Like I said, the quickest way."

I didn't doubt that. Kalinpar was about twice the size of the biggest horse I'd ever seen. I'd never seen a sentry dragon this close, but I'd heard they were nimble and quick enough to fly and land pretty much anywhere they wanted to. They were popular with law enforcement in the bigger cities. Looking at this big brute, I understood why.

Kalinpar looked pissed, too. Though he hadn't met me yet, so it couldn't have been my fault. Or maybe it was. He'd had to wait out here on account of me. Or maybe that was just his normal expression. Either way, I was in no hurry to share the saddle that was strapped to his scaled back. I'd had enough close calls for one day.

"Can't we just walk back to the citadel?" I asked Mychael. In addition to Vegard and Riston, there were at least a dozen armed Guardians with us. "I don't think anyone's going to try anything. I'm safe."

Mychael raised one brow and didn't say a word.

I stared back at him. "I'm not going to try anything, either." I sighed and raised the hand that wasn't holding the books. "I promise not to attack anyone, steal anything, or break any more of your laws." I stopped and thought for a moment. "Tonight. The way things have been going I can't make any guarantees about tomorrow."

Mychael regarded me for a moment, then turned to the Guardian holding the dragon's reins. "Allyn, would you take Kalinpar back to the stables? We'll be escorting Miss Benares back to the citadel on foot."

"Yes, sir." The Guardian hesitated. "When I land, would you like me to send reinforcements?"

"Only if we're not back within the hour."

I looked from one to the other. I think they were joking. Vegard chuckled from behind me. I resisted the urge to punch him and Mychael. Too bad I'd just promised not to attack anyone.

The Guardian swung into the saddle, strapped down his leg restraints, and with two strong wingbeats the dragon had cleared the tops of the surrounding buildings. With a parting plume of flame, he and his rider were gone.

Mychael took my hand and linked my arm through his. It could have been a gallant gesture of a gentleman walking a lady home, or it could have been Mychael making sure I stayed out of trouble. He had one of my hands; my other hand clutched the books. Regardless of his reasons, it was nice and cozy—even if we were surrounded by heavily armed Guardians. The night was cool; Mychael was warm. My night was starting to look much better than my day.

Mychael glanced down at me. "Tell me about Carnades."

So much for nice and cozy.

I hit the high points. Mychael's frown became more pronounced with each point. I didn't know if that look of stern disapproval was for Carnades Silvanus or me.

"I just had his hand in a vise," I protested indignantly. "It wasn't like I had a dagger in his ribs. 'Hand in a vise' is simple assault or, in my case, self-defense. 'Dagger in the ribs' is attempted murder. My family did teach me the difference."

"Do you want to press charges?" Mychael asked.

I blinked in surprise. Apparently the disapproving look was for Carnades Silvanus.

"Me press charges?" That'd be a first for a Benares.

"Yes, you press charges. A questing spell is considered assault. Do you want to press charges?"

"I think he knows not to do it anymore."

"Did it ever occur to you to let Vegard and Riston handle it?"

"She asked us not to, sir," Vegard said from behind us.

Mychael just looked at me. "You asked them not to? They're bodyguards, Raine, not armed accessories."

If my hands had been free, they would have been planted indignantly on my hips. "Carnades raked through my memories. I take that personally. If I take something personally, I settle it the same way."

Mychael glanced at the retreating fire bloom in the sky that was Kalinpar. If the dragon had been closer, Mychael probably would have called them back, and I'd end up tossed over the saddle.

I could only see his face in profile, but there was no missing the clenched jaw. "What about the books?"

I told him what they were and who they were both written by.

Mychael stopped. So did our escort. "Are you certain?" he asked.

"Positive. Though I didn't have time to do more than flip through the one in modern Goblin." I lowered my voice. "Rudra Muralin used spellsinging to wake the Saghred, use it, and then put it back to sleep. And he was probably not much older than Piaras when he and the Saghred did their worst damage. It might explain why the stone responded to Piaras and not to you and Ronan Cayle."

"Perhaps." Mychael's face didn't betray a thing, but I could tell I'd just lit a spark in those blue eyes. I swore silently. As paladin, Mychael needed to know everything I found out, but I hoped I hadn't just earned Piaras the same watch-first-lockup-later vibe I'd felt since I got here.

I suddenly didn't want the books out in the open. I tucked them both into my jerkin. It was a tight fit, but I felt safer with them out of sight. I also felt safer by freeing up one of my hands.

Then I saw them. Six goblins, all armed and armored in sleek black. Khrynsani temple guards. Sarad Nukpana's enforcers.

The Khrynsani were transparent. They were remnants, a psychic impression left behind after a person had left a place. Some sorcerers saw them constantly; I never could. Until now. The Khrynsani—and the young goblin they hunted—had been here just minutes before. I could see the filmy trail of the direction they'd gone in.

"Six Khrynsani were just here," I told Mychael.

He didn't question how I knew; his magic just heated the air around us as he shielded me. The remnants instantly vanished.

"Stop it!"

"What?"

"Your shields. I can't see their remnants anymore."

"You can't see remnants."

"I can now." Apparently another unwanted gift courtesy of the Saghred. "They're after a goblin, student age."

Mychael swore. The shields went down, but his sword came out, the steel glowing blue. "Which way?"

A distant scream answered his question.

The woman had seen the Khrynsani, screamed, and slammed her door by the time we got there. The goblins and their quarry were no longer there, either, but I could tell where they'd gone.

I tried to pull away to follow them. Mychael pulled me back.

"They could be after you."

I jerked away. "Not now, they're not."

Mychael glared. "Which way?"

"Around the corner there."

"Vegard?" Mychael called over his shoulder.

"Sir?"

"You and Riston take Raine back to the citadel."

"Yes, sir."

I wasn't going anywhere with anybody. "You can't see them. I can."

"No, but we can track them."

"I can see *and* track them. They're heading toward the central city. You're going to lose them in there."

"Maybe."

"Shouldn't that be my decision?"

"Not here, it's not," he growled.

I had a couple of choice words ready to let fly, but shouts and the sounds of fighting from ahead stopped me. It was probably a good thing; they weren't nice words. I took off in the direction of the shouts before Mychael could get a hand on me again, though I knew he was right on my heels. He wasn't going to be happy with me, but he'd have to get in line.

The shops and nightclubs gave way to a more residential section. The streets were darker with fewer witnesses for whatever the Khrynsani had in mind. I had blades on me but considering who I was chasing, my alternate arsenal might be a better choice. You didn't just run Khrynsani temple guards into a dark alley without a plan. What I had wasn't exactly a plan, but it'd keep me from getting roasted until Mychael and his Guardians could catch up with me. I wasn't going to let the Khrynsani get that kid.

It wasn't a dark alley. But if the goblins were looking for some privacy, the deserted courtyard they dragged their captured quarry into worked just fine.

One of the Khrynsani had a knife to the young goblin's throat. Another had leather strips out and was binding the kid's wrists. This wasn't a hit; it was a kidnapping.

Mychael caught up with me on cat feet. Vegard and Riston were close behind. There was no sense rushing in. We were standing in the only way out. Possibly. Mid had plenty of buildings that led to basements that led to tunnels. I'd heard you could get from the harbor to the center city and never see the sky. I really didn't want to test that rumor for the first time while chasing Khrynsani in the pitch dark. Elven sight was decent in the dark, but goblins could see like cats. Mychael peered into the courtyard. He saw what I saw and, judging from his confused expression, he knew the kid.

There was lamplight in the courtyard, and the goblin was in plain view. He was slender and probably not much older than Piaras, with waist-length black hair that shimmered in the lamplight. His silvery gray skin was suspiciously light, and when the lamp caught his pale eyes, my suspicions were confirmed. A half-breed, probably elven, definitely beautiful. He was stylishly dressed, though his clothing was a bit showy, more like a stage costume than anything. Probably a performer in one of the nightclubs.

A Khrynsani uncorked a small glass vial. I stifled a growl. Tied up wasn't enough; they wanted him drugged, too. The goblin tried to struggle, but with the knife at his throat he was helpless to do anything about it.

I'd seen enough.

Mychael's arm blocked me. He looked at Vegard, pointed at me and then emphatically to the ground. I had a feeling if I tried to follow Mychael into that courtyard, Vegard had just been ordered to sit on me.

Mychael stepped out into the courtyard entrance. Some of the Guardians went with him; some didn't. Vegard and two Guardians armed with crossbows didn't. There was a tree next to the courtyard entrance. One moment the two Guardians were in the street with us; then they weren't. I imagine they were making themselves at home on the building's roof.

A Khrynsani temple guard stepped in front of his captive. He wore tooled leather covered with a combination of black steel plate and scale armor. The single serpent of the Khrynsani insignia gleamed in vivid, red enamel over his heart. The etching in the steel made the armor look delicate, but experience had taught me better.

Mychael's sword glowed with pale blue fire. "You're not taking him out of here."

"I think he's the only way I am getting out of here." The temple guard smiled, slow and eager, and full of fang.

Great. Someone was feeling challenged this evening.

I peeked over Mychael's shoulder and saw that the two Guardians had reached their perches. They weren't making any effort to hide.

"Teris?" Mychael called to one of them.

"Sir?"

"Would you be so kind as to put a bolt behind this Khrynsani's ear if he doesn't comply with my order?"

"No problem, sir. I was thinking along those lines myself."

I looked back at the Khrynsani. I saw the beginnings of doubt in his black eyes. Mychael didn't need him to be afraid, just sensible.

"Don't worry," Mychael told him. "You won't feel a thing when it hits. You also won't have time to take the boy with you."

Teris's crossbow creaked as he cranked the string back. The sound effect was a nice touch. It also changed the Khrynsani's mind. He didn't move, but I saw it in his eyes—the goblin wasn't worth it to him.

Mychael stood perfectly still. He was getting what he

wanted, and saw no sense in spooking the Khrynsani. "Tell your men to take the blade away from his throat, let him go, and step back. Way back."

No one moved for nearly a minute. Then the Khrynsani guard hissed something under his breath, and the others backed away from the young goblin. The guard never took his eyes from Mychael.

Mychael motioned to the boy. The goblin ripped away the still-loose leather bindings and crossed the distance to us.

Mychael took two steps toward the boy, and the Khrynsani temple guard smiled, though it looked more like a wolf baring his fangs at a new option that'd just appeared on the menu.

He'd seen me.

"It appears I'm in your debt, Paladin Eiliesor. You take one prize away and bring me another."

Mychael stepped protectively in front of me.

"Darshan?" the Khrynsani guard called over his shoulder.

A figure stepped out of a darkened doorway wearing a black robe lined in silver. A Khrynsani shaman.

Oh hell.

I could see others in the shadows behind him. So much for there being only one entrance to the courtyard.

The guard laughed softly. "Before the paladin so gallantly shielded his fair lady, did you see her?"

"Yes, I did. She is the one. Take her."

So I was on the Khrynsani's dance card this evening.

I heard a pair of thumps, and suddenly there were two fewer Khrynsani. A crossbow bolt had taken one in the chest, another in the back.

Teris looked wildly behind him. The shot had come from the roof next door. The marksmen were goblins, they were heavily armed—and best of all, they weren't Khrynsani.

The Khrynsani scattered like roaches in torchlight. Apparently there were other exits from the courtyard into the street and the Khrynsani took full advantage. Within seconds the temple guards and shamans were moving to surround us.

Crossbow bolts weren't the only things flying through the air as the Guardians, Khrynsani, and our mystery goblin allies launched spells, counterspells, and enough nasty crossfire to fry anything left standing. I wasn't standing. I'd hit the cobbles during the first volley. In a serious fight, mages launched spells at an opponent's torso or head for a quick kill. Anything below the knees didn't warrant attention. The same went for personal shields.

I never ignored any target, especially ankles. A little focused will and a quick yank would jerk a mage's feet right out from underneath him. It'd worked for me in the past, and was doing a fine job now as another Khrynsani landed on his back in the street. That most were knocking themselves unconscious when their heads hit the cobblestones was just an added bonus.

A spell ricocheted off someone's shields. I rolled to keep from getting fried and ended up facedown in a gutter—and face-to-face with the kid. Eyes of the clearest aquamarine; eyes of a pure-blooded high elf. About eighteen years ago, a goblin had ventured way out of his or her family tree. Another explosion made us both cover our heads.

"Looks like someone doesn't like you, either," he said.

There was a momentary lull in the shooting and spell-slinging, and the kid started scrambling to his feet. I grabbed his arm and pulled him back down. "In my family that's not silence; it's reloading."

I felt cold air down the front of my shirt. I looked down. My jerkin laces had come undone. I frantically felt down the front of my jerkin and shirt. The kid's eyes followed my every move. I'd lost one of the books. Dammit. Then I saw it, lying about ten feet away against the curb. A Khrynsani shaman spotted it at the same time. His eyes went wide and he dove for the book and snatched it up. I scrambled to my feet. He tried to run, but he didn't get far. I tackled him at the knees and we both went down. Ugly wrestling ensued. The shaman had been taught in a temple. I'd been taught to beat the crap out of anyone who took something of mine. It didn't take me long to get my book back.

A pair of strong hands jerked me to my feet and dragged me into an alley.

I went for my switchblade, but he got there first. Only two men knew where I kept it. Phaelan was one. The other was the tall goblin wearing rough leathers whose entire body had me pinned against the alley wall. His hair fell in a dark, silken curtain around us both. He had my switchblade, but I had his wrist.

Tamnais Nathrach.

I was breathing heavily and so was he. I'd just wrestled a Khrynsani shaman. I didn't know what Tam's excuse was—or what the hell he was doing here.

I drew breath to ask, then held it when a Khrynsani shaman ducked around the corner into the alley. His back was to us, his hands glowing red with an unreleased spell. Tam clapped his other hand over my mouth. He needn't have bothered; I wasn't going to make a sound. It was Darshan, the shaman who had recognized me. Neither one of us moved, but the shaman must have sensed that he wasn't alone in the alley. He turned, and when he saw the two of us, he smiled slowly and the red glow faded from his hands.

"Primaru Nathrach, I'm glad to see you've come to your senses. You arrived just in time to keep your end of our bargain."

Bargain?

Darshan wanted me—and he knew Tam by a title he'd tried to bury along with his past.

The Khrynsani held a small vial in his hand. I'd seen its twin a few minutes ago.

His smile twisted into a leer, fangs peeking into view. "Do you require this, or do you wish to subdue her yourself?"

Tam violently hissed a single word and Darshan froze, his eyes wide with disbelief, strangled sounds coming from between paralyzed lips. Lips that I knew no air would ever pass through again. Strangled turned to gurgling. Tam repeated the same word over and over, each time deeper, softer, and more sibilant until the word resolved itself into a serpent's hiss.

A death curse in Old Goblin. The blackest of black magic.

And Tam was wielding it with a master's touch.

The Khrynsani's eyes went vacant as he slid lifelessly down the alley wall.

The Saghred responded. I didn't know if it was to Tam's touch, the sound of Old Goblin, the death curse, or the potent scent of Tam's black magic lingering in the air.

The Saghred didn't care.

I felt heat coil tightly like a fiery serpent in the center of my chest. It uncoiled and ignited, spreading through my body, heating and awakening. Eager and quivering. I couldn't hear anything past the pounding of my heart. Tam held me pressed against the wall, his lean body hard against mine. He looked down at me in shock and disbelief—and beyond that lay something darker and uncontrolled. His large eyes were bottomless black pools with barely any white exposed. His breathing became ragged and the sharp tips of his fangs appeared behind parted lips.

"The Saghred?" Tam's question came out as a raw whisper.

It was, but I didn't answer. I couldn't. I started to panic as the power between us continued to build, my breath coming in shallow gasps. I couldn't fight it; I couldn't stop it.

And I didn't want to.

Tam slid his hand from my mouth to my throat, the heated trail of his fingers burning away all instinct to defend myself. He bent his head until his lips hovered over mine. His breath was warm, the sting of his fangs a sharp sweetness as he softly bit my bottom lip. Then his mouth met mine and the Saghred's power coursed like liquid fire through my veins, meeting and melding with Tam's black magic until what was mine and his became ours in a searing blaze of power. A pulsing, living thing ripe with dark promise.

No!

"Back," I gasped. I managed to wedge my hands between Tam and me and pushed hard against his chest. "Dammit Tam, get back!"

My effort wasn't necessary. Tam staggered back from me like I was the edge of an abyss and he'd almost fallen in. I dimly realized the fighting in the street had stopped.

"What are you doing here?" Tam's words came out half strangled.

"The boy," I heard myself say. "The Khrynsani want him."

And me. A Khrynsani shaman knew Tam well enough to lower his defenses—and expected Tam to hand me over to him.

But Tam had killed him. With black magic.

I bent and retrieved my switchblade from where Tam had dropped it, never taking my eyes from the goblin that until two minutes ago, I had considered more than a friend. I flipped the blade open. It was in perfect working order. Good.

"Just what the hell are *you* doing here?" I growled. My eyes widened in realization. "You followed me here from Mermeia." I looked at the dead Darshan. "Why? As a favor for the Khrynsani?"

Goblins had what they called "intricate alliances"—and even more intricate betrayals. I couldn't believe that Tam would betray me.

I couldn't deny that Tam was a dark mage.

Tam had always wanted me. Now Tam's black magic wanted the Saghred. He'd come close to getting both.

"Raine!" It was Mychael's desperate shout from somewhere in the street or the courtyard. I didn't know. Hell, I could barely think. I put Rudra Muralin's journal back in my jerkin, and saw that my hands were shaking. Fear, shock, rage—take your pick.

"Answer me, Tam!" I snapped.

Silence.

"Raine!" Mychael was closer.

"She's here," Tam called, loud enough to be heard by Mychael, but no one else.

Mychael appeared at the alley entrance, saw us, and noted the dead shaman. His eyes went back to Tam, his face an expressionless mask. The air around us still crackled with the remnants of our melded powers—and the acrid scent of Tam's death curse.

I knew a little about Tam's past. He'd reluctantly volunteered some things, and I'd heard whispered rumors of a few more. None of it was anything to be proud of. Mychael had known Tam long before I'd met him. As a lawman, I imagine Mychael had made it his business to know the name of every skeleton in Tam's closet.

Mychael didn't need to say a word; his blue eyes were blazing and so was his blade. They were doing his talking for him. Tam's black eyes matched Mychael's for intensity, and the red glow of a spell in readiness flared to life on his hands. The two of them were packing enough firepower to wipe out most of a city block. I'd seen this kind of behavior before—at high noon on a quickly deserted street. I was going to put a stop to it right now.

I stepped between them. It wasn't the smartest idea I'd had today, but it'd keep either one of them from doing anything potentially lethal and definitely stupid.

"Mychael, I'm fine. Tam killed the Khrynsani to protect me."

My voice was firm and assured, and Mychael didn't buy it for a second. I wasn't sure how I felt about it myself. Mychael didn't get to be paladin without being able to recognize black magic, stop it in its tracks, and take down its practitioners. He held out his hand to me, never taking his eyes from Tam.

I didn't take his hand, I didn't look at Tam, and I walked out of the alley without either one of them.

The city watch had arrived and were helping the Guardians clean up the mess we'd made. There was a wagon being filled with dead Khrynsani. Mychael came out of the alley and after a glance at me, went to speak with the watcher in charge. When Tam emerged, he stayed in the shadows until he reached his men, also known as our mystery goblin allies. They were standing to the side, out of the streetlights, and the boy was with them. Like Tam, they were armed for trouble and wearing dark, rough leathers—dressed for doing something you didn't want anyone to see you doing.

"You okay, ma'am?"

It was Vegard. He was close enough to protect me, far enough away to give me space. I wondered if he could smell the black magic on me.

"I'm good, but I could be better," I told him, glancing over to where Tam and his men had been standing. They were gone. I wasn't surprised.

Vegard looked where I was looking and nodded. "I understand, ma'am." The blond Guardian's ax was sheathed over his back, but the blade still held a faint glow. He hesitated uncomfortably. "You just let me know if there's anything I can do to help." His voice was soft, but his pale blue eyes were solemn with resolve.

My throat felt suddenly tight. "Thank you, Vegard."

Mychael finished speaking with the watcher and crossed the street to where we were.

I took a breath and blew it out. "So, who was the kid?" My question sounded brisk and businesslike. Good for me.

"Talon Tandu. He works in Tam's nightclub as a spellsinger."

I knew Tam valued his people. I wondered what my value was.

A dragon landed with a plume of flame. Kalinpar. I could swear he was grinning at me. I didn't feel like grinning back.

"My ride to the citadel, I take it?"

Mychael's expression darkened. "I want you out of the central city now. Kalinpar is the fastest—"

"And quickest way to get around," I finished for him. "I know. Let's just get out of here."

Chapter 10

"In my office, please."

That was a pleasant surprise. I half expected Mychael to say, "In my containment rooms," without the "please."

Those were the first words he'd said to me since Kalinpar had landed with us in the citadel's courtyard. While airborne, the noise from the wind had made it difficult to carry on a conversation. Difficult, but not impossible. Yet Mychael had been silent in the saddle behind me the entire time. I think he hadn't said anything because he wanted to make sure that I heard every word he said.

I had a real good idea what some of those words were going to be.

Mychael kept up his self-imposed vow of silence all the way to his office. The Guardians we passed saluted their paladin, but no one said anything. They took one look at Mychael's expression, made the smart choice, and kept their mouths shut. Guardians weren't stupid. Mychael was keeping his thoughts to himself. I was doing the same. His thoughts were probably along the lines of getting an explanation from me.

I was thinking about possible escape routes.

Mychael closed his office door behind us and went straight for the cabinet where he kept the whiskey. Now there was a thought I could agree with. He started pouring himself a glass.

I plopped down in a guest chair. I wasn't going to wait for an invitation to sit down that might not come. I ran my hands over my face and left them there. They could make themselves useful and help me hold up my head. I didn't think I'd ever been this tired.

"Do I get one of those, too?" I muttered through my hands. "Or are the condemned not allowed a last drink?"

Moments later I sensed Mychael standing beside my chair. I opened two of my fingers and looked through. He held a glass of the blessed amber ambrosia in both hands, and was offering one of them to me.

I took it. "Thank you. I really need it."

"I imagine you do." Mychael didn't go behind his desk to his office chair as I'd expected. Instead he pulled the other guest chair next to mine. He sat down with the weary sigh of a man who's had way too much dumped on his already overburdened shoulders. I didn't need a flash of brilliance to know whose fault that was.

I sat back in my chair and took a good, long swig. The whiskey burned all the way down, spreading wonderful warmth as it went. It felt good.

Tam's burn had felt better.

I thought it before I could stop myself. I set the glass aside, suddenly feeling nauseous. Best to get it over with. "I bet you want to know what happened in that alley."

Mychael's glass of whiskey sat untouched on his desk. "I know what happened; the question is, do you?" There was no anger in his voice, no edge of accusation, but some strong emotions lay just beneath his carefully composed exterior.

I had a good idea what had happened—and what had nearly happened—but I didn't want to come out and say it. The answer just might earn me an extended stay in the containment room of my choice. Not to mention what had happened had been better than the best sex I'd ever had. Mychael so did not need to hear that.

"What happened wasn't your fault," Mychael said quietly. "It was the Saghred. Even if you hadn't been caught off guard, it's doubtful that you could have prevented it." His eyes were on mine. "But it's something I can never allow to happen again. It's too dangerous."

It might not have been my fault or Tam's, but that didn't change what had happened, or how good it had felt then, or how creeped out I was now. All that hot-blooded panting and searing and melding that Tam and I had done against that alley wall wasn't just us. The Saghred had been there, between us. A threesome featuring me, Tam, and a soul-sucking rock. I wondered if I could get the rest of my drink to go when Mychael took me down to the containment rooms.

"Mychael, I'm not a public menace."

"I never said you were. The danger would be to you." He paused. "How much do you know about black magic?"

"Enough to know I shouldn't have anything to do with it."

"It's addictive, Raine. Like a drug, the most vile and addictive you can imagine. Except this drug does more than give pleasure. It gives power—and it exacts a price you do not want to pay. I've seen it."

I met Mychael's eyes. "In Tam."

He nodded. "And many others. When Tam left the goblin court, he got help. Most black-magic practitioners don't want help. To the best of my knowledge, Tam hasn't had a relapse since then—that is, until tonight."

"Wonderful. First Carnades Silvanus says I'm infected with a filthy goblin rock; now you're saying that Tam fell off the black-magic recovery wagon because of me." I snorted. "I'm just spreading all kinds of good cheer around this place, aren't I?"

"Tam hasn't fallen yet." Mychael leveled those blue eyes on me. "But if he does, he's not going to take you with him. How long have you known each other?"

"Tam came to Mermeia two years ago; we met soon after."

Like I could have forgotten that. Tam had turned Mermeia's Goblin District on its collective pointed ear. He was a primaru, or shaman of the royal blood. Primaru Tamnais Nathrach was the ex–chief shaman of the soon-to-be-assassinated goblin queen, and a supposedly grieving husband of a recently murdered noble wife. Rumor had it that Tam leaving the goblin court and his wife's murder were connected. Tam arrived in town as a goblin of wealth and influence. He purchased the palazzo of an old but impoverished Mermeian family, and transformed it into Sirens—the most notorious nightclub and gambling parlor in the city. Some people said he bought the palazzo; others said he won it in a card game with the Mermeian family's foolish young heir. A few whispered that he'd all but stolen it using blackmail or black magic.

Knowing Tam back then, I would have believed any combination of any of the above.

I thought he'd changed. I thought I'd played a big part in that change.

Maybe I thought wrong.

I didn't want to be wrong. I didn't like it when I was wrong, and I sure as hell didn't want the Tam I thought I knew to have reverted to the Tam I'd never want to meet.

We'd met when a cash-strapped noble started working his way through his wife's jewelry to support his gambling habit. The wife hired me to find her grandmother's favorite ring. I tailed the ring—and her husband—right to Sirens's high-stakes card table. I'd heard that the owner of Sirens was a scoundrel and an opportunist, but he was also a savvy businessman. It looked good for him to return the lady's ring. Tam told me later he did it to impress me.

He needn't have bothered. Being a Benares, I've always been attracted to rogues. Kind of like a moth to flame. Most times I had the good sense to steer clear, but with Tam I'd come close to getting my wings singed more than once.

Tonight I damned near got fried.

"Has Tam ever told you what his job duties for his queen entailed?" Mychael asked quietly.

"He always kind of glossed over that part, but I've heard things."

"He was Queen Glicara Mal'Salin's enforcer—her *magical* enforcer—for five years."

I blew out my breath. It was a little shaky. "That's not the kind of job you get and keep for that long by helping little old goblin ladies cross the street."

"No, it's not."

I knew what else five years meant. I'd heard that chief shamans for the House of Mal'Salin tended to have short lifespans. The lifespan shortening was usually done by others who wanted to be chief shaman. I couldn't understand why anyone would want to fight to get and keep a job that was just going to get them killed, but I was an elf and not a goblin. I didn't give a damn about politics and intrigue. Goblins thrived on it. For Tam to have survived that long at the queen's side meant that he'd left his conscience and any morals he possessed at the throne room door. No wonder Tam had been so proficient with that death curse; I imagine he'd gotten a lot of practice.

I squeezed my eyes shut and pinched the bridge of my nose. "Okay, I'm confused by something. Actually a lot of somethings, but one at a time. Tam told me that A'Zahra Nuru was his teacher. I only ran into her a time or two last week, but she seemed to be a nice, rational sort of lady. Brave, noble, and all that. Definitely not a dark mage."

"Primari Nuru was only one of Tam's teachers," Mychael told me, "and probably the only one he'd acknowledge now. Unfortunately, others were more influential in his early education. But when he left the queen's service, Tam went straight to A'Zahra Nuru."

My throat felt tight. "He knew she could help him."

Mychael nodded. "He's not the first that she's helped. She does good work."

Black-magic rehab. Just when I thought I'd heard it all.

I didn't want to tell Mychael about Darshan thinking that Tam was in that alley to capture me for the Khrynsani, but he needed to know. Mychael was protecting me, and if I had any information that'd help him protect me and not get himself killed in the process, I owed it to him to be completely up-front. Tam didn't hand me over to Darshan, but he'd clearly been blackmailed, coerced, threatened, or all of the above to do just that. Tam didn't scare, so that left the first two. Whatever the Khrynsani were holding over Tam's head had nearly been enough to put me in Khrynsani hands. It wouldn't be the first time someone's past had come back to bite them in the ass. I just didn't appreciate being there to share the teeth marks.

I told Mychael about Darshan.

Mychael listened, his expression grim. "What were the shaman's exact words?"

"He said he was glad that Tam had come to his senses, and that he'd arrived just in time to keep his end of their bargain." I left out the part where Darshan offered Tam a drug to use on me. Tam was in deep enough shit as it was, and Mychael got the picture without it. "I think the Khrynsani have something on Tam. And I was trying to get him to tell me what that something was when you came into the alley." I knew what I was going to say next wasn't going to go over well. "I'd like to ask him again."

Mychael almost smiled. "Now what do you think my answer to that ill-considered request is going to be?"

"I asked you first."

"No," he said.

"No, what?"

Mychael leaned forward, until there were only inches between us. "No, you're not going to question Tam. I am. It's safer for you—and for everyone else."

"To avoid temptation, avoid being tempted."

"Exactly."

I couldn't blame Mychael. I wanted to disagree with him, but the truth was I just didn't have the energy to argue. He must have sensed it; either that, or he read my tired little mind. I didn't know and quite frankly I was too exhausted to care.

Mychael reached out and took one of my hands in both

of his. It was warm. No liquid fire, no blazing heat. Just warm, and comforting, and nice. Really nice. Mychael was right. Tam was an apparently not-quite-recovered dark mage. I was a dark-mage magnet. We were a kaboom waiting to happen.

Mychael squeezed my hand. "And I promise I'll tell you everything I find out."

That was a surprise. "Everything?"

"Everything. For your continued safety, you need to know—and you deserve to know."

"What's Justinius going to have to say about this?"

"Nothing, because until I speak with Tam, I'm not going to report what happened. Justinius trusts my judgment. If anything happens on this island that he needs to officially act on, he knows that I'll tell him. For now, we're the only ones that know, and until I get an explanation from Tam, that's the way it will stay."

I was shocked, but mostly I was grateful. Regardless of what he'd just said, Mychael had to be going against a whole handful of regulations not to report Tam and me—and he was doing it for the same reason he'd done everything else since I'd met him.

To protect me.

Chapter 11

*When I woke up the next morning I wasn't on a cot in a contain-*ment room or a pallet in a jail cell.

I was in my soft bed in my luxurious guest room. Sure, the Khrynsani wanted to get their hands on me, the goblin lawyers wanted to extradite me, and Carnades Silvanus wanted a warrant for my arrest, but as of this glorious, sun-filled morning, not a one of them had gotten what they wanted. Bad guys temporarily thwarted.

I loved it when my day got off to a good start.

It'd probably go straight down the crapper the moment my feet hit the floor, but for now it was all good.

Except for Tam. What had happened last night and what-ever agreement he'd made with the Khrynsani were defi-nitely not good. Before last night, I would have said without hesitation that Tam would never betray me and that I would trust him with my life. I smiled. I'd never trusted him with the rest of me, but then I didn't exactly trust me with the rest of him, either.

Tam was tall, lean, silvery skinned, black eyed, and wicked sexy. Though after last night, tall, silver, and sexy was consorting with the enemy. Not so sexy.

I felt a lump under my pillow. Rudra Muralin's books. I couldn't believe I'd actually slept with those things under my pillow, but even here in the supposed safety of the citadel, I wasn't about to take any chances of them walking away. I pulled them out. They were written a thousand years apart, both by the same sicko shaman, and both were creepy. Definitely not first-thing-in-the-morning reading material.

The bag with the kidnapped girls' hairbrush and locket was on my bedside table where I'd left it. Last night I'd tried to use the brush to link with Megan Jacobs. I didn't know if my tangle of emotions from Tam had interfered, or if I'd simply been too tired. Either way, contact didn't happen. I sat up in bed and pulled the wrapped hairbrush out of the bag. I closed my eyes and took a couple of deep breaths and tried not to think about Tam. I peeled back the cloth and took the brush in both hands.

Once again my contact was immediate and crystal clear.

Megan was still scared, but now she was almost too exhausted to care. Ailia Aurillac was wide-awake and looked furious. Good for her. The candle in their cell had been exchanged for a small lightglobe. It gave off a little more light, but it didn't show me anything new about where they were being held.

Someone walked in front of Megan, then out of her line of vision, then back into view again. A new prisoner, and not female. He also wasn't blond or petite. He was young, dark haired, and muscular. Banan Ryce had kidnapped another student and, judging from the bruises on the kid's face, he'd fought back.

Megan whimpered and then started to cry. Ailia put an arm around her shoulders and pulled her close. The boy knelt in front of Megan and took one of her hands. It gave me a better look at him. Hazel eyes, good bone structure under the bruises, dark hair cropped short, athletic build. Enough to give Sedge Rinker a good description.

Their comforting just made Megan cry harder. Dammit. I could be inside someone's head and see, hear, feel, and smell what they did, but I couldn't do a thing to help a terrified girl. No seeker could do that.

Or could I? Just how much of a boost had the Saghred given me? Only one way to find out.

I felt Megan's slender body shaking with sobs. I started taking deep, long, soothing breaths. I kept breathing, and the girl kept right on sobbing. Then she drew a shuddering breath. The next one was definitely calmer, and she wiped her eyes. The boy squeezed her hand and smiled encouragingly. That kid was a keeper.

"Come on, sweetie," I whispered to Megan, even though I knew she couldn't hear me, at least not with her ears. "Work with me."

Soon her shaking stopped, and her breathing and my breathing became our breathing. I continued taking slow, deep breaths and felt Megan doing the same. The boy traded places with Ailia, and put his arms around Megan. With a contented little sound, she nestled her head against his shoulder. Soon she slipped into an exhausted sleep.

I released the link with her as carefully as you'd tiptoe out of a sleeping child's room and close the door silently behind you.

I snuggled down into my pillows with a satisfied little smile. I did it. Now *that's* a new talent worth keeping. I could use a couple of more gifts like that from the Saghred.

I got up, pulled a robe on over my gown, and started reading Rudra Muralin's more recent literary effort. Usually I curled up in a chair with a good book. Neither Muralin nor his book was good, so I felt safer reading it standing up. As I read, I started to pace.

Okon Nusair—as Muralin was calling himself in the last century—had uncanny insight into the Saghred's use for someone who'd supposedly lived hundreds of years after the stone had done its worst. No wonder Nusair's work had been filed in the fiction section under myths and legends.

But to all legends there is a grain of truth.

From what I had read already, this little book had enough grains to fill a silo. It also explained how my father was able to keep the Saghred dormant for hundreds of years.

He starved it.

The Saghred fed on life essence, the living souls of those who were sacrificed to it. Rudra Muralin sacrificed victims to the Saghred before he wanted to use it. My father didn't give the rock a damned thing—no wonder it took him the first chance it got. That was last year. Last week, to save Piaras and myself, I tricked Sarad Nukpana into lowering his shields and touching the stone with his bloody hand. Nukpana had taken the bait, and the Saghred had taken Nukpana.

Yesterday Piaras had sung the Saghred to sleep, but from what I was reading, I had a sinking feeling it wasn't dormant or even fully asleep. The peace and quiet we were enjoying was a catnap. A cat eats, dozes off, and wakes up when it expects to be fed again. The Saghred had been fed only twice in the past thousand years.

It was going to wake up—and when it did, it was going to be really hungry.

"You must be reading the dirty part," said a voice from behind me.

I jumped, dropped the book, and barely caught it before it hit the floor.

Phaelan.

"Don't sneak up on me like that!"

He raised his hands defensively. "I didn't sneak. *I* knocked. *You* didn't answer, so I let myself in. It's not my fault you weren't paying attention."

"I was distracted."

"Obviously. Must be a really hot book. So who's doing what to whom and how long have they been going at it?"

"About a thousand years." I sat down and squeezed my eyes shut against the headache I knew was on the way from the link with Megan.

Phaelan whistled. "Impressive."

"And scary." I told him what I'd read yesterday and just now. I didn't have to explain why any of it was scary; that part was obvious.

What I didn't tell him was about Tam. Phaelan was a rogue and a scoundrel himself, so you'd think he wouldn't mind his cousin being semi-involved with someone of like character. You'd be wrong. It wasn't the obvious elf/goblin prejudice. I think it was that in Phaelan's opinion, no man would ever be good enough for me. I had enough problems right now without Phaelan finding out what had happened last night.

My cousin sat down in the chair across from me. "So let me get this straight. When you fed Sarad Nukpana to the rock, you basically rang the dinner bell. And the antique goblin shaman who's probably still alive and kicking—"

"Rudra Muralin," I told him.

"Right. The really old guy. He'd always fed the rock all the souls it could hold, so the next time it wakes up, the Saghred will expect you to serve it breakfast, lunch, and dinner on a silver platter since you're its . . . What did you say Nukpana called you?"

I leaned back in the chair and closed my eyes. "Bond servant." My headache had officially arrived and was setting up house between my eyes.

Phaelan didn't say anything else. I kept my eyes closed; the darkness and silence felt wonderful. Too bad it couldn't last.

"You ready to get out of here?" Phaelan asked quietly.

I opened my eyes into a squint. My cousin looked as grim as I'd ever seen him.

"I can't. I wish I could, but I can't."

"Why not?" Grim turned into angry. "You did your seeker thing and found the Saghred for that paladin. Hell, you even retrieved it for him. End of job. You don't owe anyone here a damned thing. The only thing you should be seeking now is a way to get off this island." He lowered his voice. "I've told the crew to be quiet about it, but to get the *Fortune* ready to leave in a hurry."

"I mean I *really* can't leave yet. I'm still connected to the Saghred. Bond servant, remember?"

Phaelan's dark eyes flashed. "Yeah, I do. And from what I've seen, no one here's breaking much of a sweat to do anything about it."

"It's only been two days. Things have happened." Entirely too much had happened. "It's complicated."

"When someone I'm doing business with tells me there's been a complication, that means the only problem they're having is deciding which way to screw me over. I'm not going to stand by and watch that happen to you or Piaras."

I froze. "What about Piaras?" It occurred to me I hadn't even seen him since his inadvertent audition yesterday afternoon.

"First Nightshades collapse the stage so somebody can watch you pick it up," Phaelan said. "Then somebody slashes the shields on the music room so Piaras can knock out the Guardians in the citadel. Banan Ryce as much as said you auditioned for whoever hired him—and I think Piaras auditioned for someone besides Ronan Cayle. Maybe Ryce's employer, maybe someone else. It could be anyone. Every mage on this island knows by now that you and Piaras are packing some serious firepower. They're either thinking the two of you are a threat—or a really valuable commodity."

Carnades Silvanus thought I was a threat. The Khrynsani saw me as a commodity to be acquired—and last night in that alley they'd damned near succeeded. Did anyone think Piaras needed to be locked up or acquired?

I closed the book and got out of the chair. I needed to get dressed and find Piaras.

"Don't worry. I've been keeping an eye on him for you," Phaelan said. "What he did yesterday impressed the maestro and whoever slashed the shields, but some of the Guardians the kid put nighty-night might not be so impressed. A couple of them could be really pissed off."

I hadn't thought of that. "Where is he?"

"Having another lesson with 'the maestro.' " Phaelan scowled. "By the way, Ronan Cayle's a mean bastard and I don't like him."

"He's a mage, and you don't like any of them."

"I'm keeping an eye on you, too," he said quietly.

I started pulling my leathers out of the closet. "Thank you. I'm sure my Guardians will appreciate any help they can get. I seem to be a challenge."

"Who's protecting you from them?"

I stopped. "I don't need protecting from them."

Phaelan snorted. "Are you so sure about that? What about the paladin?"

"What about him?"

"He has his duty. He's also not completely in charge here. He takes his orders from the archmagus, and possibly from this Seat of Twelve I keep hearing about."

"I know." I pulled out my daggers. "I met one of them yesterday."

"Did you like anything about him?"

"Not a thing."

"That's what I'm talking about, Raine. A lot of these mages want what you can do, but they don't want to go insane to get it. You haven't gone off the deep end yet. That makes you very valuable to a lot of powerful people. There's bound to be competition, and it's going to get ugly. So you just say the word—I'll get Piaras, and we'll get the hell out of here. Nothing the Guardians have at their docks can catch the *Fortune*."

I didn't remind Phaelan about the sentry dragons or weather wizards who could suck the wind right out of his ship's sails. Leaving Mid would mean leaving my only chance at getting my life back, but I wasn't going to put Piaras in danger doing it.

"You'll be the first to know when I'm ready."

The pair of Guardians on duty outside Mychael's office saw me coming. I was dressed in my working clothes: trousers, above-the-knee boots, and my favorite doublet, all in form-fitting, supple brown leather. I liked the doublet because it had steel links woven between the outer leather and inner lining. It also had leather sleeves to hide the weapons, a pair of knives in forearm sheaths I carried when I knew someone was going to jump me, but I just didn't know when.

Vegard walking by my side was probably all that kept Mychael's sentries from drawing steel. They stepped in front of the door to stop me from barging in, but they did step politely.

"I need to see the paladin," I told them. "And no, I don't have an appointment; and no, he's not expecting me."

"We can't open the door, ma'am." He was a young Guardian and sounded almost apologetic.

"Can't or won't?"

"Can't, ma'am. The paladin sealed the room."

"What for?" Vegard demanded.

"The spellsinger is in there." His eyes were a little wide.

"Ronan Cayle?" I asked.

The other sentry nervously cleared his throat. "Him, too. But it's the other one, the young one from yesterday."

I bit my lip to keep from laughing. They were afraid of Piaras. Then Phaelan's words came back to me. If these two were afraid, there just might be some who were pissed. My intention had been to tell Mychael about Banan Ryce's newest prisoner, and then find Piaras. I could do both here. Good.

I assumed my most reasonable tone. "Surely you can—"

"Just tell the paladin Miss Benares is here to see him," Vegard interrupted. "Now."

"Yes, Sir Vegard."

One of the Guardians passed his hand over a crystal mounted next to the door. The crystal flashed once and within a minute, I heard muted voices and a few seconds later Mychael opened the door.

And Sarad Nukpana was standing right behind him. He was smiling.

I knocked Mychael out of the way, whipped out a knife and slashed the goblin's throat.

My knife passed straight through.

It was a mirage. What kind of sick mage bastard creates a mirage of Sarad Nukpana?

The sentries behind me had drawn steel, and all of it was pointing at yours truly. I froze, keeping my hands where they could see them.

"Stand down," Mychael ordered. "Miss Benares was startled by the mirage. Sheath your weapons."

They did, and so did I.

"Dismissed," Mychael told them.

They saluted, left, and closed the door behind them.

"My mirage hasn't dissipated yet," Ronan Cayle told me. "My apologies if it startled you."

Piaras was standing next to a raised music stand. "Maestro Cayle was helping me improve my repelling spellsongs. He wanted to know what I was most afraid of."

Phaelan was right—Ronan Cayle was a mean bastard.

"An amazing likeness, don't you think?" The flame-robed maniac was actually pleased with himself.

My empty knife hand twitched. "Yeah, amazing. Uncanny even."

Mychael moved between me and the maestro. He didn't think I was going to do anything; he was just being prudent. I knew I wasn't going to do anything, either, but that didn't mean I wasn't thinking about it.

"Raine, a spellsinger must be able to stop *anything* in its tracks," Mychael said. "And they can't let their fears get in their way."

"If you can't think, you're dead," I muttered.

"Exactly."

"So what's wrong with using spiders and snakes?"

"I'm not afraid of spiders and snakes," Piaras said. "I'm afraid of Sarad Nukpana."

Yeah, me, too. I understood Cayle's motivation, but that didn't mean I liked him subjecting Piaras to his little exercise in terror.

"So, did you stop him?" I asked Piaras.

"It took a couple of tries, but, yes, I stopped him." He sounded pleased—and relieved.

"A *couple*? You've done this more than once?"

"Three with the Nukpana mirage," Cayle chimed in.

"Five with Magh'Sceadu. After a number of attempts, the fear begins to fade and the exercise isn't as effective."

My knife hand started to twitch again.

Magh'Sceadu were a Khrynsani creation made from goblin elemental magics. They were tall and hulking, almost hobgoblin in shape—if hobgoblins were made of black ink. They absorbed magic in those who had it, the life force of those who didn't, and the bodies of both. Khrynsani shamans used what was taken to power their own sorceries.

Piaras had taken on six Magh'Sceadu last week—and had failed to stop them. That had been the first of only two times that I'd directly used the Saghred. I had destroyed all six Magh'Sceadu.

"Did you stop the Magh'Sceadu?" I asked Piaras.

He winced. "Not exactly. Apparently I think they're scarier than Sarad Nukpana."

I nodded. I could understand that. Sarad Nukpana had only wanted to plunge a sacrificial dagger through Piaras's heart. The Magh'Sceadu wanted to suck his soul out one slurp at a time.

"You did fine, Piaras," Mychael told him. "You've made definite improvements."

Piaras smiled and blushed slightly at the compliment. "Thank you, sir."

"I need to speak with you," I told Mychael quietly.

"Concerning?"

I hesitated. "The missing students." I didn't say "kidnapped" since I wasn't sure if that had been made public knowledge. Piaras knew some of it. I didn't know about the maestro.

Ronan Cayle froze. "They've found Megan?"

"You know her?"

"She's one of my best students. Have they found her?"

I looked to Mychael.

"It's all right. I've told Ronan you're helping us."

"I linked with her this morning," I told the maestro. "She's unharmed."

His amber eyes bored into mine. "Do you know where she is?"

"Unfortunately I haven't been able to see enough to pinpoint their location." And most unfortunately, my way had been deliberately blocked. "I did see another prisoner," I told Mychael. "A boy. Student age, dark hair cut short, hazel eyes, athletic build. Does that match any new missing-persons report?"

Mychael shook his head. "I met with Sedge this morning. No students or citizens have been reported missing in the last twenty-four hours. I'll send a man to watch headquarters with the boy's description. Something may have come in by now."

Ronan Cayle took the music off of Piaras's stand and filed it in a leather case, and apparently his emotions along with it. "Master Rivalin, why don't you get some water and rest for a few minutes, and we'll meet downstairs in an hour to go to the dress rehearsal." He was brisk and all business.

I blinked. "Pardon?"

"For the recital tomorrow night," Cayle said.

"What . . . ?"

"At the beginning of each school year, Ronan's students give a recital for select alumni and parents, and returning faculty," Mychael explained.

"It's turned into a gala event over the years," Cayle added. "Only my best students are invited to perform." His lips tightened. "Megan Jacobs was one of them. Master Rivalin may be my newest student, but after what happened here yesterday, many have expressed an interest in hearing him perform."

Damn. I'll bet they have.

"A few of them have asked to attend the dress rehearsal."

And I was going to be right there with them. I glanced at Mychael, he looked at me, and the battlelines were drawn. There was no way in hell Piaras was walking into that without me.

"It's a courtesy that I extend to certain choice patrons," Ronan continued.

"If you don't mind, maestro, I'd like to go with Piaras." I gave him what I'd been told was a winning smile. "Moral support and all that."

Ronan beamed. "I would love for you to hear—"

"Ronan, it would be safer if Raine remained in the citadel," Mychael told him, and me.

Piaras shot me a look. "You're not safe outside the citadel?"

I shrugged. "Safe is relative."

He knew what I meant. I'd told him the same thing last week when we'd been between near-death experiences and had about a mile between us and Sarad Nukpana or anyone with the last name Mal'Salin.

I turned to Mychael. "With Vegard, Riston, and the boys, I think I'll be safe in a concert hall."

"We won't be using my concert hall," Ronan told me. "It's being renovated. Tamnais Nathrach, the proprietor of Sirens, has graciously agreed to host the festivities. Next to my concert hall, Sirens has the best acoustics on the island."

So *that* was Mychael's real reason. I understood it, but that didn't mean I was going to agree to it. Tam had been a busy boy—from possible Khrynsani conspirator to gracious gala host.

"I'll be going to Sirens with Ronan and Piaras," Mychael told me, his expression giving nothing away, least of all that he and Tam were going to have a long talk, and he was determined that talk was going to be without me.

I smiled at Piaras and Ronan. "Would you gentlemen excuse us for a moment?" I crooked a finger at Mychael. "Paladin Eiliesor, a moment of your time in private, please?"

If Ronan hadn't resumed putting away music in a rustle of papers, I could have sworn I heard Mychael growl. He may have growled, but he did follow me to a corner of his office.

"I won't go anywhere near Tam," I assured Mychael in my most emphatic whisper. "Hell, I won't even look at him." Tam wasn't important right now; sticking to Piaras like glue was.

"Good, because you're not going to Sirens."

"Mychael, somebody slashed those shields while Piaras was practicing. Now there's suddenly a lot of interest in hearing him sing. Powerful people kind of interest. I'd like to see just who these choice patrons are."

Phaelan's opinion of why those shields had been disabled was sounding more like truth than theory every second. And I'd seen it more times than I'd care to count in my line of work. Talented magic users kidnapped to be used and exploited by the rich and powerful. For obvious reasons, alchemists had the top spot on the list of mages most often kidnapped, but spellsingers ranked right up there. I'd done more than my share of magic user "seek and rescues." Piaras was *not* going to be one of them.

I lowered my voice even further. "What if whoever slashed those shields wasn't interested in killing you or me, or getting the Saghred?" I said. "What if they wanted to see just how much damage Piaras was capable of? You said it yourself that he's a weapon; Ronan said he's lethal. One of those choice patrons might be in the black market for a spellsinger." I stared hard at him. "I hear you were a kick-ass prodigy in your day. Did anyone try to kidnap you?"

Mychael looked down at me, his jaw clenching and unclenching. "If you take one step toward Tam, Vegard *will* sit on you."

Chapter 12

I'd been inside Sirens in Mermeia, so I knew what to expect. Piaras had never seen the inside of either one of Tam's nightclubs. His brown eyes were wide as he took it all in.

The Sirens nightclub in Mermeia was mainly a gambling parlor. The Sirens on the Isle of Mid offered spellsinging as the featured specialty. So far there were only two links in what Tam planned to become a chain of Sirens nightclubs.

On the outside, Sirens looked less like what one would expect of a nightclub, and more like an expensive manor house. The diamond-shaped, lead-paned windows belonged to the restaurant part of the establishment. We were in the interior theatre where the shows took place.

On the main floor of the theatre were small tables, each covered in a crisp white cloth and set with a single pale lightglobe in its center. There were either two or four chairs at each table, with enough room between each for servers to discreetly fill drink orders—and to give Sirens's guests privacy to enjoy the show. The second-floor dining suites were like private boxes in a fine theatre. Columns stretched from the floor to the high, vaulted ceiling, carved with mermaids and mermen—sirens that could sing men or women to their doom—or somewhere much more enjoyable. From what I could see, "frolicsome" didn't even begin to describe the activities the carvings were engaged in. I steered Piaras around the columns.

The stage wasn't large; it didn't need to be. Sirens was about spellsingers, and what they could do to an audience. Spellsingers didn't need space, just flawless acoustics, so that a whispered word sounded like it was being whispered directly into the ear of a patron at the farthest table from the stage.

Mychael had gone to Tam's office. I stayed with Piaras.

Close to two dozen people were seated at various tables near the stage. When Ronan had said "choice patrons," what I saw was pretty much what I'd expected. The mixture of elves, goblins, and humans had the air of privilege that only came with obscene wealth. Not surprisingly, the elves sat on one side of the theatre, the goblins on the other. The humans had arranged themselves more or less in the middle. Some of the patrons were magically talented; most were just rich. Of the talents, I didn't sense any nefarious purpose, but that didn't mean it wasn't there.

Ronan was conferring with one of his students onstage. She'd just finished a love song that quite frankly hadn't done a thing for me. There were shields at the base of the stage that would prevent spellsongs from having their full effect. They could be strengthened or lowered as needed. They could have turned them off for this girl. Maybe it was just me she left cold, but I didn't think so. With spellsinging, the sex of the singer and the listener shouldn't matter. A truly gifted spellsinger could make you forget that you even had a sexual preference. Ronan's student was a regally beautiful goblin who came complete with her own entourage. Two armed and leather-armored bodyguards stood nearby, their eyes alert to her and everyone else in the room. The goblin girl was dressed in the height of fashion, and wore more jewelry than was tasteful. I thought one piece was particularly tasteless. A mirror pendant hung from a rope of diamonds around the girl's neck. A mirror mage. Figures. A human hairstylist fussed with elaborately jeweled clips holding back the girl's waist-length blue-black hair. One of the clips pulled the goblin's hair and the girl spun and hissed something, the back of her hand stopping just short of the human's face.

"Countess Sanura Mal'Salin," Piaras told me as if that explained everything.

It did.

Apparently Ronan invited his best students—or the most politically advantageous. For years the goblin royal family had snubbed the Conclave college, until about ten years ago when goblin aristocrats started filtering into the college classrooms—and their gold started flooding into the college coffers. I wondered if Mal'Salin gold was paying for Ronan's recital hall renovation.

Six students lounged at a cluster of tables at the base of the stage: three elves, two humans, and another goblin. None of them had entourages. I chuckled. It looked like Piaras had a small platoon in his wake. The platoon was for me, but no one here knew that. Vegard and Riston hung back a few feet to give Piaras and me the semblance of privacy. The others deployed themselves around the theatre. I saw a familiar young goblin leaning casually against one of the siren-covered columns, his arms crossed over his chest, watching the countess with amusement.

"Is the goblin next to the column one of Ronan's students?" I asked Piaras.

Piaras nodded. "Talon Tandu. He also works here."

"Do you know if he's any good?" I asked.

"I heard him briefly in the maestro's tower yesterday. I thought he was very good." Piaras was silent for a moment. "Paladin Eiliesor didn't want you to come here."

"He didn't want me to leave the citadel," I corrected.

Piaras's lips turned up in a brief smile. "No, I distinctly heard the words 'Tam' and 'Sirens.' I also heard my name more than once. You don't go into a corner to argue about giving someone moral support."

Crap. The kid's got elf ears, Raine. You've got a pair yourself. They're not just there to look good.

"Sounds like we should have left the room," I told him. "Eavesdropping is rude."

"I'm sorry, but when I heard my name, I thought it might be something I needed to know." He hesitated. "And when Paladin Eiliesor said it wasn't safe for you to leave the citadel, he looked like he meant it. I needed to hear why. I can't do a good job of worrying about you unless I know what I'm supposed to be worried about."

"The only thing you need to be worried about is singing. And you don't need to worry about that. You'll be splendid as usual."

"You're avoiding my question."

"You're ignoring my avoiding."

"How else am I supposed to find out what's going on? Whenever I walk by, everyone stops talking. I walk down the halls at the citadel, and the Guardians stare. I think some of them are afraid of me. They don't need to be." He looked down. "I don't want them to be," he said quietly.

Crap again.

Piaras wanted to be a Guardian more than anything. It looked like yesterday's damage wasn't only to sabotaged shields. Nothing stomped on a teenager's already fragile self-esteem like being ostracized from day one by the men you most admired.

"Now everyone knows what I did to those Guardians." A muscle twitched in his jaw. "All this is just the maestro displaying the freak."

I looked directly into those liquid brown eyes. "You are *not* a freak. Just because you didn't mean to put those Guardians to sleep doesn't change what you accomplished. And yes, I said 'accomplished.' If you were on a battlefield aiming at the enemy, what you did would get you called a hero, not a freak. You have a rare and powerful gift, and that can intimidate people, because they only see the gift and not the person behind it. You are *not* a freak—and don't you dare let anyone tell you otherwise."

I saw a flicker of what may have been belief in his dark eyes. "Thank you."

"You're welcome, but I was just telling the truth. No thanks needed for that."

"You're not a freak, either," Piaras said solemnly.

"The jury's still out on that one."

"*I* know you're not a freak."

I exhaled slowly. "Thank you, sweetie. You can't know how much I needed to hear that today."

One of the other spellsingers—a pretty, dark-haired human girl—was stealing shy glances at Piaras.

I gave him a lopsided smile. "Who's that?"

Piaras looked where I was looking, blushed, and quickly looked away.

"Katelyn," he said so softly I barely heard him.

My smile broadened into a grin. I bit my lip to make myself stop. "Katelyn who?"

"Valerian," he whispered.

"*That* Valerian?"

Piaras nodded. "The archmagus's granddaughter." He glanced at her, and she caught him looking. She smiled and gave him a shy wave. The tips of Piaras's ears flushed pink.

"Have you heard her sing?" I asked.

He looked at Katelyn and kept looking. The kid was enraptured. "It was beautiful."

I nudged him playfully. "Has she heard you sing?"

Piaras nodded. "Yesterday in the maestro's tower. Her lesson was after mine."

"And . . . ?"

"And what?"

"What did she think?"

Piaras flushed scarlet. "She said I had the most magnificent voice she had ever heard."

I grinned and nodded approvingly. "Beautiful *and* she has flawless taste in men and music. I could like this girl."

Piaras risked another quick look at her. "Me, too."

"Piaras!" Ronan Cayle yelled. We both jumped. "It's your turn. Quickly now. Our host needs his theatre back in another hour."

I punched him on the arm. "Break a leg, sweetie."

As Piaras made his way to the stage, I pulled out one of the chairs and made myself comfortable. I was far enough back to see anyone who came into the theatre. When I looked up, Talon Tandu was sauntering toward me like a sleek young cat, all cocky bravado, those aquamarine eyes checking me out from head to toe and taking their sweet time doing it.

I bit back a laugh, and heard Vegard's muffled snort from behind me. Talon couldn't have been much older than Piaras—at least in age. Though with his looks, he'd probably already had plenty of experience way beyond his years.

Talon's pale eyes sparkled. "You don't look the worse for wear from last night."

Now that was a pickup line I hadn't heard before.

"Silver-tongued little minx. I'll bet you say that to all the girls you roll in the gutter with."

He pulled out a chair, straddled it, and folded his lean arms across the backrest. His grin was full of fang. "I liked watching you wrestle last night. I think I heard a few of that shaman's bones break. You went to a lot of trouble for one little book."

"I take my education very seriously." I folded my arms across my chest. It was the only way to get the kid to quit staring at my breasts.

Talon jerked his head toward Piaras. "Did he really knock out every Guardian in the citadel?"

"Not all," I said. "Some of them couldn't hear him."

Talon laughed, a bright silvery ring. "Damn, what I wouldn't give to have seen that. So you've come to hear the trained songbirds perform?"

"Sounds like you're feeling less than honored."

"Ronan opens the cage once a year and has us warble and trill for wealthy alumni and filthy rich parents." His eyes were hard as they looked at something over my left shoulder. "How am I supposed to feel?"

I turned slightly. Sanura Mal'Salin had gathered up her entourage and was leaving the theatre.

"I'm here to listen to Piaras," I said. "But I'd like to hear more about what happened last night. The men who tried to snatch you aren't known for music appreciation." I slouched down in the chair and crossed my legs at the ankles. "So what happened?"

"I was on my way to work, and somebody's hired goons tried to kidnap me," Talon said casually. "When you do what I do, and look how I look, you attract more than your share of pervs and overzealous fans."

"You say it like it's not the first time."

The goblin shrugged. "I've been kidnapped twice before."

I just looked at him for a moment. "Did Tam come after you those times, too?"

He arched one flawless eyebrow. "*Tam?* You know the boss?" He grinned slowly. "Exactly how well do you know him?"

"Yeah, I know him. How or how well I know him is none of your business. I asked you a question. Did Tam rescue you those other two times?"

Talon shook his head. "They happened at my previous gig, a spellsinging club in Mipor. It paid well enough, but the owner had an arrangement with certain patrons—wealthy and influential patrons, if you get my meaning."

"Yeah, I get it." I didn't even try to keep the disgust out of my voice.

"If a patron liked what they heard and saw onstage, they'd pay the owner to arrange a private performance. I went once. I tried to leave, but the patron's bodyguards had other ideas." The kid's voice was nonchalant; the rapid pulse in his throat wasn't. "The next morning, I told the owner I wasn't going again. Next time he didn't ask me—"

"He just charged the patron more and had you kidnapped and delivered."

"Pretty much." Talon's bravado was back. "That's when I came here. I heard Nathrach took good care of his people and paid well. And last night he and some of the bouncers from the club came after me. I've never worked for anyone who'd do that." He scowled. "Though what he makes me do is almost as bad."

I didn't move. "What does he make you do?"

"He's making me go to college." The kid was indignant. "It's actually in my contract. If I don't go to classes during the day, I don't get to work at night." He slouched down in his chair. "So that's how I ended up in the maestro's flock of performing songbirds."

"Talon!"

We both jumped. It was Ronan again. I growled. Talon heard me and grinned. If the maestro did that one more time, I was going to give him a quick and dirty lesson in volume control.

"You'll be after Piaras," Ronan yelled. "Go warm up."

Talon stood and gave the maestro a little mock salute. "Yes, sir. Be right there, sir." Then the kid muttered something under his breath in Goblin.

It was highly creative and physically impossible. I think.

He winked at me. "Later, gorgeous."

As he made his way to the stage, I saw a tall figure in black robes enter the theatre through a door near the foot of the stage.

Carnades Silvanus.

Two other elves were with him. One looked like a bureaucrat. He was a full head and a half shorter than Carnades, blinking in the dim light as he fidgeted with a pair of spectacles perched on the bridge of his nose. The other elf was more familiar. Not him personally. I didn't know him, just his type. He entered behind Carnades, not from deference, but to let the senior mage attract all the attention. This one didn't want to be noticed, either personally or magically. He was using Carnades's arrogant aura of power to cover whatever magic he was packing. Generally, if someone doesn't want you to see what they've got, it means they've got a lot. I'd found that out once or twice the hard way. Today wasn't going to be my third.

I half turned to Vegard. "The elves with Carnades. Who are they?"

"The little one's Giles Keril, the elven ambassador to Mid. The other is Taltek Balmorlan. He's with elven intelligence. Don't know what he does."

Which was exactly how Taltek Balmorlan and anyone else who worked for the agency liked it.

I'd done consulting work for elven intelligence. I was recruited by Duke Markus Sevelien, the agency's chief officer in Mermeia, and I'd only worked with him. That's exactly the way *I* liked it. Markus was an up-front and moral sort, which was a rare find in the agency. I'd always wanted to think that Markus sought me out because of my superior seeking skills, but I knew differently. Markus thought my being related to criminals helped me know the criminal mind. I didn't want to come right out and admit it, but he was right. Truth be told, if it can be picked up, pried off, or in any way pilfered, my family's made off with it at one time or another. Unfortunately those pilfered goods have occasionally included people. It's not something I'm proud of, but it's not something I can deny.

Most of my work for Markus involved finding pilfered elves—diplomats, intelligence agents, assorted nobles. The kind of people the less savory members of my family would love to get their ransom-grubbing hands on. It was gratifying work and I was good at it.

The agency was always looking to acquire fresh talent.

I sat up slowly. Sometimes they acquired without asking the talent.

Carnades spotted me—I'd already seen him—and the tension in the room popped up a couple of notches real quick.

"Ma'am," Vegard warned.

"Don't worry. I'll be good if he will. But if he's looking for trouble, I *will* give it to him."

"I've been ordered to sit on you, ma'am," the Guardian told me. He didn't sound very enthused about trying.

"I know." I gave him my best evil grin, then turned back to watching Carnades and his merry minions.

They sat at one of the tables closest to the stage. Piaras had just finished his warm-up.

I tensed, but kept my seat. Me going to Piaras would just get him the wrong kind of attention. He would be performing a sleepsong, but this version wasn't for a battlefield; it was for a nursery. If Taltek Balmorlan or anyone else in the theatre came to hear a weapon, they were going to be really disappointed. But that didn't mean we couldn't let everyone know that messing with Piaras would be a very bad idea.

"Vegard?"

"Ma'am?"

"I know all these Guardians are for me, but could you spare a few to discreetly, but obviously, arrange themselves at the base of the stage when Piaras is singing?"

The big Guardian was instantly beside me. "The boy's in danger?"

"Not immediately, but someone here might be spell-singer shopping."

Vegard knew exactly what I meant and growled something that summed up my thoughts perfectly. "I'll take care of it."

"Thank you, Vegard."

"Always my pleasure, ma'am."

He went to Riston and they spoke quickly in lowered voices. Even I couldn't hear what they were saying, but I didn't need to. Within half a minute, five fully armed and really good-sized Guardians had arranged themselves around the base of the stage, their broad backs to Piaras, their stony expressions toward the audience. Piaras looked out at me; his eyes widened briefly. I smiled and gave him an encouraging nod. Piaras didn't know what was wrong, if anything, but he knew that me and the boys had it under control.

Piaras walked to the middle of the stage. He looked out

and saw who was in the audience. He didn't know any of them, but he couldn't have liked that every eye was on him, anticipating his first note. Piaras closed his eyes and took a breath and let it out. It was shaky. Then he raised his head and resolutely fixed his gaze on the back of the theatre where there was no one staring at him.

Piaras sang without accompaniment. No instrument marred his voice's pure, unadorned perfection. The words and tune were a soothing lullaby, but flowing beneath them was a depth of power most spellsingers could only dream of. The sleepsong was for a baby, not a battalion, but that didn't matter. Piaras couldn't hide his strength. And he had the rapt attention of everyone in the theatre. There had been talking during the other spellsingers' practices. No one spoke now or even moved. Entirely too many people in that audience had just had their suspicions confirmed. Damn. I couldn't see the faces of anyone at Carnades Silvanus's table. But I could see some of the goblins, and I didn't like the looks Piaras was getting. To them the Guardians were just furniture to be pushed aside or ignored, and Piaras a treat to be taken and enjoyed. In that moment, I understood why Carnades hated goblins.

I didn't hate goblins, but I could have a momentary change of heart for that bunch.

Piaras finished his song to thunderous applause. One of the goblins gave him a standing ovation. He had the high cheekbones and handsome, angled features of a pure, old-blood goblin. His black eyes were bright as he shouted, "Bravo!"

The bastard.

Piaras left the stage and stopped to confer with Ronan. Two of the Guardians moved closer to him, blocking anyone from access. No one tried. I had to hand it to Mychael's men—they had the bodyguard thing down pat.

I felt a presence brush my skin like fingertips. I sat perfectly still.

It was Tam.

I couldn't see him, but I didn't need to. I could feel him just fine.

"Raine, you shouldn't be here."

I gasped at the sudden intimate contact. Tam's voice brushed against my mind like dark silk.

Vegard looked at me, and I quickly coughed.

"Dry throat," I rasped at his concerned expression.

Tam and I had spoken mind-to-mind before. Many times.

"Mychael didn't want me here, either," I said. *"You know I never do as told. Especially when I haven't been given a good reason. Now what the hell is going on?"*

I slouched in my chair. Keep it casual, Raine. I wanted answers from Tam; I didn't want to tip off Vegard. I turned my head toward the stage as if the human kid up there now running through scales was simply fascinating. My eyes flicked up to the right of the stage, then up to the first dining suite.

There he was. The dining suites were dark and Tam blended in perfectly. My elven eyes could just see him, his beautiful, silvery face silhouetted against the shadows. Vegard was human and if he looked at the suite, he would only see the shadows.

I had promised Mychael I wasn't going anywhere near Tam. I could keep my promise and talk to Tam at the same time. And I could stay safe while doing it.

"Trust your instincts, Raine. You are not *safe here. You're being watched."*

I kept my face neutral. *"By who?"*

Tam met my question with silence.

"What have the Khrynsani got on you?"

No response.

"You can't tell me—or won't?"

I saw Mychael on the opposite side of the theatre conferring with some newly arrived blue-robed mages. He stopped and looked at me. I gave him a little smile and a wave—and held my breath. He shouldn't be able to sense me mindspeaking to Tam. If he could, he'd have been over here in an instant. Mychael held my gaze a moment longer, then turned back to the mages.

"The men in blue robes are Conclave shield weavers," Tam told me. *"They're reinforcing the stage's shields. Since these are Ronan's best students, I can't risk anyone being hurt."*

"Some risks are worth taking, Tam. I want to help you."

"Sometimes you can risk hurting someone just standing close to them."

"What happened in that alley won't happen again. I won't let it."

Tam's low laugh brushed against me like the softest fur. I shivered and gripped the chair's armrests. Tam had never been able to do *that* before.

"Stop it."

His laughter stopped. *"Just a demonstration, Raine. What happened between us is still there. We're not entirely separate anymore. Mychael knows this. Some things are beyond mortal control—and some things are impossible to resist. Like you. Please stay away from me."*

Don't think about Tam. Don't think about what we did, or what I'd like to be doing again right now. Eternal damnation versus amazing sex. Close, but no contest. Amazing sex didn't last nearly long enough—damnation lasted an eternity. That tossed a bucket of ice water on my lust.

"What have the Khrynsani got on you?"

Silence. *"It's complicated,"* he finally said.

"With you it always is," I muttered. *"I'm a bright girl, Tam. I can handle complicated. You'd be surprised at the knots I can untangle. You made a bargain, but you didn't keep it. Then you killed the person you made the bargain with. In my family that makes any and all deals null and void. How does it work in your family?"*

"You saw last night how it works in my family." His voice in my head was tight with repressed rage.

"The Khrynsani aren't your family." I stopped, thought, and concluded in the span of two seconds.

Oh hell.

The Khrynsani worked for Tam's family. The Mal'-Salins.

I just sat there. A Khrynsani shaman could have popped out of the floor right next to me and I don't think I would have batted an eye.

Things fell into place for me and it wasn't pretty.

The Khrynsani wanted me, which meant the Mal'Salins wanted me. Their lawyers were taking the legal road. Their shamans were going for dark alleys—and Tam. You didn't get to pick either your enemies or your family, and both were just as likely to stick a dagger in your back.

Tam's presence in my mind vanished. My glance flicked back to the dining suite. He was gone.

Piaras appeared at my side and I damned near jumped out of my skin.

"You looked like you were concentrating on something. I didn't want to disturb you."

"You didn't disturb me, kid. You scared the crap out of me."

"Sorry."

"It's okay. It's my fault; I wasn't paying attention." I was too busy realizing that Tam's family had somehow roped him back into service, and had come close to lassoing me along with him.

I felt someone watching us. I had a feeling who the voyeur was, but I turned and looked to the front table anyway. Yep, it was Carnades. I was half tempted to stick my tongue out at him.

Piaras grinned sheepishly. "Well, how did I do?"

"Absolutely beautiful." I didn't mention the people in the audience who thought the same thing but wanted more. "If it hadn't been for those stage shields, everybody out here would've been—"

I sucked in my breath and froze. Something was lightly brushing the skin between my breasts. I looked down. Nothing there except me and mine.

I stood as calmly as I could considering I was being groped by invisible fingers. I stepped back and the touching didn't stop. I blew out my breath in short puffs and looked at

Carnades's table. He was turned away from me, talking to someone. It wasn't him.

And it wasn't Tam.

Piaras's hand gripped my arm. "Raine, what is it?"

"Someone's touching me."

"I'm touching you."

"It's . . . not you." My breath came in gasps. I couldn't get any air.

Vegard was beside me. "Ma'am, what's wrong?"

The fingers suddenly splayed, the tips pressing into my breasts, the palm pushing hard against the center of my chest. Power radiated inward from that invisible hand. Searching. Summoning.

The Saghred surged against the hand from inside of me. The pressure from both inside and out held my rib cage like a vise. I couldn't breathe at all. Piaras's face blurred and faded. I was going to pass out.

"Raine!" It was Vegard. I could see his face, but his voice sounded like he was yelling down a well. I dimly heard him call for Mychael.

With the pressure came a presence. Not just old. Ancient. Its weight crushed me, thickened the air that I couldn't breathe. Filled my gasping mouth and nose with the sharp, coppery scent of blood. More blood than one body could hold, the blood of hundreds, thousands of screaming victims.

It was magic. Ancient and malignant. And evil. Gleefully evil.

Black flowers bloomed on the edge of my vision. The hand on my chest suddenly blazed into a white-hot brand, searing my flesh, burning through bone. My silent scream became one of the thousands as I fell into darkness.

Chapter 13

"It wasn't Tam," *I said for the umpteenth time.*

I could almost sit up in bed now. I was perfectly fine. Well, at least better.

Mychael wasn't listening to me.

It didn't help my case any that when I came around, I didn't have the strength to get my head off the pillow. Hard to be defiant and have a decent argument when you couldn't lift your own head. I was surprised to find that I didn't have any burns. It felt like someone had hauled off and punched me in the center of the chest with a branding iron.

Apparently I was out cold all the way back from Sirens to the citadel. And judging from the cramp in my neck and the dark outside my window, I'd added a couple of hours of sleep on top of that. I felt better, still crappy, but better.

Once he determined that I could speak, Mychael had started in with the questioning. You'd think that air-deprived impressions and images wouldn't stick around in your head all that long, but you'd be wrong. Like the phantom hand in the center of my chest, those images were seared into my mind. There was going to be no forgetting those anytime soon. By the next time I went to sleep, they'd probably have taken a place of honor in the parade of nightmares that made me go scream in the night.

I wondered how long I could go without sleep.

"All I know is that the Saghred responded to him," I told Mychael wearily. "Big-time."

His blue eyes narrowed. "Like Tam?"

"Nothing like Tam."

Tam had been amazing; this had been amazingly painful and nearly deadly.

My tone must have implied my enjoyment of the former, because Mychael's scowl deepened. Great. Jealousy was rearing its ugly head. Normally I'd feel flattered; now I knew it was only adding unwanted trouble to an already-too-long list.

"The Saghred just said hello to Tam," I explained. "It greeted Mr. Fiery Fingers like a long-lost friend."

I knew who it had to be. He was an ancient, powerful, bullying slaughterer who enjoyed his work way too much. I'd read all about him and his antics—in his own words and his own handwriting. All the blood, the thousands of screaming victims had been Saghred sacrifices.

"You've got a seriously unwanted guest on your island," I told Mychael.

"I've got a lot of those right now."

"This one makes Banan Ryce look like a choirboy."

Mychael didn't move. "Do you have a name?"

"Rudra Muralin."

Mychael sat back in the chair he'd pulled beside my bed. He didn't say anything for a while. "Are you certain?"

"I can't imagine the Saghred reacting that way to anyone else. He kept it fed and happy. The rock was trying to rip me apart to get to him."

Mychael knew what Rudra Muralin being here meant. I could see it in his eyes. The Khrynsani and the Night-shades had just been downgraded from dangerous to a mere nuisance.

Mychael had himself a big problem. Mine was catastrophic.

A thousand-year-old psychotic goblin teenage spell-singer wanted his rock back.

"Rudra Muralin was in Sirens," I said. "It doesn't tell us what the Khrynsani have on Tam, but it might go a long way toward explaining why he had to act like he was going along. And it would also explain why he didn't want me there."

Mychael's lips quirked in a sardonic grin. "Tam can be a wise man sometimes."

I pressed my lips into a thin line. "So what did the fount of wisdom have to say for himself?"

"Probably nothing more than what he told you."

I blinked. "You were eavesdropping."

"I was doing my job."

"I thought your job was to keep us apart."

"My job is to keep what happened in that alley from happening again. Tam was less than forthcoming with me. I thought he might tell you things that he'd kept hidden from me."

"So you struck out?"

"What he told me, I already knew. When he discovered that the Khrynsani were going to kidnap one of his employees, he and some of his men went to retrieve the boy."

I nodded. "That matches the story the kid told me. Either it's the truth, or Tam told the kid what he was supposed to say if anyone asked. That adds another question. What do the Khrynsani want with a nightclub spellsinger? And then it just so happened that I was there while Tam was there, and Darshan the shaman was tickled to see us both. I take it Tam didn't say why."

"He refused to give details. I could have arrested him, but I know Tam and that wouldn't have made him talk. Though if the Mal'Salins are threatening or coercing him, a containment room might be the safest place for him right now. And if the Khrynsani discover Tam killed one of their own with a death curse, he may wish that I had arrested him."

I almost couldn't believe what I was hearing. "You threatened to lock him up?"

"I never threaten; I merely told him what my duty as paladin required of me."

"Sounds like a threat to me."

"I would have been entirely within my rights as paladin to take Tam into custody. I can't trust him, but I can't deny that he saved your life. I'm having him closely watched. No doubt, his reaction to the Saghred was as much a surprise to him as it was to you. I don't think it was premeditated. The last time he saw you in Mermeia before we set sail, the Saghred was secure in its casket and wrapped in containment spells. At that time, those containments actually worked. There was no reaction then between the two of you and the Saghred."

No, but there'd been plenty of reaction between Tam and me. Now there was a good-bye a girl could remember. I think I can safely say that I'd never been slammed against a mainmast and kissed quite like that before. Tam wanted to make sure I wouldn't forget him. No chance of that.

Mychael hadn't seen that farewell, and I wasn't about to tell him. Especially now.

"The containments aren't working so great anymore," was what I said. Piaras's song put the Saghred down for a light nap. It was snoozing just fine until it got a whiff of Tam's magic. "I'm not surprised you couldn't get Tam to admit to anything. Goblins are notorious for talking in circles. Tam's elevated it to an art form. If he doesn't want you to know something, trying to pry it out of him will just make you dizzy." Tam's answer to a question was very often another question. Not one of his more endearing qualities.

One thought kept popping into my head with annoying frequency.

"Mychael, has anyone actually tried to steal the Saghred?"

"No one."

Mychael's stony expression told me that fact confused and concerned him even more than it did me. He didn't want anyone to steal the Saghred, but he expected someone to at least try. Apparently there were no takers—at least not yet.

"Maybe Piaras putting most of the Guardians to sleep actually *was* a trial run for a Khrynsani robbery attempt," I ventured.

"Perhaps. But Piaras didn't knock out all of my men. With the wards, spells, and guards I have down on the containment levels, no one can stroll in, pick up the Saghred, and walk out." He paused. "The only treasure anyone has tried to take is you," he said softly.

Oh boy.

I tried to sit up in bed and winced; my muscles screamed in protest. Mychael arranged my pillows, and with his hands on my shoulders, gently eased me back. Those sea blue eyes looked at me a couple seconds longer than was comfortable for either one of us.

"Would you like me to help with the pain?" he asked.

"Uh, I'm not sure that'd be the best idea."

"Why not?"

I put my hand where it felt like Rudra Muralin had punched me—right between my breasts. "Right here's where it hurts the most."

"Oh." Mychael's color rose slightly. With a visible effort, he forced any awkwardness down. The proper paladin was back. "I am a healer, a medical professional. You are in pain. It is my sacred duty to ease that pain."

He held up his right hand with a questioning glance.

Now if it'd been any other man, I'd say he just wanted to get his hands on me. Mychael was most definitely a man, though I would think that having his hand where he proposed to put it would tempt even the most professional healer to nonprofessional conduct. It wasn't a problem for me. I was just a seeker; my ethical values were safe.

Far be it from me to prevent a man from doing his sacred duty.

"Okay." My voice came out kind of husky. Whoa. My professional values were safe, but apparently my body was ready to toss my morals out the nearest window. I knew why. Yesterday, Mychael had used both his hands *and* his lips to heal my headache. I swallowed. If he did that now, I could not be held responsible for my actions.

Mychael took a few moments to steady and still his breathing. I'd already given up on mine. I didn't know if Mychael's little breathing exercise was to prepare him to heal, or to prepare him to put his hand between my breasts.

"What about the Saghred?" I asked. I cringed inwardly. Way to ruin the mood, Raine.

Mychael stopped with his hand halfway between us. "Since I'm not a dark mage, there should be no reaction from the Saghred at all."

"Are you sure?" I wasn't. And the more I thought about it, the more I thought this might be a really bad idea. "You wrapped it in containment spells, tried to bind it with a spellsong, and then carried me out of Sirens before Rudra Muralin could finish what he started. The rock might be feeling a tad vindictive." I exhaled slowly. "I don't want to hurt you." My voice shook, and I couldn't stop it. "I don't want to hurt anyone."

There. I'd said it. My chest and throat felt tight and the Saghred didn't have a thing to do with it.

Mychael's calm blue eyes held mine. I couldn't look away and I didn't want to.

"Raine, you're not going to hurt anyone. The Saghred is dangerous; *you* are not. You may be linked to the stone for the time being, but we will find a way to break that link. And I swear to you on my honor that I will not stop trying until that link is broken and you're free."

Okay, that did it. I had to clench my jaw to keep the tightness in my throat from turning into tears in my eyes. I was not going to cry. Mychael's steadfast and reassuring gaze wasn't helping things any.

"You're hurting." His voice was low and soft. "And that pain goes far deeper than physical injury. Let me help."

I took a deep breath, sniffed, and nodded.

Mychael placed his hand very carefully in the exact center of my chest. I looked down and held my breath. No

Saghred retaliation. No blazing heat. Just warmth. Mychael's warmth. It radiated outward from his steady hand, comforting and soothing. I took one breath and let it out, then another, the tightness and pain in my chest lessening with each breath until it was completely gone.

I raised my eyes and met Mychael's gaze. The pain in my chest was gone, but his right hand remained on me, resting over my heart as if making a solemn promise, or taking a sacred oath.

"I will see the Saghred gone. You have my word."

Chapter 14

Once I'd had a good meal and an even better night's sleep, I wasn't exactly ready to take on the world, just the bad guys infesting my little corner of it.

After breakfast, Mychael arranged to have a bathtub brought up to my room and had it filled with steaming hot water complete with bubble bath. His healing had taken care of Rudra Muralin's handwork, and his assurances that he was going to somehow get me out of this mess had made the rest of me feel better. A little. Promises and oaths were all well and good, but I knew he could only do so much. I had a feeling when it came time to put the cards on the table, it was going to be up to me.

I felt like everyone on this island knew more than I did. It was high time to play catch-up. No way was Rudra Muralin going to catch me with my magical britches down again. I put his books on the table next to the tub, then dipped my hand in the water. Perfect.

I started undressing. Whoever said ignorance is bliss must have died a horrible death with a really surprised look on his face. I needed to know what the bad guys knew, and I needed to know it now. Rudra Muralin was the biggest problem on my plate, but there were plenty of others to keep him company.

I was no closer to finding those kidnapped students, or why Banan Ryce had taken them. He didn't do anything for free or without a reason. Someone had hired him, and chances were that someone was local.

I eased myself into the steaming tub with a groan of mixed pain and pleasure. What muscles weren't still sore were in tense knots. The hot water made them feel better, and the bubbles made me feel better. Best of all, thanks to the small heatglobe bobbing among the bubbles, the water would stay hot for as long as I wanted to stay in the tub. You gotta love magic.

I reached for Rudra Muralin's journal. I just had to smile. I would love to see Lucan Kalta's face if he knew I was reading a thousand-year-old manuscript in the bathtub.

Muralin's journal was filled with more smiting, conquering, and an awful lot of enslaving—and most of the slaves were elves. The majority of them were sent to Rheskilia to work in the goblins' mines; choice captives were kept for the Saghred. I understood the physical act of sacrificing someone to the Saghred. I'd witnessed it firsthand last week with Sarad Nukpana—and gotten a history lesson directly from Rudra Muralin in Sirens. Blood and physical contact with the stone was all that was needed— the rock took it from there. But something I kept finding throughout the journal didn't make sense. Muralin referred to himself as the Saghred's "bond servant." Believe me, I got that part. What I didn't understand was that on occasion sacrifices were brought to Muralin—not to the Saghred— and he would "accept the gifts" on behalf of his master. The word "master" was used interchangeably with "Saghred." And in two instances, Muralin was referred to as "the vessel." Maybe my Old Goblin language skills weren't as good as I thought, but from what I read, Muralin's "gift acceptance" was always fatal to the poor, elven gift.

The next pages took something I already knew one big, scary step further. To use the Saghred, you didn't have to be anywhere near the stone itself. I'd used the Saghred only twice before, last week in Mermeia. The stone and I were in the same city, within only a mile or two of each other. Yet according to Rudra Muralin, distance was no barrier whatsoever. As long as the Saghred was awake, Muralin could use it. Whether he was one mile from the stone or a thousand, it didn't matter. Sometimes the Saghred traveled with the goblin armies; sometimes only Muralin did. The level of death and destruction never changed.

Rudra Muralin wrote that for all intents and purposes, he and the Saghred were one and the same. His link with the Saghred was that strong. I wasn't a spellsinger, and before my contact with the Saghred, I was only a marginal sorceress, and I'd only been connected to the Saghred for a little under two weeks. Nowhere near long enough to forge the kind of bond that could level cities. Or was it? Was my link as strong as Rudra Muralin's? And if not, just how strong was it? I didn't plan on having the link long enough to find out.

When I finished Muralin's journal, I put it on the table well out of splashing range, and opened the Saghred legend book that Muralin had written under his pen name. I started reading where Phaelan had interrupted me last time. There was more on the power of spellsinging to command the Saghred. Obviously you didn't have to be a spellsinger to command the Saghred. It occurred to me that I didn't know if my father was a spellsinger. Mychael probably would. I'd have to ask. The rest of the book was either things I already knew or had heard about, such as the Saghred's preference for shamans or powerful magic users as sacrifices.

According to legend, shamans who had fallen from royal favor were fed to the stone. The shaman doing the sacrificing received enhanced powers, near immortality and eventual insanity. The shaman getting sacrificed had his soul trapped for eternity inside the stone. I couldn't decide who got the worst end of that deal.

I finished the book and put it on the table with the journal.

I sank down lower into the hot, bubbly water. It took a while, but I felt myself finally start to relax, and caught myself dozing off. I didn't try to stop it. I'd wake up before I drowned. Probably. I drifted between sleep and wake. When I opened my eyes, my room was kind of blurry.

Sarad Nukpana was in sharp focus. He was smiling.

"Mind if I join you?" he asked.

The goblin looked entirely too happy to be sitting in a chair next to my tub, my bubbles had become noticeably less bubbly, and worst of all, he had my towel.

The goblin saw my glance, and his smile broadened, a hint of fang peeking into view. "You can come and get it."

I told myself I wasn't going to be intimidated. Scared, I had no control over and it was too late for that; I was already scared. Intimidated I could do something about. My last encounter with Nukpana had proved that anything he could do to me, I could do worse back to him. Physically speaking, I'd fought while naked before. Once you got past the embarrassment, it was actually kind of liberating.

I took a slow breath and, trying not to expose too much of myself in the process, strategically arranged what bubbles I had left. Then I crossed my arms over my chest. It didn't cover everything, but it'd have to do. Nukpana's dark eyes hungrily devoured my every move. I guess naked female elves were a scarce commodity inside the Saghred.

I tried to ignore where that thought led and glanced around. "Not enough power left to repair your own bedroom?"

Sarad Nukpana trailed his hand in my bathwater, parting my largest cluster of bubbles. "You've seen mine," he murmured, peering down into the water. "I wanted to see yours. By the way, this is your dream; I merely invited myself inside. Your bond with the Saghred allows me to exist in your waking thoughts or dreams. So I can come and go as I please."

I resisted the urge to look where he was looking. He

shouldn't be able to be here. "The Saghred's asleep." I said it, but I suspected the cat was waking up.

"Merely conserving power."

"By desire or necessity?"

"Both. Power is precious, little seeker. It should not be wasted on trifles."

"I'm not a trifle?"

"You are a necessity." The hand trailed deeper into the water, his fingers brushing my skin. "A most precious and desirable necessity."

I forced down a shiver. It wasn't entirely due to Nukpana's hand in my bathwater. My heatglobe had gone out. "If you want to talk or gloat, get on with it. My water's not getting any warmer."

He grinned, exposing alarmingly sharp fangs. "You're welcome to step out of the tub."

"You're welcome to go to hell."

"Such vehemence, little seeker. And when all I wanted to do was congratulate you."

"On what?"

"On your newfound skills. Even though I enjoyed your primitive dispatching of my shamans last night—inept though their attempt was—I have been truly impressed by your evolving contact with the abducted students." He removed his hand from the tub, negligently flicking the water from his fingers.

I resisted the urge to slink down farther into the water. I didn't know if Nukpana had continuous contact with me, or just got the information once he'd infested my dream. Either way it had to stop.

"What do you know about the students?" I asked.

"I have retained Banan Ryce's unique services from time to time. He is most proficient at his craft, but he does have his weaknesses, most notably blondes. I prefer redheads."

"One of your shamans apparently still has Banan's business card."

"My people are not responsible for Banan Ryce or your

missing students." The goblin's smile held secrets he had no intention of sharing. "You'll have to look among your own people for that. As to Darshan's rather clumsy attempt against you last night, Primaru Nathrach gave him precisely what he deserved." Sarad Nukpana nodded in grudging approval. "It was exceptionally well done. Darshan was an impulsive idiot. Now he's a dead one."

"So Darshan screwed up your orders?"

"That fiasco was on no order of mine." Nukpana's smile was slow and full of intent. "I have you exactly where I want you—as did Primaru Nathrach in that alley. You let a rare opportunity slip through your fingers, little seeker. It's not often that an elf has a chance to taste goblin black magic." His dark eyes lingered where my bubbles weren't. "No doubt Primaru Nathrach found you utterly delectable. You glisten with the Saghred's power. He keeps you at a distance because if you get within arm's reach again, he *will* take you. He will not be able to stop himself." Nukpana laughed softly. "Once a dark mage, always a dark mage."

I was sure there could be worse circumstances I could be in, but being naked in a tub with an evil megalomaniac sitting next to me definitely warranted an honorable mention. Too bad I hadn't used bath oil instead of bubbles. At least Sarad Nukpana wouldn't be able to get a grip on me should he decide to try.

He was using Tam to bait me. I wasn't going to bite. "So the Mal'Salins set their Khrynsani lapdogs on me?"

"The Mal'Salin family controls the Khrynsani in name only. Their master is the one who has come to reclaim what your father stole from him." Nukpana dropped my towel and picked up Muralin's journal. "I always found his writing style to be rather pompous, though the content is entertaining enough. Old Goblin is hardly light reading suitable for the bath, little seeker."

Tam had lied. His family wasn't running the Khrynsani show. Rudra Muralin was. Or maybe no one had told the Mal'Salins that their attack dogs were answering to someone else's whistle. Who knew what kind of tangled knot

Tam had gotten himself tied up in. Goblins lived for intrigue, deception, betrayal, and all the backstabbing that went with it.

Nukpana leaned back in his chair. "I wish you luck finding Rudra Muralin. He was nineteen years old when he fell into the Great Rift. Mid is teeming with college students, many of them goblin." Nukpana's expression grew thoughtful. "What *is* that quaint expression involving a needle and a haystack? Perhaps while Grand Shaman Muralin is here he can hear my favorite nightingale sing." He smiled. "Who knows? Perhaps he already has."

Nukpana referred to Piaras as a nightingale. Piaras didn't like it, and neither did I.

"Stay away from him," I growled.

The goblin raised his hands defensively. "It's Rudra Muralin you should be threatening, little seeker—but first you have to find him. Piaras's skill is astonishing for such a young age. And the way he sang us all to sleep—the Saghred hasn't received such a treat in years. Those with the sweetest magic are the most delicious. Is he being properly trained?"

I didn't answer.

"I'll take that as a yes. And considering his skill level, Ronan Cayle would be his voice master. I know of a master more suitable to develop his unique talent." Nukpana smiled slowly. "Maestro Cayle should take care; he could soon find himself with competition."

I sat up in the tub, sloshing water over the side. My remaining bubbles parted and I didn't give a damn. "What the hell is that supposed to mean?" My tone told him in no uncertain terms that if he didn't answer, I was out of that tub with my hands around his throat, buck naked or not.

"If I told you, it would spoil the surprise." He leaned forward. "And I can guarantee that you will be very surprised." His black eyes shone in the half-light. "Was that response evasive enough to make you come out of the tub after me? I would enjoy that very much."

I sat back, this time intentionally sloshing water over the

side and soaking Nukpana's feet. "Live with disappointment," I said with calm I didn't feel.

The goblin was staring in the direction of my bedroom door. I heard a distant pounding. Something or someone was trying to get in. Nukpana started to fade.

"Enjoy your freedom, little seeker. You will not have it for long."

Chapter 15

I woke up. I was shivering and my teeth were chattering. My water was ice-cold.

The pounding was someone kicking in my door. Then the kicking stopped and I felt a massive surge of power.

Dammit. I jumped out of the tub and ran to get a dagger. Then I faced the door, braced and ready for whatever was coming through it. I shivered and realized I was standing in a puddle of water, dripping wet, and I was *still naked*. I swore again and scurried back for my towel.

I was reaching for it when most of the door simply disintegrated.

Mychael all but fell into the room, his hands glowing white-hot with an unreleased spell. Instead of whatever he expected to find, he saw a soaking wet, naked seeker holding a dagger and a towel.

I clutched the towel in front me. "What the hell?"

I didn't know who was more stunned, him or me. But I knew who was more embarrassed.

Mychael's face went through several shades of pink in search of a blush. "You were shouting . . . The door was locked and you didn't answer—"

"So you blew away my door?" I felt laughter bubbling up, probably a prelude to hysteria.

Mychael's blush turned into a paladin's indignation. "Yes, I blew away your door!"

"I was in the tub—" I managed through chattering teeth.

"I can see that." His voice had a rough edge—and his sea blue eyes were looking at where my towel wasn't.

I clenched my dagger between my teeth while I wrapped the towel around myself, restoring some semblance of decency. It wasn't a particularly big towel, but it covered most of what needed to be covered.

"I fell asleep in the tub," I said. "Sarad Nukpana was in my dream, sitting right there." I pointed to the chair near the tub. "Your kicking chased him off." I shivered with cold, and tried to smile. "Thanks. Good timing."

There was a commotion in the hall. Vegard burst into the room, his ax drawn.

"Sir, we heard . . . Whoa!" He saw me and stopped dead in his tracks. He looked from me to Mychael, then at the door—or what was left of it. "I'll come back later."

"It was a misunderstanding, Vegard," Mychael told him. "Wait for us at the end of the hall. In the meantime, see that no one comes in."

"I'll take care of it, sir." And he was gone.

"Bring a new door," I called after him. I looked at Mychael. "What do you mean, wait for *us*?"

In response, he pulled the blanket off my bed and crossed the room to me in three strides. He held the blanket between us, and kept his eyes on mine.

"Drop the towel," he said, his voice low.

I gaped up at him. *"Excuse me?"*

A smile tugged at the corners of his mouth. "You'll need it to dry off. I promise I won't look."

I snorted. "You've already seen everything."

"Yes, I have." He didn't blush again, but the tips of his ears were pink—and his blue eyes had darkened.

He averted those eyes and resolutely kept them that way while I dried off. When I finished, he carefully wrapped the blanket around me, his expression serious.

"You need to get dressed."

"That doesn't sound good."

"It's not."

Great. First I got to be Sarad Nukpana's tub toy; now Mychael had news so bad even he admitted I wouldn't like hearing it.

"The Seat of Twelve have requested to see you and Piaras. Immediately."

I hadn't been in this part of the citadel before. It was less military, more formal. Imposingly formal. We had a dozen armed Guardians as an escort. Vegard and Riston were among them. They didn't look happy with where we were going. Maybe it was just me, but going somewhere *inside* the citadel with that many Guardians didn't bode well. Mychael's grim expression confirmed it.

"Do you know what kind of questions they'll ask?" Piaras asked Mychael.

Piaras's voice was steady, but I knew the kid had to be shaking like a leaf inside. He had absolutely no business being here. The only fear he should be dealing with today was recital stage fright.

"No, I don't," Mychael said. "But if any of their questions are for you, I'll be responding to them. You won't have to say a word."

"Who called the meeting?" I asked, though I had a sneaking suspicion who was responsible.

"Justinius's secretary delivered the Twelve's summons."

"Is that how it's normally done?" I asked.

"No. Usually Justinius comes to see me himself."

I smelled a setup. "Carnades will be there." I didn't ask it as a question.

"He will."

"Who's that?" Piaras asked.

"Carnades Silvanus is the senior mage on the Seat of Twelve," Mychael told him.

"I thought the archmagus was the senior mage."

"He is," I told Piaras. "Carnades is one step down." And that fact probably galled him every day of his life.

It could just be a question-and-answer session, but with Carnades Silvanus there, he'd probably find some way to turn it into a witch hunt. I knew Carnades had it in for me, but what I didn't understand—and didn't like one bit—was why the Twelve had asked to see Piaras. When I was getting dressed, I added enough discreet steel to make me feel comfortable. Mychael had seen me adding the last dagger and didn't say a word. That told me a lot about what we were walking into.

"Am I in trouble for what I did the other day?" Piaras asked quietly.

"I'm in charge of the Guardians," Mychael told him. "If you were in trouble for putting my men to sleep, you'd be in trouble with me. It was sabotage. You're not in trouble."

"Then why am I here?"

"I don't know," Mychael said honestly. "But you're both guests of the archmagus and under his protection. And at this moment, you're in my citadel and under my protection." His eyes narrowed dangerously. "No one will touch either one of you."

The old man was only going to be able to play that guest card for so long. I knew it. Mychael had to know it. Piaras didn't need to.

Our destination was behind a pair of massive bronze doors with an only slightly less massive pair of black-robed mages standing guard. The welcoming committee had Carnades's name written all over it.

Mychael stopped me with a hand on my arm. "Raine, when we get inside, let me answer *all* of the questions."

"What, you don't trust my diplomatic skills?"

"You don't have any."

"What if they ask me a direct question?"

"Just let me handle it."

I didn't respond. I didn't make promises I couldn't keep.

The mages opened the doors and stepped aside for us to enter.

This wasn't a room for the Seat of Twelve to meet—it was a star chamber for passing judgment. The Twelve were seated on a raised dais in chairs that looked more like thrones than anything. There were a few humans; most were elves. They were highborns just like Carnades. Great. The big chair in the middle, which I assumed belonged to Justinius Valerian, was conspicuously vacant. Carnades Silvanus was standing in front of it.

Oh yeah, this was a setup.

I also knew where this was going. Piaras didn't need to be anywhere near this room. Carnades wanted Piaras here for a reason, and I knew I wasn't going to like it.

There were observation balconies on either side of the room. Both were occupied. Now it looked less like a setup, and more like a trap. I kept my face expressionless. I wouldn't give anyone in the room the satisfaction.

In the balcony to the left were four black-garbed goblins. They looked like Khrynsani wannabes—they had the desire to be evil, but not the athletic ability to get through the boot camp. Bookish looking plus the desire to make the lives of others as miserable as possible. Had to be the Khrynsani lawyers.

In the other balcony were two elves. I recognized both of them. Giles Keril, the elven ambassador to Mid; and Taltek Balmorlan from elven intelligence.

I swore silently.

Mychael stepped forward. "I received a summons from the archmagus." His voice was perfectly controlled. "Where is he?"

"The summons was in the name of the Seat of Twelve," Carnades corrected him.

"Where is the archmagus?"

"He is unable to join us."

"An inquest cannot take place without the full Seat of Twelve—that includes the archmagus."

"This isn't an inquest, Paladin Eiliesor. My colleagues and I merely want to ask a few questions. We are *unanimous* in that request."

Mychael's face betrayed no emotion as he glanced at the balcony with the two elves. "And your guests?"

"Have a vested interest in the answers."

Vegard was standing by my right side, and bent to whisper in my ear. "Unanimous means the boss can't stop them from asking."

"We have received requests from our honored elven and goblin guests," Carnades said. "Most of these requests concern Mistress Benares. We acknowledge that she is also a guest with us and under the protection of the archmagus. But as a courtesy to our other guests, we have asked you all here to answer their questions and hear their petitions in an open meeting—where we can all hear the answers."

"We will hear our guests' questions and petitions," Mychael said formally.

"Like we have a choice," Vegard muttered under his breath.

Carnades sat in his own chair, not the old man's. I have to say I was surprised.

"The legal representatives of the royal House of Mal'Salin and the Brotherhood of the Khrynsani have filed a request with Ambassador Keril that Mistress Benares be turned over to them for extradition."

"The archmagus and I are aware of their request," Mychael replied coolly.

"Their request has now turned into a demand," Carnades said. "They claim that Mistress Benares is an agent for elven intelligence."

I resisted the urge to roll my eyes. "Do a little contract work for the agency and it comes back to bite you in the ass," I muttered loud enough for everyone to hear. The human lady on the Twelve chuckled behind her hand. There was one potential ally.

"Raine, I will respond for you." Mychael's voice was terse, and inside my head.

"Maybe later."

I stepped forward. "In the past, I have used my seeking skills to find kidnapped elven agents and government officials," I said, out loud. "The last time I checked that kind of thing would earn you a medal, not extradition."

"Our Khrynsani guests do not share your perspective," Carnades said.

"I'm sure they don't."

Out of the corner of my eye I saw one of the goblin lawyers stand. "Magus Silvanus, if I may?"

Carnades stiffly inclined his head. "Of course."

"Our presence here is to reclaim a treasured object that was illegally taken from the goblin people. The fear of His Majesty, King Sathrik Mal'Salin, is for the safety and very life of his trusted royal counselor, Grand Shaman Sarad Nukpana. We have signed affidavits from the Khrynsani temple guards who were with Grand Shaman Nukpana the night he was absorbed by the Saghred. Their testimonies confirm that Mistress Raine Benares did knowingly trick our king's loyal counselor into touching the activated Saghred, resulting in his imprisonment within the stone. The archmagus and the paladin have refused numerous requests to return the Saghred to its legal and rightful owners—the goblin people."

Mychael stepped forward. "The legality of that claim has been denied repeatedly by the Conclave. The first such claim was made by your government nearly nine hundred years ago. It was denied then, and I am very doubtful that judgment will change now. As I'm sure you are aware, the Conclave of Sorcerers was founded to control and prevent the abuse of magic. Keeping the Saghred in a controlled—and neutral—location is the only way to do that." He paused meaningfully. "I'm sure you are also aware that neither goblin nor elven laws apply in matters of the Conclave."

The Khrynsani lawyer slowly sat down, never taking his black eyes from Mychael. Once seated, he spoke in hurried and hushed tones with his colleagues.

Carnades looked to the two elves. "Inquisitor Taltek Balmorlan has petitioned the archmagus repeatedly for permission to question Mistress Benares on behalf of the elven government. His requests have also been denied."

Inquisitor? Oh hell.

I looked up at Taltek Balmorlan and bared my teeth in a smile. "And just what would you like to ask me?"

Unlike the goblin, Balmorlan remained seated. "Our questions concern elven government security and center on your continued association with a member of the Mal'Salin family. This same person was recently seen in the company of a high-ranking Khrynsani shaman." He courteously inclined his head to the goblin lawyers in the opposite balcony. "Begging your pardon."

Tam. I swore silently. "Who would that be?" I asked out loud. Act ignorant, not guilty.

"Primaru Tamnais Nathrach."

"Tamnais Nathrach *used to be* married to a Mal'Salin duchess. Past tense." I kept my voice even, and my tone reasonable. "I fail to see how an acquaintance with a goblin can be of concern to the elven government. I'm sure you count goblins among your acquaintances, as do most in this room."

"Normally such an acquaintance would not be cause for alarm," Balmorlan replied smoothly. "Concern, yes; but not alarm. It is your relationship with Primaru Nathrach combined with your bond to the Saghred. Your actions in the square the other day indicate that your abilities now match or exceed those of every mage on this island. And according to testimony of Magus Silvanus, your soul has been inside the Saghred itself on two occasions."

So much for what Carnades gleaned with his questing spell.

"On the first occasion, you spoke with Eamaliel Anguis, who is also your father and a known Conclave traitor."

Mychael's hand on my arm stopped the response I really wanted to give Balmorlan.

"Paladin Anguis was one of the finest of our order."

Mychael's voice was calm, but cold. "He kept the Saghred safe for nearly nine hundred years."

Carnades spoke. "His previously honorable service record to the Conclave does not alter the fact that he stole a Conclave artifact."

"To keep it out of the hands of four mages on the Seat of Twelve who wanted to abuse that power," Mychael responded.

"Mistress Benares's second time inside the Saghred was to meet with Grand Shaman Sarad Nukpana." Carnades's voice was quiet. "He has referred to her as a partner and a bond servant of the Saghred. As you can understand, Paladin Eiliesor, this is of grave concern to the Twelve."

Balmorlan nudged Giles Keril. The elven ambassador to Mid stood and licked his lips nervously. "Raine Benares is a member of the most notorious criminal family in the seven kingdoms, and has been in an intimate relationship with Tamnais Nathrach, formerly the chief shaman for the House of Mal'Salin." He sounded like he had actually memorized this. I wondered how long it had taken him. "Now she is the bond servant of the Saghred. In the opinion of the elven government, she needs to be in strict custody and control. If the Conclave Guardians are unable—or unwilling—to provide it, the elven government will."

So there it was. Carnades thought I needed to be locked up and he'd teamed with the agency to get it done.

Mychael spoke. "There has been no indication that Mistress Benares has been affected in any way by her contact with the Saghred. Unless any ill effects are proven to Guardian satisfaction, we will not take her into custody, but will continue to offer her our protection."

"I have spent my academic career studying the Saghred," Carnades countered. "You and the archmagus may not be fully aware of the effects contact with the Saghred has on mental stability. They are seldom apparent to inexperienced observers. Mistress Benares's soul has been contaminated by dark forces." His arctic gaze came to rest on Piaras.

"Dark forces that have seduced an innocent into doing her will." He said it almost too softly to be heard.

I felt sick. "No."

"Master Piaras Rivalin's sleepsong put nearly a hundred Guardians to sleep." Carnades's eyes were on mine. "And he put them to sleep while you were in the same room with the Saghred. I find it difficult to believe that is a coincidence, Mistress Benares. I think it is a conspiracy to steal the Saghred—just like your father did."

I was not believing this.

"Master Rivalin is being corrupted by your influence, and he is far too powerful a spellsinger to remain where you can use him again. For the boy's own safety we recommend that he be confined to—"

"My care and protection," boomed a voice from the doorway. It was the commanding voice of a born orator, and of a really pissed-off old man. "Master Rivalin is a minor and a student of this college." Justinius Valerian's bright blue eyes landed on Carnades like a block of granite. "He came to Mid under Guardian protection and he will remain there until such time as any charge against him is proven in a formal—and open—court of law, not a clandestine gathering of rumor and innuendo."

The archmagus turned to Mychael. "Is everything all right here?"

"It will be."

"Glad to hear it. Mychael, you and yours, Master Rivalin, and Miss Benares are dismissed. I need to have a few words alone with some of my esteemed colleagues."

Chapter 16

"Seduced an innocent?"

Piaras was furious—and was having a real problem getting past those three words.

"Like I don't have a mind of my own and the sense to use it!" Now Piaras was furious and pacing.

I had fully expected Carnades to go after me. I didn't know what he'd wanted with Piaras, and now I did. At least some of his cards were on the table. But I knew he and Balmorlan had plenty more cards in their hands they weren't showing until they were good and ready.

I'd seen Carnades's type before. He'd spent his life studying the horrors that the goblins had inflicted on the elven people in past centuries. He was full of hate and prejudice, and fed both of them three square meals every day. No doubt he saw himself as a defender of the elven people. To him, I truly was a traitor and a criminal and a danger to all he held dear. To him, Piaras was a corrupted innocent. Carnades Silvanus believed every word he said. But the scary part was that he was powerful and influential enough to convince others that he was right.

Piaras and I were in my room. Mychael was in Justinius's office planning their next move. I hadn't insisted on joining them because I could plan my next move just fine from here.

I'd sent for Phaelan.

Mychael wasn't letting Piaras or me out of his sight, let alone out of the citadel. Tonight's recital would take us to Sirens, which was conveniently located next to the harbor and our quickest way out of here if things continued to go sour. The Benares family was good at a lot of things, but what we did best was elude the law. I didn't want to have to elude Mychael, but he was the law. If the law told him he had to lock Piaras and me up, he would have no choice.

I planned on acting while I still had the right and ability to make my own choices.

I took a deep breath. "Piaras, I need to ask you something."

He stopped pacing, but the fury was still there. Good. Carnades would claim that what I was about to say was corrupting an innocent. And he'd be right; that was exactly what I was about to do. Piaras had always known what the law could do *for* him—defend and uphold his rights. He idolized the Guardians and wanted someday to become one. An hour ago, he'd gotten his first taste of what the law could do *to* him—imprison him and take away his rights. And sometimes guilt or innocence had nothing to do with which end of the law you got. I muttered a word I rarely used. I saved it for special occasions like close calls with death, or when I had to give someone really bad news. Piaras was about to have his innocence shattered, possibly along with his dreams, and I was the one throwing the rock.

"What is it?" He perched on the edge of my bed, then stood restlessly like he was looking around for something to hit.

I bit back a smile. Just like a man.

"Mychael and the archmagus are going to do everything they can to keep either one of us from being locked up," I told him, "but there is the possibility that they won't be able to prevent it."

"We didn't do anything!"

I held up a hand. "We know that and so do Mychael and the archmagus." I hesitated. "The law doesn't care what we know; it only recognizes what can be proven."

Piaras sat back down on my bed. "But we didn't do anything wrong."

"No, we didn't. But the law can see things differently. A lot of what was said in that room about me was the truth. I did trick Sarad Nukpana into touching the Saghred, knowing full well that the stone would take him as a sacrifice. I am a Benares. I do know Tam—though I wouldn't exactly call our relationship 'intimate,' at least not in the strictly physical sense of the word. I am linked to the Saghred, though contrary to popular belief, I haven't gone off the deep end." I paused, mostly for air. "My point is, the truth and the law can be used against you—even if you didn't do what you've been accused of."

Piaras's eyes were solemn and calm as he sat looking at me. "You said you wanted to ask me something. You haven't done that yet."

I muttered the rarely used word again, this time to myself.

"All of this will probably work out," I told him. "You'll go to school; I'll get rid of my link to the Saghred; our lives will go on as planned. But there is a possibility that Mychael and Justinius won't be able to keep the Khrynsani or elven intelligence from using the law against us. If that's the case . . . well, some very bad things could happen."

"We'd be locked up."

"For starters. I can use the Saghred. You're probably the most powerful spellsinger since Mychael or Ronan Cayle. People like the Khrynsani or the agency like to have powerful weapons like us."

"I would never be anyone's weapon," Piaras said vehemently.

"Sometimes no one asks you what you want . . . and persuasion can take many forms." I stopped and just looked at him. He'd done a lot of growing up in the past two weeks, and it'd all been my fault.

"I'm sorry," I said.

"For what?"

"For getting you into all of this. You're in some serious danger and it's all my fault."

"No, it is not your fault." His dark eyes met mine unwaveringly. "You didn't ask for any of this, and you have tried from the very beginning to protect me." He took a deep breath and carefully let it out. Any fear he was feeling was firmly under control, and he was determined to keep it that way. "You said you had a question. You still haven't asked me anything." His voice was quiet, but resolute.

For a few seconds the only sound was fire crackling in the fireplace.

"Do you want to leave Mid?"

I expected a stunned reaction from Piaras. He didn't even bat an eye.

"Will it be necessary?"

"Maybe not. But it might reach that point. Soon."

"How soon?"

"Tonight."

"But if we're convinced that the paladin and the archmagus can keep us safe—"

"Then we will stay. I want to be rid of the Saghred." I smiled a little. "And even the best spellsinger in the world can still learn a few things at college."

"How would we leave?"

"I've asked Phaelan to come here so we can work out the details. He should be here anytime."

"I want to stay, but I won't stay if that means being imprisoned for something I didn't do . . . and be used."

"Me, either."

"If we have to leave, how do we get out of the citadel?"

"We'll be going to the recital tonight. It's closer to the part of the harbor—"

Piaras blew his breath out and it almost sounded like a laugh. "The recital. I've never sung for people who wanted to use me or lock me up."

Or both.

"Taltek Balmorlan has heard you; he knows what you're capable of," I said. "I wouldn't be surprised to find out he was behind slashing the shields in the music room. Anything you do tonight's not going to make any difference to them." I hesitated. "Your gift is going to attract unwanted attention from people you'd never want to meet."

"The same as you."

I frowned. "Exactly."

"They've already decided what they want to do with me—and with you." Piaras's voice was solemn. "All they need now is an excuse to do it."

"Pretty much."

Except they didn't need an excuse. The agency and the Khrynsani were like certain members of my family. If they saw something they wanted, they didn't ask; they just took it.

Piaras froze. "Raine, if we have to leave, who'll find the kidnapped students?"

Crap. I hadn't thought of that. I hadn't even tried to link with them today.

"Katelyn said Megan has the most flawless soprano voice she's ever heard," Piaras said.

I remembered something Carnades had said in the Scriptorium. Ailia Aurillac studied mirror magic, alchemy—and spellsinging.

"Is Ailia Aurillac one of Ronan's students, too?" I asked.

Piaras thought for a moment. "I don't think so. But she could still be a spellsinger. The college has an entire department for it. Maestro Cayle isn't the only professor. I'll be taking a class with one of the other maestros next term." He smiled ruefully. "If I'm still here."

I wondered about the boy I'd seen in the room with Megan and Ailia. Was he a spellsinger? I'd ask Mychael if Sedge Rinker had a missing-person name to go with the description I'd given him.

Two spellsingers in Banan Ryce's possession could be a coincidence. Three spellsingers was a collection.

If I wouldn't be here to find those students, I'd do everything to make sure Sedge Rinker could.

I went over to my bed and slipped my hand under the mattress until I felt the bag with the hairbrush and locket. The last time I'd linked with Ailia I hadn't been able to see any more of their surroundings than I had before. I took out the cloth bundle with Megan's hairbrush and unwrapped it.

"Is that Megan's?" Piaras asked.

"Yes, it is." I sat in one of the chairs by the fireplace and held the brush in both hands. The link took longer to establish than it had before. Maybe Banan had strengthened the wards around them or . . . The connection came, sharp and clear.

The students had been moved. And I could see where they were.

They weren't in a room. They were in a cell, and the walls were solid rock. This wasn't anywhere in the city—it was under the city. I clutched the brush harder. Now we were getting somewhere.

There was still only Megan, Ailia, and the boy. Banan hadn't kidnapped any more students, or if he had, I couldn't see them through Megan's eyes. The bars of their cell weren't rounded as they were in more modern cells; these were flat pieces of iron overlapping each other to form squares. These cells were old, but apparently still in working order. They didn't make them like that anymore. Their age should make where they were easier to find. Megan and the boy were holding hands. He was protective of her, but Megan looked like she needed it less than she had before. Good. Ailia was pacing.

The light was good enough for Megan to see outside the cell. There were two Nightshade guards, and there was another cell across from theirs. A cell block. That should be even easier to pinpoint. I broke the contact.

Mychael needed to know what I'd seen.

Vegard and Riston were on guard duty outside my newly replaced door.

"I need to see the paladin," I told Vegard.

"He's not here, ma'am." He paused uncomfortably. "He and the archmagus had to go to the elven embassy."

My stomach tried to do a flip. Taltek Balmorlan just wouldn't give up. If Mychael and Justinius had to go to the elven embassy in person, then the old man was probably playing the last card in his hand. I hoped for my and Piaras's sakes that it was a good one.

I took a breath and stood straighter. "Fine. Then I need to get a message to Sedge Rinker—directly to him, no one else. Can you arrange that for me?"

"I can," Vegard said.

"Good. I'll just need a pen and some paper. And have the messenger wait for a response. I need to know if Rinker has the name of the boy who was taken yesterday. I also need to know if he's a spellsinger. The two kidnapped girls are spellsingers."

Vegard stood motionless. "Are you certain?"

"Positive." I smiled in grim satisfaction. "But if your chief watcher knows this island as well as he should, he could be on the verge of finding them all."

Vegard left to deliver my note to a Guardian courier; he came back accompanied by a swaggering vision in scarlet.

Phaelan was wearing his on-shore-leave-and-getting-laid clothes. His doublet was scarlet buckskin with matching breeches topped with high, black leather boots. At his side was his favorite swept-hilt rapier, and a single ruby earring gleamed in the lobe of one elegantly pointed ear.

I looked him up and down. "Going out this evening?"

"Absolutely. With you and Piaras."

"You're going to the recital." Piaras's relieved smile was like the sun coming out.

Phaelan nodded. "I thought I'd sample Mid's cultural riches."

I raised a brow. "And?"

"And what?"

"You hate mages, you barely tolerate academics, and you told me once that highborn elves give you a rash."

"I'm prepared to deal with the discomfort to ensure the safety of my family. That includes you, too," he told Piaras.

"Thank you," Piaras said earnestly.

"Don't mention it."

I approved of family-ensured safety. The Guardians would arrest first, ask questions later. Phaelan would kill first, no questions asked.

"I've told Piaras what we might have to do tonight," I said.

Phaelan nodded. "I know you don't like it, kid. But trust me—the view's a lot better from outside cell bars. I speak from experience."

"I don't want that experience," Piaras said.

My cousin grinned wolfishly. "That's why I'm here. And that's why I'm going to the recital. Aside from my incomparable bodyguard services, there's the entertainment value of rich people clutching their jewels when I walk through the door. You just can't buy that kind of fun."

"We want you there," I told him. "The question is, will Mychael let you?"

"My presence is paladin approved."

I snorted. "Since when?"

Phaelan's grin vanished. "Since I told him there was no way in hell the two of you were going into that hornet's nest without me."

"Thank you." And I meant it.

His dark eyes were as serious as I'd ever seen them. "That's what family is for." Then the rogue was back. "That and jailbreaks. Speaking of which, Tanik Ozal is in port."

I swore silently. Next to our family, the Ozals were the second-most-notorious criminal family in the seven kingdoms. What Tanik Ozal was doing here boded no good for local law enforcement or anyone else. Anything he and Phaelan tried to pull would come back to splatter on me. After today, I wasn't in the mood to be splattered.

"Phaelan," I said in warning.

My cousin raised his hands defensively. "We're not up to anything. Tanik wants to help."

An Ozal promising help was like a shark promising not to eat you.

"Tanik's here to bring his son back to school," Phaelan continued. "I told him about the two of you getting hung out to dry, and he wants to help in any way he can." Phaelan's grin was cheerfully evil. "And he said if it involves blowing anything up, all the better. But for starters, I've asked him to keep an eye on his neighbors. He's docked in a prime slip; Mal'Salin and Khrynsani craft on one side, and that elven intelligence agent's yacht on the other. And if you buy a lot of drinks for some of Balmorlan's crew, you find out all sorts of fascinating things, like their captain's told them to be ready to leave fast. They even have a pair of weather wizards on board to help it happen."

I swore.

"Yeah, I thought it was interesting, too. And the Khrynsani ship has her bow pointed toward open water. Tanik said they had to do a lot of maneuvering to get her that way. Anyway, Tanik says he'll keep watch for us."

"Thank him for me," I said.

"I already have. And if we do this thing, you'll get a chance to thank him yourself."

I frowned. "Phaelan, no. Absolutely no."

"Cousin, if we want to leave this island, it's not going to be on the *Fortune*. Stealth is called for, and the paladin has got my lady wrapped in cloaking spells, and a few other things my men discovered when they tried to raise anchor. Key word there is 'tried.' "

I didn't move. "You couldn't raise anchor?"

"Not an inch. The paladin has made sure we're not going anywhere."

"Mychael wouldn't do that." I said it, but I wasn't so sure.

His duty was to keep the Saghred on the island. Until I was no longer bonded to the Saghred, that same mind-set would have to apply to me. Mychael would do his duty at all costs.

"Damn," I muttered.

Phaelan nodded slowly. "Now you're getting the picture. Since he cut off one exit, we'll just take another. Tanik's *Zephyr* is a nimble little craft, no high tides needed for her to leave the harbor. He'll drop us off at Mermeia. I sent a message to Dad before we left Mermeia last week. By now he'll be waiting there just in case we need him."

"Commodore" Ryn Benares was Phaelan's dad, my uncle, and the main reason the name Benares struck terror everywhere it was mentioned. Beneath his reputation lurked a softy, at least to his children—and Uncle Ryn considered me one of his own. It'd be nice to see him again. From Mermeia we could go anywhere.

"What about your crew?" I asked.

"What about them?"

"When Mychael finds out I'm missing, if he doesn't put your ship on lockdown, the Twelve will. Your crew will probably be taken into custody."

Phaelan shrugged. "Wouldn't be the first time. And they'll probably be confined to the ship, not taken into the citadel. No lawman I've ever run afoul of wants to take a pirate crew off their ship and through town. Too many chances for bad things to happen. And my crew's known for bad things. Mychael, or whoever, will leave my men right where they are. They'll just post more guards. My men know what to do. Lay low, keep quiet, and sit tight until I get back. It's not like they haven't done it before. They know the drill."

I exhaled. "I don't like it, but it's like you said—we're not exactly flush with options here. Okay, listen up. One block down from Sirens is a row of town houses. There's a street that runs behind them. That time of night that street should be nice and dark, and from there it's a straight shot to the harbor. We'll meet there if we get separated."

I looked questioningly at Piaras. He nodded grimly.

Phaelan clapped and rubbed his hands together. "Good, that's settled." He took a small velvet pouch out of his doublet. "You said your gown's black, right?"

I nodded. Riston's wife had gone shopping for me this

morning. The fruit of her labor hung in my closet. Normally I didn't care for gowns, but I had to admit I liked this one. It was the softest black velvet I'd ever felt, its long sleeves were tight, and the gown itself was perfectly cut, sleekly styled, with a short train. With my pale skin and red gold hair, black had always been my best friend. If I had to walk into a hornet's nest tonight—or make a quick getaway—at least I'd look good doing it.

"Here." Phaelan tossed a drawstring bag to me. I opened it and a choker of creamy gray pearls spilled out into my hand. The clasp was an ornate, diamond bow. Very nice.

I gave him my best fess-up look. "How hot is it?"

Phaelan's dark eyes went wide and innocent. "Pardon?"

"Hot, stolen, missing, no longer where it's supposed to be—"

He grinned crookedly. "They've cooled down."

"Is there any chance the former owner will be at Sirens tonight?"

"That would depend on who's invited."

"Maybe a better question would be, 'Who should I avoid?' "

He shrugged. "I took it off a ship going to Nebia."

"Are there any Nebian royals or merchants among Ronan's students?" I asked Piaras.

"Not that I'm aware of." The kid was fighting a grin and losing. I should have known better than to think anyone in my family could set a good moral example. Though it was nice to see Piaras smile.

I sighed. "They are beautiful. I'll chance it."

"There's a matching bracelet and earrings in the bag, too," Phaelan said brightly.

Of course there were. Never let it be said my cousin stole anything halfway.

Chapter 17

I was bejeweled, my hair was up, and I was dressed—at least from the front.

Riston's wife had bought a gown for me, but what she didn't get was an extra pair of hands to lace the thing up. The gown laced up the back, starting near the base of my spine and ending just below my shoulder blades. All I saw when I looked over my shoulder were open silk laces and a lot of exposed skin.

Crap.

Vegard's duties were about to expand to include dresser.

I went to the door and yanked it open. Mychael was standing there in his steel gray formal uniform, his fist raised to knock.

I loved a man in uniform. I especially loved seeing this particular man in that uniform. Mychael's auburn hair was damp from a recent bath—and those sea blue eyes were tracing every velvety curve of my gown. I smiled at him. A girl does like to feel appreciated.

"You were actually going to knock this time," I said. "No kicking or blasting."

Mychael met my eyes. "I knocked last time. When you didn't answer, then I kicked and blasted. May I come in?"

I stepped aside so he could.

Mychael closed the door behind him. "Riston's wife wasn't sure what you'd like, so I—"

"Told her what you would like?" I finished suggestively.

A smile tugged at the corners of his mouth. "I thought you would agree with my choice."

"I do. Do you like it?"

"Very much so," he murmured. "And the pearls match your eyes."

My hand went to the choker at my throat. "Phaelan brought them to me."

"Legal purchase or illegal acquisition?"

I let out a short laugh. "Guess. However, he did say they've cooled off enough to wear in public."

The gown slipped off my shoulder. I quickly pulled it back up, and clutched the front of my bodice with the other hand.

Mychael stepped back toward the door. "I can see you're not finished dressing. I'll wait in—"

"No, no. I need your hands."

"My what?"

I half turned so Mychael could see my predicament. "I can't go like this."

I heard a muffled noise and looked over my shoulder at him. He was laughing silently.

"No, you definitely shouldn't go anywhere like that." Mychael's smile had reached his eyes. He was looking at my bare back, but making no move to do anything about making it less bare.

"If you lace me up, we can go." I turned my back to him. I waited and nothing happened. "You've never done this before, have you?" I glanced over my shoulder at him.

Mychael was grinning like a little boy. "I can honestly say that you're my first."

I felt my face getting warm, and quickly turned away. "It's easy. You just start at the bottom and work your way up."

A moment later, I felt his fingers on the base of my spine. His touch was like a shock. I let out a little gasp before I could stop it.

He paused. "I'm sorry."

"Fine," I managed. "I'm fine. I must be a little ticklish down there. Go on."

He did and I bit my lip against the incredible sensations running up and down my spine and spreading to other places. It was all I could do to stand still. I was glad my back was to him and he couldn't see my face.

"I think I threaded the laces evenly before I put it on." My mouth was suddenly dry. "So all you should have to do is tighten them."

Mychael hesitated, his hands on my waist. "How tight do you like it?"

Oh my.

"Breathing's good," I told him. "I need air." And I could use some more of it right now.

I felt four tugs in sharp succession. If he kept that up, I was going to have to hold on to the bedpost.

"How's that?" His voice had turned husky.

"That's good." And then some. "Wait a minute. Let me . . ." I squirmed a little in the bodice, took a good breath, then put my hands on my waist and pushed the fabric toward the back. "There. That should work even better."

Mychael's hands were warm against my bare back as he worked at the laces, and he was standing so close that I could feel the heat from the rest of him.

Talk, Raine. Talking will help.

"Vegard said you and Justinius went to the elven embassy. You didn't bring any embassy guards with you, so I assume that I'm still a free woman, and Piaras isn't under protective custody."

Mychael gave the laces a sharp tug and I bit back a squeak.

"It wasn't for lack of trying on their part." All signs of playful were gone. "Giles Keril argued that since you're a subject of the elven king, you should be in their custody, not ours. I reminded him that the Isle of Mid is neutral and that any person, regardless of their race or kingdom of birth—unless convicted of a crime in an open court—is granted political asylum for as long as they desire it."

As he talked, his hands became firm and sure on the laces. "So I have to officially ask you." His voice was low and close to my ear. "Do you desire it?"

I froze. "Desire it?"

"Political asylum."

Oh, that. "Yes, I desire it very much."

"Good. There's a document in my office you'll need to sign. Piaras will need to do the same. I'll take it from there."

"So that will just delay things until the Khrynsani and Balmorlan can get this into open court."

"Time was something we were running out of. This will buy us some more. I *will* find a solution."

I wondered if my father had heard the same promise from his paladin before he was forced to take the Saghred and run. Or in my case, just run. Time to change the subject.

"I sent a message to Sedge Rinker. I linked with—"

"I know. Sedge was here when I got back. There are only a few places on the island that we know of with cells like you described. I have some men checking them out now."

Mychael put his hands firmly around my waist, lifted me a scant inch or two off the floor, turned me so I was facing the door, and set me back down. "I need more light," he explained. "The fireplace is over here."

Of course.

"Did Sedge know if the kidnapped boy is a spellsinger?" I asked.

Mychael resumed tugging and tightening. "His name is Gustin Sorenson, and he graduated two years ago. He's a spellsinger in one of the nightclubs."

"Mychael, three spellsingers are no coincidence," I said.

"I agree."

"And Banan Ryce has yet to do anything with them or to them. That tells me he's probably not finished collecting.

When I was in the tub, Sarad Nukpana said I should look to my own people for who's behind the kidnappings. I'm ashamed to say it, but Taltek Balmorlan is an elf. That means he's 'my people.' Banan and his boys don't come cheap, and the agency has some very deep pockets. Carnades has me in his sights, but today he and Balmorlan went after Piaras with a vengeance, and they almost got him. And in less than two hours, Ronan's best spellsingers— including Piaras—will be on Sirens's stage."

Mychael finished my lacing with one last tug. "Yes, I know. I've already requested that the recital be canceled, or at least postponed."

"And?"

"Justinius said no."

I turned and stared at him in disbelief. "*Justinius* said no? The Twelve I could understand, but Justinius? His granddaughter is singing tonight. He can't possibly want her there. Students are missing, Mychael. They're all spellsingers. I've linked with them and they're together."

"I believe you. But the recital is in less than two hours. As archmagus, Justinius would need nothing short of a signed confession from Banan Ryce himself to stop it now. His official stance is that three kidnapped students, regardless of them all being spellsingers, doesn't necessarily constitute a conspiracy. Justinius said that warding the dressing-room mirrors at Sirens and posting guards at the exits will be adequate to prevent any incident."

I was dumbfounded. "Is this the same Justinius who chewed out the Twelve this afternoon?"

Mychael took a breath and let it out. "Yes. He didn't doubt what I told him; he just knew the ramifications of canceling the recital."

"I can tell him what the ramifications will be if he doesn't."

"Raine, it's political." Mychael said it like it left a foul taste in his mouth. "The Twelve would outvote him, and after the dressing-down he gave most of them after we left, they'd do just that, for spite if nothing else. He can't afford to jeopardize alumni goodwill on anything less than cold, hard facts."

"Can't afford?"

"The office of archmagus is an elected position."

I blinked. "He's afraid of losing his job?"

"Yes, he's afraid of losing his job because he knows what will happen if he does. Carnades Silvanus has enough support on the Twelve and enough influence with the wealthier alumni to get himself elected if Justinius loses the support base he has. After what nearly happened to you and Piaras this afternoon, I don't have to tell you what the Isle of Mid would be like with Carnades as archmagus."

"So the old man picks his battles carefully and watches his back."

Mychael nodded. "And tonight he's depending on me to do the watching. And he's told me to protect those children as best as I can. According to Sedge Rinker's report, even though Gustin Sorensen is a spellsinger, he's no longer a student. And he wasn't abducted through a mirror. There were witnesses, and they can't say whether the kidnappers were human or elven."

"But I've seen him. He's there with those two girls. They were guarded by Nightshades."

Mychael's silence told me more than I needed to know.

"No one other than you and Justinius is going to believe the word of a Benares whose soul has been 'contaminated by dark forces.' "

"Unfortunately, they're not. Carnades doesn't even believe you've linked with the students. He's demanding a test of your abilities—that is, after you're in elven intelligence custody."

I swore. "It's not my seeking abilities he wants tested." I resisted the urge to pace. "Mychael, it's just a recital."

"I know it's just a recital. But to the Twelve and the department deans, it's the college's most profitable alumni fundraiser."

I was incredulous. "This is about *money*? Tell me you're joking."

Mychael's lips were a thin, angry line. "Some of the college's biggest financial supporters have traveled a great distance for this event. If it were up to me, I'd tell them all to go home. But it's not up to me."

"Meanwhile, you're told to protect and defend. And if anything happens to those spellsingers tonight, it's your ass."

"It won't be the first time it's been on the line. Unfortunately, my job is as much about politics as protecting the citizens of this island."

"Then why do you do it? No, let me rephrase that. How *can* you do it?"

"Because I know I'm better at it than anyone else," he said with an intensity and conviction that was almost frightening. "And if I didn't do it, mages like Carnades would reduce the Guardians to ceremonial guards—or personal enforcers. It has happened before, and I will fight to my last breath to keep it from *ever* happening again."

I nodded in grim approval. "Not on your watch."

Mychael eyes were like blue steel. "Not on my watch."

"If elven intelligence wants to get their collective hands on me, it's not because of who I am or what they say I've done," I told him. "As to me being dangerous, they don't fear that; they want it for themselves. Most of all, they want it before the goblins can get it."

I stopped talking. What I'd read in the tub clicked into place with what I'd just said.

"What is it?" Mychael asked.

"Rudra Muralin said in his journal that his bond with the Saghred was so strong that he could use it from anywhere to do whatever he wanted. Distance didn't matter. The stone only had to be two things—awake and fed—and it didn't have to be anywhere near him. He claimed that he and the Saghred were one and the same." More pieces fell into place. "Mychael, no one's actually tried to steal the Saghred, but the Khrynsani and elven intelligence want me really bad. When Sarad Nukpana came to me in the tub, he said that the Saghred was conserving power. In his journal,

Rudra Muralin wrote that before he did anything big and deadly with the Saghred, he had to sacrifice souls to it—magically gifted souls were preferred."

It all came together, and I realized with dawning horror what had happened and what was going to happen.

"Was my father a spellsinger?"

Mychael was puzzled. "He was. Why?"

"What about Sarad Nukpana?"

Mychael's blue eyes widened in realization. "Before he became the Khrynsani grand shaman, yes, he was a spellsinger."

"When Piaras sang the Saghred to sleep, Nukpana told me that the Saghred hasn't had such a treat in years. Then he said those with the sweetest magic are the most delicious. Does that mean what I think it means?"

Mychael stood utterly still. "Spellsinging is known as the 'sweet magic.' "

Sarad Nukpana had told me that I was doing the Saghred's will and I hadn't believed him.

"Mychael, we've just brought the Saghred back to the biggest buffet in the seven kingdoms, and Banan Ryce has been gathering dinner. Tonight he's going after dessert."

Phaelan knocked as he opened my door. "You decent, cousin?"

I scowled. "And I'm dressed, too."

He looked from me to Mychael. "Something I should know about?"

"The kidnapped students are all spellsingers, the Saghred likes spellsingers as sacrifices, and tonight Sirens is hosting the cream of Ronan's crop."

"That's a trap waiting to happen. So just cancel the damned thing and lock down your spellsingers."

"The Twelve won't cancel the recital," I told him. "It's political."

"Sounds like you need to get yourself a new Twelve," Phaelan told Mychael. "Just get me the names of the ones you don't want to keep." He glanced back over his shoulder for eavesdroppers and lowered his voice. "I know people."

Mychael's smile was more like a baring of teeth. "I just might take you up on that." He looked down at Phaelan's rapier and sighed. "I really hate to tell you this, but I can only allow Guardians to have swords in Sirens this evening."

I couldn't believe what I was hearing. "Even now?"

"Especially now."

"And especially considering who he is," I shot back.

"Raine, I can't make any exceptions."

Phaelan shrugged, unbuckled his sword belt, and tossed it on my bed. "As a guest here, I humbly comply with my host's wishes."

Mychael just looked at him. "You're bristling with daggers, aren't you?"

" 'Bristling' is such a negative term, I prefer 'amply armed.' " My cousin turned to me. "Speaking of ample, there's no room in that bodice for anything other than you. You wearing a thigh sheath?"

I linked my arm through Mychael's. "Now what would be the sense of wearing just one? I have two thighs." I glanced up at Mychael. "Welcome to a night on the town with the Benares family."

Chapter 18

It's tough to go against your upbringing. Most times I try. From now on I wasn't even going to bother.

I was a Benares. As far as Taltek Balmorlan was concerned, I was also one of the most powerful mages in Sirens. Yes, my power came from an evil rock locked in the Guardians' basement, and I had no intention of using that power, but no one knew that and I wasn't going to tell them.

I was going to keep them guessing and shaking in their designer robes.

But if anyone so much as laid one finger on Ronan's spellsingers, all bets were off.

Mychael had taken every precaution to protect those kids. He'd ordered all of Sirens's mirrors bespelled to prevent their use by mirror mages. Mirror mages needed a crisp, clear image to do their thing. Mychael's spells distorted whatever was reflected in the mirror as an undulating wave, its pattern constantly changing. Try putting on makeup, doing your hair, or getting dressed in front of an undulating wave. Some people it'd make sick; most people it'd just make ugly. All the dressing rooms at Sirens had big, full-length mirrors. If any of Ronan's spellsingers wanted to admire themselves, they'd better have done it before they got here.

Seeing someone or something step out of my reflection was one of the reasons why I owned only one mirror and it was just big enough to see my face in. Anything that popped out through that mirror would be small enough for me to stomp on.

Ronan had gathered his students and Mychael told them that, due to the recent student abductions through mirrors, Sirens's mirrors had been warded as a safety precaution. That didn't go over well, especially with Countess Sanura Mal'Salin. Mychael ignored the goblin girl's outburst and proceeded to lay down the law for the evening: no going out the stage door into the alley, and if they needed to leave the dressing-room area during the recital, they would have to do so in the company of a Guardian escort. He didn't want to scare the kids, just make them aware of the safety precautions being taken and that he expected nothing less than their full and complete cooperation.

Mychael's talk left out the words "Saghred" and "sacrifice." Like he'd said, until we had irrefutable proof—meaning from a source other than me—we had to keep our private suspicions from becoming public allegations.

I had all the irrefutable proof I needed. I had told Piaras everything—and made sure he had enough steel on him to discourage any takers.

When Mychael finished talking, every last one of Ronan's students still insisted on singing. The show would go on. Dammit.

I was backstage looking out into the rapidly filling theatre. I wanted to know who was here and where they were. Phaelan was standing next to me looking cool and confident, even without his rapier. He noted my glance at his side and chuckled.

"Since you only have two daggers, just let me know if you need to borrow anything. I've got you covered."

"I just might take you up on that."

The house lights were still up, so we could see everyone as they entered and were escorted to their tables. That made it impossible to miss when Taltek Balmorlan, Giles Keril, and party arrived.

Phaelan saw where I was looking. "A shark and a weasel. Are those our primary targets for the evening?"

I nodded. "They're two of them. Unfortunately, there are a lot more. I'm also keeping an eye out for a thousand-year-old psychotic goblin teenage spellsinger."

"Rudra Muralin?"

"The very same."

I had warned Mychael about the possibility of Muralin masquerading as a student, or as one of the many Mal'Salins here for Countess Sanura's performance. There were a lot of young and good-looking goblins in Sirens tonight. But Rudra Muralin had fallen into the Great Rift. I'd imagine bouncing down a ravine hadn't done him any good, though if contact with the Saghred kept him alive for a millennium, it could certainly repair any damage. So that meant any young male goblin was a potential candidate.

Phaelan and I were within sight of the dressing room that Piaras was sharing with Talon Tandu. I had checked their mirror myself. Even glancing at it made me nauseous. Nothing was coming through that mirror.

The door opened and Talon Tandu sauntered out. I guess it was taking Piaras longer to dress because he had more clothes to put on. Talon's costume consisted solely of silver silk trousers, slung low on narrow hips and leaving little to the imagination. His otherwise bare chest was covered by a long, aqua, silk dressing gown that perfectly matched his eyes. Eyes that saw me and liked what they saw.

"Evening, gorgeous. Since all the mirrors in this place are warded, I thought I'd let you tell me how hot I look."

I gave him a flat look. "You're sizzling. I can barely stand the heat."

"Likewise. You should doll up more often. It suits you."

Ronan swept by, his robes this evening edging more toward the gold and orange end of the flame spectrum. "Talon, you're first. Get dressed."

The goblin gave the maestro a little salute. "Yes, sir."

I waited until Ronan had gone. "You are dressed, aren't you?"

"Oh yeah. I'll drop the robe before I go on and whatever else is left is what I'm wearing." He shrugged. "Most of the people out there have seen me perform. They'd be disappointed if I wore too many clothes."

"And you can't disappoint your adoring fans."

Talon's crooked grin was full of fang. "Finally, someone who understands."

"And your song?"

"Ronan said to keep it tasteful and decent," Talon said smugly.

"Is that possible?"

"It was during rehearsals." The kid had a sparkle in his eyes that he shouldn't be old enough to have. "It won't be onstage."

"And you wanted to go first?"

"I wanted to get it over with. We drew numbers for our singing order. Naturally, I cheated. Then there's the added plus of Ronan being too busy with the rest of his songbirds to be pissed at me after what I'm going to do out there."

Phaelan nodded approvingly. "Cheating to get what you want, ignoring the rules, and defying authority. And to think some people are worried about the next generation."

The dressing-room door opened and Piaras came out. Riston's wife had gone shopping for Piaras, too. I looked at him and just couldn't stop looking. Formal and formfitting black velvet doublet, black buckskin trousers, black boots. A fine, white linen shirt gleamed through the slits in the velvet doublet. The clothes were undeniably elegant.

And Piaras was unmistakably grown up.

"Our somber songbird is singing right after my exhibitionist self," Talon was saying. "That should soothe any offended sensibilities."

Piaras looked at me. "I wanted to go second."

And I knew why. The sooner he sang, the quicker we could leave.

Talon clapped Piaras on the back and lowered his voice. "I knew which end of the box the number two tile was in, so I helped him out."

And Piaras had to cheat to get it. First cheating, then possibly going on the run from the law. I didn't like that he was being forced to do any of it.

"Well, I'm off to warm up my pipes," Talon told me. "Don't miss my act, gorgeous."

"No chance of that."

Talon left and it was just the three of us.

"Where are the two of you going to be while I'm singing?" Piaras asked Phaelan and me.

"Right here," I promised him. "I'm not moving from this spot."

Phaelan was looking out into the theatre. "The old man just arrived."

Justinius Valerian was entering the best box in the house. Normally Mychael would be by his side. Tonight it was Riston and three other Guardians I didn't recognize. Mychael was doing his best to be everywhere at once. If there was any trouble, he wanted to either be there when it happened or just a few seconds away. Vegard was backstage, along with enough Guardians to make me feel safe if we decided to stay, or seriously outnumbered should we opt to leave. I wanted to trust Mychael's promised political asylum. Piaras and I had signed the papers before leaving the citadel, but when push came to shove, some documents weren't worth the parchment they were scratched on.

In the next box were Carnades Silvanus and a too-beautiful-to-be-real elven lady wearing a gown of silver gossamer. Carnades had a date. I guess someone had to find him appealing.

"I need to go warm up, too," Piaras said, and he didn't sound excited about it.

I didn't want him to leave, and he clearly didn't want to go.

"I'll be right here," I promised. "Phaelan, I want you to go with Piaras."

Neither Phaelan nor Piaras liked that idea. I held up a

hand to stave off any arguments. "I've got a soul-sucking rock at my beck and call, and anyone who wants to get their hands on me knows that. I've got plenty of magic muscle of my own. And Vegard's back there lurking somewhere in the shadows, aren't you Vegard?" I called over my shoulder.

"Lurking and ready, ma'am," came his voice from the dark.

I spread my hands. "Plenty of firepower. Ample backup." I lowered my voice. "Phaelan, just take care of Piaras. And if things go to hell in a handbasket later, just stick to the plan."

I stood on tiptoe and wrapped my arms around Piaras's neck. He hugged me back, tightly. We just stood there holding each other for a few moments; then I stepped back, my hands on his upper arms.

"You're going to be magnificent," I told him. I looked up into his dark eyes. "And we're going to be just fine," I whispered. "Go warm up."

He and Phaelan disappeared into the area directly behind the stage where Ronan waited to go through warm-ups with each of his students.

I looked across the stage to the opposite wing. Tam was staring at me.

My heart skipped a couple of beats. Of course Tam was here; it was his club. There was nothing odd about him being backstage, nothing in the least. I instinctively ran a hand down the side of my gown. One dagger, check.

Tam and his nightclub staff wore all black, but no one wore black like Tam. Unless my eyes deceived me, his shirt didn't have any buttons. When it came to Tam, at least my eyes had never lied to me. The shirt fell open, treating me to a view of smooth, silvery chest.

I had weapons. Hell, I *was* a weapon. So what if Tam was stalking around backstage? I'd protect myself any way I had to. Problem was, I didn't know if I could do that to Tam. Bigger problem was, I didn't know if I really wanted to protect myself.

Moments later the house lights blinked, and those in the audience who hadn't yet taken their seats hurried to do so.

The lightglobes in the backstage area dimmed to near nothing. I looked back across the stage.

Tam was gone.

Shit.

Propriety be damned. I slid the velvet of my gown up to my thigh and put one of my daggers where it belonged—in my hand.

The house lights went down and unseen musicians began to play in the near darkness. I slipped into the shadows near the stage curtains where I could see anything coming at me. Drums and two other percussion instruments established a languid beat, and then the low, vibrant tones of a goblin flute joined with the melody.

Talon Tandu appeared in a single, silvery spotlight, his slender form lithe, his movements impossibly smooth and slow. In the stage light, it was nearly impossible to tell where Talon's silver silk trousers ended and Talon began. His hair cascaded in ebony waves to just above hips that moved slowly in time with the music, languorous, hypnotic. Every ear in the room was enslaved to his voice; every eye was on his body.

His tenor voice was rich and vibrant. His words were Goblin, his intent seduction. His song reached every corner of the theatre, but the intimacy of his words was sung for each listener.

Part of me wanted to throw a tablecloth over him. Another part wanted to see more. One word described him—feral. Talon was generating enough sexual energy to power every lightglobe in the club. It was almost too intimate to be watched, but I couldn't look away—and I didn't want to.

The stage's shields were to diffuse the effect of the spellsingers' songs. They ran from the footlights to the rafters, invisible unless you saw them from the stage wings. From where I stood, they shimmered like a silvery net.

None of Ronan's students were going to do anything potentially lethal. Talon's song would make everyone horny, then Piaras's lullaby would make them sleepy. There was nothing wrong with either one.

Once Talon's final note evaporated, the audience erupted in thunderous applause. If anyone had been offended, it sounded like they'd gotten over it.

The stage had gone dark and Talon exited off the other side. I could just barely see Piaras walking out onto the stage. When he reached the center, he stopped and bowed his head. He stood that way for a few moments, then raised his head, the light coming up with him. The single light illuminating him looked like moonlight. The effect was enchanting.

If Piaras was scared to death, I couldn't see or sense it. His voice was rock solid. There was no sign of nerves whatsoever, no hesitation or lessening of intensity in the higher notes, and his low notes were resonant waves washing over the audience, again and again. If the shields hadn't been at full power, they'd all be asleep. I looked out over the sea of upturned faces. Piaras had them all in the palm of his hand. He could have done anything with them and they would have loved him for it.

I heard a sibilant whisper, and goose bumps prickled at the back of my neck and ran down my spine. Only one thing did that—magic, power of the worst kind. The whisper evolved into a singing voice, heartbreakingly beautiful and hypnotic.

And gleefully malevolent. The voice carried whispered promises of unbearable agony or the heights of ecstasy. Or both.

An instant later, that voice hit me in the chest like a battering ram, knocking the air out of my lungs and driving me to my knees.

Not this time, you bastard.

I took short, shallow breaths and fought to stay conscious. I grabbed the velvet curtain and hauled myself to my feet. The voice was coming from above me. A metal catwalk spanned the width of the stage. I couldn't see him, but he was up there. I had his psychic footprint in the center of my chest to prove it.

I tried to swallow. "Vegard?" I whispered.

No response.

"Vegard?"

Silence. Really bad silence.

I muttered my personal shields into place. I pushed down the pain and forcibly dragged air into my lungs.

There was a ladder mounted against the wall and I used it. I clenched my dagger between my teeth, hiked up my gown, and climbed as fast as I could. Anyone looking up from below would get one hell of a view.

I reached the top and stepped out onto the catwalk.

There he was, standing directly over the center of the stage. He was young and he was perfect, like a fine sculpture, and just as ageless. His youthful beauty was no glamour, no spell to trick the eye; it was all him. He turned and looked at me, and the air between us wavered, his eyes becoming pools of darkness I could gladly fall into and never want to find my way out of. I shook my head and pressed the pommel of my dagger into my thigh until the pain was greater than the desire to drown in those black eyes. I clenched my teeth and reminded myself that those eyes had been the last thing thousands of elves had seen before they were slaughtered in bloody sacrifice.

Rudra Muralin smiled at me, never ceasing his poisonous song. He pointed in a direct line out into the audience, and his smile broadened until his fangs were showing.

The stage's shields were solidly in place—except for the foot-long gash where Muralin had aimed his voice. I looked where the goblin proudly pointed.

Justinius Valerian staggered to his feet, his hands clutching his chest—just as Piaras finished his lullaby.

I stared in dawning horror. I knew what he'd done. Rudra Muralin had attached his song like a malignant leech to Piaras's voice. A true master spellsinger could kill with a lullaby. It was all in the intent.

To everyone in Sirens, it looked like Piaras had just assassinated the archmagus.

Chapter 19

There were gasps from the audience and then the screams started.

"Two birds with one stone," Rudra Muralin said. "Or in this case, one song." His beautiful black eyes glittered. "Now it's your turn."

My horror turned to disbelief as armed Guardians grabbed Piaras and forced him off the stage. He had no idea what had just happened. The Guardians thought they knew.

"*No!* He's up here!" I screamed at them.

"They can't hear you, Raine. Even if they could, they wouldn't believe you." Muralin chuckled. Even his chuckle was beautiful. "No one believes you."

The smarmy punk was right. He was also between me and the quickest way to Piaras. He closed the distance between us and I let him. When he was close enough, I tossed my dagger from my right hand to my left. When the goblin's eyes involuntarily flicked to the blade, my right fist took him hard in the temple.

The cocky ones never shielded. I smiled in a baring of teeth.

The ancient goblin absorbed the punch, and then he smiled right back at me.

Oh crap.

I never saw his fist coming. My shoulder and head

slammed into the catwalk's metal grille. This is really bad, I thought while I could still feel my head. My dagger clattered down the catwalk behind me, well out of reach. Then Muralin's full weight was on top of me, his lean body warm, his lips next to my ear, whispering, discordant, feeding my disorientation, softly seducing me into submission, coaxing me into unconsciousness.

Son of a bitch! I raised my head and sank my teeth into his ear.

His whispers turned to screams, then hissing. The spellsong lost its hold on me, my vision cleared, and I used my knees and fists anywhere on Muralin that I could reach. My growls joined the goblin's hisses. I let go of Muralin's ear and, using every bit of body weight and leverage I had, shoved him off of me. I tried to get to my feet, but my legs tangled in my gown. No gowns again. *Ever.* The goblin grabbed for me. I rolled away and out into empty air.

I desperately grabbed the railing at the base of the catwalk. I didn't fall, but I was dangling at least thirty feet above the stage. A fall would either break my legs or kill me. The backstage area suddenly erupted in shouts and panicked screams. Terrified female shrieks.

The dressing rooms. The spellsingers.

Muralin's hands grabbed my arms just above the wrist. Hands that felt like living stone: cold, hard, and unyielding. I gripped the railing harder.

The goblin actually laughed. "I'm trying to save you. I can't let you die yet." His lips curved into a slow grin. "But I can't help you unless you let go."

The sound of steel-on-steel combat joined the screaming from backstage.

My hands were starting to sweat—and slip. My breath came in shallow bursts. I'd never realized how hard it was to breathe with your arms stretched over your head.

"Back . . . off," I managed.

"Very well."

Muralin abruptly let me go; I gasped and slipped some more.

The goblin stood up; the tips of his boots were entirely too close to my fingers. He looked down to the stage. "A drop of that distance is nothing for us, Raine. The Saghred would save you. Just ask and I'll tell you how to do it. It's simple—even an elf could understand it."

"Back. Off!"

Muralin shrugged and walked a few steps down the catwalk, turned, and leaned against the railing. He glanced down into the backstage area and smiled. "Nightshades," he noted. "Once again elves are doing my bidding without me even asking. You and your people have been most accommodating."

I pulled myself up inch by inch. I thought my fingers were going to snap off gripping the flat bars that made up the catwalk floor. It hurt like hell and I ignored it. The only thing that motivated a Benares more than greed was vengeance. I pulled myself up onto the catwalk, lay on my belly, and panted. When I thought I had enough air to do it, I got to my feet.

And stared.

Tam was standing about ten feet behind Rudra Muralin. His face gave nothing away, but his eyes promised murder.

To Rudra Muralin.

Muralin spoke without turning. "Your services are no longer required, Tamnais. I have what I came for."

Tam didn't budge. "I'm still protecting my investment."

A pair of armed goblins stepped onto the other end of the catwalk. They weren't in uniform, but they were big and wearing identical arrogant smirks. Had to be Khrynsani temple guards. A trio of Tam's bouncers came up the ladder to stand behind their boss. I was trapped smack dab in the middle of everybody, with straight down being my only way out.

Rudra Muralin slowly half turned so he could see Tam. Unfortunately, he didn't turn his back on me. I swore. I had one dagger left and it had Muralin's name all over it—all dressed up and nowhere to go.

"Your *investment* is safe." Muralin sneered the word like it was something he'd scrape off the bottom of his boot.

"Is it?" The tiniest smile creased Tam's lips, but the gleam in his eyes was chilling. "Are you quite certain?"

"You *dare* doubt my word?"

Tam laughed, low and dark. "Doubting your word would imply that its validity once existed."

Point for Tam. Painful death for me.

Tam hadn't looked at me, not once.

Muralin stood utterly still, like sculpted marble. "You forget your place."

"My place is here. Yours is not."

"I have destroyed men for less than—"

A crossbow bolt whizzed past my left ear, and I dove for the catwalk. Others wisely followed suit.

A volley of bolts followed, pinging and ricocheting off of the metal railing. One punched through a rail and kept right on going, taking one of the temple guards in the thigh. He screamed and fell over the edge, landing with a sickening thud on the stage below.

Crap in a bucket. Wooden bolts didn't puncture metal. But steel did.

They were shooting freaking armor-piercing steel bolts at us—and "us" included me. The shooters were a pair of Guardians and four fancy-looking elves in someone's private guard livery. Finding out who didn't take long. Carnades Silvanus pushed his way through the panicked crowd toward the stage, roaring orders at those fancy guards. I heard the word "kill" at least twice.

I didn't know if he meant me or the goblins, and I wasn't sticking around to find out. The second Khrynsani guard behind me was gone. Over the railing or down the ladder, I didn't care which exit he'd taken. My way out was wide-open.

Until Rudra Muralin grabbed my ankle.

I snarled, twisting from my stomach onto my back, and looked up into a blazing nightmare.

The goblin's entire body was alight with power, red and glowing like a bloody sun. I felt the power that was building in him and recognized it.

It wasn't a death curse.

It was *really* going to hurt.

Muralin tightened his grip on my ankle, his hand like a white-hot brand. I screamed in pain, then in rage. I drew back my free leg and kicked him solidly in the knee.

He laughed.

Not the reaction I was going for.

"Soon," he promised me. Then he released me and vaulted effortlessly over the railing, landing lightly on the stage.

Impressive. Scary as hell, but impressive.

Two of the elves turned their crossbows on him, and Muralin hissed a single dismissive word, turning the bows to molten metal slag in their hands. The elves' agonized screams just added to the chaos. With another word, the goblin extinguished the footlights, plunging the stage into near darkness. When they came back up, Rudra Muralin was gone.

Tam hauled me to my feet.

I hauled off and punched him.

His head snapped back. Not as much as I would have liked, but it was gratifying.

Tam wiped his bloody lip with the back of his hand. "What the hell is wrong with you?"

I think my mouth fell open. "Everything!"

A bolt fired from below barely missed us. Tam grabbed my hand and pulled me toward the same ladder I'd come up. I dug in my heels.

"Raine, please come with me."

Tam rarely said "please." I wasn't the only one who saved certain words for special occasions. My word had four letters. Tam's word was "please." He'd said it to me at the rehearsal to warn me to stay away from him. Now that same word was asking me to trust him.

Regaining my trust was going to take a lot more than one word, but it was a start. We had to get off this catwalk.

By now the Guardians must be halfway to the citadel with Piaras. And where the hell was Phaelan?

When I reached the bottom of the ladder, Tam took my arm and pulled me past the dressing-room area and into the back of the theatre.

"Where the hell are we going?" I muttered between clenched teeth.

I caught a glimpse of Sedge Rinker and two of his watchers talking with unfamiliar Guardians, and a dead Nightshade sprawled on the floor nearby, blood pooling beneath his head.

"Do not call out to them," Tam warned and walked faster.

I let out a bitter laugh. "I'm safer with you than them?"

"For now, yes. Sanura Mal'Salin unwarded her mirror to admire herself, and the Nightshades were waiting." Tam's voice was tight with barely contained rage. "They took Talon, Valerian's granddaughter, and Ronan Cayle."

Dammit. I pulled back against Tam's grip.

"Nathrach!" It was Sedge Rinker. The chief watcher had seen me and was after Tam.

Tam hissed a curse in Goblin, tossed me over his shoulder, and ran.

The back of the theatre was dark; Tam knew it like the back of his hand, and he was a goblin. Rinker and his men were human. No night vision. There were plenty of things to trip them up, and from the thumps and swearing, the watchers had found them. But Rinker wasn't chief watcher for nothing. He cleared his path and kept coming.

All I could see was Tam's ass and the floor.

Tam opened a door and closed it behind us, and went down a flight of stairs entirely too fast for my comfort.

"Put me—"

"Shhh!"

I shushed, but I wasn't going to stay shushed for long.

Tam stopped at the bottom of the stairs. Above us, Sedge Rinker and his men ran by and didn't come back.

"Put. Me. Down," I said from behind clenched teeth.

Tam didn't put me down. He slid his hand under my gown and up my bare leg to my thigh sheath. Finding that one empty, he went in search of the other one.

No way in hell.

Tam and I had wrestled before—once with intent soon after we'd met, and a couple of other times since then for fun. He knew my moves. This probably wasn't going to end well, but I wasn't giving up my last dagger without a fight.

I clasped both of my hands together into one big fist and hit Tam in the back as hard as I could. When he grunted in pain and surprise, I twisted. We both went down, and I got to be on top this time.

A single globe offered meager light, but it was enough for me to see that Tam wasn't fighting back.

He held his hands up, palms out. "No weapons," he whispered.

"Because you didn't get mine!" It was all I could do to keep my voice down.

"To keep you from carving me up."

I sat back, still straddling him. "What the hell is going on?"

Tam looked as tired as I felt, but he languidly moved his hips beneath me. "This is the best thing to happen to me all week."

I gasped at the source of the contact and the delicious shock of sensation that followed. Focus, Raine. I glared at him. "I repeat, what the hell?"

"I'm touching you."

"Yes, I'm aware of that." Parts of me were much more aware than others. "That doesn't answer what—"

I realized what he meant; I shut up and didn't dare move.

Tam was touching me. I was touching Tam . . .

. . . and the Saghred wasn't touching either one of us.

But it was there; I could feel it, hot and coiled, ready to

strike at the slightest provocation. I knew it'd be a good idea to get off of Tam, but I thought it'd be a bad idea to move.

"How?" I whispered.

"I haven't used a death curse lately?"

I narrowed my eyes. "You mean no überevil black magic."

"Don't act surprised."

"How am I supposed to act? You're a dark mage."

Tam was incredulous. "I was the queen's chief shaman. What did you think I was?"

"Shush!" I heard, felt, or sensed something like a snake's angry hiss.

Tam froze and didn't even blink. He'd heard, felt, or sensed it, too.

Apparently passion ignited it—that or strong emotion. Great. That's all Tam and I had. Ever since we'd met, either he was trying to seduce me, or I was arguing with him.

I sat quietly and waited. Tam closed his eyes, took a deep breath, and slowly let it out. When he opened those glorious midnight eyes, he had himself under control. Possibly. Me straddling him while wearing a slinky, black velvet gown wasn't helping matters any.

The pissed-off-firesnake sensation didn't entirely go away, but it had lessened. I'd take that for now.

"Raine, what did you think I was?" Tam asked again, softer this time.

"I don't know."

Tam hadn't talked much about his past; I hadn't asked him to tell me. I thought we had a fine arrangement.

My family's big on denial. And if we denied something long enough, we thought it'd go away. I know that's not how it works, but we're in denial about that, too.

In my mind's eye, Tam's dark-mage nature paced restlessly on the edge of the shadows, eager and hungry. The Saghred was coiled like a fiery serpent near his feet, tongue flicking, tasting the air, searching, wanting the black magic Tam held in check.

So long as Tam didn't antagonize that snake, it wouldn't bite me. Maybe.

I didn't feel like taking that chance. Time to leave.

Tam's hands tightened around my waist. "Wait."

"I'm helping you control yourself. You're a fuse. I'm explosives. Remember?"

The goblin's lips curved into a slow, wicked grin. "Yeah, I do."

I just looked at him. "If the Saghred strikes a match, that *fuse* of yours is going to get us both into trouble."

"I like playing with fire." Tam's hands explored my velvet bodice with a mind of their own.

"I know you do." And after some heavy breathing in a dark alley, I did, too. "So the farther I stay from you, the better."

Tam ran his hands down the length of my bodice from ribs to hips, like he was memorizing the curves for later. "It would be the smart thing to do." His breathing had taken on a ragged edge.

I dismounted. I had to take the moral high road sometime.

I hate moral high roads.

I sat on a nearby crate and crossed my arms. "Now talk. What have the Khrynsani got on you, and why is Rudra Muralin your houseguest?"

Tam sat up. "Talon."

"Huh?"

"The Nightshades took Talon." A muscle worked in Tam's jaw. "So no one has anything on me anymore. Tonight, I'm going to make the Nightshades permanently sorry."

I did the math, made some assumptions, and when that got too convoluted, I just trusted the answer my gut gave me. Talon's swagger, the bravado, the feline grace, but most of all the eyes. Tam's eyes were black. Talon's were aquamarine, but they had the same bad-boy sparkle—and the same intent.

And Tam had taken on the Khrynsani to protect him.

"Talon's your son."

"Yes, he's mine."

Talon obviously wasn't a result of Tam's only marriage to a pure-blooded Mal'Salin duchess. Tam liked elves. Tam liked me. Judging from Talon's eyes and pale, silvery skin, I wasn't the only elf Tam had liked.

"And he doesn't know."

"I don't want him to. Considering who and what I used to be, it's not safe for him to know." Tam's expression darkened. "Until a few days ago, no one knew. Muralin said that unless I turned you over to him, he was going have Talon kidnapped—and sold in the Nebian slave markets. The Khrynsani have a long reach, so I knew I couldn't send Talon away to keep him safe. The closer he stayed to me, the better."

Tam didn't have to spell it out for me. I knew full well what kind of slavery awaited a half-breed as beautiful as Talon.

"If I tried to warn you, Rudra Muralin said he would kill Talon outright. I tried to keep Talon safe." Tam's eyes narrowed accusingly. "*You* were supposed to stay in the citadel."

The citadel. Piaras.

Crap.

"I've got to find Piaras."

"Then you'll be going to the elven embassy," came Phaelan's voice from the dark. Lantern light flared, illuminating my cousin leaning against a closed door.

"You were supposed to wait outside," Tam told him.

"You weren't supposed to be late."

I was incredulous. "You knew about all this?"

"Hey, I just found out," Phaelan said. His dark eyes flashed in anger. "You might say Tam and I ran into each other backstage. He was kind enough to hit the high spots for me. It all sounded just crazy enough to be true."

"But Guardians would take Piaras to the citadel, not—"

Phaelan snorted. "If they had made it that far. Six Guardians took Piaras out the backstage door. I couldn't get to him without getting nabbed myself, so I hung back. Glad I did. Those Guardians were ambushed. Within a couple seconds there were six dead Guardians and one unconscious Piaras being loaded into a coach—by elves who knew which end of a crossbow was up."

"Were they wearing fancy livery?" If Carnades was responsible, there wasn't a hole deep enough for him to hide in.

"Nope, uniforms. Definitely embassy guards, and that's the direction they were headed."

"Any witnesses?"

"Just yours truly. And I don't think I should go anywhere near a Guardian just now."

I didn't want to ask, but I had to know. "Is Justinius dead?"

Tam spoke. "The last I saw, Mychael was working on the archmagus. Mychael is a fine healer, but it didn't look like it was going well. Though Mychael didn't look like he was giving up."

Oh shit.

"Gentlemen, the Isle of Mid just got itself a new archmagus," I said. "If Justinius dies or until he's in a condition to take command again, Carnades Silvanus is in charge—and Mychael has to take his orders from him."

Chapter 20

Carnades was probably living his dream, and Mychael had to be in a living nightmare.

I told Tam what I knew about where the Nightshades were holding the spellsingers—and their eventual fate unless they were found.

"The Saghred is still in the citadel's containment rooms," I said. "They can't sacrifice anyone if they don't have anything to sacrifice them to." This was supposed to make Tam feel marginally better. It didn't.

"Can Carnades order Mychael to turn over the Saghred?" Phaelan asked.

"He can. But Mychael won't do it."

"Sounds like mutiny."

It would be mutiny, though Carnades would probably prefer to call it treason. He could have Mychael locked up in one of his own containment rooms and pick a paladin who'd give him the Saghred, and anything else he wanted.

I couldn't let myself think about Mychael right now. I had to get Piaras out of that embassy. One catastrophe at a time.

"Tam, I wish we could—"

Tam held up a hand. "I know. You'd help if you could.

You have to get Piaras. I understand. I have to get my son back." His dark eyes were hard and resolute. "Once Talon's safe, I'm going after Rudra Muralin." He grinned in a cold flash of fangs. "I have a busy night planned."

Tam sounded like he was looking forward to it. I would have, too. I guess I'd have to settle for having left my teeth marks in Muralin's ear.

Tam went to one of the racks against the wall and pulled off the sheet that was covering it. There were costumes zbeneath. We were in a prop room two levels below the stage. Tam selected two cloaks, one black and the other dark green. He tossed the black one to Phaelan and held the green cloak open for me. I stepped up to him and he swept the green velvet around me and I fastened the clasp.

"I won't be going in alone," he assured me. "I have men I can trust. They're good in a fight." He almost smiled. "And they'll love the chance to get their hands on Nightshades and Khrynsani in one night."

Phaelan opened a low door in the far wall. Beyond was a pitch-dark tunnel that Tam said emptied five blocks from Sirens, well away from the chaos that was probably still going on upstairs.

I held out my hand and stared at my palm. I'd seen light-globes created, but I'd never done one myself. Since the Saghred had come into my life, I'd found all kinds of new things that I could do. Lightglobe making was small magic. It should be no problem.

After a few moments, a pinpoint of white light flickered to life from the center of my hand, beneath the skin. It was no larger than a firefly. It spun, weaving a trail of light until a globe, the size of my fist, hung suspended above my open hand, glowing steadily. It floated a few feet down the tunnel, then stopped, hovering, waiting for us. I felt a little thrill of accomplishment.

I looked up. Tam was gone.

Phaelan stepped into the tunnel. "We men aren't good at good-byes."

• • •

"*I've strolled past the embassy a couple of times,*" Phaelan said. Even at a whisper, his voice echoed off the tunnel walls.

I didn't like tunnels. I liked it even less that I had never seen the elven embassy. Phaelan had scoped out the city soon after we'd docked. Pirate instincts, I guess. He'd been all around the outside of the embassy. I'd rather have a detailed floor plan of the inside, but I'd take what I could get.

Water dripped and ran in thin rivulets down the cracked walls. Cracks weren't good. Last year, I'd taken a contract job for the Mermeia city watch. They needed my help in finding a smuggling ring's hideout. In my search of one of Mermeia's many tunnels, I opened an innocent-looking metal door and a canal's worth of water just fell on me. Though the same water that fell on me made it easy to find William Lark's smuggling ring. My opening that door caused a tunnel wall to collapse. The canal flooded the place and shot Bill and his gang out the Dock Street sewer tunnels like rats out of a hole. I don't know how I managed to avoid the same fate. It was a sight my nightmares wouldn't let me soon forget.

The only thing I wanted to know when I went into a tunnel was how soon I could get out.

"For a place that's supposed to be a safe haven for elves, it didn't look like it'd be safe for me," Phaelan was saying. "Too many guards, and too many of those magical . . ." He wiggled his fingers in the air.

"Wards." I sounded as drained as I felt. "They're called wards, Phaelan."

"Whatever. They were red, they were sizzling, and they were at every gate entrance. Like I said, not a friendly place, for elves or anyone else. I know I wouldn't be welcome."

"So you're saying you're not going to help me."

"On the contrary. You know I love to go where I'm not welcome." His grin was slow. "Our friend has been inside the embassy, but never through the front door. Better yet, he wants to help us."

"Tanik Ozal." My lack of enthusiasm was evident.

"The very friend."

"Ozal is not our friend."

Phaelan's grin vanished, and I saw a glimpse of the Captain Benares who struck terror into the hearts of every merchant in the seven kingdoms. "Tanik would try to screw me over on a business deal, and I'd cheerfully do the same to him. It's business; it's expected. What happened to Piaras is personal; it's family. Tanik will do everything he can to help. And he would never turn a brother pirate over to the law—and especially not to any stinking mage."

I opted not to remind Phaelan that I was officially now a stinking mage.

I'd like to have shared his confidence, but it'd been my experience that with someone like Tanik Ozal, allegiances changed direction as often as the wind.

But Piaras was in the embassy. I needed information. Tanik had information.

So I'd roll the dice and take my chances.

The tunnel ended in someone's storeroom. I assumed it was someone Tam trusted or did business with. I was glad they weren't working tonight since we didn't have Tam with us to do the introductions. The door at the back of the storeroom opened onto a narrow, and blessedly empty, side street. The street beyond wasn't empty. It was one of Mid's main thoroughfares. Great. Just great.

I stopped Phaelan with a hand on his arm. "Wait."

"What for?"

"The streets are crowded, and chances are I'm now at the top of more than a few wanted lists. The two of us walking side by side to the harbor is going to look odd. I have an idea. I don't like it, but it's probably the safest way for us to attract as little attention as possible."

"Dazzle me with your brilliance."

"I'm shorter than you and smaller, and my cloak is very

nice. Fortunately, it's also got a deep hood. So it's obvious that I'm a woman. It's also obvious that you're a man."

"Thank you for noticing. Your point is?"

"Anyone looking for me is going to expect me to either be alone, or with you, my cousin. So I don't think we should act like cousins."

Phaelan's grin was slow and wicked. "You're a naughty girl."

"I'm a girl whose not about to get recognized and arrested. To keep either from happening, I think that from here to the harbor, I'm officially your doxy for the evening."

"I don't do doxies."

"Phaelan, you do anything female, attractive, and breathing. Just don't let your hands get carried away while playacting and I won't have to stab you."

"Deal."

"Good."

Phaelan put his arm around me and pulled me close to his side. It worked out well. My right hand was free, and so was Phaelan's left. I was right-handed; Phaelan was a lefty. We'd have to separate to draw any substantial weapon. But if we ran into that much trouble, our charade was officially over anyway.

The nighttime streets of Mid were full of students, in groups and in pairs. The taverns and nightclubs were doing a brisk business. A door to one of the clubs opened to admit a young couple, and the sound of a spellsinger drifted out into the street. His voice was low, his song simple and beautiful. Phaelan tightened his grip on my waist and hurried me past.

"How far is the elven embassy from Tanik's ship?" I asked.

Phaelan didn't stop, but he did slow down. "That's risky, cousin."

"I thought 'risk' was your middle name."

"It is. I mean it's risky to let you anywhere near that embassy right now."

"I'm not going to do anything."

"I'll believe that when I don't see it."

"I just want to be sure Piaras is there. No use breaking in if Balmorlan has already moved him."

"Good point. So that means you're not going to blast holes through the walls."

"No blasting. You have my word."

Phaelan smiled and it was warm, no trace of bravado. "You're a Benares, Raine. Never forget that our word isn't worth the air it's spoken into unless we want it to be."

Phaelan was right. The elven embassy's wards were red and siz-zling. And the place was a virtual fortress. The damned thing actually had battlements complete with armed and pa-trolling guards. Some of those guards had partners—nearly waist high, dark, sleek, and red eyed. Werehounds.

"Shit," Phaelan whispered. "Those weren't there last time."

"They didn't have Piaras inside last time. Taltek Balmor-lan has his treasure; he doesn't want anyone taking it away from him."

Phaelan chuckled. "Stealing treasure is what we do best."

No one was getting in there who didn't belong, and no prisoner was getting out without some high-powered help.

I was high-powered help. Thanks to the boost the Saghred had given what I already had, all the brawn I needed was at my beck and call. But magical brawn was noisy. Stealth was called for, so I'd give my brain the first shot at it. No building was impenetrable, every ward had a weak spot, and werehounds could be drugged. I had done all of the above before.

We went around the side of the compound, keeping to the shadows until we found a cozy little alley across the street from the back entrance. Staff and lesser guards came in through the back; the people I didn't want to see me went in through the front.

"Can you do your seeking thing through those?" Phaelan indicated the gate wards.

"I thought I'd just go over them."

"I was going to suggest that." His smile flashed in the dim light. "Great minds think alike."

I didn't have an object from Piaras to link with him, but I didn't need anything to find him. He wasn't related to me by blood, but that didn't stop me from loving him like a brother. Family knew their own, no linking objects required.

I used my memories to create a vivid image of Piaras in my mind. Not the terrified and disbelieving Piaras from tonight. I relaxed and breathed deep, and tried to relax some more until I had an almost tangible image of the Piaras I knew and loved. Then I reached out, over the warded gates, through the stone of the embassy walls into the interior. The interior was blurred and indistinct, like looking through greasy glass. An upstairs room was thickly warded and bespelled. I knew Piaras was in that room. I couldn't actually see him; the wards were too thick, but I knew he was there. Now all I had to do was get in, get him, and get us both out.

And Taltek Balmorlan better hope he wasn't in my way when I did it.

I pulled back slowly, carefully going out the same way I'd gone in. Wards on buildings were generally for preventing physical entry or high-powered magic from getting through. Seeking wasn't high-powered. More like a gnat flying through a fishnet. Nothing disturbed, no one would notice.

I squeezed my eyes shut and blinked a few times to clear them. Seeking through thick wards always made my eyes hurt.

"Well?" Phaelan asked.

"He's in there. Balmorlan has him cocooned in wards and spells. And I'm sure one of them is to keep Piaras's voice from knocking out every guard in the place." I chuckled darkly. "Turn Balmorlan's new weapon against him. I like it."

"Sounds like a damned fine way to get us out of there."

"First we need a damned fine way to get in."

"Tanik's done some arms smuggling for the elven ambassador. He knows the basements of that place. Let's get ourselves down to the harbor and reap the benefits of Tanik's expertise."

Chapter 21

Tanik Ozal's yacht was the Zephyr. *She was sleek, beautiful, and* expensive—the same way I'd heard that Ozal liked his women. She was also docked uncomfortably close to the yachts of the people who most wanted to get their hands on me.

My father had hidden the Saghred in the catacombs of the Mal'Salin family estate in Mermeia. He claimed the safest place to hide something was under the very noses of the people who most wanted to find it. If that was true, right now I was about the safest woman on the island.

The wind was down and the harbor was a dark mirror reflecting the yachts' deck lightglobes. One slip over from the *Zephyr* was a yacht flying the royal elven standard. Had to be Taltek Balmorlan's. She looked fast, and she was definitely armed. Enough slender brass cannons gleamed on her well-lit decks to discourage anyone from boarding—or giving chase once she was under way.

On the *Zephyr*'s port side were two goblin yachts. One flew the royal Mal'Salin standard with two intertwined serpents battling for dominance, both surmounted by a crown. The flag of the other goblin yacht bore the single red serpent of the Khrynsani. Phaelan had been right; the bow of the Khrynsani ship was pointed toward open water. The deck and the interior were almost completely dark. A few red lightglobes cast a dim glow. Spooky. The only way I could see the Khrynsani flag was from the large harbor lightglobes mounted on posts along the dock.

All of the yachts looked like they had minimum crew on board. Hopefully their captains had given them shore leave for the evening. Even the most disciplined crew couldn't resist having a few too many while out on the town. I'd take a tipsy or drunk crew over sober and alert any day.

"Looks like no one's home," I noted. "Tanik expecting us?"

"He's expecting me. You'll be an added bonus."

My lips narrowed into a thin, angry line. "If he grabs my ass again, I *will* punch him."

Phaelan flashed a quick grin. "I think he remembers that from last time."

Tanik Ozal looked like someone's jovial uncle. He was human. He was also big, bearded, and barrel-chested, with a booming voice and laugh. Tanik liked to enjoy himself, and most of the time he could be enjoyable to be around.

I still didn't trust him. Maybe I just didn't know him well enough. Maybe it was because I didn't want to. Tanik Ozal would smuggle pretty much anything if the price was right. His fees were obscenely high, but I'd found over the years that when wealthy people wanted something badly enough, they were willing to pay for it.

Occasionally Tanik's cargo was a human, elf, or goblin. *That* was why I didn't like him. Most smugglers had lines they wouldn't cross. I don't think Tanik had found his yet.

Phaelan hit the high points of what had happened at Sirens. I wasn't in the mood to explain anything to anybody.

I parted the curtain and peered out the window of Tanik's main salon. It was still too quiet. I trusted quiet even less than Tanik Ozal. "So where are your neighbors?"

Tanik passed a drink to Phaelan. "Let's see. The

Mal'Salins were at that recital. One of their nieces was singing or something."

I snorted. "Or something." Like letting in enough Nightshades to kidnap two spellsingers and their maestro.

"Balmorlan's probably still at the embassy. And who the hell knows where those Khrynsani bastards are. You see them come and go at all hours, but you never hear them. It's not natural."

"Nothing about them is," I muttered.

"You sure I can't get you something, love?"

"No, thank you." So far Tanik's hospitality had been faultless. He'd even given me some clothes better suited for breaking into an embassy, and a much-welcome assortment of bladed weapons. I'd asked for picklocks, and Tanik had provided a professional-quality set. I knew Piaras was being held behind wards, not iron locks, but I liked being prepared for any possibility.

And Tanik didn't try to grab my ass, even when he'd seen me in my gown. I think he saw my mood when I walked through the door and knew better than to even think about touching me.

"Understood," Tanik told me. "You've got a job to do, and you want to keep a clear head."

"And I'm in a hurry."

"Getting into that embassy isn't quick work."

"There's a first time for everything."

"If you're worried about Balmorlan getting young Piaras on his yacht and out of this harbor, you can rest assured that will not happen." Tanik smiled, showing all of his teeth.

"Thank you. But what I'm worried about is what might be happening to Piaras in that embassy right now. I want him out of there. Phaelan tells me you know it inside and out."

"Do you know where he's being held?"

"Upstairs."

Tanik leaned back in his chair and the wood creaked in protest. "You're a seeker."

I was instantly wary. "I am."

"I understand you're more than a seeker now."

I answered by not answering.

"You haven't exactly kept a low profile since you got here," Tanik noted. "I heard about what you did with the stage. I could tell you all about the embassy basements, and I will. I've delivered many a shipment for Giles Keril over the years. The ambassador has expensive tastes. But trying to get from those basements to the upper floors using mundane means is going to get you killed. If you've got something up those sleeves of yours other than my throwing knives—"

"Just say it, Tanik."

His dark eyes shone. "Rumor has it you can do anything you want to, magically speaking. Why don't you just walk in through the front doors?"

Phaelan chuckled. "She promised not to blast holes in the walls."

"Magic makes noise," I told Tanik.

"Not the little kind. I'm talking glamours. My son's gotten quite good at them. Though it irritates the hell out of me never knowing what he looks like. He thinks it's funny."

I just stared at him.

"You know, a glamour," Tanik said.

"I know what a glamour is, and I know how one is done." I resisted the urge to snap at him. "I just can't do one."

Phaelan cleared his throat. "Have you tried since"—he made a fist-sized circle with his fingers—"you met you-know-what?"

The Saghred. "No."

"Well, then you don't know until you try."

Tanik spoke. "Guards walk in and out the front gates of the embassy all the time—they don't stop you if they know you. But to get in as a guard, you're going to have to go in as a man."

"Excuse me?"

Tanik raised his hands defensively. "Just looking like one. Your glamour will include a uniform; it's not like you have to make yourself anatomically correct or anything. Embassy guards have been coming and going at all hours to Balmorlan's yacht. I'll just have my boys borrow one for a while so you can get a good look at him." He paused and grinned. "And of course keep him occupied until you get back with Piaras." He chuckled. "It'd suck to almost get out of the embassy and run into your double."

I gave him a flat look. "Yes, it would." I didn't like the idea of a glamour, but I had to admit it was inspired.

"Though you have to ask yourself something, girl," Tanik said. "And you have to be honest about it. Do you have the brass to walk through those front gates and into that embassy? The ambassador has some nasty mages on his staff. I think those bastards can smell fear."

"I've got the brass to get in and the brains to get out," I said quietly. "I'm a Benares, remember?"

Tanik laughed. "Just wanted to be sure. I didn't want to have your death on my conscience."

It was my turn to laugh. "You don't have one."

He leaned forward eagerly. "Well then, before I have my boys deplete the embassy guard population by one, why don't you do a test run on Phaelan here?"

My cousin tensed in his chair. "Wait a minute. I don't like magic. I especially don't like magic done on me."

I sighed in exasperation. "I won't do anything to you. You're just a model. I'm the one who'll be doing the work. Stand up."

He hesitated, then stood slowly.

I knew the mechanics of doing a glamour, but I'd never tried one before. I'd seen someone get stuck halfway through their transformation. It wasn't pretty. That had put a damper on any curiosity I had. I walked around Phaelan, committing to memory how he looked, internalizing the smallest detail and then releasing the slightest touch of power into the image in my mind, projecting it outward.

I hesitantly looked down at myself. Tanik whistled and applauded. Phaelan turned and took one look, and his mouth fell open.

It looked like I owed the Saghred another thank-you.

Phaelan shook his head in wonder. "I never realized what a devastatingly handsome devil I am."

"Nice work," Tanik said. "How long can you hold it?"

"As long as necessary," I told him. I gasped. I had Phaelan's voice.

My cousin's eyes went wide. So did mine.

"Are you supposed to be able to do that?" he asked me.

"No." I stopped again at Phaelan's voice coming out of my—I mean his—mouth. "A glamour is just an illusion to trick the eye. I've never heard of one being this thorough."

Apparently the Saghred didn't do anything halfway.

Phaelan's grin was wicked. "How thorough is it?"

I looked down, way down. Now my mouth fell open.

I definitely felt different. I mean I was still me, but I now had things dangling where things had never dangled before. I resisted the urge to reach down and touch.

I was horrified. "How the hell do you walk with these things?"

Phaelan's grin turned wolfish. "Proudly."

Tanik Ozal was red in the face from laughing so hard.

"Oh, shut up!"

"I'm sorry, girl . . . Captain . . . whatever."

"Okay, so I can do a glamour," I told them both. "That's all well and good to get through the front doors, but I can't just walk out of there with Piaras."

Tanik's laughter had subsided to chuckles. He grinned and raised a finger, indicating that I wait. He went to a chest in the corner and started rummaging through it. He pulled out a pendant on the end of a long chain.

"Oh shit," Phaelan said, saving me the trouble.

A pendant linked to the Saghred was what got me into this entire mess. I was less than enthused about wearing another one.

"My son's majoring in magical instrument design," Tanik told us. "This little gadget was his summer school project. And unlike some of his other efforts, this one actually works." He paused and looked embarrassed. "Well, for about fifteen minutes. It makes the wearer invisible, so you can get in as an embassy guard, free Piaras, have him wear the pendant, and stroll out."

I just looked at him. "In less than fifteen minutes."

"You'll get to find out how good you really are."

"I'd rather not have to find that out. Can Piaras take it off and then put it right back on for another fifteen minutes?"

Tanik grimaced. "Unfortunately, no. It takes about an hour to recharge after it's been used. My boy only got a C on this project."

I blew out my breath and took the pendant. "Then I'll work with what I have. Okay, have your crew get me an embassy guard. And make him an officer. I don't want to get stuck cleaning latrines."

Chapter 22

It took Tanik's boys nearly two hours to get what I needed, but what they brought me didn't disappoint. An elf lay trussed and mostly unconscious at my feet. An embassy guard captain. Perfect. High enough of a rank to get respect, low enough not to attract too much attention. Plus he was good-looking. If I had to be a man, at least I got to be a handsome one.

"I need his name," I told Tanik's first mate.

The man grinned and pulled a disk and chain out of the guard's tunic and over his head.

Dog tags. Excellent.

Captain Baran Ratharil. Serial number 847364. My identity for the evening. I hung the tags around my neck. Captain Ratharil was about to take Taltek Balmorlan's newest prized possession out of the embassy right under his nose.

At least that was the plan. It was my plan, I liked it, and I was going to do everything in my ability and power to make certain that it happened.

I was going into the embassy alone. Phaelan didn't like that.

"I'll be waiting across the street," he said, his expression as dark as his mood.

"With six of my best men," Tanik added.

"If something goes wrong, there'll be nothing you can do to help," I told them both. "You won't even know I'm in trouble."

Phaelan almost smiled. "If you and Piaras get into trouble, everyone within a ten-mile radius is going to know about it."

He was probably right.

"Phaelan, if anything happens to me—"

"Nothing is going to happen to you." He said it like he personally dared Fate to defy him.

"Okay then, in the unlikely event that a mishap should befall me . . ."

Phaelan scowled.

"I want you and Tanik to promise me that you'll do everything you can to keep Balmorlan from taking Piaras off of this island." I looked from one of them to the other. "And if he does, you will find Piaras, regardless of where he is—or how long it takes. Promise me."

Phaelan's dark eyes were solemn. "I swear to you that Piaras will not leave this island without me—and Taltek Balmorlan will not leave this island alive."

"That's all I could possibly ask for. Thank you."

I looked down at the embassy captain. Tanik's boys had done clean work, but they hadn't been gentle.

"Captain Ratharil is going to have one hell of a headache when he comes around," I noted.

Tanik grinned. "By the time that happens, he'll be blind-folded and kept literally in the dark about where he is. I'm not a coward, but I don't go around asking for trouble in the cities where I do business. When we're finished with him, the boys will dump him in an alley, loosen his knots, and run like hell."

I knelt behind the guard and lifted one of his eyelids. Dark green eyes, a few freckles, strong features, slight stubble on his face. He hadn't shaved today. I hoped that didn't violate some kind of embassy guard rule. With my luck, it would.

"Could you stand him up for me?" I asked Tanik's first mate. "I need to get a look at all of him. Tied up and on the floor doesn't get it. Plus I need to see how tall he is."

"Ask and receive," he said brightly. "Boys, you heard the lady. Stand our guest up."

They stood him up and held him up. I walked around him twice, and went through the same process that I had with Phaelan. When I looked in the mirror on the salon's wall, I saw two Captain Baran Ratharils.

I straightened my/his tunic. "Wish me luck, gentlemen." My new voice was a baritone, commanding and authoritative. I detected a hint of arrogant jerk. Wonderful. Ratharil was probably an asshole, hated by one and all.

Phaelan stepped up and hugged me, man body be damned. "Good hunting, cousin."

I wore a large cloak until I'd cleared the harbor area, and once I got within a half mile of the embassy, I ditched it and walked briskly the rest of the way. I didn't go too fast, but Captain Ratharil didn't seem to be the type to tolerate dawdling, either in himself or anyone else. I combined Mychael's confident stride with a touch of Phaelan's swagger. Somehow it felt right for Ratharil.

Something didn't feel right for me. That something was what put the pride in Phaelan's stride. There were entirely too many things crowding the front of my trousers. I had to resist the urge to adjust myself every few steps. Whenever I'd seen a man do that before, I thought it was rather disgusting; now I found it absolutely necessary. I ducked down a side street, reached down, and did what a man's gotta do.

Whoa.

When I came out of that side street, I felt justified putting a little more swagger in Ratharil's step.

True to his word, Tanik didn't just tell me about the embassy basements, he had an actual floor plan of the whole building. While I had waited for his boys to bring me a guard to copy, I memorized the plans—especially the fastest ways out of there. If it involved survival, it was amazing what I could memorize. Lucky for me, there were several likely routes.

I was two blocks from the embassy when I saw the Guardians.

They were armed and armored for patrol. I wasn't sure if Guardians routinely patrolled the city, but that's what it looked like they were doing now. Even if Mychael knew where Piaras was being held, there wasn't a damned thing he could do about it. The elven embassy was elven soil, and even though Mychael was an elf, he was also paladin of the Conclave Guardians. He couldn't enter the embassy in an official capacity, let alone search the place. Taltek Balmorlan, Giles Keril, and the entire embassy staff including the guards, had diplomatic immunity and any crime they committed had to go through the elven legal system.

Mychael had to be looking everywhere for me and Piaras—that is if he'd been able to leave Justinius's bedside—if the archmagus was still alive. I hoped he was, and not just for Mid's sake. I liked the old guy. The Guardians coming toward me could also be patrolling the streets looking for me on Acting Archmagus Carnades's orders.

I wanted to duck into the shadows, but I had to remind myself that I wasn't me, at least not to these four Guardians. I didn't know any of them, which was good. I also didn't know what the relationship was between Guardians and elven embassy guards, and I wasn't keen to find out. Being a captain—but mostly being male—I decided that direct eye contact was called for. Not confrontational, but not evasive, either. The Guardians went with a give-us-an-excuse-to-beat-the-crap-out-of-you look.

So much for Guardian/embassy guard relations.

As we approached each other on the narrow sidewalk, the Guardians didn't make room for me to pass. I knew what was coming, so when we passed each other and one of the Guardian's shoulders rammed into mine, my shoulder met him halfway and just as hard. He grunted with the impact. I didn't. I also didn't get a dagger between the shoulder blades once I was past them. I guess according to man rules that meant I'd won.

It was just after midnight, but the elven embassy still looked like it was expecting a full-scale attack at any moment. Taltek Balmorlan must be feeling a little insecure this evening. He had Piaras. No one had me. That had to make the inquisitor just a tad bit nervous. He knew what I was capable of, and he knew how I felt about Piaras. The guards patrolling the battlements looked ready to shoot the first thing that moved wrong. I made sure I was moving as much like Captain Baran Ratharil as I knew how when I crossed the street and approached the embassy gates.

There were a major and two lieutenants on duty in the small guardhouse next to the warded gate. I saluted the major and ignored the lieutenants. It felt like what Ratharil would do. The major responded with a sharp salute, as did the lieutenants after they'd snapped to attention. A disciplined and alert group of guys. Just what I didn't need.

While I waited for the ward to open to admit me, I tried to clear my mind of me, Piaras, and the desire to strangle Taltek Balmorlan and kick Giles Keril's bony butt from here to the harbor. I was Captain Baran Ratharil, it had been a long day, it was after midnight, and I was tired.

The ward parted just enough to let me in.

"Ratharil!" It was the major.

Damn. I stopped midstride.

"Ambassador Keril has been asking for you for the past hour." The major grinned and chuckled. "I think he's lost his reading spectacles again. You're to go straight to his office."

I saluted again, this time with less enthusiasm. "Yes, sir."

I went through the wards and they closed behind me with a sizzle. Forget Keril—I was going to kick Tanik's crew's butts from here to the harbor. Thanks to them, I was now Captain Baran Ratharil—the ambassador's lackey.

• • •

Logic, Raine. Just use logic.

I was inside the embassy in an overly ornate, marble-floored reception hall, and I had absolutely no idea where Keril's office was. Not that I had any intention of going there, but since I was trying to avoid Keril, it'd be good to know where the little weasel was.

Continuing to stand there looking confused would attract attention I didn't need. I'd been inside one or two government offices before. This was basically the same thing, I told myself; it was just a little fancier than I was used to. In my limited experience, the first floor was for reception and underlings' offices. The important people worked upstairs—or in Keril's case, the self-important people.

Piaras was upstairs.

I took a deep breath, adjusted myself, and started up the stairs.

At the top the first flight was a wide corridor, and the walls down both sides were covered floor to ceiling in massive mirrored panels. No doors, just mirrors. Crap.

Naturally, the stairs to the next floor were at the other end. I started walking, and tried to keep my mind off who or what could be lurking on the other side of any mirrored panel. I took a casual glance at my reflection. Yep, still the captain.

"Baran, where have you been?"

I nearly jumped out of my borrowed skin. I recognized the voice, which was the only reason my dagger was still in my hand instead of embedded in the elven ambassador. For all I knew, Ratharil may have wanted to kill his boss, but I didn't think now was a good time to do it, as much as I'd like to.

Giles Keril stood just inside an open panel. The mirrors concealed the doors to offices.

That was just wrong.

I smoothly sheathed my dagger. "Forgive me, Your Excellency. You startled me."

Keril's eyes were a little wide. "When did you start carrying throwing knives?"

"Since this evening, sir. I felt it was prudent considering the circumstances."

"Quite true." He swallowed. "You are wise to be so well prepared."

I inclined my head respectfully. "Thank you, sir. I understand you have been looking for me. My apologies for keeping you waiting. My errand took longer than I expected."

"I've lost my reading spectacles again and I can't find them."

I swore silently and followed him back into his office, and went through the motions of looking around. From the looks of things, Keril wasn't a patient man. He'd essentially trashed his own office. I hoped he didn't expect me to clean it up.

"Have you looked in all the usual places where you've left them before?" I kept my voice casual, as if I had all the time in the world for this.

Keril shot me an indignant look. "Of course."

One of my hands curled into a fist. "Have you been outside of your office today, in another part of the embassy?"

"I've had several meetings."

"Where, if I may ask?"

"Down the hall earlier this afternoon, and upstairs this evening."

Upstairs. Perhaps Giles Keril wasn't a colossal waste of my time.

"Have you searched either place?"

"No, I was certain they were here."

"Sir, I would be glad to check both locations for you, if you would like."

"I can look upstairs, if you would take Symeon's office down the hall," Keril suggested. "I believe he's gone for the evening but his assistant can let you in."

No way, no how. "Sir, you've searched your office very thoroughly." I made a show of looking around at the disaster that was Keril's office. "And you must be exhausted from what happened this evening."

The little elf cleared the papers from his office chair and sat down with a sigh. "I am quite fatigued."

"Then I insist on going upstairs for you. Was your meeting on the top floor?"

"Yes."

"Did you have your spectacles with you then?"

Keril beamed in realization. "Why yes, I did. It's been so hectic tonight that I'd forgotten. Inquisitor Balmorlan needed my signature on a prisoner extradition document. I would have needed my spectacles to sign it."

Son of a bitch.

"Then I'm certain your spectacles are still there." I smiled at him. "If not, I promise I'll turn this place upside down until I find what I'm looking for."

There were two guards on duty on the top floor. One was leaning back in a chair at the end of the hall; the other was walking toward me. A captain. Good. No salutes needed.

"Evening, Baran," he said as he passed me.

Sometimes it was nice to be recognized.

"Evening," I replied.

"And make it strong," the other guard yelled.

"Yeah, yeah, Rance. I hear you. Next time, you're going for the damned coffee."

It didn't take any acting for me to look tired, but amiable took some work. I saw what Rance and Captain Whoever were guarding. The last room on the right was layered and crackling with wards. Somebody had laid them on thick.

Piaras was in there. I knew it.

From the bars on his uniform, Rance was also a captain—and a prison mage. All they did was ward and guard. Chances were he'd constructed those wards himself, and if I tried to take them down, the alarms would bring everyone in the entire compound.

He didn't have the key to Piaras's cell—he *was* the key.

Rance leaned forward, the front legs of the chair coming to rest on the floor. "What brings you up here this time of night?"

"Guess," I said, my voice flat.

Rance chuckled. "What'd he lose this time?"

"His specs. Again." I ran my hand over my stubble. "He's positive he left them up here, and he sent me to look. Do you know which room he was in tonight?"

Rance swore and jerked his head toward Piaras's warded door. "Guess."

"Damn."

"Yeah."

"I hate to ask, but could you . . . ?" I made a parting motion with my hands.

"Do you know how long it took me to put those up?"

"Couldn't have been quick; it's impressive work."

"Damned right it is. And that inquisitor's been making me let him in and out all night."

"Is he coming back soon?" I resisted the urge to look behind me.

Rance yawned and shook his head. "Not for another hour. But the room will be empty then and you can look for specs all you like."

I stood completely still. "Empty?"

"He'll be taking his prisoner with him. Fast ship to somewhere that's not here. Good riddance, too. That inquisitor's been a pain in everyone's ass since he got here. But then they all are."

"It's been a long day, Rance." I tried to sound tired and speak slowly, which wasn't easy since my heart had just jumped into my throat. "An hour's a long time to wait." I paused meaningfully. "I'd owe you one."

"Yeah, you would." He regarded me for a second or two, then pushed himself out of his chair with a grunt. "You might want to stand behind me. Wouldn't want you to get hit with the backlash."

"I wouldn't want that, either." I stepped behind him and reached inside my tunic for one of Tanik's gifts.

Rance deftly parted a section of the wards. "There you go; that'll stay for a minute or two. Be quick—"

I was, with a blackjack to the back of his head.

Piaras was on a pallet in the corner. He was either unconscious or asleep. I was hoping for asleep. I leaned over him, my hands gripping his shoulders, shaking him gently.

"Sweetie, wake up."

Piaras opened his eyes, took one look at the man leaning over him and calling him "sweetie," and punched that man squarely in the balls.

Chapter 23

I swore I'd never punch, knee, or kick a man in the balls ever again—if I lived through the next few seconds.

I couldn't breathe; I couldn't move—at least not out of the fetal position I was in—and chances were good that I was going to throw up.

Piaras was headed for the open door and wards.

"Raine," I croaked. "Me."

Piaras stopped, looked, then stared in disbelief, his eyes huge.

"Raine, I'm so sorry . . . I didn't know it was you. I didn't mean to . . . Are you hurt badly?" His words tripped over each other in a rush to get out of his mouth. His feet did the same getting to me.

I suddenly became aware that I still hurt, but not in quite the same way as before. I took my hands from where they'd been clutched between my legs. They were my hands, not Ratharil's. My body, not his. My dangly bits were gone. My eyes went as wide as Piaras's.

I'd lost Ratharil's glamour.

Oh no.

Rance was going to come to; Captain Whoever would be back anytime; and Balmorlan would be here within the hour.

Breathe deep, Raine. Calm down.

I could breathe, but calm was not going to happen. Fine. Nerves could be productive.

Piaras helped me up.

Captain Rance was lying motionless just outside the door. Guess who was about to become my second glamour subject of the evening.

I reached in my pocket for Tanik's kid's pendant and gave it to Piaras. "When I tell you to, put this on," I told him. "It'll make you invisible for fifteen minutes."

I went to the door and peered out into the hall. It was empty, and better yet, I didn't hear boot steps indicating the impending arrival of coffee and trouble.

"Come on, let's—"

"They said I murdered the archmagus," Piaras said hoarsely.

I looked back over my shoulder. Piaras was still standing in the middle of the cell, the pendant dangling loosely from his hand. He looked like he was about to be sick.

Any nerves I had gave way to cold rage. "Who said that?"

"Inquisitor Balmorlan and the ambassador."

"They lied," I snarled. "You didn't kill anyone."

Hope flared in Piaras's dark eyes. "He's alive?"

"We don't know yet." Best to tell the truth. "Regardless, it wasn't your fault. Your song was used to cover up the real attack."

Piaras stood there, absorbing what I'd just said. I could see his anger building. "They tried to force me to sign a confession. Admitting that I'd done it with your help." His voice had taken on a steely edge. "Balmorlan said you were on the catwalk above me with a goblin spellsinger. I knew he was lying, but I didn't know what had really happened."

"That goblin attacked Justinius, not you. I was trying to stop him."

Taltek Balmorlan had just joined Rudra Muralin on my personal shit list.

I looked back down the hall. Still empty. "Let's get out of here first, talk later."

We carefully stepped past the wards and out of the cell. I stared down at Rance, quickly memorizing every detail, internalizing his appearance. I pushed outward with a touch of power. I looked down.

And I was still me.

Oh crap.

Personal pep talk time. Just relax, Raine. You and Piaras are perfectly safe; no one wants to lock both of you up or use and abuse you for the rest of your lives; the Saghred's not going to eat your soul or drive you crazy. Everything's good; everything's fine.

I tried again. No dice.

"Dammit!"

Sometimes nerves weren't so productive.

If you ignored his clenched jaw, Piaras looked surprisingly calm. "It's not going to work, is it?"

I rolled Rance over, started stripping him of his weapons and giving them to Piaras. "Doesn't look like it. We'll just do it the old-fashioned way. I talked my way into this place. If I have to, I'll blast our way out. You wouldn't happen to know any quick and *really* dirty spellsongs, would you?"

His slow grin told me he did and that he'd welcome the chance to use them.

"Are these sleepsongs or slam-people-into-walls songs?" I asked.

Piaras's grin broadened. "Dealer's choice."

I was glad to see that grin and the resolve growing behind it. I smiled up at him. "Phaelan's been teaching you cards, hasn't he?"

Piaras tucked the last dagger into his belt. "And most times now I win."

And I thought I had corrupted the innocent.

I gave him the blackjack. "Put on the pendant, and let's see if at least that works."

Piaras slipped the chain over his head and vanished along with all of his new lethal toys.

I nodded in approval. "Okay, this could work nicely."

"What could work?"

Piaras's voice coming from Piaras's invisible body. Creepy.

"We've only got fifteen minutes—or less if that pendant craps out on us," I told him. "Listen up."

Everything was right where Tanik Ozal's embassy blueprints said it'd be, including the narrow service stairwell Piaras and I were now in. I'd told him my plan, but the reality of any plan was that it was subject to change at any time for better or worse.

My plan had just lost most of its options. There were several exits we could have taken from the embassy, but those were for Captain Ratharil strolling out of the embassy with his new invisible friend—not for Raine Benares, elven public enemy number one.

We were moving fast. Any moment, that captain would return with coffee and find Rance, or Rance would come to and sound the alarm himself. Our minutes were numbered. So I was nothing short of stunned when we reached the first floor without running into anyone. There was a definite advantage to after-midnight jailbreaks. I'd have to remember that. According to the blueprints, we had to cross an open office area at the back of the embassy, as well as the main corridor, to reach the entrance to the basements and the tunnel that was our final goal.

That tunnel led to the harbor and freedom.

"Piaras?" I whispered.

Silence.

"Piaras!"

"I'm right here."

"Why didn't you answer me?"

"You told me not to talk."

Couldn't fault his logic. "We need to cross—"

Sirens wailed and lightglobes set into the walls flashed red. Prison break discovered.

I swore. "Take my hand. I can't see you and we can't get separated."

He did and we ran.

Shouts and the pounding of booted feet joined the sirens. One voice bellowed over the chaos.

"Lockdown! Lockdown!"

The sirens went ominously silent, though the red lights continued to flash. Then I saw them, descending from the top of every hall opening and doorway. Gate wards. Glowing green and nasty. They looked like the bars of a jail cell, except these bars made sure magic users stayed put.

We ducked under one gate ward and ran faster.

"One to go," I panted.

It was on the other side of an open office area. It was going to be close, too close.

"We can't make it holding hands," came Piaras's voice from beside me. "Let me go."

He was right. I didn't like it, but I did it.

I dove under the ward and it hissed when it reached the marble, leaving black scorch marks on the floor.

"Piaras?" I whispered.

The sharp point of a blade pressed into the back of my neck. I froze. I was still on my belly. Two pairs of black boots stepped into my line of vision.

"Put your hands behind your back," ordered a deep, male voice from above me. "Slowly."

I couldn't see the speaker, but both sets of boots were military issue. One of those boots planted itself in the middle of my back, knocking the air out of me, and pinning me to the floor like a bug.

"I said hands behind your back!"

I heard two sharp thumps of a blackjack, two grunts, and then two unconscious embassy guards were sharing the floor with me.

"It was the least I could do after punching you in the balls." Piaras sounded pleased with himself.

I wanted to smack him. I wanted to hug him. I couldn't see him, so I couldn't do either one.

I got to my feet. "We're almost there. Stay close."

Set into the wall just ahead was a curved alcove with a bench. Cozy. According to the blueprints, that coziness came complete with its own concealed door. Tanik said the trigger looked like a knot in the wood. There it was. I pressed and a small section of the bench and wall opened into darkness. I might just have to start liking Tanik Ozal.

We went through and the wall clicked securely closed behind us.

"Will they look down here?" Piaras asked almost too softly to be heard.

"I don't know, but let's act like they will."

I had to risk making a lightglobe. It was completely dark and a light would announce us to anyone lurking down here, but I'd take that over falling and breaking a leg.

I focused on my palm. A spark bloomed and wove itself into a sphere. I could see Piaras now. "Your fifteen minutes of invisibility must be up," I told him.

Piaras looked down at himself. "That timed out right."

"Yeah, it did. Take off the pendant and put it somewhere safe. You should be able to use it again in another hour. Hopefully you won't need to."

I smelled damp earth, wooden crates, and not much else. I shone the globe in an arc in front of us to get my bearings. I saw something on the floor and stopped.

Piaras saw what I saw and went for a dagger. I thought it was a good idea and joined him.

A dead elf was sprawled on the edge of the globe's light. We moved closer. Oh yeah, he was definitely dead, and from the blood still pooling around him, he hadn't been that way for long. He was lying on his side. I used the tip of my boot to roll him the rest of the way over. Piaras sucked in his breath.

I recognized him. He had been one of Banan Ryce's boys. A Nightshade.

He'd literally been sliced to ribbons.

The first cut hadn't killed him, and neither had the next dozen or so. I thought it was a safe assumption that the slit throat had done the trick. From the angle of the cuts, the blade had been razor sharp and curved. Someone liked to play with their prey first. I increased the globe's glow. Farther down was another corpse.

The lightglobe would announce us to what was down here, if it hadn't already. Dousing it would leave us fumbling in the dark; and the dark would just make the things that'd killed the Nightshades more comfortable while they killed us.

I exhaled. We'd probably be safer back in the embassy. Taltek Balmorlan was the lesser of the evil that was down here with us.

Playful, sadistic bastards with curved blades.

Khrynsani.

Chapter 24

Piaras swallowed hard and stared at the body. He didn't know what had killed the Nightshade, and I was going to tell him. He needed to know. From talking to Tanik, I knew there were two ways into, and out of, the embassy basements—through the embassy itself or through the harbor tunnel.

Khrynsani goblins certainly hadn't strolled in through the front door of the elven embassy. That meant there was an undetermined number of Khrynsani between us and our only way out.

I had plenty of questions, no answers. One question rudely elbowed its way to the front of my mind. What the hell were Khrynsani doing under the elven embassy?

Piaras started to say or ask something.

I shook my head with the least motion possible. Piaras remained absolutely still, his dark eyes intent on shadows where there could be anything or nothing.

I dimmed the lightglobe and motioned for Piaras to follow me. There were two crates stacked on top of each other that would give us some cover but still let us see anything coming at us. Maybe. Goblins were fast, especially these goblins.

I stood on tiptoe, my lips next to his ear. "Khrynsani." I said it in a whisper so light that I barely heard it.

Piaras's only sign that he'd heard was a single nod. I was impressed. Though after being arrested, kidnapped, imprisoned, charged with murder, and interrogated, and escaping in the span of just a few hours, being told there were murderous goblins in the basement couldn't come as that big of a shock.

Time for a brilliant plan, Raine. Problem was, the bad guys were sitting back with the good cards and a heaping pile of chips. We were stuck with a really crappy hand and were down to our last, lousy chip.

I was at the top of the Khrynsani's most-wanted list, and worse yet, their boss wanted me alive. Rudra Muralin had used Piaras to attack Justinius, but I didn't know if he had an interest in Piaras beyond that, though Muralin knew that gifted spellsingers like Piaras were rare and highly prized.

Highly prized for their voices—the sweet magic.

Oh hell.

I knew why the Nightshades were down here.

I knew why the Khrynsani were down here killing Nightshades.

I knew Piaras and I didn't need to be anywhere near here.

Sarad Nukpana said Muralin had come to Mid to reclaim what my father had stolen from him. Muralin had no use for the pitiful efforts of a starved Saghred. He needed it at full power, and for that he needed sacrifices. And the Saghred liked nothing better than spellsingers. Banan Ryce and his Nightshades had been gathering spellsingers. Tonight they'd captured three more. What better place for the Nightshades to keep their growing collection than under the one building on the island that Mychael, his Guardians, and the city watch couldn't legally search.

Banan Ryce had done the work; Rudra Muralin was moving in to reap the benefits. When the Nightshades had stormed the dressing rooms at Sirens, Muralin had said that once again elves were unknowingly doing his work for him.

Ugly didn't begin to describe how bad this was going to get. Bloodbath sounded about right. Me, Piaras, and those spellsingers were going to be caught in the middle.

Piaras's eyes were intent on my face, noting every change in my expression. I hadn't bothered to keep what I was thinking from showing on my face.

"Tell me." He kept his voice down, but his tone told me he wanted to know. Now.

Piaras knew about the first three spellsingers. He didn't know who had been taken this evening—and that Katelyn Valerian was one of them.

"The spellsingers may be down here. I need to check."

Tanik had told me the basic layout of what lay beneath the elven embassy. Piaras and I were in the main basement, directly beneath the embassy building. More than likely the dead Nightshades had been trying to get upstairs for help. They obviously hadn't made it. If they had, Giles Keril would have been looking for a place to hide, not for his specs.

Beyond this room were storerooms of various sizes on several levels. Naturally, it wasn't a straight shot from where we were to the tunnel. We had to go through some of those storerooms, and down three levels. Tanik hadn't mentioned any rooms with prison cells. But from Piaras's encounter tonight with elven government hospitality, I'd be willing to bet there was a prison block tucked away down here somewhere. A place where inquisitors wouldn't have to worry about screams disturbing the nice bureaucrats upstairs.

I didn't have Megan's brush or Ailia's locket with me, but I'd linked with both girls a few times. If they were close by, finding them shouldn't be a problem.

"Keep watch," I mouthed silently to Piaras.

He nodded.

Seeking was quiet. If Muralin or Ryce were down here, they wouldn't hear what I was about to do.

I didn't close my eyes, but stared instead at the side of the crate. I clasped my hands loosely together as if I actually held Megan's hairbrush. I remembered the sharpness of the bristles against my bare palm, the cool smoothness of the silver, the feel of the intricate scrollwork.

I linked and I saw.

Khrynsani shamans had the spellsingers, and they were all in one cell. Katelyn was kneeling next to an unconscious Ronan Cayle, wrapping what looked like a strip of fabric from her gown to bind a nasty gash on the maestro's head. Talon was pacing in feline fury. I had been able to hear the spellsingers before, but not now. Was Rudra Muralin using stronger wards? He'd been sacrificing spellsingers for a long time. If anyone knew how to protect himself from terrified spellsingers who knew they were going to die, it would be Muralin.

I couldn't see Rudra Muralin.

That could be good—or that could be really bad. He had to be somewhere, and just because I couldn't see him in that cell block didn't mean he wasn't down here.

And down here was dark. Really scary dark.

The spellsingers were somewhere below us. There was no doubt in my mind. The link pulled at me through the soles of my feet like weights attached to my ankles, dragging me down.

I didn't want to go down; I wanted to get out. But no one had asked me what I wanted.

No one had asked those kids or Ronan what they wanted, either.

I unclasped my hands and broke the link. "All six spellsingers are down here." I sounded about as enthused as I felt.

Piaras looked confused. "Six? I thought you said there were—"

"There were three; now there are six." I really didn't want to tell him, but he needed to know. "After you were arrested, three more were taken from Sirens: Talon Tandu, Maestro Cayle . . . and Katelyn."

Piaras's face drained of all color. It wasn't from fear. It was all rage, cold and focused.

"Now the Khrynsani have taken them from the Nightshades," I said. "A goblin named Rudra Muralin is their leader." I didn't mention that Muralin was ancient and psychotic. I was holding on to the slim hope that Piaras wouldn't be finding that out. "He's a shaman and a spellsinger. He used to wield the Saghred, and now he wants it back." I paused. "He's also the goblin who used your song against the archmagus."

Piaras's dark eyes narrowed. "What did you see?"

"The spellsingers are in one cell. Ronan is unconscious."

It was my turn to watch the thoughts flow across Piaras's face. Frustration put in an appearance several times. Piaras was realizing what I already knew only too well.

We were the only hope of help for those six spellsingers.

"Even if we could get out of here, we couldn't go to the paladin or the watch." Piaras didn't ask it as a question. He knew the answer as well as I did. "We'd be arrested if we showed our faces in the city."

I nodded. "And if we didn't get ourselves arrested, they still couldn't help. We're under the elven embassy. That makes what we're standing on sovereign elven soil. Mychael's an elf, but he's also the paladin. Neither he nor the city watch can search the embassy grounds—or what lies under it."

"They'd never find the spellsingers."

"No, they wouldn't. And with Justinius incapacitated—"

"Or dead," Piaras cut in bitterly.

"Or dead . . . Carnades Silvanus is acting archmagus. He commands the Guardians now."

Piaras couldn't believe what he was hearing. "Paladin Eiliesor has to take his orders from *him*?"

"If he doesn't, Carnades can charge him with treason and lock him up in his own containment rooms."

"So it's just the two of us." Piaras's voice was steady and resolute. He'd already decided what he was going to do.

"I'd rather it be just the one of me."

"Not this time. I want to help."

I want to help.

I'd said the same words to Mychael only a few days ago;

it seemed like so much longer. I wanted to help find Megan Jacobs. I had been determined, I knew I could help, and I refused to take no for an answer.

Just like Piaras was doing now.

He was ready to do everything he could, anything he had to do. I almost smiled. All he needed now was a suit of shining armor. It would have looked good on him. He'd get himself killed unless I had a damned fine plan going in—the kind of plan that would work regardless of how the situation changed. It'd been my experience that bad situations rarely changed for the better. They had an annoying tendency to go from bad to worse.

I didn't have a plan, damned fine or otherwise, at least not yet. If I was left with no other choice, I had firepower. The odds of success—or survival—without using the Saghred were next to none, the risk we'd be taking was too high, and failure was a virtual certainty.

Having an intact soul was overrated anyway.

Chapter 25

*Something really bothered me. Aside from the near certainty of im-*pending death or lingering insanity.

Rudra Muralin had the spellsingers, but he didn't have the Saghred to feed them to. Now I wasn't an expert on evil master plans, but it seemed to me that Muralin had a very large crimp in his. Maybe his age was getting to him. Maybe he just wasn't a strategic thinker.

Probably there was something going on that I didn't know about.

If Carnades Silvanus was acting archmagus, he had the final say over what was done with the Saghred. Knowing how he felt about goblins, there'd be icicles sprouting in the lower hells before he'd give Rudra Muralin the slightest chance to get his hands on it.

Somehow I didn't think Muralin's plan involved making an appointment with Carnades and asking nicely for the Saghred.

Piaras looked down the dark tunnel we were about to walk into. There were entirely too many unknowns, but one certainty—if we weren't at the top of our game, we were dead.

It looked like a tunnel, but as dark as it was, we could be walking into a dead-end alcove for all I knew. But that's where my seeking instinct told me we had to go. Just because it was the right direction didn't mean it was the best or healthiest direction. My seeking instinct didn't pay any attention to little things like dead ends or death-inducing goblins along the way. It just told me the most direct route and expected me to take it. Avoiding death and dismemberment was my job.

"So how are we going to do this?" Piaras sounded dubious about the whole thing. Smart kid.

"It's pretty straightforward," I told him. "We go to where the spellsingers are—killing or incapacitating any goblins or evil elves before they can do the same to us—we free Ronan and the kids, and if we're really lucky, we get out of here with all of our pieces and parts intact."

Piaras looked down at me and blinked. "This is how seekers typically work?"

"Nope, this time I have a plan."

"Good. What is it?"

"I just told you."

"That's *it*?"

"I like to keep it simple. You got a better way to get it done?"

Piaras went through the motions of thinking about it, then blew out his breath.

"Should I take that as a 'no'?" I asked him.

The kid actually snorted. "You might as well."

Reality rarely settles in lightly. Most times it lands on you like a slab of granite. Any noble illusions Piaras had about what "charging to the rescue" really meant had just been squashed flat.

"We've got plenty of blades and blunt objects." I tried to at least sound reassuring. "You've got quick-and-dirty spellsongs; I've got the Saghred. Best of all, we're both highly motivated to survive."

Piaras didn't move. "Raine, you can't use the Saghred."

"I said I've *got* it. I didn't say I wanted to use it."

"But you would."

"Yes. The Saghred taking a chunk out of me is a small price to pay to see you and those kids safe."

Piaras's eyes hardened. "Don't use it to save me."

"That's not your choice. It's mine, and I've already made it," I told him point-blank. "I'm prepared to do anything I have to." I jerked my head toward the embassy above us. "If it'd come down to it, I would have used the Saghred up there to get you out. If Rudra Muralin brings out the big guns down here, I will use everything in my arsenal to shut him down."

Piaras drew breath to retort. I held up a hand.

"Last time I checked, my brain was still in my arsenal," I told him. "It's always been my first line of defense, and it always will be. After that . . . well, I can't make any promises."

Piaras looked into the dark. "Blades and magical arsenals. How could anything possibly go wrong?"

I do believe he was being sarcastic.

"Raine?"

"What?"

"I'm scared," Piaras said. Being a teenager and male, I knew that admission had cost him a lot.

"I'm scared, too. In spades. Damned near everything that's happened since we got here has been scary."

Piaras exhaled. "Let's finish this so we can stop being scared."

I smiled at him. "Best idea I've heard in days."

I kept my tiny lightglobe.

I figured the goblins could see us whether we had the globe or not. This way, if they jumped out of the dark and tried to kill us, we'd at least get a good look at them while they did it.

I thought I'd have to link with Megan every now and then to locate the cell block. Not necessary. Piaras and I simply followed the trail of dead bodies like gruesome breadcrumbs. The first two bodies had been Nightshades; the next one was Khrynsani.

The one after that was also a goblin—but he wasn't a Khrynsani.

He was one of Tam's.

Oh no.

Piaras looked over my shoulder. "That's not a temple guard."

"No, it's not."

"Who is—"

I scowled. "Tam's down here. He's come to get Talon. Until about a half hour ago, this one was a bouncer at Sirens."

Piaras arched an eyebrow. "Talon?"

The bad guys already knew, so why shouldn't Piaras? "Talon is Tam's son."

"He didn't tell me."

"He doesn't know. People in Tam's past would come after him if they found out."

"People like Nightshades and Rudra Muralin."

That brought up a thought I didn't want to let inside my head, let alone ponder. Tam had to have known Rudra Muralin long before he showed up on Sirens's doorstep. Tam had readily admitted that Muralin had threatened Talon.

Too readily.

"Yeah, people like them," I muttered.

I could've kicked myself. Tam had done it to me again. Goblins didn't give up information that easily unless it was a diversion for something they didn't want you to find out. Tam had been the queen's chief shaman, a master of the black arts. And from what I'd heard from Mychael and witnessed firsthand, Tam hadn't forgotten a thing. He'd known all about the Saghred when we had found it in Mermeia last week. He'd known what it was, what it did—and he had to have known what it reacted to.

He'd known full well how he would react to it.

He already knew how he reacted to me.

And he followed me here from Mermeia.

Passion set the Saghred off. There were all kinds of passion. Rage was one of them. Vengeance was another.

Once Talon was safe, Tam had said he was going after Rudra Muralin, then any Khrynsani or Nightshades he and his boys could get their hands on. Tam would have enough rage and vengeance to kick any evil stone of power wide-awake.

Talon was still tightly locked in that cell.

One of Tam's bouncers was dead at my feet.

That meant Tam was down here and he was hunting. If Tam's black magic got its hooks into him and it got wind of me, I couldn't be all that certain that Tam would be able to limit his elf hunting to just Nightshades.

Tam had known that, too. He'd told me that some things were beyond mortal control. He knew what his breaking point would be.

Dark power calls to dark power. Always has, always will.

I felt Piaras watching me. "Tam's one of the good guys, right?" he asked quietly.

A couple of days ago, I would've answered that question without much hesitation. When it came to me, Tam had been one of the good guys. When it came to me and the Saghred, I wasn't so sure.

I opted for noncommittal. "Mostly," I said.

"How about now?"

"Good question."

I put my blades in my hands where they belonged.

What had happened between me and Tam in that alley was still fresh in Tam's mind. I certainly wasn't going to forget it anytime soon.

Tam had embraced black magic his entire life until A'Zahra Nuru helped him kick his addiction. Now Tam was down here after a shaman darker than he had ever thought about being. Maybe. I tried not to think that Rudra Muralin and Tam might have had more than a few atrocities in common.

I pushed that thought out of my head. I didn't care what Mychael said; Tam would never do that.

Sarad Nukpana's voice came back to me.

Once a dark mage, always a dark mage.

I told Sarad Nukpana's voice to shut up.

I'd felt black magic before the Saghred. When you find stolen objects and missing people for a living, a dark mage has been behind the pilfering more than once. The safest way to confront a dark mage was not to confront him at all. Stealth and smarts had kept me from getting myself roasted on more than one occasion. You didn't want to run into a dark mage in the dark, or in blazing sunshine, either. My family said that if you can avoid it, you can survive it. Other people called it running. I didn't care what other people called it.

My link with the Saghred was my first personal encounter with black magic. I had felt the seduction, innocent at first, to use my new powers for good to help others. I knew that desire could just as easily twist into using the power for power's sake, to revel in the feel of it, the rush, the certain knowledge that you could take on anyone and anything, and utterly destroy them.

Just like Rudra Muralin and Sarad Nukpana.

Just what I'd told Piaras I was prepared to do.

Walking down a dark tunnel while Death did some heavy breathing down the back of my neck wasn't the best time or place to have a moral debate with myself.

My morality would have to wait. Piaras and I had a more immediate problem.

Every elf or goblin we found was dead. I didn't mind dead Khrynsani or Nightshades; more dead ones meant less live ones for us to deal with. I just didn't trust it. Just because we hadn't found them yet—or they hadn't found us—didn't mean they weren't down here waiting. Any surviving Khrynsani or Nightshades were perfectly capable of shielding themselves to avoid detection.

Step into my parlor, said the spider to the fly.

Piaras and I were shielded, and Piaras had a deadly ditty ready. The ditty itself wouldn't kill; it'd just paralyze anyone he intended it for. The blades in my hands would take care of the rest. Another Benares family rule was: leave no living enemy behind you, receive no dagger in the back.

Khrynsani and Nightshades and daggers that went whoosh in the dark were bad enough, but they weren't what had scared the crap out of me and put a twitch in my left eyelid. I didn't like where we were, and I liked even less where we were going.

The Saghred was thrilled.

The more bodies we found, the heavier the pressure grew beneath my breastbone. Coiled and hot, quivering in anticipation. Maybe the Saghred knew I was prepared to use it. It might also know that Rudra Muralin was down here. Like a really big, very hungry dog that recognized who had kept it well fed in the past, it was eager for its next meal, and was pulling on its leash. Rudra Muralin had used the Saghred to lay waste to civilizations. If he got the rock back under his control, he'd use Piaras and me to pick his teeth.

Maybe the Saghred would refuse to bite the hand that had fed it—and would turn on the one holding its leash. That would be me.

I hadn't considered that.

My intuition had never lied to me. Right now it was in my face, in a panic, telling me that I was in way over my head, I was going to die, and it was really going to hurt. But I knew if I screwed this up, I wouldn't be the only one dying. Rudra Muralin was nearly a thousand years old. He'd been patiently searching for the Saghred all this time. His search was over, his work almost done. The Saghred was awake, its containment wards probably now a joke, and an arrogant and deluded elf mirror mage was in charge of the entire freaking island. Rudra Muralin was probably damned near giddy.

He'd probably make the Isle of Mid his first playground.

The air shifted.

That was all the warning I got.

"No songs, spells, or movement," Rudra Muralin said quietly from behind us. "And the half-breed gets to keep breathing."

A pair of Khrynsani stepped out of the darkness ahead of us with a tied, gagged, and blindfolded Talon Tandu between them. One of the guards yanked off the blindfold. Talon's aqua eyes blinked in the sudden light.

A sound started low in Piaras's throat.

"Khali!" Muralin snapped.

Instantly, one of Talon's guards put a curved blade to his throat.

"Your voice is splendid, Piaras," Muralin said smoothly. "I've heard it once this evening." The goblin's voice was quiet, but the menace was clear. "I do not want to hear it again. If you make one sound, or so much as clear your throat, he dies—and it will be as much your doing as if you had slit his throat yourself. Do you understand?"

Piaras hesitated and nodded mutely. There was no fear in his dark eyes, just rage. I was going to do everything possible to give him a chance to use it.

"Gentlemen, would you relieve our guests of their weapons?"

His Khrynsani did as told, and unfortunately, they did a thorough job. I didn't have any steel left on me, and I doubted Piaras did, either.

"Turn around," Muralin ordered. "Slowly."

The goblins had lightglobes of their own, and they increased their glow slightly. The goblins didn't need light to see us, but they knew we needed light to see them. After all, what's the fun of having a pair of elves at your mercy when the elves couldn't see well enough to appreciate how helpless they were?

Rudra Muralin wasn't alone. Mere psychopaths traveled alone; evil maniacs came complete with an entourage of minions.

And I hadn't heard, seen, sensed, or smelled them coming until they were on top of us.

We weren't in a tunnel. We were in a room, and it wasn't

empty. Darkened openings in the walls indicated more tunnels. The decor included a pair of chains hanging from the ceiling, each with a sturdy iron hook at the end. Iron rings were bolted to the walls, and there were a couple of other implements I couldn't identify and didn't want to. This wasn't anybody's happy place, except perhaps for sadistic maniacs like the one standing in front of me.

Rudra Muralin's onyx eyes were on mine. "Both of you put your hands behind your heads and keep them there."

When a crazy person tells you to put your hands up, you should at least think about it. When a crazy person with a dozen or so heavily armed friends says the same thing, you don't think; you just do it.

I hesitated and then slowly put my hands behind my head. Piaras did likewise. I hesitated because I didn't want Muralin to get the impression that I was a pushover.

"Bind them," Muralin said.

Like hell.

Strong hands grabbed me from behind. I slammed the heel of my boot down on the goblin's instep. He swore and hissed, but never loosened his grip.

I called up my power. All of it. If Muralin wanted the Saghred, I'd shove it down his throat.

A manacle clicked on my right wrist and icy numbness raced up my arm and kept going, paralyzing my body with burning cold. Stopping my breath. Freezing my magic. Another manacle clicked on my left wrist as a pair of hands swept my feet out from under me and pinned my legs.

"Hang her," Muralin said.

My mind screamed fight. My body couldn't respond—neither could my magic.

Two goblins lifted me and hooked the chain linking the manacles over one of the iron hooks. They released me, but not before the goblin pinning my legs ran his free hand up my body from hip to breast.

When he stepped aside, I saw Piaras sprawled unmoving on the ground.

"Best way to silence a songbird," Rudra Muralin said mildly.

"If you killed—" I snarled.

"Killing Piaras would be wasteful. I never carelessly discard a potential power source."

The balls of my feet touched the floor. Barely. It might be enough for leverage or it might not. The cold was gone, but the numbness stayed, though not in my body. I could feel every last bruise I had, and I'd collected plenty lately.

I couldn't feel my magic. I still had it—it was there, my magic and the Saghred's power—but I couldn't reach either one if my life depended on it. And it was going to.

I never thought using the rock was a good idea, but now it was the last thing I could do. My soul appreciated the reprieve; my brain didn't appreciate the pressure.

You don't need the Saghred; you can get out of this. Think, Raine. Use your head. Yeah, a hacksaw would be great. Even better if the goblins closed their eyes and counted to a hundred. Neither one's gonna happen. So *think*.

Rudra Muralin's smile was full of fang. He was still just as perfect, just as beautiful. He also didn't look old enough to buy himself a drink in a bar. Since I was chained, surrounded, and didn't have enough magic to strike a match, I thought I'd keep that observation to myself.

"You've got me," I said. "Congratulations. Now what do you want?"

The goblin's black eyes glittered. "I thought that would be obvious, even to an elf. You're the Saghred's bond servant."

"Let me guess—you need me to use the Saghred for you. That's going to be some trick with these manacles."

Muralin's smile broadened as if he'd been waiting centuries for this moment. "No, Raine, I need you to *feed* the Saghred for me."

Chapter 26

I hung there and tried to wrap my head around that one.

"You are confused," Muralin murmured sympathetically. "It must be too much for you to comprehend. I'll explain, and I'll use small words. I died when I fell into that ravine. Or to be more exact, my heart stopped. It was only for a few moments, but it was long enough. In that instant, I ceased to be the Saghred's bond servant. Your father was a mage, so when he took the Saghred, the mantle of bond servant passed to him. When the Saghred absorbed him, the stone considered him dead and the honor of bond servant remained unclaimed—until you unwittingly stumbled upon it. Then the honor passed to you by blood relation—and by what scant magical ability you possess. Unfortunately, the stone will only accept one bond servant at a time." He smiled. "I understand you attempted to read my works?"

"Yeah, I read them, cover to cover, and I even did it without moving my lips. You needed a good editor; you couldn't say anything in less than ten pages. They put me to sleep in the tub, and if it hadn't been for Sarad Nukpana, I probably would have drowned. By the way, he sends his regards."

Muralin's smile vanished. "I'm certain he does—and he can keep sending his regards from precisely where he is. When you sacrificed Nukpana to the Saghred, your methods were not only primitive, but inefficient. There is a more direct and personal way for the bond servant to feed the stone."

The last piece of the puzzle clicked into place. I couldn't tell if the twisting in my chest was the manacles' doing or my own growing panic.

I knew what he meant. I had read it myself.

Rudra Muralin hadn't always taken the Saghred with him on his king's destroy-and-enslave excursions. Sometimes the rock had stayed at home—and it had stayed at full power. As bond servant, Muralin would accept "gifts" on behalf of the Saghred.

Those gifts were sacrifices.

Magic user sacrifices. Spellsinger souls. No wonder Rudra Muralin was a raving loony.

My body was meant to contain one soul. Mine.

Rudra Muralin was watching me closely. "Now you understand. Just as the Saghred's power flows through you, the sacrifices will flow through you to the Saghred. They merely have to be killed so that their blood falls on you. I've found that slit throats work best. Once the stone has fed, I will kill you and the honor of bond servant will return to me where it belongs."

"You still won't have the Saghred," I heard myself say. But I'd be dead—and so would Piaras and every spellsinger in that cell.

"I've used the Saghred to level cities." Muralin's tone was flat. He was finished playing. "I will gladly destroy one citadel. I can feed the Saghred from any distance, and use it the same way."

The citadel destroyed. Hundreds of Guardians dead in an instant.

Mychael.

Muralin nodded. "Only the Saghred will remain. I'll have to wait until the crater cools, but then I can reclaim what is mine. This time I'll be the one giving the orders; no king will command me." His lips smiled, but his eyes were the flat black of a shark. "I may even offer my unique services on the open market—for the right price, of course."

"Megalomaniac and entrepreneur," I managed past the tightness in my throat. Unlimited death and destruction to the highest bidder.

"Merely trying to adapt to modern times."

"I won't take sacrifices," I told him. I tried to sound defiant. I don't think it worked.

"The Saghred is willing. What you want is irrelevant. Those manacles will keep you from causing me any more trouble, but they won't keep the Saghred from feeding." He drew a thin, curved dagger. "You're the bond servant; so in theory, this should work. But since you're an elf . . . Well, I wouldn't want to waste any of my *valuable* spellsingers. Tamnais's half-breed bastard will make a perfect test subject."

Talon's aqua eyes widened in disbelief, and he screamed in muffled rage from behind his gag.

"Your father didn't tell you?" Muralin asked mildly. "Or should I say your father refused to claim you. Hardly surprising. Taking pleasure from elves is permissible; procreating is not. His shame is understandable."

I should probably have kept my mouth shut, but I didn't want to.

"My father kept the Saghred away from you for eight— or was it *nine?*—hundred years. Not too shabby for an elf." I lowered my voice in commiseration. "Must have embarrassed the hell out of you. Your shame is understandable."

Rudra Muralin's hand went white-knuckled around the dagger's grip. "Since you're an elf and female, the feeding process will probably shatter your sanity. You should be grateful that I'm merciful and willing to kill you quickly." His eyes glittered with something nasty. "And if the Saghred rejects Tamnais's spawn, all I've lost is something that should have been drowned at birth."

I pushed down my rage. "What a sweetheart. If you unhook me, I'll give you a hug."

Rudra Muralin turned to Talon's guards. "Bring him."

Talon fought like a wildcat despite being tied up, and his guards had to virtually drag him across the floor to me.

"You need do nothing," Muralin told me. He came closer, circling me to stand just behind my right shoulder. My legs weren't chained and he wasn't taking any chances. "If my test is successful, I'll have the other spellsingers brought in one at a time." His voice turned soft and coaxing next to my ear. "Just relax, Raine. The Saghred has done this many times. It knows what to do."

I felt myself begin to respond to his voice, to do what he said. I fought the urge to thrash and struggle. I was still desperately trying to come up with a way to get out of this while trying not to look desperate.

One of the guards grabbed a handful of Talon's long hair and jerked his head back, exposing his throat. Rudra Muralin moved into position behind him.

I felt the Saghred. I couldn't use its power, but it was there, quivering in anticipation, waiting, eager.

But not for Talon's blood.

It was ignoring Talon completely. Its attention was elsewhere—and so was mine.

Muralin sensed something was wrong.

I met his black eyes. "It's not Talon's fault." I let one corner of my mouth curve into a crooked grin. "It's yours."

Rudra Muralin was a thousand years old, but he was still just a boy.

The lower hells must be freezing over. The Saghred and I actually agreed on something.

Why would you want a boy when you could have a man?

A voice came from the shadows, low and dark with barely contained rage. Tam's voice.

"Release my son."

Heavily armed and black-armored goblins silently emerged from the tunnels and quickly surrounded the Khrynsani. Dark power rolled in waves from each and every one of them. These weren't nightclub bouncers. Tam had called in high-powered, out-of-town talent.

The Khrynsani weren't outnumbered, but I do believe they were outgunned. The same thought was crossing their minds. They looked to Rudra Muralin for the command they had to expect but didn't want to hear. Even death-loving Khrynsani didn't want to die.

Tam's dark eyes glittered in the dim light. This wasn't the Tam I knew. This was Primaru Tamnais Nathrach: dark mage, former chief shaman for the House of Mal'Salin, magical enforcer to the goblin queen—and a really pissed-off father.

Tam was dressed for sending Rudra Muralin to his reserved place in the lower hells. He was in black from head to toe, including boots that came up to midthigh. His armor was leather and matte black steel, he was wearing blades anywhere and everywhere he had the room, and his hair was pulled back in a long, goblin battle braid. When he stepped into the room, his braid didn't move. Probably another blade.

Rudra Muralin was standing between Tam and his son. When bad people threaten your child, I imagine that could make you a little irrational. Add irrational to rage and black magic and you've got a powder keg ready and eager to explode. Most people would run screaming from that kind of blast before it happened.

Tam was going to run toward it; I could see it in his eyes. And if he got the chance, Rudra Muralin was going to do the exact same thing.

And I was hanging there like a side of beef, smack dab in the middle of the room, with Piaras sprawled in a corner, out cold.

Like I'd said, things were going to get ugly.

"I offered you a place of honor among my new disciples." Muralin's voice was ominously quiet. "You scorned my gift."

I blinked. So the petulant punk was going to slaughter Talon out of spite?

Tam looked past Rudra Muralin to me.

"Did he harm you?"

"Just my dignity for now, but I don't like his plans for later."

"Plans can change."

"I was hoping you'd say that." I tilted my head to the right. "Piaras is on the floor over there. Please get him out of here."

Tam's eyes went back to Muralin. "Done."

Muralin actually made tsking sounds. "You shouldn't make promises you can't keep, Tamnais. Your spawn means nothing to me; I have other sacrifices. But your elf whore is mine."

Whore?

Chain me, steal my magic, slaughter kids on me, kill me, *and* call me a whore? I flexed my feet. There's payback due on that one.

Rudra Muralin took the curved knife away from Talon's throat and, with a disdainful smile, shoved him to the floor. Talon's hands were still bound behind him and he landed hard on his shoulder. A muffled sound of pain came from behind his gag, but when he looked up at Rudra Muralin, his aqua eyes were crystal clear and blazing with hatred.

"There's your filthy bastard," Muralin purred. "Come and get it."

Tam did.

Now I don't mind all hell breaking loose. My family loves a good fight. But a torture chamber full of leather-clad goblin dark mages, and me dangling from the ceiling like a party favor? No, thanks.

Fortunately, most of the spellslinging was aimed elsewhere. One of Tam's men dragged Piaras clear and took up a defensive stance in front of him. Good. Piaras looked like he was starting to come around. Even better. Hopefully he'd realize that the goblins were divided into "us" and "them," and that the goblin standing guard over him was one of us.

Talon was on his feet and was looking for a way out when a Khrynsani with a wicked-looking dagger locked his arm around Talon's throat and pulled him in tight for the kill. Bad move. Talon's hands were tied behind his back and they were perfectly aligned with their intended target. The guard's shriek confirmed it. The kid traded his death grip on the Khrynsani's dangly bits for a sharp twist, and didn't let go until the guard's knees buckled. Having been a man myself for several hours this evening, I knew firsthand that there was no pain like man pain.

"Talon!" I yelled.

The kid turned. He was gagged and tied; I was chained to a hook. We were quite a pair.

"Swing me!"

The kid looked baffled for a split second; then he grinned.

I narrowed my eyes. "Not that kind of swing. Get behind me and push."

He did, and I got the intense satisfaction of kicking a Khrynsani in the back of the head.

I was on the backswing when I saw Rudra Muralin coming for me, curved dagger held low.

He wanted control of the Saghred—and if he killed me, he had it. I could not believe this. My life's goal was to get rid of the Saghred. Now to keep my life, I had to fight for the rock. Irony sucked.

Rudra Muralin ran straight at me and I used the only weapons I had. I wrapped my legs around his waist, pinned his arms to his side, and squeezed my thighs together. I felt his power building, so I twisted sharply, squeezed harder, and screamed right in his face.

Tam's blackjack came down on the back of his head.

Rudra Muralin went limp between my legs and I let him go before his weight dislocated my shoulders.

"No spells?" I gasped.

"No need." Tam grinned and tucked the blackjack back in his belt.

He bent and wrapped his arms around my hips and lifted me straight up. I unhooked the chain and lowered my arms, my shoulders screaming in protest.

I grimaced. "I am going to be so sore in the morning."

Tam loosened his hold enough that I slowly slid down

the length of him until my feet were on the floor. Tam didn't let go. I'd kind of thought and hoped he wouldn't.

"Nice work," he murmured.

I shrugged as much as my aching shoulders would let me. "If you can't fight, distract."

I looked around the room and swallowed. Tam's black-magic hit squad didn't believe in taking prisoners. If it was Khrynsani, it was dead.

Piaras was on his feet and mostly conscious. Talon was untied and ungagged.

"Garai?" Tam never took his dark eyes from mine.

One of the goblins approached. "Your will, my primaru?"

"Find the keys."

"At once."

I stopped and my eyes went wide. With all the black magic flying around the room, the Saghred should have been trying to burn a hole in my chest. It wasn't.

Oh yeah. The manacles.

Tam knew. He grinned slowly, then bent his head and kissed me even slower. One arm pulled me tight against him; his free hand cradled my face and one finger lightly traced the tip of my ear.

I told myself that my legs were still weak from hanging; Tam's kiss and nibbling fangs had nothing to do with it.

Tam raised his head and looked down at me; his dark eyes had gotten even darker.

"See, no Saghred kickback," he murmured.

"Not a peep," I managed.

His smile turned seven ways wicked. "Maybe we should keep the manacles."

I met his smile and raised him a grin. "They could come in handy. And you're very bad."

His smile faded. "That's what I've been trying to tell you."

Garai brought the keys and Tam unlocked the manacles. He pocketed the key, then held out the manacles to Talon.

"Would you care to do the honors?" Tam asked his son, indicating the still-unconscious Rudra Muralin.

Talon bared his fangs in a ferocious smile. "I'd love to."

Tam's expression went solemn. "We should talk later."

The kid snorted. "Damned right we should." He stopped and thought. "Sir," he added.

I took a couple of quick steps back from Tam. The second those manacles came off, the burn was back. With the room full of black magic—and especially Tam's proximity—the Saghred was looking for a piece of the action. It felt like it was going to take the first piece out of me.

"Raine, are you—" Tam took a concerned step toward me.

I held out my hand to stop him. He understood and didn't come any closer.

I took slow, measured breaths. "Maybe we should have left the manacles on me." I tried a grin; it didn't quite make it.

Rudra Muralin chuckled dryly. He was on the floor, he was manacled—and he was smiling. That didn't bode well.

He looked around at his dead Khrynsani guards. "Bravo, Tamnais. You've always been the thorough type. Very neat, very meticulous work. My temple guards were here with me." His black eyes were shining. "My *shamans* are with the spellsingers. And if I didn't return within the half hour . . . Well, let's just say they had their orders." He smiled, slow and horrible. "Time's up, Tamnais. The harvest has begun."

Chapter 27

Just because punching the goblin's fangs out wouldn't do those kids any good didn't mean I didn't want to do it. Really bad.

Tam grabbed the front of Rudra Muralin's doublet and jerked him to his feet.

"Talk," Tam growled.

Muralin's laugh came out as a strangled rasp. "Why? Or you'll kill me?"

"I'll make you wish I had."

"Hollow threats, Tamnais. You'll never find what's left of those spellsingers without me."

"Want to bet?" I asked.

"My shamans have put up shields, distortions, and illusions, seeker," Muralin sneered. "Even with the Saghred, your abilities are pathetic. Do you truly think what you call skill got you this far? I brought you here, exactly where I wanted you. You weren't following spellsingers, elf. You were answering my call."

Piaras was beside me. "Raine, he's lying. You *saw* the spellsingers in their cell. You were tracking them, and he knows it. You can pick up their trail again." His confidence was absolute. So was his desperation. Katelyn Valerian was down here somewhere.

The desperation part I agreed with. I had to find Ronan

and those kids now. But what I'd been following all this time—had it been the real thing or a Khrynsani shaman phantom? There was no time for doubt, no second-guessing. Tam could torture information out of Rudra Muralin, but anything he told us would be a lie.

I knew it. So did Tam. He was looking at me. There was no question reflected in those eyes; he just needed an answer. I'd backed away from him and stayed there. The Saghred was coiling and twisting at the stench of black magic in the air—and at Tam's nearness. I couldn't trust anything Rudra Muralin said. Could I trust the power boost of a starving, vindictive, and fickle rock?

No.

I was a Benares. I knew one person whose wits I could trust here and now.

Me.

I didn't need the Saghred. I'd had dark mages, crafty bastards, try to throw me off the scent in the past. It hadn't worked then, and it sure as hell wasn't going to work now.

I exhaled and let a slow smile spread across my face. "I can do it."

I had to. Ronan and those kids had no other choice.

Tam's eyes were still on me. "Raine, when Rudra said harvest, he meant Magh'Sceadu."

Oh shit.

Piaras's expression was identical to mine, and I'm sure he'd just thought the same two words.

"Magh'Sceadu are the most convenient way to store souls when living bodies become inconvenient," Muralin agreed smugly. "And they can flow through solid rock. These tunnels run under the entire island—including the citadel." Those black eyes were on mine. "As enjoyable as it would be to watch the souls flow through you, my Magh'Sceadu can flow into the Saghred's containment room and feed the stone directly. I just need you to die. I always have a backup plan, Raine. Or I believe the more modern term is 'Plan B.' " Rudra Muralin grinned until his fangs showed. "What's your Plan B?"

My stomach twisted. Plan B? Hell, my Plan As were rarely anything to write home about. Sneak in, charge out, hope not to die. That pretty much covered it. I tried to keep my plans simple. I'd discovered through near-fatal experience that the only thing fancy tactics gave you was more things that could go wrong.

I had an idea. It was simple, which was just the way I liked it, and even better, I thought it would work. If Rudra Muralin was going to play hardball, the least I could do was throw him a curve.

I showed him my teeth. "You should already know what my Plan B is; you brought him here yourself. You might say you answered *my* call." I spoke without turning. "Talon, I need you."

"The words I've been waiting to hear, doll."

"I need you to take me back to that cell block."

Talon blanched.

Muralin barked with laughter. "We brought him in blindfolded, seeker. Or didn't you notice even that?"

"Oh, I noticed. I don't need his eyes."

The laughing stopped.

"Talon, I need your memories."

"But I was blindfolded." He scowled at the dead Khrynsani around us. "And they let me fall down a couple of times. I can't lead you anywhere."

"I find people through objects that belong to them—or through psychic traces they leave behind wherever they go," I explained. "They're called remnants. Since the information that brought me this far may have been contaminated, I can use your remnant to trace your steps back to that cell." I smiled sweetly at Rudra Muralin. "The same way I tracked Talon and your guards to that courtyard a couple of nights ago."

"Will it hurt?" Talon asked quietly.

"No."

He leered a little. "Will it feel good?"

I resisted the urge to roll my eyes. "No, it won't feel good. You won't feel anything at all. Just come here."

He stood in front of me and I placed my hands on either side of his head. "Close your eyes," I told him.

He closed them, but not before he gave me a sly wink. I needed to get a sense of him, a psychic scent. I didn't need his eyes closed for that, but looking into those gorgeous aqua eyes would be a distraction I didn't need. I also didn't need Talon knowing that I'd be distracted. I closed my own eyes and inhaled with all of my senses. In seconds I had what I needed. Clear and strong, with no Khrysnani-concocted illusions between me and where I was going.

I opened my eyes and released Talon.

"Gentlemen, let's go."

My Plan Bs usually involved thinking fast and moving even faster. When you viewed it like that, everything right now was going perfectly to plan. The remnant Talon had left behind when he was brought up from that cell block was still relatively fresh and I followed it without trouble.

Trouble was what waited ahead for us. Tall, black, soul-slurping trouble.

Rudra Muralin claimed that the spellsingers were going to be fed to the Magh'Sceadu if he didn't return. I knew for a fact that hadn't happened yet. I remembered the Khryn-sani with Sarad Nukpana last week in Mermeia. The moment the Saghred sucked their leader from the world of the living, every last one of them suddenly remembered somewhere else they had to be. A Khrynsani would take a prisoner; they'd take a life, but individual initiative? Forget it. Those shamans were probably shaking in sheer terror that the moment they fed the spellsingers to the Magh'Sceadu, Rudra Muralin would come waltzing back into that cell block. No one wanted to risk making a decision and taking the flack for any resulting screwups. It was the same in any organization, be it business, government, or a military brotherhood of sadistic goblins—everyone wants to take credit; no one lines up for blame.

Those spellsingers were still alive. I knew it.

I also knew there were Magh'Sceadu down there.

Last week, I'd used the Saghred's power to destroy six of them. But that was when I'd worn the Saghred's amulet around my neck. It was a beacon my father had had made nearly nine hundred years ago to let him guard the Saghred from a safe distance.

When the Saghred had helped me destroy those Magh'Sceadu, it was still imprisoned in the vault where my father had hidden it. The Saghred had wanted me to find it, and I couldn't very well do that if the Magh'Sceadu had slurped me up. The Saghred had a vested interest in helping me then. Would it help me now? I snorted silently. No way. To the Saghred, those Magh'Sceadu and the shamans that controlled them were waiters about to serve it the biggest meal it'd had in centuries.

And Piaras and I were walking right into the middle of it.

I'd wanted him to stay near the back of our group, pro-tected along with Talon, but Piaras had refused.

Yesterday, Ronan Cayle had worked with Piaras on his repelling spellsongs, using mirage Magh'Sceadu as sub-jects. Piaras had been given five chances to stop them. He'd failed all five times. He knew that and he still wanted to be on the front line with me.

And I'd said yes.

I was either leading Piaras to what had to be one of the worst deaths imaginable, or he was going to be our best hope of stopping those Magh'Sceadu. Piaras was scared, but he was determined. And since chances weren't all that great that we were going to make it out of these tunnels alive, I owed it to him to let him choose for himself how he was going out.

I didn't like his choice, but I respected it.

Tam and his dark-mage hit squad followed me, a gagged and manacled Rudra Muralin in tow. We didn't want to bring him, but we could hardly leave him at our backs, even wearing magic-sucking manacles. Tam said he might be valuable as an incentive to get those shamans to release the spellsingers with a minimum of fuss. When we got closer to the cell block, one of Tam's men would put Muralin's lights out. An unconscious Rudra Muralin wouldn't ruin a perfectly good plan by telling his shamans to attack. It's been my experience that a bound and unconscious hostage inspired more enemy cooperation than a conscious and defiant one.

A girl screamed in pure terror. She was about to die and knew it.

"Katelyn!" Piaras bolted into the dark.

I swore and took off after him. Tam's rough hands yanked me back. I twisted and elbowed him hard in the ribs, and the Saghred's power seethed between us. I told the Saghred to shut the hell up, and glared at Tam the same way.

He turned without releasing me. "Kontar, Tau. Stop him!"

Two dark mages pushed past me and ran after Piaras.

Piaras couldn't see where he was going. Any Khrynsani shamans would see him coming. Magh'Sceadu didn't have eyes and they didn't need them.

"Raine, stay here." Tam tightened his grip—and the Saghred flared in response.

My response was to jerk away from him.

Tam and his goblins didn't need light. I did. I muttered a pale lightglobe into existence.

"Keep him here," Tam ordered the two mages guarding Rudra Muralin.

I ran after Piaras, Tam and his mages right on my heels. Any efforts at stealth had just gone down the crapper along with Plan B.

The bottom dropped out of the temperature; I could see Tam, my breath, and little else. The air thickened with Khrynsani magic of the blackest kind, the kind that created and controlled Magh'Sceadu. The air was hazy with it, disorienting my sense of direction even more.

From somewhere ahead of us came shouts in Goblin, curses, and spells.

Above it all was Piaras's voice. Sharp, staccato, piercing. Paralyzing. I didn't know if he was aiming at shamans or Magh'Sceadu, or both.

We ran into the cell block and straight into a nightmare.

Magh'Sceadu, Khrynsani shamans—and every last one of them focused on Piaras and Katelyn.

Piaras had his back to the bars of one of four cells, one arm around the girl. His voice had caught four Khrynsani shamans off guard, paralyzing them where they stood. Piaras repeated the song, reinforcing the spell, taking no chances that one of them could escape. He knew we were there, but he didn't dare take his eyes from the immobile shamans. His eyes were wide with fear, but he controlled his voice and held the spellsong.

For now.

Ten shamans either already had their shields up or got them there before Piaras nailed his first note. Good news was they were ignoring Piaras; bad news was we now had their undivided attention.

But those ten Khrynsani shamans were the least of our problems.

A Magh'Sceadu glided patiently not five feet in front of Piaras. His voice might be holding it off; maybe the thing was savoring the anticipation. It was tall and hulking, almost hobgoblin in shape, if hobgoblins were made of black ink. The cell next to Piaras had been thickly warded. Now those wards were open in a thin line from top to bottom.

Magh'Sceadu were oozing out of the cell one at a time, re-forming once they were out in all their soul-sucking horror. Two were already loose in the cell block; more shapes flowed restlessly in the shadows inside the cell, waiting their turn to escape.

A shaman in fancy robes chanted in a low, sibilant whisper, forcing a single Magh'Sceadu slowly back toward the cell. As he did, a third Magh'Sceadu oozed out of the slit in the ward, a fourth right behind him. Fancy Robes was doing his work way too slowly and far too late.

One of the paralyzed Khrynsani shamans couldn't

scream past frozen vocal cords as a Magh'Sceadu flowed into, through, and over him, leaving nothing behind. The other three paralyzed shamans were about to meet the same fate. The Magh'Sceadu would take the easy prey first, feeding and strengthening.

Then they'd be ready for a challenge. They'd come after us.

That ward had to close.

"We've got a minute, maybe less," I told Tam, reaching behind his back and relieving him of a pair of daggers. They probably wouldn't do me a damned bit of good, but being a Benares, I wanted steel in my hands.

Tam pulled a short, curved sword and tossed it to Talon. The kid expertly caught it and grinned.

"Protect yourself," Tam told him.

Talon's eyes narrowed and fixed on a Khrynsani shaman. "Yeah, that, too."

One shaman on the far side of the cell block opted for self-preservation rather than staying to fight both us and starving Magh'Sceadu. He had a clear shot at a tunnel mouth on the other side of the cell block and he ran for it.

The shaman closest to Tam drew breath to spit a death curse, and Tam's armored fist took out most of his teeth.

Tam's hired help had fully engaged the Khrynsani, and I flung myself to the side to avoid a noxious green spray that sizzled when it hit the wall behind me, leaving it blackened and pitted with holes. What kind of crazed bastard summons acid?

A shaman launched a ball of blue light from the palm of his gloved hand, slamming it full force into the wards on the spellsingers' cell. The wards blazed incandescent, sending white-hot needles of fiery light at the spellsingers.

Megan Jacobs screamed. I couldn't hear it, but I could see it. Ronan pushed two of the kids down, shielding them with his body. One of Ronan's silk sleeves caught fire and he fought his way free of the outer robe before it could spread. The kids whom Ronan couldn't shield were bleeding in thin trails from where the fire needles had struck.

Tam swore. "Attack the ward, the ward attacks the prisoners." He flung a particularly nasty orange blast that glanced off of the shaman's shields.

The shaman smiled and tossed another blue fireball in his hand; this one was bigger and darker, cobalt flames writhing inside. "That was a warning. This one goes *in* the cell. Tell your men to surrender, or I'll roast those songbirds alive."

I could have said, "Behind you," but I didn't.

A Magh'Sceadu reared up and engulfed the shaman, wrapping itself around the goblin's body like living black quicksand. The shaman managed a scream just before his head was absorbed. I thought I heard muffled screams coming from inside the Magh'Sceadu. Then they stopped. Maybe it was my exhausted imagination. If I survived, I was sure my imagination would replay it for me in my next nightmare.

The Magh'Sceadu came for us. Tam tried to get in front of me; I didn't let him.

The creature stopped, floating there, not more than five feet away. Magh'Sceadu didn't have minds, but this one was hesitating for a reason, and I think that reason was me—but mostly the Saghred. Last week in a Mermeian forest, the rock had used me as a conduit to destroy six Magh'Sceadu. I was just as scared now, but I didn't think my shortness of breath was fear's fault. I also didn't know if that shaman had been the Magh'Sceadu's first meal today—the Saghred didn't care. It just hungered. I also didn't know if some Magh'Sceadu were smarter than others, but it looked like this one might be.

Only one way to find out. I took a step toward it.

Tam sucked in his breath. "Raine!"

The Magh'Sceadu flowed back the same distance and stopped.

Nothing like a game of chicken with a soul-slurping monster. I think this one realized I was more than he wanted to bite off. Point for me.

"Can you open that ward?" I quietly asked Tam.

"Only the shaman who made it can open it."

Damn. Tam's boys were doing too good a job. Half the shamans lay dead or dying. With the way our luck was running, the ward builder was either dead or inside a Magh'Sceadu.

"But I can rip it," he said with a fierce smile.

The cell block was huge; there was at least thirty feet of shaman/mage battle-infested floor between us and the spellsinger cell. Fists and steel were flying right along with spells and death curses. The Khrynsani started it; Tam's boys were determined to finish it.

We were shielded, but I'd found out last week that Magh'Sceadu ate shields for appetizers. Control or destroy were our only options.

"Get that ward open," I told Tam, never taking my eyes from the carnivorous inkblot in front of me. "I'll worry about him."

Piaras's song abruptly changed. His warm, rich baritone turned dark and discordant, the notes booming and harsh. He was singing in Old Goblin, the language of black magic, the language of the dark spells used to create Magh'Sceadu. He wasn't trying to repel them.

He was trying to unmake them.

Oh no.

Tam spat the exact word I was thinking.

Katelyn Valerian wrapped her arms tightly around Piaras's waist, pressing her head against his chest. I actually saw Piaras's shields strengthen. The girl was sharing her power. Piaras hesitated, then wrapped his arms tightly around Katelyn, and his song became a little stronger. The pair of Magh'Sceadu stalking them hesitated, wavering— and became slightly less substantial than before.

Tam said the same word again, this time in admiration.

I saw a flash of scarlet out of the corner of my eye. Ronan Cayle was gesturing and yelling. The wards kept any sound from getting out.

There was a Magh'Sceadu in the cell with them.

Crap.

The thing had come straight through the rock wall of the adjacent cell. A second Magh'Sceadu oozed through the same way. Ronan Cayle stood protectively in front of his students, pushing them back against the far wall. That was all he was doing. Why wasn't he fighting, singing, whatever? I realized with dawning horror that those wards did more than keep sound in.

Ronan couldn't use his magic.

Chapter 28

We only had seconds before those Magh'Sceadu started feasting on Ronan and those kids.

Tam and I sliced, blasted, and beat our way across the cell block. I didn't know if the Magh'Sceadu that had been in front of us was now behind me, and I didn't have time to look or worry about it.

The boy spellsinger, Gustin Sorenson, held a sobbing Megan. He gently turned her head into his shoulder so she wouldn't see what was about to happen to them.

The Magh'Sceadu drifted almost within touching distance, as if feeding on those kids' fear. I never thought I'd be grateful for sadistic behavior, but it bought us a few critical seconds.

Tam took one look at the ward close up and snarled a string of guttural goblin curses.

I looked where he was looking. "What? You can't do it?"

"The wards are rooted in bedrock," Tam told me. "If I rip into it, the ceiling comes down."

"Any other way?"

"None."

We were at least a hundred feet underground, with an embassy on top of that. If Tam tore into those wards, all of that was going to be on top of us.

If we did nothing, those spellsingers were worse than dead.

I'd held up a stage full of mages two days ago. No Saghred, just me. But that stage was wood, not untold tons of rock. Dammit. I didn't want to die squashed like a bug, but if I screwed this up, a lot of other people would be dying along with me.

I snarled my favorite about-to-meet-Death four-letter word.

"Do it!" I snapped.

"The ceiling—"

"Is *my* problem."

Tam knew what I was saying. He stared at me, his expression unreadable. "I need you to support the ceiling above the tear I'm going to make."

"Yeah, yeah. I got it. You pull; I push. Let's go!"

"I need control and delicacy, Raine."

I snorted. "Too bad you're stuck with me."

He held out his hand to me. "And we have to work in unison."

So there it was. I knew it wouldn't be just Tam and me. The Saghred was going to want a piece of the action—and a piece of us. The Saghred had given me power when I'd used it. Would it do the same for Tam? I didn't want that power. Did the dark mage in Tam not only want it, but crave it?

Triumph was the only way I could describe what I felt coming off the Saghred. The rock was about to get what it wanted. If we all got out of this alive, I'd have what I wanted.

A win-win for everybody. Yeah, right.

Tam called his power and I felt it: dark, potent, rushing up from the deep, primal core of him. My own magic coiled and flared through my body, serpentine, seeking the source of Tam's dark power. I found it and touched it: the dark well, its source unknown, its depths unexplored. The Saghred wanted to know those depths. I just wanted to explore.

"I knew I couldn't leave you two alone."

Rudra Muralin stood smiling at a tunnel opening next to the Magh'Sceadu's cell, manacles dangling negligently from one finger.

"Always have a backup plan," he told us. "And an extra set of keys. I hope you didn't pay your two lackeys in advance, Tamnais. Gold is wasted on dead men."

Muralin laid his hand on the ward of the Magh'Sceadu's cell. It opened seamlessly and Magh'Sceadu poured out, flowing around him like a black tide. They wanted nothing to do with him. I guess evil repels evil.

"Impressive work, Piaras," Muralin called. "You have even more potential than I thought. Too bad you're about to be overrun."

"Rip it now!" I snarled at Tam. I turned my head toward Piaras, Talon, and Katelyn. "Run!" I screamed.

I grabbed Tam's hand, and his power exploded through my body; my own surged upward to meet it.

A roar tore itself from Tam's throat. His eyes were solid black orbs, his lips pulled back from his fangs in a bestial snarl as he sank his fingers like claws into the wards and tore them open. The wards screamed as if Tam was ripping into living flesh, not magic.

I gathered my will and my arm extended toward the rock above where Tam had shredded the ward. My fingers flared out to focus my magic and I pushed with everything I had. My arm shook with the effort and my shoulder was on fire.

A spiderweb of tiny cracks appeared on the ceiling where wards met rock.

Oh hell.

Tam had flung open the door to the cell and was pulling the spellsingers out and all but throwing them toward the door to the tunnel beyond. Ronan and two of Tam's mages were herding the kids, including Piaras, Talon, and Katelyn, into the tunnel.

Rudra Muralin was gone.

All that power came at a price. I was panting and tasting blood. Either I'd bitten my tongue or ruptured something.

Black blooms danced on the edges of my vision. If I didn't stop soon, I was going to pass out.

Silence hung in the air, followed by a low rumbling. A crack appeared in the ceiling at our end of the cell block and started to spread.

I was all that was holding up that ceiling and if I let go . . .

I couldn't speak. I frantically motioned for Tam to go.

His black eyes blazed. "Like hell!"

A tremor shook the room. The crack in the ceiling was as wide as my hand and expanding fast. Chunks of ceiling began to crumble and fall. Tam tightened his grip on my hand.

"Drop it!" he screamed over the din. "Now!"

I dropped it.

Tam and I ran.

Chapter 29

The tremors turned into a thunderous roar, and the ceiling simply crumbled. Dust and debris chased us in a billowing cloud.

We didn't have to run faster than the Magh'Sceadu behind us. We just had to run faster than the Khrynsani shamans in front of them.

Tam and I had a head start, and survival was a strong motivator. In fact, my motivation knew no bounds. I didn't think I could run any faster, but a panicked shriek in the tunnel behind us proved me wrong.

There had yet to be a time when I couldn't outrun a magic user wearing robes. Robes were just a pretty way to an early grave—stylish death traps in your choice of silk, brocade, or velvet. Flowing sleeves got in your way during a fight, and flowing hems tripped you when running away. Behind us, a shaman tripped over his hem and went down screaming. A Magh'Sceadu caught up to him and the screaming stopped. I quit looking back at that point. What was behind us didn't matter unless it caught up to us.

The rumbling faded and the tunnel ahead sloped up and presumably led out, and best of all, whatever was behind us wasn't going to catch up with us—or anybody else.

I smelled the salt air from the harbor. We were almost out. Problem was, I didn't know if out there was any safer than in here.

Piaras, Ronan, and the spellsingers were waiting at the exit. Tam's mages were guarding them. Ronan didn't look particularly comfortable with that arrangement, but he hadn't spellsung any of Tam's men to death yet, either.

Piaras spotted me and swept me off my feet in a rib-crushing hug. I wrapped my arms around his neck and just hung there happily. Piaras was warm and alive, just the way I liked the people I love.

I felt him smile against my cheek. "We still have all of our pieces and parts intact," he said.

"See, I told you my plan would work."

"I still require an explanation, Master Rivalin." It was Ronan and he didn't sound amused.

I felt Piaras sigh; then he put me down. "Sir, I read the spell in a songbook in the citadel's music room. Since I'm not very good at repelling songs, I thought—"

Ronan's expression was both appalled and disapproving. "You thought you'd just teach yourself something stronger."

Piaras met his eyes. "I didn't teach myself, sir. I just read it once. I didn't see the harm—and there was a need."

Ronan was incredulous. "You read an unmaking spell-song in Old Goblin *once* and you could use it down there in that hellhole?"

"Yes, sir. I memorize quickly."

"So it would appear," Ronan muttered. The maestro searched Piaras's face for something only he knew. "I understand you want to be a Guardian," he said quietly.

Piaras shot a quick glance at me. "I did, sir. Perhaps I still do."

"What the hell do you mean, 'perhaps'?"

I stepped up to the maestro. "Uh, Ronan, a lot happened since you got snatched through that mirror at Sirens."

"So tell me."

I pulled him aside and told him. I included what had happened to Piaras this evening, who was responsible, and what they had wanted. I finished with how Mychael might not be in charge anymore—and who probably was. I motioned Katelyn over and as delicately as I could, told her that Rudra Muralin had used a spellsong to attack her grandfather. I left Piaras's accused involvement completely out of it. He was innocent, so as far as I was concerned, it didn't enter into the equation. To Katelyn's credit, she controlled herself better than I thought she would; apparently she wasn't Justinius Valerian's granddaughter for nothing.

To Ronan's professional credit, he didn't vocalize the choice words he was thinking.

"Mychael Eiliesor is still in charge," Ronan insisted. He insisted, but he didn't sound completely confident. He'd been on the Isle of Mid long enough to know the kind of political, backstabbing crap that passed for civilized behavior around here.

We'd find out soon enough if Mychael was truly in command, or in command in name only. I knew he wanted to protect me, but with Carnades Silvanus in charge, he might have to lock me up in the citadel, and Piaras along with me. He'd see it as continuing to protect us while still obeying orders. To keep the Guardians from being reduced to ceremonial guards or disbanded all together, Mychael had to remain paladin, even if it was an empty title for now. Like Justinius, Mychael had to pick his battles carefully. I didn't like it, but I understood it.

Sometimes the only way to keep what you had was to do something you didn't want to do.

I wanted to keep my freedom. I also wanted be rid of the Saghred. Staying on the island was my best chance to get rid of my bond with the rock, but Mid was also full of mages and bureaucrats who would want me and Piaras kept securely under lock and key. Protect us from others, protect others from us, study us, use us—the reasons were different, but they all meant the same thing.

No freedom. No lives of our own.

No way in hell.

Piaras stepped closer to me. "So where are we going?" he asked softly.

"To see which way the wind is blowing."

Phaelan had said he was going to wait for us across the street from the elven embassy. I had no desire whatsoever to get within miles of that place, but I soon found we didn't have a choice. When I got a glimpse of the harbor, it was obvious that Tanik Ozal's slip was empty. Taltek Balmorlan's yacht was still there, as were the Khrynsani and Mal'Salin vessels, but no Tanik.

Either Tanik had to suddenly get out of port, which, knowing Tanik, was hardly surprising, or something more nefarious had happened while I was gone.

Walking gave my brain time to ponder even more disturbing possibilities. If Rudra Muralin had killed me, he would have regained control of the stone. That scenario was bad enough, but it raised some even uglier questions. Would that work only for Muralin, or could any mage powerful enough kill me and be able to command the Saghred? And would the rock take anyone, or was it picky, like taking only the mage most likely to feed it? My father had starved the Saghred and lived nearly nine hundred years.

I just wanted to live.

Worse still was a realization that rolled my stomach, and made me want to get as far away from these kids as possible. If a spellsinger or magic user was killed and a drop of their blood landed on me, would the Saghred slurp their soul, using me as the straw? Just as long as no one died in my immediate vicinity, I wouldn't have to find out.

So many questions, way too few answers.

Answers that, unfortunately, I could only find here.

I felt a touch and jumped. It was Tam; his arm had brushed my shoulder. He'd come up next to me and I'd never heard him. I was still thinking about slurping and straws.

I stopped, and Ronan and the kids waited a little distance ahead, giving us some privacy.

"It's best that I leave now." Tam lowered his voice to a bare whisper. "Whether Mychael or Carnades is in charge, it's dangerous for you to be seen with me." He glanced back at where Talon stood with Tam's mages. "And I can't risk my son, or the men who risked their lives to help me."

"A high-powered group of guys," I noted.

"Yes, they are."

"Old colleagues?"

"And good friends."

Tam was right about not being seen now. The Conclave and possibly now the Guardians saw things in black and white. Tam was gray, but now he was sometimes black. They didn't know what to make of him.

To tell you the truth, neither did I.

"Do you know what you do to me?" Tam whispered.

I remembered the cell block and the alley. "I think I've got a good idea. You do the same to me." I forced my voice to be steady. "Tam, I'm going to get rid of my link to the Saghred; once that's done, it won't be an issue anymore. We can go back to the way things were."

His dark eyes glittered in the streetlamps. "You don't believe that any more than I do."

"No, I don't. But I do believe in denial. My family's developed it to an art form. Much like goblins and deception."

"Deception for your own good," Tam corrected.

"I'd like to be the judge of that from now on."

Tam looked straight ahead, his profile stern. "When I tell you to stay away from me, I expect you to listen."

"Expect?"

He glanced down at me, a faint smile visible in the lamplight. "How about hope?"

"You can hope all you want, just don't hold your breath."

Tam was silent for a moment. "Just because I am no

longer married into the Mal'Salin family doesn't mean they don't ask favors from time to time," he said softly, and in Goblin. "They have, and they will continue to do so. Some favors I can comply with—others may prove more of a challenge."

"Like me."

His lips curled into a quick grin. "I've always considered you a challenge." The grin vanished. "Rudra Muralin has nothing to do with the Mal'Salin family, and he's merely using the Khrynsani to get what he wants. And the family's connection to the Khrynsani is—shall we say—fluid."

"Good old goblin 'shifting alliances.' "

Tam nodded. "King Sathrik Mal'Salin wants the Saghred—and you. He has made no secret of that. The same can be said of his brother Prince Chigaru."

I remembered the prince's hospitality from last week; so did Piaras. For Chigaru Mal'Salin, the end justified any means. And Sarad Nukpana was, or used to be, Sathrik's chief counselor. Both Sathrik and Chigaru wanted to get their hands on the Saghred and do some smiting of their own, starting with each other. Sathrik was a new king who wanted to prove himself; Chigaru was an exiled prince looking for a throne.

"Have they asked for a favor?" Namely me.

Tam's answer was silence.

"So what are you going to do about it?"

"Favors imply a sense of obligation or loyalty, and asking is not the same as receiving."

And for Tam, or any goblin, a response was not the same as an answer.

I shook my head. "I'm beginning to believe Phaelan has the right idea."

"What's that?"

"Trust no one."

"Do you trust me?" Tam said it almost too softly to be heard.

I hesitated, sighed, then reached down and took his hand. Tam's fingers wrapped warm and strong around mine. The magic sparked between us, though this time it was warm and tingling, not violent and lustful.

"Though you're the last thing I need," I muttered.

I heard the smile in his voice. "But I'm the first thing you want."

Chapter 30

When we got within sight of the elven embassy, it was swarming with Guardians. When we got closer, it was obvious that someone had been doing a little exterior remodeling.

The embassy had a hole in it. A big, gaping, smoking hole. An entire section of the wall was gone and smoke was pouring out of the building.

It was beautiful.

I wasn't the only one who thought so.

Phaelan and some of Tanik's crew stood admiring it from across the street like it was a work of art you had to view from several angles to truly appreciate.

"Ronan," I said. "Piaras and I are going to leave you for a while." I paused. "We might rejoin you—we might not."

The maestro nodded. "I understand." He held out his hand to Piaras and Piaras took it. "Master Rivalin, I hope you are able to resume our lessons. You have a truly rare gift and it would be a shame—and a danger—if it were not properly developed."

"Thank you, sir. I hope I can continue my studies, too."

Ronan extended his hand for mine and I was once again treated to a most proficient hand kiss. "Mistress Benares, it has been both a pleasure and an adventure—an adventure I hope to never repeat."

I grinned at him. "I'll bet you don't get to say that to many girls."

"I can honestly say that you're the first."

We watched for a minute until Ronan and the spell-singers were spotted by the Guardians at the elven embassy. They were safe; I wished I could say the same for us.

"Did you get a chance to say good-bye to Katelyn?" I asked Piaras.

He bit his lip and his eyes were sad. "No. But maybe it won't be for long."

"Maybe not."

Phaelan spotted Piaras and me and was grinning like the explosives-happy maniac he was. We quickly darted into the shadows and my cousin greeted us both with bone-crushing hugs.

I stepped back and draped an arm over my cousin's shoulder, admiring the view along with him.

"You do magnificent work. Truly awe inspiring."

Phaelan shook his head, still beaming. "Not mine."

"No?"

"Nope. Tanik's junior gunner. That boy has a true gift." He lowered his voice. "The official story is Tanik was taking the *Zephyr* to a new slip, the boy was messing around with the forward cannon, and when the *Zephyr* passed the embassy, it accidentally went off. Apparently the kid didn't know it was loaded."

Piaras and I looked at the hole and turned and noted the path the cannonball had taken. Piaras whistled. It was a straight shot down a narrow street to the harbor. An extremely narrow street, more like an alley. That was a flawlessly timed accident. The kid was gifted. Tanik might want to keep watch over his junior gunner; Phaelan was always on the lookout for new talent.

My cousin's grin turned sly. "Unofficially, I thought you two might need a distraction—and the paladin looked like he needed another way into the embassy."

I blinked in disbelief. "You're helping Mychael?"

Phaelan shrugged. "We chatted briefly from a comfortable distance. I told him who had Piaras, where he'd been taken, and that you'd gone in after him. Then Tanik's gunner had his accident. After that, the paladin and a couple dozen of his boys made use of the new door in the embassy wall. Eiliesor hasn't come out and thanked us, but he hasn't tried to have us arrested, either."

I looked around. There were curious onlookers and plenty of Guardians in full battlefield armor. Most of those Guardians were elves. I smiled. Leave it to Mychael to try to get into the elven embassy using the most legal means possible.

"It was a regrettable and embarrassing accident," Phaelan was saying. "Tanik and the boy want to personally apologize to the ambassador, but he seems to have gone missing."

I laughed. "Check under his desk."

"Where's Inquisitor Balmorlan?" Piaras asked.

"No one's seen him, either," Phaelan said.

"His yacht's still in the same slip," I told him. "The Khrynsani ship is still here, too."

The Guardians near the embassy's front gates came to attention. When I'd gone in as Captain Baran Ratharil, they'd parted the wards just enough for me to squeeze through.

They shut them down completely for Paladin Mychael Eiliesor to leave.

I grinned. In through a breach in the wall, out through the front gates. Someone in there had decided to cooperate.

Mychael saw me, and after a few brief words with one of his officers, he started toward us. When he got close enough, Piaras walked forward to meet him.

"Sir, I didn't attack the archmagus. It—"

Mychael held up an armored hand. "I know, Piaras. And so does Justinius."

"He's alive?"

"He weak, but I believe he'll recover."

Mychael slowly turned his head to look at Phaelan. "I

have no knowledge of the events immediately preceding the firing of that cannon."

"Would you like some?" Phaelan offered.

"No, I would not. I also do not want to hear rumor, innuendo, or confirmation that it was anything other than an accident. The city watch has taken Master Ozal's statement, and they are satisfied that there was no malice or forethought involved on his part or that of his crew."

"Tanik's the salt of the earth," Phaelan proclaimed, his expression solemn. "Not a malicious bone in his body."

"There will be no further investigation." Mychael paused meaningfully. "Into *this* incident. The same guarantee does not apply to any such future incidents."

"Understood. I'm sure Tanik will take the appropriate measures to ensure that his forward cannon never blows a hole in the south wall of the elven embassy ever again."

I couldn't care less about holes in the elven embassy. I had one question, a big one. "Has Acting Archmagus Carnades Silvanus ordered either my or Piaras's arrest, extradition, and/or execution?"

"He has not," Mychael assured me. "He lacks that authority."

"He's not archmagus until Justinius recovers?"

"He is, but the Isle of Mid is under martial law. *My* martial law." Mychael's gaze took in every possible threat within fifty feet of us. "Raine, we really shouldn't be standing out in the open. It's not safe for either one of us, but especially not for you."

He'd get no argument from me on that one.

"Phaelan's staked out a nice patch of dark over there," I told him.

"That will suffice."

Mychael and I stepped into the shadows of a building near where Tanik's crew was gathered. I waved to the boys and they waved and grinned back. I noticed that a quartet of elven Guardians kept their paladin in sight and within response distance.

"Phaelan, I need to speak with Raine in private," Mychael said.

My cousin looked at me. "Would you like to speak to the paladin in private?"

"I think I need to."

"Fine. Just yell if you need me—or all of us."

"I'll do that."

"Come on, Piaras. Let's give our girl some space."

I waited until Phaelan and Piaras were mostly out of earshot before saying anything. I also stayed well out of Mychael's reach. Trust is a wonderful thing; caution is even better.

"I thought Carnades took over completely if anything happened to the old man." I kept my voice down in case there were any eavesdroppers I couldn't see. This was Mid; the freaking lampposts probably had ears.

"Under normal circumstances he would be. Circumstances haven't been normal since you got here."

I couldn't keep a little smile off of my face. "Most girls get flowers or candy. I get a declaration of martial law. What's Carnades going to say about this?"

"Magus Silvanus has had his say. Until Justinius is fully recovered, Carnades is the senior-ranking mage. But until this island is secure, he is under the protection of the Guardians in the comfort of his town house."

My little smile turned into a delighted grin. "You've got Carnades under house arrest?"

"At-home security precautions for a senior mage."

"Call it what you want. You locked him up to keep him out of your way."

"Six of my Guardians were ambushed and killed with military precision behind Sirens. Piaras was knocked unconscious and put into a coach." Mychael's voice was tight with restrained anger. "Both of these acts were committed by elves. I have two eyewitnesses."

"Three if you count Phaelan," I told him. "They were embassy guards. Taltek Balmorlan wanted Piaras, so he took him."

"I had assumed as much. That's why I came here."

"To rescue Piaras?"

Mychael nodded. "And you. If Piaras was here, I knew you wouldn't be far behind."

"Correct on both counts." I hit the high points of the rest of our night, culminating with Rudra Muralin's vanishing act.

Mychael listened, his face expressionless, his mind working, no doubt separating our multiple near-death experiences into cold, hard facts he could legally act upon, and nonprosecutable incidents. I had a sinking feeling where most of them would fall—under nonprosecutable incidents with untouchable perpetrators. And I couldn't be entirely sure that he didn't consider Tam one of those perpetrators.

"Balmorlan's going to walk, isn't he?"

"Probably. Diplomatic immunity being the first of a long list of reasons. The confession Balmorlan wanted Piaras to sign was that he had attempted to assassinate the archmagus. To virtually everyone in Sirens, that's exactly what it looked like. Piaras is an elven citizen. No doubt Balmorlan will claim he was acting in the best interests of the elven people, and the Conclave."

I couldn't believe what I was hearing. Then again, I could. "He only acted in the best interest of Taltek Balmorlan. He wanted to take Piaras off of this island because of his voice, not his guilt."

"Unfortunately, we can't prove intent."

I spat a word that expressed my feelings perfectly.

"I agree. But that doesn't change the law."

"Then the law sucks."

"Sometimes it doesn't."

I snorted. "How?"

"After Piaras was taken and you disappeared, Carnades wanted to convene the Seat of Twelve and discuss our next steps. I didn't agree with his plan. The archmagus was nearly assassinated by a Khrynsani spellsinger, Nightshades had kidnapped five students and our top maestro, six of my Guardians were murdered, Piaras was abducted, and the first person to be able to wield the Saghred in centuries was missing. In my opinion, martial law was not only justified, but called for."

"So you declared martial law."

One corner of Mychael's mouth turned upward. "There's a statute that says there has to be a two-thirds majority vote from the Twelve before martial law can be declared. It's a safety measure to keep a paladin from wresting power from the Conclave."

I was stunned. "Two-thirds actually voted for martial law?"

"No paladin has ever declared martial law, so it's a little-known statute." Mychael's blue eyes gleamed in boyish mischief. "So I didn't ask them."

I grinned slowly in delighted amazement. "You broke the law."

"Not broken, merely bent it in the direction it needed to go."

"Until it squealed. First I corrupt Piaras, now you." I laughed. "I'm a bad influence. You want me to go home?"

Mychael reached me in two strides, gripped my shoulders, and pulled me to him in a kiss of desperate relief and long-denied need. His hands slid down my arms and around my waist and back, enfolding and crushing me against him.

Heat flared and spread through every part of me, and I felt breathless and disoriented. Though that may have been from being crushed against plate steel. I didn't mind. I also couldn't feel my feet on the cobblestones. It took a moment to register that Mychael had lifted me off my feet.

He raised his head and gazed down at me, his sea blue eyes as dark as sapphires. "I didn't know where you were, who had you, if you were hurt or dead. I was tearing this island apart looking for you."

"You trashed your island for me?"

"I thought I'd lost you."

"You almost did."

He briefly rested his lips against my forehead. "And I still could."

He gently set me back on my feet and reluctantly took his arms from around me, but he didn't step away. I was glad he didn't. I could still feel his warmth—and I wanted it.

Mychael was worried about losing me to someone like Rudra Muralin or Taltek Balmorlan. I didn't tell him about the Mal'Salin family—and Tam and goblin favors and shifting alliances. He'd probably find all that out soon enough.

Mostly he meant the Saghred.

"Are you ready to go home?" he asked quietly.

I knew what he meant. The citadel. I knew I didn't have a home anymore. Home was where you felt safe, and until I felt safe in my own skin, I couldn't call anyplace home. Oddly enough, that didn't bother me nearly as much as I thought it would. In fact, it was liberating. I started to smile. Must be the Benares seafarer in me.

"You're smiling." Mychael's voice was a husky whisper. "What is it?"

My smile broadened and I took a step back from him. "No."

He was confused. "No, what?"

"No, I'm not ready to go home. Mychael, I'm not going to be locked up, put in protective custody, safe keeping, whatever. That's not home. I can't live that way, and I won't."

He stood utterly still. "Then you might not live."

I put my hand gently on his armored chest. "My choice," I whispered. "And it has to stay mine."

"What is your choice?"

I thought for a moment. "For now, I'll stay on the *Fortune*."

"But I can't protect—"

"Mychael, you can't protect me anywhere. No one can." I chuckled. "I'm way beyond protection. You could lock me in the deepest containment room you had and I wouldn't be protected." I paused and looked into those sea blue eyes. "You know that."

I took his silence as a yes.

"I want my family around me right now," I said.

"Then Phaelan's told you."

I was instantly wary. "Told me what?"

"Apparently Phaelan's father was on his way to Mermeia in case the two of you needed to make a quick getaway."

I grinned crookedly. "That I knew."

"He also told his father that once he made port in Mermeia and if he hadn't heard from either Phaelan or you in three days, that he was to sail directly here." Mychael blew out his breath; it came out as a long-suffering sigh. "If the wind's good, you'll have all the family *I* can handle by sundown tomorrow."

"Uncle Ryn's coming to visit!" I couldn't keep the excitement out of my voice and I didn't even try.

"And he'll stay as long as it takes," came Phaelan's voice from behind me. "The paladin here has said there are mages on this island who can help you. Dad and I will be around to ensure that it happens. The quicker it happens, the faster we'll leave. If the high-and-mighty mages don't want pirates in their harbor and town, they'd better start looking for some solutions to your problem. The good paladin has agreed to uncloak and unward the *Fortune*. Kind of defeats the purpose of having a ship if it's just a big, wooden float."

I turned to Mychael. "And you approved this?"

"With the understanding that Ryn Benares is here only as your concerned uncle, not as Commodore Benares."

I snorted. "And you actually believe that'll happen?"

"Yes, it will," said the steely-eyed paladin. "This island isn't secure—but it will be."

If it could be done, Mychael would do it; of that I had no doubt.

And he was right—Mid was anything but secure.

Rudra Muralin wasn't going anywhere. Neither were the Khrynsani unless their lawyers could work some serious legal magic. No one had seen Banan Ryce, but vanishing into the woodwork was what Nightshades did best. Banan didn't lead by example; he led from behind. At the first whiff of Khrynsani, Banan had probably bolted. No body, no Banan.

The Nightshades we found in the embassy basements had been goblin bait, pure and simple. Banan had lost some; he'd just recruit more. There were always plenty of goblin-hating elves to fill his ranks.

Once it became known that Piaras didn't assassinate the archmagus and that we both had played a big role in rescuing the spellsingers, some of Carnades's supporters might just switch sides. But the same ones who condemned us one day and congratulated us the next could be back to witch hunting tomorrow.

And some of them would never stop.

My life's goal was to get rid of the Saghred. Until I could get rid of my link to it, to keep my life, I had to fight for the rock. Meanwhile, the temptation would be there. The danger sure as hell wasn't going anywhere.

I could live with that.

Like a starved monster crouching in a dark corner, the Saghred was waiting for me to yield to temptation, turn my back, make a mistake, let my guard down.

I smiled. I had some bad news for the rock—and worse news for anyone who tried to take either it or me.

I'm Raine Benares. My guard never comes down.

About the Author

Lisa is the editor at an advertising agency. She has been a magazine editor and writer of corporate marketing materials of every description. She lives in North Carolina with her husband, two cats, two spoiled-rotten, retired racing greyhounds, and a Jack Russell terrier who rules them all.

For more information on Lisa and her books, visit her at www.lisashearin.com.